Glass Houses

Melanie Murphy is an award-winning lifestyle YouTuber and best-selling author from Dublin, Ireland where she lives with her husband and children.

Melanie's online content about creativity, relationships, motherhood, sexuality, confidence and mental health has attracted hundreds of thousands of followers across social media platforms and her YouTube videos have amassed over 72 million views to date. She was named Blogosphere's 'Influencer of the Year' in 2018 and 'Best Social Media Star' at the 2020 Gossies. Her first short film, *Choice*, premiered at Buffer Festival in 2017, where it won the 'Excellence in Cultural Experience' award.

Glass Houses is her second novel.

Also by Melanie Murphy

Fiction
If Only

Non-Fiction
Fully Functioning Human (Almost)

Melanie Murphy

Glass Houses

HACHETTE
BOOKS
IRELAND

First published in Ireland in 2022
HACHETTE BOOKS IRELAND
First published in paperback in 2023
1

Cataloguing in Publication Data is available from the British Library

ISBN 9781473691827

Typeset in Century Old Style Std by Palimpsest Book Production Limited,
Falkirk, Stirlingshire

Printed and bound in Great Britain by
Clays Ltd, Elcograf S.p.A.

Hachette Books Ireland policy is to use papers that are natural, renewable
and recyclable products and made from wood grown in sustainable forests.
The logging and manufacturing processes are expected to conform to the
environmental regulations of the country of origin.

Hachette Books Ireland
8 Castlecourt Centre
Castleknock
Dublin 15, Ireland

A division of Hachette UK Ltd
Carmelite House, 50 Victoria Embankment,
London EC4Y 0DZ

www.hachettebooksireland.ie

For Johann Hari, whose work inspired the story, for Jessica, and for Thomas, without whom this book wouldn't exist. Glass Houses *was like the One Ring that I had to get to the top of 'Mount Doom' – pregnancy and birth during a pandemic. Thank you for carrying me, my dear Sam.*

Please note that this book explores subjects such as suicide, eating disorders, self-harm, bereavement and revenge porn which may be upsetting to some readers.

PROLOGUE

Dublin sleeps. A delicate stillness permeates the cluttered study where David Dolan settles into his desk chair with a warm can of stout. He pushes back the curtains of silver hair from his forehead with an arthritis-twisted hand and takes a celebratory swig. For a long moment, David regards the open Word document on his laptop and the tall stack of journals beside it, each filled with sticky tabs and folded edges – research pertaining to *the project*. Pride floods his waxy face. Finally, he knows what he has to do.

His late wife, June, always showed him the way, and even now – four years on from her death – she's penning his future with the invisible ink of the essence of her.

'It's perfect.' David says it aloud to the empty room. He closes his eyes, and there she is: bright eyes behind glasses, a vision of thick, dark curls with that one grey streak that frames her face.

The first time David ever saw June she was leafing

through a magazine in the waiting room of his medical practice, visibly out of breath with nerves ahead of her interview to be the new receptionist. With legs wrapped around one another like tangled tree roots, June took an apple from her handbag only to leave it half-eaten on her chair upon hearing her name sound from the hallway. David presented it to her at the back door before she left, told her 'Hygiene is important in a place like this – remember that'. June snatched the chewed-up apple from David's un-gloved hand and took another bite, right in front of him. Winked. Left him reeling. June didn't get the job, but David – in spite of himself – wanted to know everything about her.

He would soon discover that the woman loathed traditional medicine – except, of course, when an antibiotic would save her from developing sepsis or when a simple tube of medicated cream could soothe her skin, splitting in pain from an allergic rash spawned from God only knows where. 'So, you're one of *those people* – you'd sooner jig on broken glass than accept some help,' he'd teased over dinner and wine on their first date. Hot with attraction, they wound each other up in the town's finest Italian restaurant, La Scarpetta – a phrase in Italian referring to mopping up the sauce left on your plate with a piece of bread, which they did. Apple crumble for dessert.

Their love's first breath spanned months on a mattress on his sitting-room floor under a high ceiling where they lay drenched in sweat and sunset, high on the ecstasy of living – for it was as much living as David had ever done after years studying medicine, hunched like a hiker in a too-bright campus library. In her silk underwear and bare skin, *always* smelling of lavender and peppermint, June talked about spiritual dimensions and sound healing, that sort of malarky, malarky that almost put him off her entirely – not her fiery temperament, not the hair growing from her armpits and covering her legs, not the gap in her teeth, not even her wild laugh. June was completely at odds with his first love: science. Fairy doors and crystals and hippy-dippy through and through. They clashed all the time, but night would come and David would hold her and he'd stroke her hair because she was *his girl*.

For a long time, it's been David's greatest secret that sometimes they communicate like this now, that in death June plants ideas in his mind and pulls him this way and that, helping him to decide what colour shirt to wear or what brand of bread to buy or what Meat Loaf song to play in the car. He's sure that she's even responsible for saving his life on more than one occasion. But he doesn't attempt to explain any of it to his siblings or his friends for fear of the looks and the whisperings behind his back that might dismantle his solid reputation as the 'dependable ex-doctor', one who always picks up the phone, even in retirement.

David ran two medical practices during his long career. Almost everyone in Skerries – his small coastal hometown, where he'd worked for over thirty years – recognised him. They smiled, waved; some would even wish him a lovely afternoon when passing him in the cereal aisle. Others felt so comfortable with David, they would divulge their deepest secrets to him while he analysed their heartbeats. He had hoped to work in Skerries until his retirement but after losing his wife, the fear of ostracism pushed David miles away and into the city, where he finished out his years with the stethoscope. He was afraid that people would read madness all over his face. And he couldn't have that.

She still exists.

Without her, there's no me.

Yet here I am.

The table clock ticks. David's laptop screen lights up the smattering of photos strewn across the desk. He downs another mouthful of stout then examines the photograph again, the one with June's message – the one that started him off down this rabbit hole – scrawled across the back in blue biro.

It'll serve as centre stage. They will grow fast and tall, like sunflowers. Thank you, thank you, the world will thank you, my dearest love! J x

The photo was taken back in 1993 when their adopted son, Peter, was only as tall as David's dodgy hips and when June still had her eighties perm. Their faces smile up at him from the aged, glossy paper.

The family then lived in a big house tucked away in the hills of Milverton, Skerries, on the outskirts of Ireland's capital city, but of course David couldn't stay there after losing June. To be home without her was to ache all over with a grief so fierce it could bruise his living flesh. Peter moved back from New York to live with David in Dublin city, the pair of them motherless and wifeless – lost boys in the Big Smoke.

David's eyes examine the glasshouse forming the backdrop of the photo – back then, it flourished, full to the brim with blossoming plants. It winks at him.

He had decided to sell the house off-market – to ensure it would go to a young family who would look after it, not some institution or investor with euro signs for eyes. Peter has been handling the house viewings; *he* doesn't experience the same insurmountable dread when faced with the prospect of walking across floorboards that used to press against June's feet, or the agony of hearing her voice carry through the mist of memories that cloud every corner of every room. But last week came the first sign that he wasn't supposed to sell up: Peter told David that the old glasshouse was putting off potential buyers. He recalls the conversation. 'We might as well advertise it as a bird-shit palace with a house out the front. The glasshouse is in bits . . .'

'Let it put them off.' David says it now, under his breath, knowing June will hear and will nod approvingly.

It'll serve as centre stage.

JENNA
Two months later

Don't assume I'm inconveniencing my sister for the fun of it, right? Rosie would want you to think that little of me – that I love being a pain in the arse. In the conversation we won't be able to have, I'd tell her everything. I'd apologise for dumping myself on her like this and, mostly, for what's to come.

'He won't last long, Jenna. Might be time to consider putting him down,' the vet said on Bertie's thirteenth birthday – two years ago now. On a planet of nearly eight billion people, Bert is all I have left – this old, tailless fur bag of bones that can't even speak. I look down at Bertie, all crusty and frightened in his cage now, paws in piss but breathing, *still breathing*. Fifteen for a cat is seventy-six in human years, apparently. Bet that prick vet doesn't think it ethical to put sick human beings down when they're frail and in *their* seventies. Not everyone who's suffering wants to die.

I mean, *I* do. But it's just so – I don't know – arrogant, isn't it? To believe you can make that decision for someone else?

I inhale a lungful of strawberry vape and look down into the open-air atrium from the ninth – top – floor of Rosie's building, wondering where my baby will have to wander during his last days on earth. Of course Rosie had to buy the least animal-friendly property going: a one-bedroom apartment in Grand Canal Dock. It's the stuff of my sister's fantasies to live in such a wanky building, though – a fat glass cylinder housed within steel pillars and all snuggled up with the Dublin elite. Her kitchen table is likely as see-through as her decision to live here. *This* is where you live if you grew up in the sort of family to holiday in Disneyland. Dublin's upper middle class is a cohort Rosie has loathed not being part of ever since we were kids, when we'd be sent to school wearing uniforms that didn't fit.

I sent Rosie a long (admittedly desperate) Facebook message a few hours ago and asked if I could stay with her for a bit. Rosie replied to my message with her address and nothing more. No emojis, no 'can't wait to see you', no funny GIFs, no 'how've you been?!', no updates about her life. I thought she'd at least feign concern so I wouldn't be standing here feeling so fucking awkward. A cup of coffee here, a phone call there, that one evening after Auntie Bridie's funeral, and then radio silence for coming on thirteen months now.

I plonk Bertie down and look at my phone to double check I'm at the right apartment.

I'm in number 203.

Two knocks with my weak knuckles, small as Skittles.

Rosie opens the door a couple of seconds later, like she was waiting. It catches me off guard in a choking cloud of strawberry vapour. She eyeballs my vape like it's a loaded gun so I bury it in my pocket. A silence clings while she glances from my face to Bertie's cage then back to my face.

Bottle blonde and caked in make-up, she's dressed in a black blazer over a white tank top and dark skinny jeans that look a bit too small for her. We still share the same crooked face: my straight, dark eyebrows, my slightly-too-big nose, my wonky mouth, all looking back at me.

'Are you not freezing?'

I am, but I tell her that I'm grand. I'm wearing black denim shorts in October. Irish October never sees pale, stubbly legs, but I deserve the sting of cold, so it's fine, really. I hang like a limp puppet and wait for her to invite me in.

Rosie crosses her arms. Her pointed cream heel makes a clicking sound against the gleaming marble tiles inside the doorway where she stands and I wonder why she's bothered with torture shoes: they can't be for my benefit. 'You know the landlords around here don't allow pets?'

I remind her that she owns the place.

'Yeah. But . . .' she starts, clearly trying to make something up to save herself, 'one of the neighbours hates animals. He'll need to stay inside.'

Who *hates* animals? 'If you don't want us here . . .' It escapes me before I've thought it through.

'I don't have a choice, do I?' She already sounds exhausted by me. I don't answer her. I don't think she wants me to. 'It's not for long, anyway, this arrangement. I've only one bedroom.'

My God, what? She must be repaying the bank a couple of grand a month for this place – for one bedroom? Isn't it well for some! I tug at the sleeve of my oversized hoodie and think about how Rosie's couch in la-di-da land is my best and only option: I have to stay where I'm not welcome.

'You could've told me that,' I say, my voice smaller than I intend it to be. 'How was I supposed to know?'

'Know what?'

I feel pathetic. 'That you wouldn't have a bed for me.'

She looks away. More silence. More strangled-sounding meows from Bertie and the distant coaxing of melodies from a keyboard from one of the other apartments. Rosie notices it, too. The sides of her mouth curl up ever so slightly, just before she notices my lack of a suitcase.

'Hang on. Jenna, where's your stuff?'

I swallow all the spit that's gathered in my mouth. My head was in a dark place leaving Deb's – I needed to get out of there quickly and I didn't know anyone with a car who could help me to transport my stuff, so I left most of my (few) belongings behind. All I have with me is inside the fake leather backpack from Penneys that's hanging off my shoulder: my laptop, my chargers, my wallet, a sketchpad with some pen and ink, a knot of costume jewellery on top of about fifty muddled earrings and a half packet of Mentos. 'I don't need stuff,' I lie.

Of course, I do need stuff. Mostly for Bertie. A comfy bed, cat food, some oil for his coat, some catnip toys . . . I'm running low on funds, to be honest, but Rosie's tone isn't really inviting of a loan request. Better sign on before the week is out. I don't have the energy to look for another job.

Rosie's reply is air forced through her nostrils. Then, 'You'll need *my* stuff.' Her snarky voice. My least favourite of her voices.

I chew my lip.

Bertie yelps.

'Just come in.'

Martian soil. We walk single file. The only sound is the click of Rosie's heels. Her hallway leads to a spotless open-plan living area with a kitchen kitted with everything you could possibly need and more. Her blender looks more expensive than my second-hand MacBook, and crisp clear views of Dublin City beckon through the massive curved windows on the other side of the couch and TV. The place is decorated with fake plants, pretentious quotes in frames, minimalist 'art' posters that represent nothing at all. It looks like a magazine ad, not a home.

The *actual* grimness of my student accommodation in contrast with the divine order of Rosie's – it's like hopping from the piping hot Blue Lagoon into an ice bath. I could do with a warm towel for a minute.

After Jason inevitably broke up with me, I moved in with a right old wagon named Deb, an hour's walk away from the National Academy of Art and Design in Dublin where I am – *was* – studying. Although my room was forever Baltic and I had to 'keep to myself' in the house, I was grateful to have somewhere to sleep in Dublin for under five hundred quid a month and my own (very tiny) press where I managed to stuff my bits and pieces.

But this morning Deb rang me during my walk home. Said she needed to talk. When I got back, she sat me down and laid out a bunch of new rules. 'Bertie has to stay in your room. I don't want him wandering the rest of the house or shitting on my patio. You can turn on the hot water when I've given permission, so remember to *ask me* before you run a shower. Oh . . . and tell me when you are coming or going ahead of time, please. I'd actually really appreciate it if you could text me a picture of your full class schedule. Is that all right? Hmm. What else. Ah! Yes! Don't go out after 7 p.m. for any reason. No friends are allowed to stay over. No blokes, either. If you can't verbally agree to all of this, Jenna, I'm afraid I'll have to raise your monthly rent of €460 to €620.'

I'm not even exaggerating. Can you even imagine a bigger bitch?

Honestly, I think that one-way conversation just tipped me over the edge. I stood up, found Bertie, walked out. Fuck the stupid course, fuck funnelling the last of my earnings from countless retail hours into Deb's pockets . . .

'What do you think?' Rosie eyes me, seemingly desperate

for any glimmer of jealousy, for a sign that I'm inordinately impressed by her home. She tucks her chin and raises her eyebrows, awaiting a gasp. 'It's a Victorian gasometer, this building. One of a kind.'

I don't know what that means, so I just stare into space.

'We're inside an old gas storage tank. That's why the building looks so . . . unique! See how the wall there is curved?'

I shrug my shoulders.

Rosie tucks flyaway hairs behind her ear and rounds her shoulders as her chest caves with disappointment. 'Anyway. You'll be sleeping on the couch, there. It pulls out. There're blankets down the hall to the right, in the hot press, beside my bathroom. No bath,' she says, touching the side of her head and staring at the floor, as if having no bath is something to be embarrassed about. 'But, sure, this isn't a five-star hotel.'

Isn't it?

We both look around to avoid eye contact. I wait for her to say something else. You'd think she'd at least ask me how I am. Offer me a toastie. A shower. A cup of tea. *Anything*.

'Listen, Jenna, I've to go.'

My jaw falls.

'You were late! And Mam needs her dinner. Plus, I work evening shifts, in . . .' she diverts, breathless, 'anyway, I'll be back late – 1 a.m. ish.'

Rosie used to be an airline pilot. Over the years her Instagram feed spat out photos of her smiling in her uniform, on flights and with her arms in the air, showing off whatever country she was in by posing in frame alongside famous landmarks: the Eiffel tower, the pyramids, the Hollywood sign. She's never mentioned why she quit, or where she works now, and I've never asked.

'Grand, yeah. Sure, that's early,' I say without inquiry – mirroring her lack of interest.

Rosie gives me this look that says *I'm dreading having you around*. I wish I could tell her I won't be around for long, but I'd rather chew my own arm to shreds – the tattoos, the cartilage, the veins: I've tried to talk about it before, with Rosie, with Jason, but the words never come. I've just accepted my lot as a lonely burden, like how you accept a broken-bone diagnosis.

'Do you?'

'Do I what?'

'Work? You were between jobs the last time we . . . spoke.'

I lie and say *yeah* instead of admitting I was fired from Ladybug last month for tinting some girl's eyebrows without doing a patch test first. It was an accident. Really. Concentration feels so out of reach these days. I usually blame my depression, but it could just as well be the meds. 'Decreased alertness' is listed as a common side effect. Suppose I'll have to make myself scarce with some regularity now or she'll cop on that I'm full of shit.

'There's a spare key beside the fridge,' Rosie tells me, squeezing the back of her neck. 'And I bought a couple of frozen lasagnes. Vegan ones. Saw online that you're doing that whole vegan thing.' Before I can acknowledge the gesture, she continues, 'You should go and buy a litter tray and whatever else you need for him. The smell of wee from his box, Jenna. Sort that, yeah?'

She *knows* Bertie's name. I want to ask her to stop acting like he's not worth the two syllables, but I don't. 'Yeah,' I sigh.

'Right.'

That's the last thing she says before tip-tapping out of her little palace in her ugly heels. Bertie won't set foot out of his cage (which really does stink at this stage) so I stick my arm in for a bit to comfort him – and to comfort myself, too.

Lying cow. She said she has one bedroom but there are two: she just has one *bed*.

I can't resist the closed door in the middle of the hallway . . . Look, there's no such thing as respect for privacy when literally nothing matters any more. It's obviously meant to be bedroom number two – *her* room has a king with a velvet headboard, made up all pretty with pillows and a throw. I dug through that room too, found a surprising collection of condoms and lube in her bedside locker (let's call it her wish drawer). Rosie has this second bedroom full to the brim with clothing racks weighed down with designer gear, much of it with price tags still attached, and with shoeboxes and shelves stacked with probably unread self-help books. She's even bought herself a treadmill, though it's serving as a hanger for wet pyjamas. Scarlet for her. Some two-pound purple dumbbells are propped up at its base. Rosie's always been the type to start a new routine only to stick with it for approximately two and a half days.

I must be masochistic or something because nosing through Rosie's shit makes me feel more like the pauper to her princess than I ever have and still I don't stop. I mean, I knew she was making bank on long haul, but *my God*. I examine the picture-perfect polaroid wall of her travels as a pilot and look through her expensive department-store make-up, stored neatly on her dressing table. So many tokens of her sensible choices – the apartment, all of it. You don't get tokens like these for artistic flair, not unless you're the lucky one in a million.

After a good rummage I lay down half of Rosie's kitchen roll across some tiles in front of the cat carrier – just in case Bertie needs a wee.

I need sleep.

And alcohol.

After raiding her kitchen presses I find a half-full bottle of gin. I take it and my bare feet outside the front door onto the floor-nine balcony to sit cross-legged in front of the glass panelling. There's a single tree in the middle of the courtyard below: scrawny, alone, branches so weak they'd likely snap if someone gave them a funny look. Hard relate.

I clutch my e-cig and swig from the gin bottle until my thoughts turn to slush.

*

From behind and to my right along the shared circular balcony, the pull and thud of a door, and a dog, panting. I glance over my shoulder with foggy eyes and see a shaggy red dachshund showing just a touch of grey, with a lead strapped to his neon collar. A guy, too, somewhere on the twenties spectrum. Eyes as kind and curious as a child's behind round glasses find mine. His smile is a wonky line drawn onto his face, like one of my cartoon illustrations. He looks back at his door while he locks it, and I quickly hide my e-cig and the near-empty bottle of gin from his view by leaning back onto my palms to watch him. He's got a thick mop of dark, wavy hair and the most radiant skin I've ever seen without a filter. Definitely too cool for this yuppie nest in his retro T-shirt.

He fully turns to face me.

I know him.

From where?

'Hi,' I blurt out, wishing I wasn't so carelessly dressed.

'Why did you hide the booze?' With one hand in his pocket and the other holding the lead, he goes right there, with a faintly familiar voice. *Holy shit*. Awareness takes over like pins and needles.

That's *lowercase pete*!

You could describe me as a casual listener of his music. I know his more popular songs but I've never actually bought an album. God, though, I must have listened to his new single, 'Postcards to Autumn', a hundred times in the last week on Spotify. The music video – pete, fully clothed in a bath tub, broodingly playing his green ukulele – had over a million views on YouTube the last time I checked. He's 'online famous' – certainly not a household name, but he's got his own dedicated following.

My sister lives next door to, basically, a celebrity.

Of course she does.

I offer up a resigned shrug so he doesn't know that I recognise him. Then, 'Didn't want to make a bad impression on the new neighbours. I've got enough problems.'

His eyes dance across my face then down to the scars on my wrists, my legs, my feet.

He sees. He sees what I've been doing to myself.

Rosie didn't. She didn't even look.

'You're so much like Rosie Walker.' His eyes smile as he says her name. They've met, then. Relief folds up with insult – I'm glad he didn't ask about the marks, but also . . . he thinks I look like Rosie. Sure, she's *pretty*, but in a kind of flawed, accessible way. It's not exactly a compliment. 'A Walker too, right?'

I hate acknowledging my surname. *Wanker Walker walked right on out* – they'd chant that at Rosie and me during lunch-break. Dad left for a takeaway one day and never came back. Not the juiciest story, nothing you'd base a movie on or anything, but news got around.

I carefully control my face so I don't look like some pathetic fangirl. I give him nothing.

His smile climbs up his face. 'You are, I can tell. Sisters?'

'Maybe I'm her daughter.' I'm teasing, but also hoping he'll think more of me than someone who looks like Rosie. Funny girl. Cool girl. Hot girl. He's a lighthouse blinking in the darkness and I want him to like me. Rosie is completely unlikable . . .

He takes me in. 'You seem lonely.' His friendly voice slices through my long-built wall like it's fresh pie dough. 'Want to be lonely together?'

I can't help but hope that he's flirting, but something tells me he's just uncommonly approachable. I eye the dog and forcefully raise an eyebrow. 'The thing about lonely people is their whole vibe involves, y'know, being alone.'

He considers me. 'You never find yourself lonely in the cinema?'

My lips vanish into my face.

'I mean . . . we sit with hundreds of strangers who'll carry on being strangers after the credits roll two hours later, even though we've just been on this . . . emotional rollercoaster together.'

He sidestepped my dog joke and went straight for real talk. Who does that? Jason wasn't able for real talk . . . never asked me a question like that, either.

I tilt my head so my hair falls away from my face. 'I mean. Sure. But you've got a dog. Everybody knows you can't be lonely with a dog.' I feel my tongue peek from between my lips. It's the performative giddiness I know well, the kind I whip out when I want to shield people from myself. But pete is trying to see me. He's not just glancing over the paint job – he's examining it up close for blotches, streaks, blistering.

'You mean this guy? Moss?' he goes on. '*Pfft*. Moss is lonelier than I am. Look at him. Miserable dog.' Moss wags his tail. He pants and stares up at pete, who reaches down to rub his head without breaking eye contact with me. 'How d'you like to pass time, Rosie's sister?'

'It's Jenna,' I tell him, grabbing at possible answers to his question. Why does he care? Am I safe to go with partial honesty? I've nothing to lose. 'Christopher Nolan movies. Iced coffees. Screaming into a pillow when nobody's around to hear me. You?' I have his full attention. The way he stares, it's like he can't quite believe he's lucky enough to be talking to someone who's actively listening. Maybe his confidence is for consumption only: fake, like Rosie's banana plant just inside the door.

Maybe he really is lonely.

His phone vibrates and the skin between his eyebrows wrinkles into a frown. Stealthily, he checks his notifications while carrying on the conversation. 'I make music,' he says, distracted now.

'Is it any good?' I feel gross for being so sly, but I don't want to embarrass myself.

'That's debatable.' Whatever pete just read on his phone screen has shifted his demeanour a few miles to the left: he's curled up a bit, like he's afraid of an invisible somebody standing behind him. 'I'm all about lyrics. When I open my mouth all my guts fall out. You've probably noticed. Actually, it causes me nothing but trouble . . .' I remember the sound of music earlier and Rosie smiling. Maybe she has a sad little crush on him. Poor thing! He must be a good four years younger than her. He's not much older than me. pete ruffles his hair as though to self-soothe. Discomfort dissipates. 'Come on.' He nods at the lift. 'Join us,' he says, resolute confidence showing in his features once again. 'Moss needs a friend.'

'Moss. Why *Moss*?'

'Why *Jenna*?'

I feel something. An unfamiliar swelling in my chest. I really should stay here, make sure Bertie doesn't destroy the place, sober up, get settled in. But I decide to surrender myself to pete's pull. It's not every day a celebrity wants to hang out with you and my days are numbered. I've caught lightning in my fist – I'm hardly going to turn my nose up. 'I'll come. *For the dog*, obviously.'

'For Moss.' He nods formally.

I ask pete for his name. He tells me it's Peter Dolan.

The dulcet tones of Rosie shouting wake me up. She was asleep when I got back from walking around Dublin City with pete – Peter – and Moss, drunk on gin and attention, listening to Peter's alternative indie pop songs, pretending I'd never heard them before and talking about everything and nothing: about how we rate different flavours of Doritos, about what kinds of insecurities Ryan Gosling could possibly have, about the future, about the stars.

'Later, Jenna,' he'd said when it was all over. So casual. *Later*. He could've said goodbye, but he didn't. Later implies that he wants to see me again . . . doesn't it?

There's cat piss everywhere, my sister announces. Then she moans about how I didn't eat the lasagne she bought and how I used her new toothbrush and how I stomped muck through the house and how I need to grow up and learn to take responsibility for myself. On and on she goes; meanwhile, my brain is a neon arcade as Peter's demo recording for his song 'Entwined' swirls and echoes on repeat. I just gaze at the ceiling and I think about the little wisp of hair at the back of Peter's neck.

ROSIE

My head is *fried* after another night of Jenna streaming *Friends* till 5 a.m. Sleep punctuated by studio-audience laughter could be used as a form of torture, honest to God. Not only that, but after she finally went to sleep, the manky cat scratched my doorframe for at least half an hour, and when I eventually got up to shoo him away, I stepped in a little brown gift he left for me in the hall.

I can only imagine how sour I look right now – on all fours in fuzzy socks, disinfecting the floor because, of course, Jenna won't do it. She hasn't once in the two weeks she's been here. Jenna expending the energy she needs to walk from the couch to the fridge once a day . . . perish the thought! On my hands and knees, gloved up, I glance down the hall at the litter I bought for her cat. It's still unturned. The little bastard prefers to shit and piss anywhere but where he's supposed to.

She is out. Probably off with Peter again. Obviously not

at the job she lied about having or the course she's evidently bailed on. According to Peter, it's become a regular thing – the pair of them hanging out during the day – and the last time I checked, it's impossible to be in two places at once. Peter's told me all about befriending my sister; meanwhile, Jenna – weirdly – hasn't mentioned him. Not once! I think she's got a bloody thing for him. She was doodling a face that looked remarkably like Peter's the other night while the rotten fake 'ice cream' I bought her went untouched and melted into a bowl of sticky, processed non-milk. I caught a glimpse over her shoulder on a run to the loo. Pretty sure she tried to tilt the sketch pad to hide it from my view . . .

It's nothing serious between myself and Peter, but *it* is an *it* nonetheless. We've been sleeping together since late summer. They say blood is thicker than water, but in my experience, blood is more jealous and all. I can't imagine jealousy is something Jenna could contend with right now.

As much as she does my head in, I'm worried about her. Genuinely. I've never seen her like this before.

I think about how much my sister has changed since she first pulled away from Mam and me. This big shadow stretches out behind her, one that was never there before. Such a slight girl shouldn't cast a shadow so big, and now it's all I can see as she moves about the apartment. The dark circles under them are almost bigger than her eyes and, God, the *scars* – they're all over her thumbs, her wrists, her ankles, her knees. I can't draw attention to them, obviously . . . I can't even begin to process the sight of them inside my head, let alone *out loud*. Then there's the nightmarish portraits she draws and posts to Instagram. Her feed has done a 360-degree turn. I had another look yesterday, and her last post was a charcoal drawing of a naked woman with a load of violent scribbles in place of a head . . .

I fill my lungs with air and carry on with my never-ending to-do list.

When I'm *doing* there's less opportunity to worry.

For fuck's sake. There are cat hairs all over the couch. I faux-threateningly point at Bertie with the head of the hoover and curl my upper lip with disdain. 'You'll only have eight lives left soon. No joke.' Red-cheeked and sweaty, I pull the cushions apart. When I see what is hidden underneath, I stop dead.

Several sheets of painkillers, foil intact, surrounded by a well-worn red hair tie.

The white noise of the vacuum just about covers up the sound of my heartbeat in my ears. I chew my knuckles. An interrogative *mew* from the corner of the room. I can't pull my eyes from the stash. 'Don't suppose these are yours, eh?' My voice is shaking.

I pace in front of the TV for as long as it takes Mam to answer the phone. Then I spend about five minutes telling her what's just happened.

'Mam, try to keep up with me—'

'Pet, breathe. You're getting yourself into a state over nothing.'

'I *am* breathing,' I say, hardly breathing at all. She's not listening – or, worse, she's not hearing. Maybe it's another bad memory day. I'm usually more understanding of Mam's condition but I need her right now. 'This,' I say, looking down at my discovery, 'isn't . . . attention-seeking behaviour. She doesn't want me to see these. She's *hiding pills*.' My thoughts flicker to the bathroom cabinet, where I keep my own medication. I wonder if she's taken any of my painkillers, if she's seen my anxiety prescription . . .

'Meaning?' Mam snaps me out of my spiral.

'Meaning, maybe she's planning on *doing something*—'

'No, no, Rosie, your baby sister is—'

'Jenna is twenty-two, Mam, she's not a stupid child any more, she's a stupid fully grown woman now—'

'I didn't raise you to speak like that about your family.' Mam says it with the sharpness of a blade.

'Family.' I roll my eyes. Jenna hasn't visited Mam in years, but my mother finds reality easier to look at with a pretty bow on. Honestly, my sister could murder someone and Mam would defend her to the bone. 'There are at least *seventy* tablets here, Mam.' I only realise my hands are trembling as I say it out loud.

I just want Mam to tell me that everything will be fine. I need to hear that, even if it's not true.

'That many?' she says and pauses. 'Probably just, just, for her terrible headaches,' she assures me. 'She's always had them. A wet towel, a dark room, she'll be right as—'

The sound of the front door closing interrupts the call.

'*Crap*. Mam, she's back,' I whisper into the phone. 'Crap, crap, I'll see you later.' I hang up, stuff the phone into my pocket and frantically shove the full packets of painkillers back under the couch cushion where I found them. I push the hoover over towards the TV and mutter *crap, crap, crap*, then I pitter-patter to the opposite end of the corner couch and throw myself into a resting position.

I hear Jenna sigh. She hunts through the fridge. A veil of sweat starts to form across my face. A moment later she appears by the couch. I smell body odour mixed with roll-on deodorant. The Pixies or some similar misery rock pulses through the headphones resting on her shoulders.

'Oh. Hi,' I say, feigning surprise, stretching my arms above my head like I've just woken up from a nap. 'Where were you?'

'Out,' she says flatly. She's not the least bit suspicious.

I notice she's somehow thinner than yesterday, standing there in my old uni clothes; I dug out a bunch of skinny-me relics from 2013 that were hidden at the bottom of my wardrobe soon after she arrived, because she brought nothing to wear – they're somehow baggy on her. Looks like she hasn't washed her hair either. A minimum of seven bad dye jobs mulch together into two greasy mini pigtails. If I had to describe her current hair colour, I'd have to go with 'something attempting to look like green'.

This girl hardly resembles my sister.

I curl up my toes, hoping we can sit together and have an *actual* conversation. 'You want a can of fizzy lemon? Stocked up last night! Used to be your favourite.'

Without glancing my way, Jenna lifts her right hand to show me she's already got herself a can. She slides a nail coated in chipped black varnish under the tab and pops it.

Then she sits on the cushion hiding enough painkillers to kill a rhino.

I gnaw at the insides of my cheeks so I can't snap 'Thanks for offering.'

Jenna pulls out her laptop and sticks my headphones back over her ears, mutilated by twenty or more piercings.

I don't know this person. But this person needs me, maybe even more than Mam does.

The worst part about caring for someone with chronic pain is knowing that nothing you do will take the pain away.

I cross the Samuel Beckett bridge and hop on a tram out to Stoneybatter, just north of the river Liffey, where Mam lives in her two-up two-down house, the size of a mini-fridge, that's over a hundred years old. Stoneywey Road is the kind of place where most of the neighbours know your middle name and your ex's name and your boss's home address and the name of your boss's dog, and they all absolutely know about my mother's advanced multiple sclerosis – a neurological condition affecting her optic nerves, brain and spine – even though she still does her utmost to hide it away. 'They'll only pity me,' she's said, 'or, God forbid, they might even think I brought it on myself!'

Sclerosis. Not exactly a nice-sounding word, like aurora, or elixir, or lullaby. It's a pointed word for a disease Mam can't fight. Like Peter said, 'Fight kind-of indicates you can win.'

'Maybe she doesn't see a point because she knows there'll be no running up the *Rocky* steps, no victory dance.' I explained my situation to Peter during our first post-sex smog – about six months ago now. He's the first person I've told about my role as Mam's carer since my ex, Ger. *Not* because I'm in love with Peter or anything, but because he'd probably listen to me fill a dishwasher, and because I was in dire need of a vent!

Mam has difficulty walking and rarely gets out of bed. Her balance is awful and she's proper terrified of falling – understandably! If the woman lands herself with an injury, it'll be even harder for her to get around – she'll be even *less* independent. I've made her house as fall-proof as possible, though: no rugs to trip over, no more cane (the bloody cane was a fall magnet, I swear. Now, she just uses it to bang the floor if she needs me while I'm downstairs). I installed handrails and, for her last birthday, bought her an alarm bracelet that I had to mentally wrestle her into – she called it 'minging' and said it would make her look like 'an invalid'. The doctor told her to do some mild exercise to strengthen herself against falls, but I'd say she's done all of two ten-minute sessions in six months. When she does get up out of bed, Mam needs one of her two walkers – the upstairs one or the downstairs one – or, to be pushed in her wheelchair.

Spasms sometimes break up Mam's words and leave her mortified. Her concentration and memory are affected, too. We both leave post-it notes all over the house to jog her memory – like *defrost the broken meat* (that's what my mother calls beef mince). But bigger things are starting to slip through the net, the kinds of things you'd never write down as reminders, the kinds of things that a quick google has told me hint at early-onset dementia . . .

MS looks different on everyone, mind. It can even change year to year. Unfortunately for Mam, it just keeps getting worse, and watching is like having a front-row seat to the sinking of *Titanic*. The actual sinking – not the movie with Kate Winslet and the romantic gesture of *I'll freeze to death so long as you're safe on that very spacious floating door!*

A professional carer from a local agency – this lovely woman called Emma – calls out to Mam for a couple of hours each morning, every day of the week but Sunday, when I usually spend the guts of a whole day with Mam myself. Emma will make Mam some breakfast and she'll keep on top of the smaller chores like emptying the dishwasher. Apart from that, Mam's on her own till I visit before work in the evenings, usually landing out to her at around five o'clock.

Yes, I've tried living with her.

No, it didn't work out.

Our relationship is stronger when we have our own space away from one another, but also, like, I can't have dates around in Mam's (you can *literally* hear a fart in one end of the house from the other – allow your imagination to run wild) and Mam simply refuses to live anywhere else. 'The only way I'm moving out of here is in a box, on my way to the graveyard!'

But I do all that I can. Every single evening, I dress Mam in a clean pair of pyjamas. She rarely wears proper clothes so I keep her PJs freshly ironed to give her some sense of pride in her presentation. I clean for her. I prepare her dinner, and when things get *bad* during a relapse – or a 'flare' as she'd say – I feed her. I bathe her, too. There's nobody else to help out any more. Mam's sister, Bridie, passed away a few years ago – she'd always been on hand when I was flying for Aer Lingus. When she died, I kissed my dream career goodbye, because Jenna, well . . . 'bathe Mother' was never going to top any sixteen-year-old's to-do list. I got it when she moved out at eighteen and I get it now. I do! But if I recoiled as Jenna did, Mam would be on her own. And, well, she's our mother. The only one we'll ever have. The literal reason we're both alive. When she cries in pain, I'm there. When the fatigue saps her and makes her grumpy, I grin and bear it. I massage her when she asks me to. I fill her water bottle before she has to ask, because you care for your family. And now I've one more on my back where there's no room. Not a square fucking *inch*.

Maybe that floating door in *Titanic* just looked like it had enough space for Jack . . . Maybe that ending was realistic . . .

When I arrive at Mam's in the champagne shimmer of evening, with cheeks chewed to bits from stress, I realise she must be having a bad day. It's Emma's day off, and the curtains are still closed from last night when I left for work.

I see Dotty Byrne from next door spy on me through her window netting, rollers in her hair, a puckered mouth like a dog's bum. 'Hi, Dotty.' I say it as she retreats in a way that says *wasn't even looking*. It's our nightly peekaboo routine.

I let myself in to number 14 and my heart skitters when I hear Mam's piano.

'Of course, it's not me,' Mam says, looking from her piano to me, like I'm thick. 'That's Beethoven. It's on the, what you call it, the playlist you made me. I've only 5 per cent battery, pet.' Her mobile phone glows in the dark bedroom from the ridge of her legs all wrapped in blankets. I scramble over and pull up the charger cable from beside her bed; the Sellotape I'd used to keep it within her reach has come unstuck from the wall and pulled a chunk of paint with it. I stick the cable into her phone and sit at the edge of her bed, then I look from her to the dust-coated piano in the corner by the window.

Piano *was* Mary Walker. It wasn't just what she did: it was who she was. Piano taught me that my mother is her own person. Before I really understood that, I'd glimpse it – like the time I watched Mam seductively wiggle her waist to 'Dancing Queen' at a party downstairs when I was supposed to be in bed, or the time Dad loaded the back of his car with cans of cider ahead of a weekend away and Mam excitedly shouted goodbyes from the passenger seat, her favourite Marian Keyes novel in hand. Watching Mam's fingers move across piano keys eventually solidified her separateness from me. She'd sit and play and she'd be just Mary for a while. Piano was how she stood out as the second of eight children, before going on to teach private lessons to teenagers all around the county. But the numbness in Mam's hands from the MS means she can't play like before, which is depressing to think about – and it certainly depresses her. The soundtrack to my childhood is completely inaccessible, a scratched-up CD I can no longer listen to.

I got Big Jim from over the road to help me move Mam's piano upstairs – the house is so small, she has no option but to sleep up beside the bathroom. I figured having it in her bedroom might tempt her to at least *try* to play sometimes, seeing as she spends half her day in bed.

'That's not for me any more,' Mam says eventually, her voice full with defeat. She's seated upright with one tiny, hand placed upon the other in front of her. Her round, soft face hovers and she stares at me expectantly, doing that very Irish thing of not asking for what she wants. But I can suss her out in seconds. I can tell that she can't remember anything I've called her about, because if she could, she'd be interrogating me about Jenna, about the pills, about all of it. She reaches up to her hair and pulls at her ends, and then I know.

'How about I put on some tea, find you a nice cardigan and we can get to work on that mop of yours?' Her grey roots are showing through hair tinged with deep-red dye. In spite of everything, Mam likes to keep on top of covering up her age, even though it's rare she sees anyone but myself and Emma.

A smile melts across her face. 'Lovely, yeah. And tell me some good news, please. A *nice* story.'

I want to vent about what's happening back home but I squash my feelings down. Today, she's not able to be there for me and that *has to be* OK. The alternative means turning everything in her small world murky, unclear, even frightening.

I open Mam's musty curtains and fill a teapot. Two mugs,

plenty of milk and four teaspoons of sugar between us. When we finish warming our hands and catching up, I wrap her up and help her into the bathroom, where I've propped a chair by the bath. I start her dye job and waffle about a non-existent promotion opportunity because I've no real happy stories to tell her. Not today . . .

'And what about the Peter boy? Is he still showing up at the bar?' I stiffen as I brush the red goop across her scalp. 'He's keen on you,' she continues. 'I used to show up anywhere your dad went, like a fly on shite. Resisted me at first, he did . . .'

She keeps talking but I've stopped listening. I want to make a smart remark about how all of that turned out. But I don't. For all I know, she's momentarily forgotten he left at all. Usually, she'll only forget things that have just happened, but nothing would surprise me at this stage. There's no rhyme or reason to her symptoms any more. So, I say the other thing that's bubbling.

'I don't have time for that, Mam.'

She's quiet. 'What d'you mean?'

'Just that I'm not looking for – a relationship. I've enough going on.'

She turns to me, transverse wrinkles on her forehead. 'By the time I was your age, I had two daughters. Life just . . . happens!'

'Not any more, it doesn't. Contraception has been legal since the eighties. Autonomy – it's *a thing* now!'

Mam scoffs at me. 'There was no waiting around in my day. "I don't have time." We *made* time.'

I say nothing and, instead, concentrate on dabbing my red mixture along her hairline, so I don't stain the delicate skin on her face.

'The old crow was right,' she goes on. '*My* mother. "We lie best when we lie to ourselves" – that's what she used to say. You take note of that, pet.'

Mam just wants me to end up with my own front garden and a respectable husband, because *she* never had a front garden – or a respectable husband, for that matter. And she really wants some grandchildren, like, yesterday. *To breed or not to breed?* That is the question that Mam *won't* ask because, to her, it's not a question to be asked of a childless twenty-eight-year-old. To her, it's a question of when. Only when.

My mind has been divided on having kids for most of my twenties, and if I'm being completely candid, I'd rather birth a scrapbook of memories filled with trips to Vegas and white beaches and good sex than with screaming babies – more people who'll grow up likely fatherless and damaged and in a world drowning in plastic and iPads. But because of Mam's situation, I never get to travel any more, so I can't pull that one as a get-out-of-motherhood-free card. The truth is that, even if I wanted a child, I'm simply not in the best position to pop one out: I'm running out of money, and after caring for Mam, I have so little left to give at the end of a long day.

'I'm here for you, and I work. There's no space in my life for a man.' I bite my lip as I focus on the patch of hair behind her ears. 'Especially not for one with a rake of teenage fans who write fan fiction about riding him when they should be doing their homework.' I say it mindlessly, more so to myself. Mam doesn't understand the internet.

Concern twists her face. She turns back to face the bath, maybe considering the fact that my evenings are dedicated to keeping her ticking, maybe wondering how difficult it would be to date an up-and-coming celebrity who'll likely be touring Europe in a few months while I rot, waiting for him to return, unable to get my orgasm fix with someone else, someone hot skinned, someone actually present. I can't do without. It's my one real release.

'*Rubbish*, Rosie.' She lifts her nose in the air. Right then, maybe not considering any of that at all. 'You're free all day every day till the evenings. You're keeping him out. Why?' She's pure snapping at me now. 'Not every man is like that bloody *Gerard*.'

Daytime is my time, I want to say. My time for escape. For porn; for examining my pores in a magnifying mirror; for scrolling through ASOS; for frozen mac and cheese meals; for no-strings-attached sex; for trying and failing to read books about mindfulness when anxiety wraps a cold hand around my throat. Can't I prioritise myself for just a few hours?

'I like my life as it is right now.'

Any more complications and I'd cease to function. Peter may not be anything like Ger, but he's a man, and men – in my experience – bring nothing but disappointment.

'You're not seeing him any more, then?'

'Well,' I mutter, 'I am. Sort-of. It's just . . . not serious.'

She tuts at me. 'Forgive me for wanting a bigger family around me as I get on in life. Lord, give me patience.'

If you're actually there, Lord, please keep some. For me!

I arrive at Skelligs on King Street for my four-hour shift. After tying up my hair and reapplying my favourite nude lippie, I sink into the usual routine till Peter shows up to whisk me away.

I wonder where we'll go.

I need it.

Tonight.

Skelligs – the intimate, rough-around-the-edges bar where I work, complete with traditional decor and nightly live music – is near Mam's, which is handy, and I probably *should* focus on being grateful for how accommodating my manager, Tom, is of my carer's schedule (I doubt I'd find many jobs with such flexible hours) but honestly I just don't want to be here, pulling pints. I didn't want to wave my dream job farewell for *this*.

And I hate that I feel I have to justify whinging about my job. For one, Tom doesn't pay me nearly enough money to cover my mortgage, that expensive noose I just had to have. As a pilot, I managed to save enough to put me through two more years of flirty barflies, but I really need to find a better-paying job and soon – one that'll slot seamlessly into my glamourous caregiver lifestyle. Then, on top of whistles from tourists and Jimmy's unwelcome comments about how I look (our leering resident who has his very own stool), there's the relentless waterfall of questions, like 'What are you studying while you work here?' and 'So, what's the end goal? You won't do this forever, right?'

My shift is almost over and the nondescript man in the football jersey who's been here all evening winks at me from across the bar like I've only arrived. 'Two pints of Carlsberg, love. One for my right hand, one for my left!' I offer up lightning-quick service with a smile.

The customers drink and talk and I get on with it. A four-piece band with their fiddles and flutes have taken over the corner table, by the window. They fill the air with a tune that has them all tapping their shoes and slapping their thighs. Anyone who comes to Skelligs with an instrument is welcome to play a song. Tonight, we got lucky – these guys are bloody great! They're making the shift just about bearable. So bearable that I *almost* manage to push Jenna and my awful discovery out of my head . . .

Then, long before I'm expecting him, I spot Peter amazing-in-bed Dolan walking through the double doors. Tonight, of all nights, he's carrying a black case slung over his shoulder. I read his up-to-something expression.

Fuck. No!

Peter moves through the pub's crowd to the side of the bar so he can see me from top to toe. This is his little ritual. He consumes me with his eyes long before he comes anywhere near me, to get all my cogs in motion. I find myself pulling my stomach in and throwing my shoulders back, preparing for his eyes to flash with thirst when he spots that I'm in the heels I wore the last time we slept together two weeks ago, right before Jenna showed up. I wore these and nothing else while we had sex in front of the full-length mirror right inside my front door. Some might assume it's impossible to be detached with sticky skin on skin, but it's not. Detachment is perfectly achievable. It's all about avoiding the dreaded mid-shag eye contact . . .

Peter looks me up and down. I feel that unmistakable, ecstatic ache low in my body. He leans over the bar, eyes soft. 'So, I wrote something for you,' he says all too enthusiastically.

I double blink.

'It'll be on the new album,' he explains, knowing full well I understood him the first time. 'I'm going to play it when these guys finish up.' He points to the black case. Opens it an inch. His mini wireless keyboard practically waves at me.

'You will not!' My eyes dart around, looking for Tom. I remember he's outside, having a cigarette. I hope he stays out there. For the love of Christ, don't come in!

'Not really up to you.' Peter nods towards the sign on a nearby pillar, welcoming all local musicians.

'Ah, Peter, *come on*. You know me. You know I'm—'

'Afraid? Difficult? A pain in my ass? Hot as hell?' He scans me with his eyes and a dorky half-smile, trying to be sexy and – succeeding.

'What if someone here knows who you are?'

Peter glances around. 'Eh . . . pretty sure we're safe.' Unspoken, between his words, I hear *not a young girl with blue hair in sight.*

I'm not so sure. I know Peter gets harassed by trolls, and for all I know, that tall thirty-something woman in the corner could be one of them. Or the sexy ginger lad by the door. My palms start to sweat. If a troll posted a picture of us together online, I'd fucking *die*. I don't want people knowing about us. Romance makes my skin itch and I'm allergic to the idea of a relationship, let alone one that plays out in the public eye – entirely unerasable from the internet.

'You can't know that,' I hiss. 'What if—?'

The hum of folk music abruptly ends. Customers clap all around us. 'I just love how spontaneous you are, Peter . . .' He mimics my voice as he unpacks his keyboard. His movements are soft and gentle, like he's in no hurry.

'You can't.' He ignores me. 'Peter.'

'Rosie.' He says it with all the warmth of breath against flesh, mid-kiss. I keep my face hard and serious but I find myself moving slightly towards him, a melting magnet, my body at odds with my head. We share uncomfortably intense eye contact, the kind that makes you feel all exposed: Bambi's mam in the meadow, right before she gets shot. 'Remember we talked about you loosening up? Letting go?' Peter's goofy smile. *Yes, I remember.* I concluded that very uncomfortable conversation about my emotional unavailability by 'letting go' in the only way I know how to – in bed. 'Enjoy, neighbour.'

Peter turns.

He's off.

Everything slows and speeds all at once as I cower inside my brain from the anxious knot that's burst through from wherever anxiety lives right into my belly. My hand shoots upwards to brush at my hair like a wide-toothed comb as Peter chats to the head fiddler to request a slot. I grab the

wood of the bar, mutter 'crap' under my breath. Customers
pile up to order drinks, Tom's not here to help me, I have
to smile, I have to serve them . . .

Peter starts to sing. His voice sounds like the lovechild of
Hozier and Brandon Flowers. The chorus of the song he's
written for me makes my insides fizz – but *not* in the good
way. Not like . . . Prosecco. More like lacquer thinner that's
accidentally dripped all over a painting, causing bubbles that'll
change it in a way it doesn't want to be changed.

And he just. Keeps. *Going*.

> let's stay here
> she says
> you and I
> she says
> safe from fear
> she lies
> oh, my dear
>
> can't bluff a bluffer
> girl
> here's not good enough
> girl
> pull back the curtains
> open the door
>
> clinging to the space between
> hiding from those shapes
> in the mirror, otherworldly us

                    darling
                    please just have the guts
                    to feel it

                    letting go
                    of all the things you can't know
                    letting go
                    feel it
                    letting go

Don't get me wrong. It's a *lovely* song. But I've made it clear countless times that what we have here is A Casual Thing, and Peter's ruining it! This perfect, casual *thing*.

Tom appears at the bar in the middle of Peter's song, a sort of vinegary knowingness plastered across his face. I'm dead.

Peter finishes.

Everyone cheers.

And just as he's putting his mini keyboard back inside its case, right when I think things can't get any worse, Peter winks at me. People notice. I see random heads follow his eyeline. Some of them wolf whistle.

Repressing a snarl, I politely beckon Romeo. Seemingly delighted with his asinine self, he practically bounds over to me. I pull him behind the pillar by the bar so we're at least shielded from some of the customers now watching us intently.

'What was that?' I ask him in an angry whisper.

His face drops. 'You . . . you didn't like it?'

I hesitate. I'm not sure 'the one' exists – maybe there are lots of ones for me – and if there are, Peter isn't even one of those, because if he were, surely I'd have visualised tonight happening in slow motion or, at the very least, I'd be gooey in the chest after that little performance. But we're just . . . friends. Friends who have sex. I want the sex without the expectation of anything more because more never ends well, does it?

There's a reason Hollywood movies fade to black before happily ever after: *it doesn't exist.*

'You knew exactly how I'd react, so don't even *pretend* to be surprised that I'm not giddy about you embarrassing me at *work.*'

'Embarrassing . . .' he repeats, his face blank, like it's a word he's never heard before.

'Call the taxi. I'll get my coat.'

'Well, this is uncomfortable,' Peter says it from the other side of the perfectly comfortable Skoda's back seat.

'*This* is what you get,' I say absentmindedly as I refresh Twitter. I've searched pete alongside keywords like 'pub' and 'girlfriend' to see if anyone has posted anything within the last hour. Thankfully, there's nothing – the most recent tweets referencing Peter are from faceless accounts set up by people with far too much time on their hands.

anyone else think pete is overrated? he was good like five years ago when he was less popular but think the views have gone to his head lol

> I used to stan lowercase pete but now when I see updates from him I just feel old!!! He's in his late twenties and dresses like a teenager, cannot COPE

> pete's working on ANOTHER album? after the last one flopped? he should quit while he's ahead tbh, this will be pure cringe . . .

I click out fast, hoping he didn't spot what I was doing in the window's reflection, then I interrupt the silence in the taxi, asking the driver to drop us off at the side of the road. 'We'll walk the rest of the way. Thanks.'

'Rosie?'

I have to tell Peter everything I've been bottling up since this morning – even though I'm mad at him, even though he's being bashed online – because there's literally no one else I can go to. But all he wants to talk about is us. And the song. And us. And *oh my God*.

'I know you hate the big gestures, OK?' he starts after the taxi pulls away, all hands and inflection. 'You let my flowers die and, well, you liked the chocolates but not 'cause I gave them to you, 'cause *everyone* likes chocolates, and—'

'I can't talk about this stuff right now,' I say bluntly. 'Things aren't . . . OK. At home.'

Peter pauses. 'Shit. I'm sorry.' He stops walking, holds my shoulders. Moonlight highlights the worry on his face. 'Tell me.' His expression is reminiscent of his online persona – *super-deep musician* – and once again I have the sensation that I'm trespassing by being in his offline company. I just

sort of forget who he is sometimes. This weird realisation
– that he's the guy from the small rectangle on the laptop
screen – always feels like a smack in the face.

'It's my sister. I think she's planning to do something
stupid.' He says nothing and keeps looking at me. My teeth
start to chatter. In my rage, I forgot my coat. I was too busy
silently screaming with my fist shoved inside my mouth.

'Here,' he says, and pulls off his denim jacket. 'It's winter.
A blazer isn't going to cut it.' As Peter wraps me up, I want
to collapse into his arms, into a heaving heap of our limbs,
in bed, soft and safe and distracted. Even an alleyway would
do. *Where can we go?* Not my place – not with Jenna there.
And Peter's dad is *always* in their place on a Friday night;
Peter could easily afford some eight-bedroom mansion
somewhere, but he chooses to live in his dad's second
bedroom. The mind boggles.

He squeezes my shoulders. 'Go on.'

My face is literally stinging with stress. I make myself focus.
I can't run from this – no temporary pleasure high will make
it go away. 'I found a kind of . . . collection of painkillers,' I
mumble, 'all unopened. Way too many and way too hidden
to be an innocent just-in-case stash, you know?' Just a hint of
him scrunching his face up. 'Mam and Jenna aren't close and
– and anyway, Mam doesn't understand what this might mean.
She reckons they're just there for Jenna's headaches.'

Peter's eyes widen. He looks away in thought.

'But what if she's keeping them for – something else?'

He rubs his face and stares at the ground. 'I didn't get the
vibe things were that bad.' He sounds genuinely surprised. I

want to ask him what exactly he and Jenna talk about, where they go when they hang out, what he thinks of her. He told me he's been 'keeping an eye on her' ever since they met, said he could see my face in hers. I haven't asked about their friendship. If I do, he'll misconstrue it – he'll think I'm in jealous-girlfriend territory when I absolutely am *not*. Besides. He might run a mile if he finds out Jenna is sweet on him.

I won't allow it.

I need the option of the escape of him and I'm sure Jenna does, too.

He walks again, but slowly. I follow. 'The self-harm . . . that alone is, that's . . . that's big stuff,' he says, because of course he's noticed the scars, too, 'but *this* is next level, Rosie. You shouldn't take this on alone.'

'She hasn't said anything to you?'

'About wanting to kill herself? No. No way! You think I wouldn't tell you that?'

I shrug and chew some more at my cheeks, pushing the flesh into my teeth with my knuckles so pain can calm my nerves. I'm really glad he's taking me seriously, but in doing so he's helped me lift my worries to new heights.

'Stop that. Stress makes you cannibalise,' he says. 'I like Jenna. She's cool. And I want her to be alright. Besides, your family is my concern because you're my concern.'

'I shouldn't be.'

'Whatever.' A gentle smirk. 'But look, if I thought she was, y'know,' he says, shying away from the ugliest word of all, 'I'd have said. Especially after hearing my dad talk about this stuff for months.'

'Your dad? What stuff?'

A pause. 'Eh, like, research he's been doing, ex-patients . . . pretty heavy shit.' I hang on his every word. 'Some of them still call him, text, e-mail, even though he's not practising medicine any more. Nobody else to talk to.'

I gulp. Peter doesn't know his dad was my doctor till he retired last year. It's none of his business, but still – it's strange to be hearing about the man from the other side of the big desk: the one who was in charge of doling out my favourite calm pills before his replacement took over. The maximum benzodiazepine prescription length I've ever been able to squeeze out of the Dolan practice on Manor Street is three weeks of 0.25mg, three times a day. Peter's dad told me that benzos can be addictive, that I should learn to manage my anxiety in other ways instead of continually returning, begging for more alprazolam. He failed to elaborate on how I might accomplish this. I presumed he was tiptoeing around telling me to 'just eat better and move more', the usual lousy advice that is demonstrably difficult to put into practice. A total stranger couldn't pry the M&Ms from my clenched fist after a midnight panic attack – how could I expect *myself* to willingly put them down and go try downward-facing dog instead? Peter's father could never really offer me the help – the relief – I was looking for. But I always appreciated his kindness; even though he couldn't hand me a neatly packaged solution to my anxiety, I always felt like he cared.

'Dad had a lot of people come to him over the years with all kinds of issues, and some of them took the meds he prescribed and were fine, that was that, but others kept coming back, complaining that stuff wasn't getting any better, and, well—'

'What?' I ask, my tone sharp. I'm one of the people he's talking about – the ones who returned, over and over, hoping for some new answers about why my anxiety was so bad sometimes that I'd ache all over. I'd wake at night, my brain cold, my throat tightening, alone in the dark with nobody to call but his out-of-hours emergency number.

Peter stiffens. 'Not sure I should be saying this stuff.'

I tilt my face forward to make my eyes appear bigger, so he'll tell me things. It always works. 'It's just me.' I gaze up at him, my fake lashes flat against the folds of my eyes.

'This is all off the record, OK?'

I cross my arms, annoyed. What does he think I'm going to do? Run to Reddit to gossip about his family? Sell his secrets to those websites that run juicy headlines about YouTubers?

He reads me like a text in all caps. 'I trust you completely. It's just, my dad's a retired physician. He's not really supposed to . . . I just don't want it getting out.'

He's annoying me now. 'What's this got to do with my sister? The pills?'

Peter breathes deeply. 'Sometimes Dad reads right through the night. It's all kind of mad, actually. He forgets to eat, like, he's *so* absorbed in the stuff. Last night I made him some pizza, brought it to him – the whole thing was still there this morning.'

'Cold pizza makes for great breakfast,' I say, hoping to

lighten the mood. I'm not used to seeing Peter so concerned. We don't often talk about other people. We don't often talk much at all, actually, unless we're naked and in that mess of skin where you feel safe to talk about anything – for fifteen minutes tops after the deed's done, before reality hits and you want to disappear. I find men to be more honest right after they've finished. Tinder has given me a pretty solid bird's eye view of typical post-sex male behaviour.

Peter ignores my pizza comment. Licks his lips. Adjusts his glasses. 'Dad never really bothered to find out what was actually going on with his patients. Said he just went by the book. Ask a few questions, suggest pills . . .'

We linger in silence. Peter looks off to the side, plays with his fingers. Like he's reflecting. I don't press him, but I'm aware of the skeletons hanging by his retro T-shirt collection, even though I've not seen them close up. Peter doesn't feel like he deserves his money, his rising fame – any of it. But if I entertain him when he tries to swim in deep water with me, he'll only become more attached, so I don't give him much opportunity to offload. Anyone looking in at our dynamic might consider me to be a massive hypocrite – involving him in this Jenna nightmare – but that's . . . that's different. *I have nobody else to turn to.*

Peter clears his throat. 'Dad reckons he could've done more to help all those people who kept coming back, desperate for him to fix things. He wants to see for himself.'

I swallow. 'See what for himself?'

'See if Mom's "plan" holds any weight. Mom is . . . well. Mom isn't anything like dad. She—'

'Isn't your mother . . .?'

'Dead?'

My eyes say yes.

His say the same. 'Sorry. My dad – he doesn't like using the past tense when we talk about her.'

Peter waits for me to dig, his eyes hopeful. I don't. I circle the conversation back to what matters most right now.

Jenna.

We stroll back to our apartment building and Peter tells me about his father's plans, how my sister might fit into them. Afterwards, we hang about in the space between our apartments in quiet contemplation. He eventually says goodnight; brushes his little finger against mine. Dopamine floods me. My faulty wiring threatens to start an electrical fire if I don't tempt Peter to make me come, right here, in the cold of night.

If my twenties have taught me anything so far, it's this: there's nothing like a bit of exhibitionism to ward off a looming panic attack.

JENNA

I wake wrapped in clammy skin with no idea of the day or the time. My lock screen says it's the afternoon. Judge away. Honestly, be my guest. Even I judge me.

Back to that place between dreams and reality.

Awake.

Asleep.

Quick trip to the bathroom.

Half doze.

Back to the couch, where I lie on my side, vaping and scrolling on my phone, with Bertie purring across my chest, his paws tucked underneath his body so he looks like a stale loaf of bread with eyes. I don't actually know what I'm hoping to gain from this thing; whatever it used to give me is missing. The dopamine reward loop is broken. Even the headlines that scream *this one thing will change your life, guaranteed!* can't grab my attention any more. The one thing never changes shit.

My thumb continues to refresh the Instagram feed as my brain attempts to process the 'You're all caught up' notification. I click back onto my profile. My likes have stagnated. Don't know why I'm surprised – I've not posted any new work in weeks. For a while, when nowhere else did, #AlternativeArt felt like home. Other artists would find my page through the hashtag and they'd like or comment on my latest offering. One of my ink sketches – a satire of the Irish housing crisis – racked up almost five hundred likes after a popular Instagrammer shared it on her story. That was six months ago.

Nothing remotely exciting has happened since.

No wonder I've not felt inspired.

I do nothing.

I *feel* nothing.

Do I have a pulse? I check. There's something all right. A weak, rhythmic sense of pressure against my forefinger. Mild surprise: does that count as a feeling?

The TV is on for some semblance of normality but I couldn't tell you a thing about whatever's been playing or anything about my mood in general. Trying to find a feeling on a day like today is like trying to squeeze a spot while looking in a mirror smudged with greasy fingerprints: a lot of guesswork, prodding and blood. Because it's one of those days. The lights are on but nobody's home. Jason used to say that to me when I'd be catatonic like this back in his place. I'm surprised he stayed with me for so long – someone so well-functioning, someone who woke up at 6 a.m. to go for a run along the river every single day, someone who remembered to water his wheatgrass and who batch-cooked his meals for the week on a Sunday and who actually *ironed his clothes*.

At least I remembered to leave out extra dry food for Bertie before I went to bed last night. At least *he's* OK. I whisper some endearments into his ear and get back to mindless scrolling.

Minutes or hours later, my sister comes home, a tornado of sharp shoes and keys clanking and bag chain against marble. Bertie jolts awake. Rosie flicks on the lamp that's practically inches from my head and I moan, raising my arms to cover my eyes. She keeps doing this. She knows I'm asleep and she does it anyway. The room is shades of black, orange and midnight blue, and I can smell something on her.

Is that . . . Peter's cologne?

'Another productive day, yeah?' she says snidely as she trots over to the kitchen area.

'Don't start.' I can't even think straight. Am I imagining the whiff? 'Time is it?' I ask.

'Nearly two' – a.m., of course. Rosie rummages through the fridge and the presses. Plastic packets, a plate, a butter knife. 'But, sure, you're always up all night, keeping me awake. Thought this was "early" for you.'

I sit up straight so I can see her over the back of the couch, my eyes squinting against the harsh light of the room. Her hair is unusually dishevelled. I don't often look at her, to be honest, but when I do, her precious locks are always waved to perfection.

Her jacket. It's Peter's.

Bertie jumps to the floor and runs off to hide. Must be able to sense my blood simmering. 'Where'd you go after work? You're, like, an hour late.'

Rosie spreads mayonnaise onto some white bread and pulls apart a packet of crisps. 'Want a crisp sambo?'

'No. They're muck,' I say, wincing. 'Where've you been, then?'

She licks some mayo from her finger before looking at me. Leaning forward, she plants both hands on the island and her eyes are more alive than every cell in my body combined. The intensity throws me off. 'Out.'

I look away.

I hear Rosie press a second slice of bread onto her sandwich, smushing the crisps to pieces with a satisfying crunch. It's how Dad used to make crisp sandwiches, when him and Mam would pull their mattress down to the front room and we'd all camp out with cheese-and-onion breath and fight about which videotape to play.

'If you have to know,' she goes on, 'I was with a friend.' I see Rosie fiddle with her food in my peripheral vision. 'A mutual friend, actually. I believe you've met our resident celeb from next door. He tells me you've been hanging out. Regularly.'

Her words knock the wind out of me. I'm not imagining the Dior Fahrenheit, Peter's jacket isn't a mirage . . .

There's no way they have *a thing* in common.

'He – hangs out at the bar, where I – work.' A bar? She looks as embarrassed as I feel for her. 'This . . . I was freezing. You know what Peter's like, he's a gent,' she says, answering the question I didn't ask. 'Look,' she goes on, 'I know you don't talk to me. About . . . well, anything. But just so you know, you can.' The offer and the tone don't mesh. She doesn't mean what she's saying. Maybe she thinks she does, but, like, I know my sister. I know how self-absorbed she is. Let me translate. *You can talk to me, but I'll continue to never ask you how you are and I certainly won't be able to handle anything you might actually say.*

Peter must have put her up to this. Maybe he's worried about me. The notion alone taps like feet in my stomach, Michael Flatley performing Riverdance. I know it's bad but I can't remember the last time someone – anyone – was concerned about me. The dancing is fast replaced by the sensation of veins tying themselves in knots over the image of Rosie talking to Peter – the two of them, alone.

'Feel better now? Like you've done your bit?' Instant regret as it all escapes my cracked lips. I look around for Bertie and spy his tail nub sticking out from underneath the curtains. My chest tightens. This is his home; he's safe here. As much as I'd love to press Rosie's buttons . . . 'Sorry, sorry. I didn't mean that.' I lie back onto my pillow so the couch hides my face. Because now *I'm* lying and she can probably read me as well as I can read her.

'Of course you meant it.' Ceramic on marble as she forces the sandwich in front of her away. 'And if there's something you want to say to me, fire ahead. I'm all ears. I have been since you showed up, actually, no matter what story you want to tell yourself. You're the one who's been avoiding *me.* So, no, I'm not here trying to redeem myself for being shit, or whatever you're thinking. I'm just – saying it out loud, so the fact isn't lost on you.' I feel my foot start to shake. 'You know, Jenna, sometimes it feels like, like a helicopter could crash through that window, right into us, and you wouldn't notice.'

Adrenaline as I focus on her words: *all ears.* Furious, I feel my heart rate speed. Then I jump up and onto my knees, to face her. My nails dig into the couch cushions. 'Here it is. The bullshit. It's always bullshit between us. All ears, she says. Rosie, you don't have a *clue.* You don't know me. You don't want to know me. You're dying for me to, to leave, so you can have your perfect life back. Stop with the *bullshit.*'

Rosie walks towards me then, mumbling 'perfect life' repeatedly as she moves, closer, closer, till she's standing right over me. I flinch. 'I've been thinking about you all fucking day!'

'I'm sure you have. Gossiping about me to him too, yeah? Giving you something to actually talk about, am I?' I don't really know where I'm going with this. I mean, it's not like she hasn't done a million cool things with her life, but she's definitely the type of person to love a gossip.

She's moving her eyes around, trying to think of what to say. Screams of guilt. 'Is that what you think of me? Big gossip who slags you off for the craic? Peter—'

I snort. I hate hearing her say his name like I hated sharing a bed with her for sixteen years. 'Probably off telling him I "ruined your life" when I moved out of Mam's, that, that now I'm back, ruining it all over again.'

Rosie's nostrils flare. 'Oh, would you stop! You don't know what you're—'

'Telling him what a disaster your waste-of-space sister is,' I say, my voice like venom now. I really don't know where any of this is coming from. I'm very clearly projecting – I have no evidence – but the self-awareness doesn't hold me back: it swims under a murky surface. 'Bitching and moaning and playing your mini violin. Well, guess what? The world doesn't revolve around you.' I'm not far off shouting now. Spit flies from my mouth as I talk and I don't care. All I can think about is Peter spending time with Rosie when he could've been spending time with me. He hasn't texted me back since the early afternoon. 'And I bet you've no *idea* about Peter and how much shit he's going through himself.' It's a big assumption on my part; I mean, Peter seems to be juggling a lot, but . . . so what? I just need to regain some ground here. Her expression is blank now. I keep going. 'And there you go, dumping your problems onto him like he has none of his own, and, like, anyway, guess what? I'm not your problem. I literally make myself *invisible* here.'

She crosses her arms as if to block out my words. 'Peter – well – look . . . my life is far from perfect.'

'I love that you're stuck on that! How dare anyone say anything about *you*. Rosie, if you can't see how great your life is then you need some fucking glasses.'

Her hands move down to her hips. She straightens her spine while one of those disbelieving fake smiles takes over her face. Then her eyes well up. 'Jesus.' She chokes on the word, blinks back tears. 'You're delusional. You're—'

'Go on. I love it when you call me names. Always did.'

'You'll talk to a guy you hardly know, but you won't talk to me.'

'Anyone but you.'

Again, that intense look that makes me feel dead inside because I couldn't possibly ever look so completely alive; my eyes are two pools of still water while hers reflect lightning bolts. Again, I think of her with Peter and I want to interrogate, I want to—

Rosie interrupts my flow of furious thought with the worst thing she could possibly come out with. 'I found the pills.'

My heart is a fist pounding a plaster wall. She's not talking about my anti-depressants: they're in my bag, and I always have that with me. She's seen my stash. I try to formulate a one-liner to explain myself but my vocal cords won't let me.

I stand up from the couch. My legs take me to the refuge of the bathroom. She follows, saying things I can't make sense of because I can't concentrate. I lock the door behind me then I sit in the scent of Rosie's jasmine shower oil, on the toilet, lid down, grasping at all possible outcomes while she shouts through the wood that separates us.

Maybe I could leave Bertie in a shelter? No. He's so clingy and he needs me. Nobody else would know how to look after him. But what if she calls an ambulance . . . tries to have me sectioned? And, like, did she tell Peter about the pills? What will he think of me? What if he stops talking to me?

'Jenna, come out. This isn't fair.'

'It's not fair to have no privacy.' I realise that I opened every last drawer in her bedroom while she was at work but this is *different*, this is—

'I have no clue how to help here, I feel so alone—'

'You obviously weren't alone tonight. Hope you had a great time making me out to be—'

'I didn't "make out" anything—'

Untamed, I grab a bottle of shampoo from the shelf to my right and throw it at the door. 'He's my friend, Rosie!'

'And he's my, well, he's—'

Some kind of guttural noise explodes out of my throat. 'Ugh, *he's just your neighbour!* You don't know *anything* about him!'

'Like I said when I was *a minute* in the door, Peter's my friend, too.' Seconds of deafening silence. 'You'd know that if you ever bothered to talk to me. I've been playing dumb for weeks, waiting for you to come out with it, but you haven't, so here it is. I know where you go when you're not here. Fine art lectures, my *bollocks!*' She sounds so full of herself. Guilt seems to crack Rosie's anger. 'Jesus, Jenna, he's as worried about you as I am. We both just . . . we want to help.'

'*He* actually *does* help.'

She slams on the door with both hands. 'Let me help, too! Come out here. Now. It's my home!' She loves rubbing that in my face. 'Don't make me ask twice. I get you don't under-stand the word *respect* right now, but you'd better bloody start learning what it means 'cause I'm not going to let you—'

'Let me what? You my mammy now?'

A primal wail from the hallway. From Rosie. I hear her slump to the floor on the other side of the bathroom door. The awful, mournful sound grows louder. It's one I haven't heard since Mam told us she didn't think we'd ever see our dad again. 'I won't let my little sister kill herself.' Gasps for air break her words apart, allowing each one to sink into me, stones in the black sea.

I don't move. I don't speak.

Minutes pass before she talks again. 'When we were little, I'd turn up the TV so you couldn't hear Mam and Dad fighting. Did you know that?'

I didn't.

'Those drives we'd go on in Dad's car, before I even had a license, that was me taking you away from the shouting, from him putting holes through the walls.'

I don't remember any of that.

'It all became so much worse after Mam's diagnosis. You were only a little mushroom of a thing. Mam complained of this – this tingling she had, in one side of her face. She started tripping over around the house, talked about her vision going dodgy . . . Remember when she gave us bowls of strawberry ice cream before telling us, after all the tests?'

I can almost feel the blood draining from my face.

'Later that same day she told Dad. Suppose he just couldn't handle it.'

I say nothing. I try to picture my mam's face, how she might look now, how she might have aged. I can't.

'I've always wanted to protect you from the world,' Rosie

says. She sounds sad. Pensive. 'Seems like the world found you, though.'

Something in my chest relaxes. The same something comes over me entirely, making me stand and shuffle over to sit against the door, to be closer to her. 'Found me is one way to put it.'

'Peter's a really good guy,' she pivots. 'He knew something was up with you right away, just like I did. But I suppose he's better at communicating . . .'

Better is an understatement. I feel less like shit around him than I do every other moment of every day. I'd have painted him into my life a long time ago if only I had a magic brush. The entire internet knows who he is, but I've found myself wishing he were my secret.

'Jenna?'

'Yeah?'

'My life isn't perfect.'

I pick at a thread sticking out of my – Rosie's – pyjamas.

'Feels like my life ended a few years ago,' she says dryly. 'I had so much to live for. All these . . . big plans. Work my way from being a first officer to captaincy . . . celebrate getting the four stripes by, I don't know . . . buying a holiday home in Portugal and calling it *I fucking did it!* Sure, I have a nice place to live, a bit of money put away. But let's be real. All I do is distract myself from my problems with, well . . . anyway.' With what? 'Doesn't matter. This isn't about me. But you know the situation. With Mam.'

Here she goes. 'I can't talk about all that.'

'If not now, when? When I bust this door down one day only to find you dead on the tiles?'

A shiver.

'Mam has no independence and no one but us. You *never* reach out, visit her—'

'I send her money.'

'What? No you don't!'

'I've sent her a quarter of my wages every month for years.' It's true, I have. Not only to relieve my guilt but because she genuinely needs it: her disability allowance only stretches so far.

'She – she's never said,' Rosie mumbles defensively.

'Look, all that, her health, just . . . scares me.'

'Of course it scares you! It would scare anyone. It's traumatic to see someone you love go through—'

'Rosie.' I try to drown out her voice. She keeps going. I focus my eyes on a stain in the paint above the loo till my eyelids become heavy.

'– and, well, your certainties kind of ebb away when you see the person who brought you up become so bloody *helpless*, because when you're a kid, your parents are – they're God. But, look, Mam isn't *the disease*, and she needs you. You can't be afraid of your own mother, Jenna.'

I snap out of my self-induced trance. 'I'm not afraid of Mam,' I assert. 'I'm afraid of . . .'

'What?'

'Becoming her.'

The only sound is the distant drone of the TV. When Rosie doesn't reply, some words manifest in the back of my throat.

'One morning, I woke up and my hand – it was completely numb . . .'

'It's not an inherited disease, Jenna. The genetic risk is tiny—'

I shrug. 'Still. I imagine being like her one day with *my brain* and it scares the life out of me.'

'Is that why you left us?'

'Well, no. This,' I say, referring to the depression without actually acknowledging it, 'all started a couple of years ago. Out of nowhere, really.' I swallow. 'I *left* because – because, well, you—'

'Me?'

'Eh, Spain! Remember?' 'A year and a half – alone – taking care of her. I was only a teenager, feeding her, changing her, washing her, while you were off living your dream. I was pissed off, Rosie!'

Her voice goes up an octave. Always does when she turns defensive. 'One of us needed to be out earning! It was cheaper for me to get qualified over there and . . . and I was just *trying* to—'

'You had this whole life I knew I'd never have.'

'What's that supposed to mean?'

I think for a minute. Then I peel myself from the floor and open the door. Rosie's eyes are bloodshot. She backs up and props herself up against the wall outside her bedroom. I sit in the doorway, facing her. Bertie quickly joins us and sits on my lap. He always knows when I need comforting.

'One time I drew a picture of this robin. I was twelve or something like that. I knew Mam loved birds, so I spent hours on this cute little robin, copying it from a page of one of those gardening magazines Mam used to buy in an effort to "manifest" her dream house: somewhere detached, out the country . . .'

Rosie half laughs. It's a glimmer of a time long ago, when it was us against the world.

'I hand the picture to Mam, pure delighted with myself, and you know what she says? She goes, "Very nice but, Jenna, remember, success is 10 per cent talent and 90 per cent hard work."'

'And?'

I pause. I pet Bertie. 'She thought I didn't have it in me to do well. Because I wasn't like you. The pressure was—'

'Oh, Jenna, I don't think she meant – she was probably trying to encourage you to keep it up.'

'No, no. She never cared about my art or about anything I was actually good at.' I can cook without recipes, style outfits, design tattoos and nail patterns, but I won't boast about my talents out loud – Rosie will only think I'm conceited, and I'm *not*. 'Meanwhile, there was clapping every time you farted.'

'There was not!'

'There was. You couldn't do wrong in Mam's eyes, and Auntie Bridie thought the sun shone out your—'

'Did you know Mam follows your Instagram page and likes everything you post? Even the really, really depressing political stuff?'

She's making stuff up now because she knows I'm right. 'She doesn't.'

'She does!' Rosie insists. 'Her account is PianoWoMan64.'

'Fuck off.' A rare half-smile threatens to crack the stone that is the corners of my mouth.

'Seriously – check! All she's ever posted is a blurry picture of us at a Daniel O'Donnell concert I brought her to.'

I consider doing an impression of a laugh but I don't have it in me. All I can think about is how absent I've been from my mother's life and how the canyon between us has grown with every year that's passed since my last time in the house. I passed the point of no return a long time ago. Liking posts on social media is one thing, but being an active participant in someone's life is another. She's not called me in over two years.

When I don't keep the conversation going, Rosie does. 'When we were little, Mam and Dad were on a tight budget. If fifty quid was spent on my birthday present and only forty-six quid on yours, Mam would insist on giving you an envelope with four pound coins, back before the euro was a thing. Remember? Just so things were fair!' I stare at the wooden floor where Bertie's tail would be swaying if he still had one. 'There's a lot happening in that head of yours, isn't there?' She leans forward. 'What about talking to – I don't know – a doctor, or some kind of professional—'

I tense my shoulders and clench my fists. 'I don't want to do that.' I say it with as much finality as I can muster. I've been to two different psychiatrists – one laughed about how traumatised I am, and spent several expensive minutes cracking jokes and talking about her own family drama; the other was seconds from slumber for the full hour, so I never went back. Then there was the counsellor who had me sit on a bean bag only to victim blame me. *Maybe you shouldn't have gone to his apartment. Maybe you shouldn't have been drinking. Maybe you didn't say no clearly enough.* I can't help but conclude that the people who say you need to shop around to find the right therapist have plenty of money at their disposal and aren't 'shopping' in TK bloody Maxx, where it's just chaos on railings. Because, quite literally, *fuck that*.

'Well, we can't live like this, Jenna. *I* can't. I don't know what else to do – do I hide the pills? Dump them? I just—'

'I'm not a problem to be fixed.' A response that can be read one of two ways: *There's no problem here to fix, so stop worrying,* or *This is completely unsolvable and there's no point in trying.*

No truth, no lie.

Bertie purrs for a moment or two till we both agree it's time for bed.

ROSIE

I finish my chat with Peter on WhatsApp. Our fumble out on the balcony last night kind-of got in the way of us making any concrete decisions.

> **Me [8:15]: Hey. What time can he meet me?**
> Peter [8:20]: morning, you. sleep well? I called dad, he said he can do 2:30 in stephen's green park. he's in town with a friend and is meeting someone else for dinner later so won't be home in between. that suit? x
> **Me [8:21]: 2:30 is fine.**

Fine. Comes across a bit frosty. I edit the text to '2:30 is perfect! Tell him to meet me at the bandstand'.

Do I return the kiss?

No.

Send!

My tired reflection stares back at me from my dressing-
table mirror. Puffy eyes, dull roots, completely gross. I
turn my make-up bag upside down and get to work on
concealing myself. 'Make-up is for enhancing your features,'
Mam said to me moons ago. For a long time, I believed
her.

Doctor Dolan. Retired doctor. Peter's dad. He's the sort
you'd call odd behind his back. Wears an awful lot of purple
for a man in his sixties, purple T-shirts and shirts and
jumpers that go over shirts, so the collars stick out – a trend
favoured by Irish granddads, ones who'd never dare brave
the colour purple. Most evenings as I leave for my mam's
David is stood outside on the front balcony, leaning over
the glass railing and almost always eating tinned fruit
straight from the can.

I make it to Stephen's Green Park, the heart of Dublin
City, just on time. On a mild Saturday like today friends
and families and lovers and loners splay themselves across
the lawns and walkways. They feed ducks, they watch
swans, they admire the plants, they stroll with headphones.
Cool air caresses my cheeks and reminds me to start
wearing my scarf and gloves, the ones Mam knitted for me
years ago before her hands started giving her so much
trouble. No designer label, but infinitely warmer than
anything I've ever bought in Brown Thomas. Love's magic
touch.

I spot Peter's dad waiting for me under the roof of the
bandstand, by the water. He's reading a book held up with

one hand – his arthritis visible from a distance – and leans
on a yellow umbrella with the other, even though there's no
rain forecast. It's not even spitting.

I wonder how to phrase everything and how much to tell
him and if this is, actually, a stupid idea.

I really hope he's never overheard my arguments with
Jenna through the wall that divides our homes. Or my
shenanigans with his son.

Oh *God* . . .

'Rosie Walker,' he says as I move towards him, stopping
a little too far away without meaning to. His sky-blue eyes
smile.

'Doctor Dolan.'

'I'm just David now.' A soft breeze bites at the white
hair framing his face. 'It's no accident that we're here
together.'

Well, obviously. I asked your son to arrange it . . .

'You're the third ex-patient I've met with today regarding
the project. It's like you're all falling out of the sky for me!'

'Ah. So that's what the brolly is for! Sorry. That . . . wasn't
funny. At all!' I grimace.

David just laughs. 'Come on,' he says, 'let's sit.'

We plonk ourselves down on opposite ends of a bench over-
looking the lake, across from the bridge. David places his
brolly and his book – Percy Thrower's *Encyclopaedia of
Gardening* – beside him and turns his body towards me. I
mirror him, nervously crossing my legs and hugging my
red coat to myself to fight the chill.

'I don't know why I'm here, to be honest,' I tell him. It's true. Really, I should've taken more time to consider this whole, ridiculous thing. Impulsivity will be my end of days. 'I suppose, I thought, this research project you're planning—'

He cuts in. 'D'you know what confluence means, Rosie?'

I shake my head.

'In a literal sense, it's about rivers,' he goes on, gesturing excitedly, 'the place where they join and become one larger river.'

'Um, right?' It's not exactly a question but it's what comes out of me.

'Anyway, it's more often used to talk about the coming together of . . . situations, ideas. That's what this is. Right now. *This* is *the project*.'

'Eh . . .'

'You want to talk about your sister.'

I feel my face twist. 'Well, yeah. What exactly did he – did Peter – tell you?'

David leans forward onto his thighs. 'My son tells me your sister is deeply depressed, is self-harming and might be considering taking her own life. Suicide.'

I open my mouth and close it again, and I glance to the path, feet away, to three power-walking mammy types, hoping they didn't hear David speak as they passed us.

'Forgive me,' he says. 'You're struggling with this. He told me that much, too.'

I bob my head up and down.

'So, what am I getting at? You girls have come into my son's life – and my life – for a reason.'

My lips scrunch up. 'Fate? Not something I'd expect a doctor to believe in.'

He steeples his fingers. 'We exist in an invisible energy soup and not one of us knows the recipe. Rosie, after all my years studying and practising medicine, I'm less certain about what is true now than I was as a doe-eyed student living off Pot Noodle.' He watches some kids throw stones into the water while their mother asks them to stop. 'Dark matter – we know it exists, yet we can't see it. There are things in this world that nobody truly understands. The placebo effect. The curved trees found in Russia's dancing forest. Why we yawn.'

As he says it, I yawn.

He smirks. 'Besides. I'm not a doctor any more, as you know.'

'Yeah. Your replacement is real shit.'

He looks concerned. 'Dolores?'

I adjust my bum on the bench to tilt myself towards him. 'Before every appointment, I tell myself to get the most of my €60 – of the time I'm paying for. But it's always the same. A couple of nods, hardly any chat, while Dolores flicks through computer files or – or writes me out a repeat prescription.'

'What's so different, then, if you don't mind me asking?'

I think for a minute. 'I'd always leave you feeling a bit lighter. You'd hear me out, ask questions.'

'No need to re-write history to massage my ego. I recall you being ever so frustrated that last time you sat opposite me.' He holds his hands up. 'I failed you. I did.'

'No! Life did that,' I tell him, unable to discern how honest I'm being with him, or myself.

He's quiet for a moment. Birdsong. The din of cars. 'Did you know this park once formed a common for public executions? Hangings?' he asks, gazing out at the trees in the distance. 'They used to burn people alive here.'

'Jesus Christ, David! Lovely dinner party fact, that.' My sarcastic words fuse with an uncomfortable laugh.

'I bring it up because, well, we've never been less likely to be killed by others, have we? And at the same time, never more likely to kill ourselves.'

I uncross my legs and shuffle my feet. 'Really? Is that actually true?'

'It is. You can look it up for yourself.'

'Why, though?'

'Why?'

'*I've* had it bad,' I start. 'Really hard times.' I think about the time my Gerard dumped me because I wouldn't 'cut the cord', because I'd sooner ensure Mam was fed and washed by me than by a stranger, because I'd sooner watch TV with her to keep her company than go down the pub with him and his obnoxious work friends. I remember how empty my bed felt and how lonely I was; the feeling of drowning, the saltwater filling me up, and having *nobody* to reach out to . . . the sense that I'd feel that way for the rest of my life. 'But even during the worst of times, I've never even dreamed of . . .' *Now* I'm telling him the truth. I know for sure that I've never even considered ending my own life.

'I'm less concerned with *why* these days.' David sees my eyes widen. 'I mean, I can talk about why I smell till the new year rolls around, or I can go have a shower. You hear what I'm saying?'

'I think so.' Not really.

He reads the lie on my face. 'Even though someone who is suicidal isn't—'

'Here, look, would you mind just not saying that word?'

'Suicidal?'

I wince. 'Please? Not here, and, just, in general, in relation to . . . her.'

'Apologies. Thirty years of necessary candour for the job. Not easy to shake.'

Again, I nod.

'Even though your sister isn't thinking logically, if she's planning to . . . do what you think she's planning to do,' he says tactfully, 'what's important is that the emotions she's feeling are real. Hundreds of thousands of people a year do – do *that*, and those are only reported cases—'

My look begs him to stop.

'Anyway. She might view . . . *checking out* as a way to stop feeling any worse. But all it'll actually do is remove the possibility of her ever feeling any better.'

I hate this. I hate it so much. I can't believe I'm even having this conversation. A memory of Jenna playing with her Barbies in Mam's old bathtub flashes before my eyes, and me pouring a jug of water over her hair – before it was whatever colour it's supposed to be right now, it was mousy brown and curly. She was so slight and pink-cheeked and

full of mischief, and I loved her more than words. I *love* her.
I can't let anything happen to her.

David is still talking. I'm not sure how long I zoned out
for. 'I'm spending retirement learning about prevention,
treatment, causes, writing about mental and spiritual healing
. . . If you're sure she's at risk, we have to act.'

Spiritual. I don't know how anyone says that word out
loud without immediately wanting to bleach their tongue.
'You think this – this project will help, then?'

He shrugs. 'Maybe.'

'Maybe?'

'She has to be open to some level of intervention. She—'

He keeps talking as I gulp and remember how she
clammed up last night when I brought up speaking with
professionals.

David re-grabs my focus. 'Is she with a therapist? On
medication?'

'No therapy, no. Not sure about meds. But she refuses
flat out to see a doctor – so even if she is taking something,
she'll likely run out soon. And then – I don't know –' A
lump in my throat like a lost slug stops my words mid-
sentence.

'That's . . . not good,' he says.

'Everything on Google is telling me that – that nothing *I*
do can—'

'Ignore Doctor Google, Rosie. Listen to someone who
worked as a doctor for thirty years and learned from his
many blunders. Did you know a tremendous majority of
people who go on to . . . well, that they visit some kind of

doctor in the year before their death, when they're at their most vulnerable?'

'Sure. I read up suicide stats all day long. My favourite hobby,' I quip.

He doesn't throw the ball back. His expression doesn't soften at all. 'I had more power than I knew. People were reaching out to me. People who still had a sliver of hope, enough hope to drive them to seek my help. Like this one older patient of mine. He always showed up well in advance of his scheduled check-ups. *Always*. I'd see him sitting there waiting and sometimes I'd call him in early if I was free, but then I stopped.'

David's face is dirty with guilt. 'Why?'

He swallows. 'I dreaded his appointments, Rosie. The desk staff dreaded him. Maggie who takes the bloods, *she* dreaded him. Even the other patients dreaded him. All he wanted to do was chit-chat – about the weather, the new shade of eggshell I'd had the office walls painted, his cousin twice removed and her bloody ingrown toenail.' David scrunches his lips so they vanish into his face. His eyes are wide-open doorways.

'What?'

'He stopped coming along. Then, weeks later, a neighbour of his informed me that he'd been found dead. Killed himself.'

I feel my face desaturate.

'The wife had left. His only child emigrated after the 2008 crash. No job, just his pension and a television set. Essentially, he was coming along early just to have somebody to talk to. In a doctor's office. In *my* office.'

'David, that's not your—'

'That's why I'm still working now, every day, researching, unpaid. I can't let it go. I won't. It's true that happiness, contentedness – these things come from inside ourselves. Sure, we're responsible for ourselves when it comes to achieving such things. But June was right all her life.'

I'm not sure who June is. Do I ask? Will he explain?

'We've lost connection to each other, to – so much,' he goes on. 'The way we *live* now, it's – well – devastating.' David observes a man walking by with his family – he's glued to his phone and his kids scrap for his attention.

My thoughts race. 'Jenna won't talk about this – any of it! When Peter told me about the glasshouse, your plan, I just thought, maybe—'

'Not too unorthodox for you, then?' He sits up straight, genuine curiosity all over his face.

I run through replies in my head for a few seconds. 'It all sounds a bit, um, forgive me, *fluffy*. Getting strangers together to work on some wasteland—'

'My wife's garden,' he corrects me. 'And that's not all there is to it. Gardening, her infertility support group, such things helped my wife immeasurably in preserving her mental health, through her—'

'Yeah, David, I just – I can't imagine it'll do much for my sister. But,' I shrug and throw my hands up, 'what else is there?'

'You think she'll agree to it? Fully commit? For seven months? Like the others?'

'Why seven months?'

A stoic smile. 'I have my reasons.'

I pull off my gloves, just so I can pick at the skin around my thumbs.

'She'll hardly notice me making notes – that, I guarantee. I'll do a lot of it up here,' he says while tapping his temple, 'but her commitment is vital. Every Saturday. Rain or hail. It's important research, Rosie. I hope to write a book about—'

I lose myself in thought again. I think about how Jenna seems to idolise Peter; she'd probably give anything to spend more time around him. 'Could you – maybe – convince that son of yours to get involved?'

David's eyes flash and the corners of his mouth turn up. 'Peter, eh? And your sister?'

'Oh! No, ha. God, *no*.' A jealous stab. I ignore it. 'But a bit of eye candy couldn't hurt,' I say, dimples out. 'You know what young girls are like. And, well, you know how popular he is. He is to her what Bowie probably was to you.'

'Popular.' David laughs. 'Try tell *him* that.' He pushes his hair out of his face. 'Peter will be helping regardless,' David tells me, and I wonder why Peter never said. I wonder who else will be there every Saturday with him, for hours . . . 'Eye candy or no eye candy, your sister needs a new way to cope. One that doesn't involve an object of affection.' His phone vibrates but he ignores it. 'Sorry, sorry, I'm not being ignorant. *That* will need my undivided attention . . .'

I assume it's one of the ex-patients Peter mentioned, so I nod and refrain from asking questions.

'Anyway. If your sister is taking her meds, that's great. If they're not helping much, then this is bigger than biology, and we can do so much more. This mental health stuff, its discourse is so narrow: "Reach out", "Go for a walk", "Just take the pills". People haven't the foggiest.'

'Why the recent interest in all this? Can I ask that?' I think about everything Peter told me last night by the canal about his dad's work.

'My wife,' he says eventually. He looks like he wants to say something else, but he holds it back.

The little hairs on my arms stand. I recall what Peter said about David always talking about her like she's still alive.

'This plan, it's all her.' He lowers his voice to say that last line, his eyes scanning the path to ensure nobody's around.

I chew my cheeks and look at my shoes.

'You know my Peter is adopted,' he continues.

'Mm-hmm.'

'June and I – we had trouble with that. With conceiving. It near killed her – to be unable to carry a child. Couldn't talk about it with anyone. Not even with me.'

Mam's words about motherhood poke at me: 'You can't know the meaning of it till you do it and if you don't, you'll regret it forever, just like your Auntie Bridie.' All the looks of concern she's thrown me amalgamate in my mind's eye. I cross my legs, then I uncross them before crossing them again.

'Fierce difficult to watch someone you love struggle with something like that. It was eating her. For a while, she wasted away. I actually thought she must be sick. There had to be some bacterial thing or a virus, some test I could do, some drug that'd help.' He blinks heavily, allowing his eyes to remain closed for a few seconds. 'And it took years, the adoption process. While we waited, June started gardening. Gardening! When we were young, we'd scoff at auld lads out tending to their flowers on a warm afternoon; we'd tell ourselves that we never wanted to become so boring. Ha! At first, she played around with a few pots here and there. It filled that gap. That longing to create. To grow life!' He smiles fondly and every line on his face becomes more pronounced. 'Then, right before Peter came to us, I had a glasshouse built in the back garden of our old house for June's thirty-fifth birthday. A glasshouse,' he says, shifting, 'has the ability to help things to grow that might otherwise not be able to. And this glasshouse, it was special, because—'

'*Was* special?'

David blinks.

'This is the glasshouse that's gone to shit, right?'

His eyes widen.

'Peter mentioned,' I say.

'And that must be remedied, for it will serve as centre stage . . . hopefully, with a little help from – Jenna, is it?'

'Jenna. Yeah.'

We walk together and I listen to David's not-so-grand plan. I tell him I'm not sure it'll help even a tiny bit.

'Only fools can be sure of anything, Rosie. You are as I was some years back. What *you* need is a pinch of faith.'

It's far removed from many of the prescriptions he's given me over the years. *Have faith*. Christ almighty! But you take everything that bit more seriously when it comes through the mouth of someone who has a medical degree, don't you? Taking a chance on him couldn't hurt any more than watching Jenna be miserable.

'All right. Let's do it.'

JENNA

My phone buzzes and wakes me from a sumptuous two, maybe three hours of sleep. The disgusting smell of bacon tells me Rosie is already up, and the munch of toast that she's in the room with me. Acknowledging her can wait: Peter's name has appeared on my lock screen. My brain convulses. I was his first waking thought.

Peter [9:35]: hihi! sorry I didn't see your last text sooner, just going through some personal stuff. would love to see a friendly face today, tbh. off to collect the new ride, WAIT till you see it! pick you up at half two? or are you busy?

No mention of the pills. I'm relief personified. She mustn't have said anything to him. Thoughts come like forks of lightning while I blink sleep from my eyes and stretch my body. Bertie stirs from my feet under the duvet while I try to come up with a flirty-but-not-desperate reply. My brain fails me, so I lie: I say I'm starting driving lessons soon and that he'd best keep an eye on the keys in case I nick them on him.

Sometimes I wonder why I make stuff up so often. Do I say things out loud that I wish were true? Am I – quite simply – an asshole? Most of the time I just do it and don't think twice. Better to fake something to say than have no words at all – to be the silent, story-less blob nobody wants to talk to. I'm pretty sure most people do it. They *must*. How can anyone possibly always have something to say?

I scroll through Peter's old Facebook albums on his personal, non-public account while I wait for his next message. It's probably the 274th time I've searched his profile this week, since he accepted my friend request. I'm not obsessed or anything. Really. There's just . . . nothing else to think about, and fixating on his world numbs me to my own.

There are pictures of Peter at YouTube conventions with queues of fans; of him on stage while hundreds of phones all glow in the dark like fireflies; shots of his ex-girlfriend, this annoyingly beautiful redhead with immaculate eyeliner and freckles perfectly placed by nature; yet more of them both wrapped up in one another by the sea at twilight and gazing into each other's eyes. Then there's my favourite picture of Peter: him leaning over his keyboard, both his eyebrows raised, wearing a *Jurassic Park* T-shirt. He just looks really like 'himself' in it. I know it was taken in his bedroom next door because the room in the photo has the same curved window wall that Rosie's room has. I'm still patiently waiting to be invited in by him, though I've already memorised every poster on his wall from the background of this one, grainy image.

My screen lights up.

Peter [9:45]: can certainly help you with the car hunt. also, how dare you assume I bought a car? ;)

My order of bubblegum e-liquid arrives – along with yet more bags of expensive made-in-China clothes Rosie doesn't need and will probably only wear once – minutes before I make my way to the underground car park, and *thank fuck* because I've somehow made it twenty-eight hours without a puff. The package contains forty bottles that were going for half price: five bottles per week to do me for the next two months or so. I unzip the pocket inside my bag to hide them, and the fact that this is probably the last batch I'll ever use starts to sink in.

Two months. The brink of despair will surely grow old after two whole months . . .

Bertie's appetite is gone again. He keeps hiding in dark spots around the apartment. Earlier, I couldn't find him. Eventually I checked behind the washing machine. There he was, balled up in the corner. Google says that when cats are really ill they can hide a lot, that it's instinct, because sick animals are targets in the wild. To want to die out of the way of any threats. I mean, make it make sense. I can't

relate to that eagerness to stay safe; just yesterday, headphones on full blast, I crossed the road without checking
for traffic. I had to hold back tears when I made it to the
other side because I had to carry on walking, weathering
the storm that is my merciless inner critic. I wish I could
extract some of Bertie's will to live.

'How much of that crap do you inhale every day, eh?'
Peter asks as I step out of the lift onto the first basement
floor, e-cig in hand. I elbow him, straight-faced.

He just grins.

'Well, where is it?' I observe all of the nearby vehicles,
trying to imagine what Peter would've gone for. 'Not a car,
then, eh?' I look at the white Transit van to our left. 'Um
. . . you *are* taking the piss?'

'Not that! Down there,' he says, twitching his head in the
other direction. A lock of his hair tumbles forward and my
eyes glue themselves to his face. Every time I look at Peter,
I try to sketch him out in my mind. He's all I've drawn since
I met him, but I've still not done the man a drop of justice.
He's hard to get right, see. Peter's most distinctive feature
is this slight misalignment in one of his eyes – I only notice
it when he makes eye contact with me or looks at something
in my direction. His left eye crosses a little towards the tear
duct. It's subtle but it's *him*, and I can't capture it.

'What?' he asks.

'Oh, er, you've – got something – on your mouth,' I lie.

He rubs his thumb across his lips. 'You actually gonna
look over there and be impressed anytime soon?'

I take a drag on my e-cig and search for something that

isn't a car. Milliseconds pass before I spot it. A shiny green Volkswagen bus practically waves at me from across the car park. I've only ever seen them online, usually pictured with 'van life' influencers who've renovated them into tiny houses on wheels so they can vlog their travels while raking in millions of views and brand deals by the shed-load.

'Isn't it awesome? It's second hand, but—'

'We don't say *awesome* in Ireland, Peter. We say *deadly*. Stop pretending to be American. And yeah. That *is* deadly.'

Confusion grabs his face. He shakes it off. 'Whatever. Anyway, I can drive nine people around in this! The seat backs are a bit too upright, but my mom always told me to sit up straight, so . . .' Weird. He's never mentioned his mam before. 'The steering wheel is super thin and old-school enormous, and –'

I breathe out all the vape in my lungs to cut him off. 'We don't say *mom* here, either. You watch too many Americans online,' I tease. 'That twang has to go! You sound like the least Irish *Irish* person that's ever lived, à la Johnny Depp in *Chocolat*.'

The confusion is back. Peter's features do a funny little dance. 'I studied in New York after school – so I guess—'

'I just wish you'd sing with more of your Irish accent, that's all . . .'

He looks at me intently. 'You sure you're not the ringleader of the group of haters out to ruin my life? The one who always calls me "lowercase Peter" instead of pete in messages on Instagram, to wind me up?'

'Wha–?'

'Because trolls say that to me, like, all the time. That I "act too American". It's just how I talk. And, well, sure, *maybe* there's pressure to sing with a bit of an American accent, but most of my followers are used to—'

I can't tell if he's being serious of if he's joking. 'Peter, I was only—'

We stop walking, now parallel with the bus. 'Look. Forget it. This one jerk is just really getting under my skin lately, with the hate comments.'

'Never, ever feed the—'

'Trolls. I *don't*. I block them. Any attempt to reason with a troll is an exercise in futility. Thing is, they keep setting up new dummy profiles to annoy me. Or maybe it's just one person with loads of profiles . . . anyway, whatever. Blocking isn't helping. And I'd like to talk about literally *anything* else. I've talked about this to death with my manager already.'

I try to refocus the conversation. 'You – you mentioned your mam. You never talk about her. How come?'

He curls his shoulders forward and crosses his arms. 'Because nobody ever asks. Let's drive.'

'CDs! I thought they were . . . extinct.'

'Nope. You can still get them online! Check it,' he says, pressing the old-school play button.

Mozart. I've often wondered what kind of music he listens to for pleasure. I suppose this makes perfect sense; in school, we learned that Mozart could compose a new work in his head on the spot, even as he copied out a different one on paper. A musician's wet dream.

Peter drums his fingers against the steering wheel as he drives, commenting some more on the bus, avoiding the subject of his mam entirely. 'Can you imagine if I released a song on Spotify nowadays with a title like 'Serenade for Winds, K. 361, 3rd Movement'? Reckon anyone would bother with that?'

The world zooms past outside with a strange sense of unreality as I attempt to catch and hold all of the questions I want to ask Peter. The stream of consciousness in my mind is distracting, something I'm not used to. It might be that I forgot to take my anti-depressants. I'm all spaced out, full of voices that sound like my own inside-head voice talking over each other, and then there's Mozart, and tyres on tarmac, and the rumble in my stomach because I forgot to eat breakfast again . . .

'Hey, so, I've been having some trouble.'

'Oh?'

'Yeah. Girl trouble.'

He's not nervous at all saying this to me. The calm in his voice makes me uneasy. What girl? What trouble? Who is she? Are we not on a date right now? Was I stupid to assume that's what this is? Why am I not answering him? He keeps talking and I keep staring into space. 'Mm?' It's all I can muster.

Peter shifts. 'It's driving me insane. So, like, my dad, he's an old romantic. He always was with Mom. And I feel like none of that stuff works nowadays.' He pauses. 'People say they want love, right? But they don't.' A pause. 'Love is straightforward. Easy. You love someone, they take your love with open arms and they return it. But . . . people seem to want things to be hard.'

Who's people?

'They need the struggle. The fight. As if the existence of problems somehow – I don't know – validates the level of love. I see opportunities; she sees obstacles.' Another pause. 'I'm writing a song about it. Struggling, actually. Because I know people online will call me all sorts . . . desperate, pathetic. Not like I'm not used to it but, yeah. Sorry. This is a lot. I'm doing it again, aren't I?'

He does tend to spill everything out – a teapot tilted, too full. But I welcome it every time. It's impressive. Something I can't do. If I were a teapot, you'd need to pull the lid off and turn me upside down and, even then, you'd be lucky to get a couple of drops from me. I'm not the teapot you'd want to find in the grip of thirst in a wide-open desert.

I decide I don't want to think about Peter with some other girl, especially not one who clearly has no concept of how fortunate she is to have someone like him in her orbit. What brand of idiot has he tangled himself up with? Sounds like it's going nowhere, though. Silver linings, am I right? Plenty of space for me to swoop in, take his mind off her. We can distract each other . . .

I lean back on the cushioned seat and stare at him. 'Your mam. You were supposed to start there. *Then* you can go off on one.'

'Ah . . . hmm. Yeah. My mom died, like, four years ago.'

He takes a breath. 'That's why Dad moved here, to the city, and why I moved back to New York for a while. It's familiar, y'know, and I needed to bury myself in – something. Settled on making music, posting my stuff, gigging.'

'And then, you moved back here to be with your dad?'

'Yeah. Last year. He's . . . not OK.'

Mam sits alone in the room of my subconscious. I manually dim and fade the image and I concentrate on Peter. *Only Peter.*

'Your music is your superpower,' I say, my voice small. 'She'd want you to use it for good, like you do.'

'That's super nice, Jenna. But I think it's more like a scar than a superpower. One that people like looking at 'cause it takes their minds off their own scars.' He gives me this sideways look, then. I instinctively pull my over-the-knee socks higher up my thighs and I tug my skirt as low as it'll go. 'You know that I *know* you hurt yourself, right? You know that I saw, like, right away?'

I think about the last time I held a cigarette against my bare flesh and I'm overwhelmed by a desire to do it right now – to realise the pain inside me – to see proof of it mapped out on my body.

'Why do you do it?'

The lapse in conversation that follows is unbearable but I don't know how to break it. I press my forefingers into my temples.

'I don't want you to do that any more,' he says, his voice firm, caring.

Though my body language says otherwise, it feels *good*

just to hear someone say that to me. I allow the words to wrap me up warm for a moment. 'I'll stop, then,' I tell him, hands either side of my face to self-soothe. He doesn't need to know where my life is headed but he should know that I appreciate his care, now, while I'm still here.

'No. Don't stop because somebody else tells you to stop. Stop because you want to stop, Jenna! Stop 'cause, 'cause . . . it's pointless. It doesn't address anything. And you don't deserve it.'

He doesn't understand. Of course he doesn't! He's this incredible, gifted, handsome, kind, enchanted thing; he'll never understand what it feels like to be anything but. It's not his fault. It's just – reality.

'Can we, please, not talk about – I – I just—'

'I hear you.'

I sigh, relieved.

'You not going to ask me what the bus is for, then?'

Thankful for the tangent, I reply immediately, eager to change the subject and to evaporate any pity he might be feeling. 'Obviously you're planning on abandoning me with Moss for a hipster life on the road.'

He laughs. 'Cold. Very cold. Come on, guess!'

'Eh, I don't know. Music video prop?'

'Freezing.'

'What could you possibly need all that space for back there if you don't plan on remodelling this thing? Or filming it. What are you up to, Dolan?'

'This is a practical purchase. We're going to need all those seats.'

'For all the friends you told me you don't actually have?'

He looks at me, hair flopped onto his forehead, cheeky smile plastered onto his face.

'Wait,' I say. 'What do you mean *we*?'

ROSIE

'Tea? Coffee?'

'Neither, thank you,' David replies. It's evening now and he's sat at my kitchen table with his jacket slung over the back of his chair and his legs crossed. 'But I wouldn't say no to a chocolate digestive.' He smiles at me and eyes up a red plastic tube on the countertop. Jenna must have had some in the middle of the night to fill the space where her dinner should've been gurgling. (My offer of homemade *vegan* cottage pie was impolitely declined.)

'Jenna aside, how've you been? Still having those panic attacks?'

Mother of divine! I can't get used to how he just comes out with this stuff. In our family we like to tiptoe around this kind of thing. Even if my mother had a knife sticking out of her neck, I wouldn't draw attention to it; I'd do everything in my power to turn her attention to something else – headlines, handbag contents, how shit the weather is. That's how she taught me to be. With my head buried a foot into the earth. That's where I'm comfortable.

I tell him, 'Not really.' It's mostly true. 'I've only had two since Jenna moved in and both passed fairly quickly.' I hand him the digestives. He struggles to take one between his thumb and forefinger.

'You agitate easily,' he says. 'Your fists, they're clenched a lot, I've noticed. Your shoulders, tense, all afternoon. Any jaw pains? Bowel troubles?'

'David! I'm fine. I just get stressed. *Everyone* gets stressed.'

'Not everyone carries it around with them all day,' he says through a mouthful of coagulated sugar and wheat. 'We're supposed to release it.' His arms fly out before him like he's throwing something invisible from his chest.

Just then, twenty minutes early, my favourite way to release stress knocks on the front door – I know it's him because he does this rhythmic seven-knock thing. Standing by the table, I intertwine my legs against the association of that knock; excitement shoots through me. My body couldn't have chosen a worse time to be at odds with my head.

'Doesn't she have her own key?' David asks.

'She does,' I say, defensive.

'Ah. A warning knock, then. Peter's a good boy. Quick. The tablets,' he says, rubbing his hands together to free them of crumbs.

I jump at my handbag as I hear Jenna's key in the lock. At Usain Bolt speed, I lay out the pills I confiscated in a way that shows how many there are: a thick fan of aluminium spreads across the table to bring Jenna face to face with the reality of how lethal such a high dose of maximum-strength painkiller would be. We won't pressure her to talk about it, though: David said we're not doing this to interrogate her, only to show her that we know where she's at and that we want her to be OK. I take a sharp, deep breath and turn to face the mouth of the hallway as Peter appears with my sister, just as we'd arranged.

'What's . . . going on?' Jenna looks from me to David then back to me. She wears an expression of the sourest confusion. 'This one here,' she says, pointing at Peter, 'is being all cryptic with me, and I've a bitch of a headache coming on, and I want to know what's happening. Who's he? Our long-lost grandad?'

'Sorry she's being rude, David, I—'

'This is my dad,' Peter says, taking over. His gaze flickers from Jenna's face to David's to mine, where it settles.

Jenna doesn't notice how he looks at me. 'Oh. Right,' she says.

'David here used to be my doctor,' I start, but as I say *doctor* Jenna slices me with a glare so fierce it stops me mid-sentence. She looks uncomfortable and on edge and I instantly feel terrible. 'But this is different, this is—'

'A fucking ambush is what it is.'

'*Jenna!*'

'Listen—' Peter tries.

'Hey,' David says, and clicks his fingers, as though to release us all from a spell. 'Let's return to introductions, shall we?' He looks at my sister. 'I don't believe we've met. Hello. I'm David, Peter's dad, I live next door.'

He holds out a hand for her to shake from across the room, but she's already turned to face Peter directly. With her arms gripping one another across her body, she bites her lip and scans his face. 'Peter, she's making stuff up, all right? She's—'

'Can we just sit down, and—?'

'Just say it. You believe her.'

'My dad isn't a practising doctor any more, he's—'

'You think I'm going to top myself, so you've enrolled daddy dearest to analyse me and you've lumped me with an audience when you – you could've – just – *talked* to me.'

Our relationship really is fractured beyond measure – she'd sooner talk to someone she's known a couple of weeks than to me, someone she's known her whole life.

'We talk, Jenna. We just . . . we don't talk about *that*, do we?' He points at the table. She hasn't looked there yet. Jenna, face crumpled with disgust, shoots the table a nasty what-are-you-talking-about look. Her eyes open wider than I've ever seen them when she spots the layout of painkillers. Immediately, she pulls her face away, and her body starts to shake, like she can't control it.

I can't stand this. 'Look, David, Peter, I think – I think this was a mistake. I'm sorry, can we just – can we leave it? Jenna, I didn't mean to—'

'Don't.' She's staring at the floor. Her eyes are fixed, wide and feral. She looks like she'd lunge at and bite me if we didn't have company.

'I'm sorry. I just wanted to show you that – that there are people who care about you! And . . . to suggest something. But, look, *it doesn't matter*. We don't have to—'

'People who care? This is the world's most pathetic intervention. I mean, *look* at us.' She throws her hands in the air. 'My sister who hasn't spoken to me for years, some auld lad I've never met . . . is this supposed to be a joke? Because it's not funny.'

'Right, fine, I shouldn't have bother—'

'Rosie,' David calmly interrupts. I look at him, and he softly shakes his head to ask that I stop. He leans forward onto his thighs, towards Jenna. 'Your sister hasn't asked me to come here as a doctor. This isn't just about you: this is about all four of us, and some others, who you'll soon meet, coming together, to—'

I stop him. 'Wait. David, *I'm* not joining.'

He just stares at me.

'Just putting that out there. In case we got our wires crossed . . .'

'I insist you do. It'll be good for you.'

What's he playing at? 'I can't. My mam—'

'You said she only needs you in the evenings.' Peter jumps in. 'This is a daytime thing. Saturdays only. You'd always be back in the city by dinner time to help her out.'

The bastard! *They're* cornering *me* just as *we're* cornering *Jenna* . . .

'What are you all on about?' Jenna begs.

'Rosie, pour Jenna some water there. Jenna, please sit.' David says it like he's known us intimately for a lifetime.

Stranger still, Jenna does as he says. She pulls out a chair, sits opposite him. Her seat is tilted slightly away from the sight of the pills on the tabletop. I do as David says too, walking as though I might wake a baby.

This all feels so illusory, like the curtain could fall at any moment. Jenna and I don't talk. Peter and I don't spend time together unless we're screwing or are about to screw or just finished screwing. Older men don't frequent my apartment because I don't know any. Yet the four of us are here, entering the deepest of conversations, to the soundtrack of Bertie's purring.

I don't even like cats.

'Do you want to know something my wife always says when life becomes too much? "David, flowers still blossom, in spite of everything. The magic of renewal can be found in the blooming of Easter lilies." Isn't that a comfort?'

It's a whole lot of discomfort. My eyes wander. I don't want him to spot the judgement in them. I look at Jenna. She's not paying attention, I can tell.

'Listen, whatever *she* said, it's not true.' Jenna points at me. 'Those pills – I just happen to have a lot of them. Headaches and stuff. I only had them in the couch because Rosie hasn't given me the spare room – like, I've nowhere to put anything. I wasn't purposefully hiding them. So, that's that. I don't know what *this* is about . . .' It could be a mouse talking, her words are so little, obviously because she's barefaced lying and feels bad about it.

David holds his hand up. 'You mentioned that it's a "pathetic intervention",' he says. 'Well, it's certainly an intervention of sorts. Not only because of these pills, but because of how worried these two are for you.' David sits still for a moment. 'Rosie,' he says, 'when you've calmed down, please read the letter I had you write. Aloud.'

Jenna twists her neck to look at me. 'Are you actually *serious* right now?' An angry whisper while I reach into my pocket. Taking deep breaths, I carefully pull out the folded sheet of A4 paper onto which I've written what I want to say to her. David told me it would help. He had Peter do the same thing.

I catch Peter's eye.

An incredulous gasp from Jenna's chair.

'Take it away,' Peter says.

'Right. Here goes.' I feel my cheeks turn hot. 'Dear sister,' I start. My voice breaks straight away.

A groan from Jenna. 'Who do you think you are? Jane Austen?'

David gestures for me to continue, so I start over, self-consciousness clawing at me from every angle. I shake off the fear like it's just dust. I have to. Or I'll actually wet myself.

'*Dear sister*. I know I haven't done all I could have to show you over these past few years, but I love you, more than you'll ever know. Ever since you came back into my life, I've been concerned about you from the moment I wake up until the moment I climb into bed. The worry shaped my dreams at night for weeks. It woke me up, it followed me to work, and after I found your stash, it grew so heavy I couldn't carry it alone any more.' I realise I've stopped breathing so I suck a ton of air into my lungs and continue. 'You don't need to explain yourself and I'm not going to press you, but you do need to hear the facts. The way you're living right now isn't healthy or sustainable for either of us. The tension that exists between these walls since you moved in is unbearable. You're an adult, as am I. I have responsibilities. I have to keep my own head above water, and you being here is making that really difficult for me. You lie to me, your routine is all over the place, you don't help out with any housework, you don't talk to me, and I've had enough of feeling how I'm feeling. It's like I'm drowning and, unlike you, I've got nobody to save me.' I hear Peter gently clear his throat and swallow: it's not an *ahem*, more like subconscious upset. I don't draw any attention to it. 'I need you to be open to what we're about to propose, and if you can't be, I'll' – I glance at her for a second, nervous that I'm about to go too far; I'm shaking like a cold, wet dog because the blood vessels in her eyes seem ready to rupture – 'I'll have to ask that you move in with Mam so I can sort myself out. Mam is allergic to cats, mind, so you won't be able to have Bertie there with you.'

I stop reading and start speaking directly to her, as if I need to explain myself. But I can't look at her, so I look at a scratch on the floor tiles. 'You – you remember how pink her eyes would get, even when you'd keep him outdoors, when he slept in the shed, and, like, now he's too old to live outside, and Mam has enough on her plate, and—' I look up. Jenna is gently waving her head in desperate protest. Fuck. I hurry back to the letter, to finish it as fast as humanly possible. 'I wasn't in the best place mentally when you moved

in, and now, I'm also trying to handle the idea that I might
. . . lose you. You're so young; you have so much life left to
live. Besides, I can't allow you to put me through the pain
of that. Not me, not Mam. You need to think about more
than just yourself.' I feel my autopilot turn off. Emotions start
to hit me like waves. I'm no longer reading a script. I'm
baring my soul in front of onlookers and I'm essentially giving
my suicidal sister an ultimatum. 'That's all,' I say, and I hide
the letter behind my back as if doing so will undo my reading,
will make Peter unhear my words, will make Jenna feel safe
enough to come up for air from her hands, where her face
is currently buried.

David's head is tilted back, his piercing eyes latched to
the ceiling. I don't think he's happy about me threatening
Jenna with a move to Mam's, but he *did* tell me to be
completely honest. I can't cope with the current situation
and I'm all out of options.

'Now, Peter,' David says, 'your turn.'

Peter pushes his glasses up his nose and walks around
to kneel in front of Jenna. She doesn't remove her face from
her hands. I so badly want to do exactly what she's doing.
I don't want to be here.

'Jenna. Or future artist of world-famous album covers
because you're so completely awesome.' She laughs weakly
from behind her hands. 'I've not known you long,' he
continues, his voice calm as his dad's, 'and I'm not just doing
this because of the pills, or because I was put up to it, or
anything like that. I just know how much you're hurting.
You're hurting inside, so you're hurting yourself on the

outside, and all that hurt, it's hurting *us*. We might not be many but hopefully we matter. We don't want to see you like this.'

I feel the hair on my arms stand against the iffy feelings that come on me then: resentment, bitterness, discontent. They're close in a way that Peter and I aren't. I imagine having him as a friend rather than a bit on the side, and envy floods me for whatever it is that they have.

'Dad is going to help,' he goes on. 'Not only you, but me and Rosie, too. You're in a . . . different kind of bad place, but you're not the only one who needs the help. We're going to be there for each other, and—'

'Tell *her* that,' Jenna says quietly. 'She wants rid of me.'

'Let me finish. We're going to get through this shit time *together*. You just have to say yes and, well, my next album . . . the cover is all yours. I mean it. I wasn't kidding there a minute ago.' He squeezes his letter into a ball and throws it to Bertie, who jabs at it with his paws from Jenna's feet.

David told me two things when we strolled together in Stephen's Green earlier today. First, that we had to give Jenna something to look forward to. Something to live for. Something she could focus on anytime dark thoughts filled her brain. He said Peter would figure that part out. David also said that Jenna needed a solid reason to agree to the plan in the first place. This was *my* job. Now I'm worried I've completely blown it by making her participation in David's plan the sole condition under which she can live here. I think I just misunderstood, I—

'Really?' Jenna says to Peter, pulling me from my worries. 'You'd let me do that?'

'It would be my honour. I'd pay you, obviously, and I'd tag you on social media, so you'd get a ton of exposure from it. Other jobs! It could totally become a whole thing. So, you need to be *around*. And I'm not only saying it because I want you to do this thing with us, I really—'

'But . . . what *thing*?' she asks, rubbing her wrist with her thumb. 'What's this thing that Rosie thinks she's too good for but that *I* have to do?'

She won't even look at me.

'So,' David jumps in excitedly. 'Jenna, let me tell you about Alice Barnes – who you'll meet – and her many talents. Peter, Rosie . . . we've some frozen pizzas next door. One of you fetch those, and one of you sort Moss out with his dinner. Let's make a night of this. This is the first day of the rest of our lives. June, *can you believe this?*'

He sits back happily in his chair and the three of us act as though we didn't hear him address his dead wife like she was in the room with us. I search Peter's expression for confusion. If he feels any, he's expert at hiding it. He must be used to this, so.

What am I getting myself into?

JENNA

The drive to Avalon – David and Peter's old house, where I've agreed to spend every Saturday until I'm, well, dead – is my kind of picturesque. Frosty winter trees, naked and gnarled. Cold-touched fields stretch out either side of Peter's bus like grey velvet blankets. If you ignore the animals dotted here and there it's like *all the world* is dead. There's something so peaceful about that.

Peter tells us that the house is named after some island from old King Arthur stories. David says his wife 'is mad into' all that.

'Mom always told me stories about this enchanted place called Avalon – King Arthur rolled up there on a boat, hanging by a hair, and all these hot mystery women with healing powers carried him off to sort him out. I mean, what more could a man hope for?'

Rosie sharply exhales. I bet she's thinking exactly what I'm thinking: how grand it must have been to have had a mother read you bedtime stories. Mam's piano tutoring always had her zapped of energy by the end of the day, when Dad would be passed out in front of the TV with a near-empty bottle of Cabernet Sauvignon.

Aside from Rosie (beside me), Peter (driving) and Moss (sprawled on David's lap with his head sticking out the window), the bus is full of people I don't recognise. They're all wrapped up in layers, hats, gloves, and I could be wrong but I'm pretty sure David's friend Alice is sitting in the row behind me, apparently she's helping him run this – *project*, or whatever it is. She caught my eye as she climbed on outside a beautiful waterfront cottage. It must be her. Everyone else appears to be in their twenties or thirties. She's got long, unkempt hair and a gaunt face with skin the colour of printer paper. Supposedly, Alice has only left the house for dog food and microwave dinners for, like, half a decade.

I wonder if she threw up before getting on the bus.
I did.
It's like my gut knows something I don't.
We all sit stiff and cloddish, saying nothing. The sound of the radio covers up the horror of silence between strangers. I fixate on that little wisp of hair at the back of Peter's neck and on his lovely smooth skin; if he wasn't part of this nonsense there's absolutely no way I'd have woken up willingly. Rosie would've had to drag me on here by the helix piercing.

'You might not feel you've made much impact in one session. But if you come with us every week, over a period of time, you *will* feel change,' David promises us at some point during the drive. I hadn't even realised he was talking.

No, I think, *I'll just see a whole lot of your son, and that's fine by me.*

Avalon is discreetly tucked away in the hills of Milverton, on the other side of a tunnel that separates the house from David's coastal hometown. Detached and sat on at least half an acre, it's tall, with bare wisteria vines on its stone walls and a peeling green door. Definitely the kind of place you'd picture a doctor owning. Big, 'look at me', beautiful, separated from other houses by a shield of trees.

We climb out of the bus and into the cold. There's an absence of the kind of man-made sounds I must usually edit out, like the roar of construction, the hum of traffic: I'm so aware that there's nothing *to* edit out.

The front garden has clearly been neglected for a long time. With an old stone well as its centrepiece, you'd be forgiven for assuming the scene was plucked from a forgotten forest. Peter tells us he's hired a well contractor for maintenance and warns us off trying to use it any time soon. He beckons for us to follow him around the back of the house through a side gate as Moss darts around and barks at birds. I trail behind, wondering why we're not going inside the house first.

Over my shoulder, I spot David lagging behind; he slowly paces, puts his hands into the pockets of his black winter coat, observes his old house. I notice he's holding back tears. An urge to comfort him overwhelms me but I don't quite know what to do with it.

David spots me hovering by the gate. 'Go ahead, Jenna. I just need a minute. You understand.'

I don't understand. But I want to.

In seconds I've caught up with everyone – I only notice when I stop hearing the crunch of my steps as grass appears beneath my Docs. I look up and drink my surroundings like I'd die if I didn't.

The back garden of Avalon is wild – somehow unstill and still all at once. It races with life, deeply serene in all its daunting unkemptness. The air is cleaner than anything I've ever had inside my lungs – I notice that as I look out at a thousand shades of green, as I smell water on rock. A sweep of woebegone winter lawn leads to a cracked stone bird bath, the remnants of a vegetable garden, patches of dark earth. The whole place is surrounded by a messy wall of ancient self-sown trees wearing thick fur coats made of moss. Don't get me wrong – I've seen places like it a million times on television and in movies, but even still, my first sentiment is shock – like my brain has never entertained the thought that nature is something that's actually accessible.

In the middle of the garden sits the old Victorian glasshouse – the reason we're all here – screaming at the life all around it. The ornate glass and iron building is bigger than I expected. It's white, with a brick base, and it's calling out to be rescued from ruin: some of the windows are smashed, there are more leaves growing on it than in it, and the glass is decorated with lashings of white bird droppings and spray paint.

A wreck.

'Told you it was bad,' Peter says, hands on his hips as he

observes the glass disaster. 'Mom always had it full of lovely plants – flowers and tomatoes, peppers, all kinds of stuff. She was really proud of it. People suck.' He's not talking to anyone in particular, but I nod in agreement anyway, feeling this odd sense of us against the world, against the people who came and made a wreck of this place.

For the first time, I look around at the others.

There's Alice, the older lady.

Then there's this plain pregnant girl with visible blood vessels all over her cheeks. She joined us in the car park of our apartment building so I assume she's another neighbour. Her belly isn't yet visible, not through her thick winter bomber anyway, but I heard David ask her how far along she was when we first took off – 'four months', she'd said excitedly.

To her left, a bit behind her, one of Peter's friends: a tall, slender man with short dreadlocks in a stylish trench coat. I recognise him from Peter's Instagram and his Facebook page, from pictures of parties, gigs, nights out; he has a hand held softly to his cheek, a finger falling in front of his lips as he sizes everything and everyone up.

The only other guy here looks like an Irish-rugby-player type. He's pale and burly, sort of hunky, if you know what I mean, with the classic brown-hair-that's-tight-around-the-sides-and-floppy-on-top. I notice how closed off he is. He looks at the ground like it's all there is.

The last group member is a girl, maybe my age. I pull my gaze away from Mister Meat and Two Veg as she walks to Peter's side. This is a girl who wears her problems on the outside. Her hair is dyed jet-black, which only draws attention to the shadows of her emaciated face. I can't see her body under all the winter gear but I imagine that her legs are as thin as my arms.

David emerges through the back door of Avalon carrying some of the stuff he and Peter had loaded into the boot of the bus: buckets full of bottles and tools, and bags of God knows what. He seems on edge, David – his lips are tightly pressed together and his eyes are in another world. He said he'd not visited this house since he moved out. 'Painful memories' something something . . . A lot of the conversation from *that night* has gone through the washing machine of my memory. Some of what he said comes to me in vivid detail but other segments of the chats we had drowned in my anger at Rosie for leaving me feeling so exposed in front of Peter, for divulging my mental state without my consent, for denying me my chosen escape route, forcing me to consider a variety of other *far less appealing*, less *quick*, less *painless* life exit strategies . . .

'It's been years since I last stood here, guys,' David starts, though it's awkward hearing him say *guys* like he's trying to seem twenty-five years younger than he is, 'and, honestly, I couldn't have made it through the front gates without each and every one of you. It's hard. To be here. To look at – at *that.*' He gestures at the glasshouse, looks like he wants to eff and blind about the damage done to it. 'Anyway. Our goal is simple,' he starts. 'It's to make this space into something beautiful again. Together.'

Shoes crumple blades of grass. Sparrows twitter from under the eaves.

'It kills me to see the place like this,' Peter says eventually. 'I get it. Kids trespass, they wreck stuff. But this . . . it feels like a slight on Mom's—'

'This wasn't just a garden that was superficially attractive – like a woman with one of those silly internet filters on her face,' David cuts in. The thin girl giggles. 'Magic once poured out of every leaf. We want to bring back the personality to the glasshouse and the garden . . . the atmosphere here was vibrant, when . . .' David trails off, turns to look at us. '"Land bonds with the people who tend to it" – my wife told me that. When a bond is formed and then that land is ignored, this is what you get,' he says, throwing his hands up. 'She'd say "a garden is like a child" and I never listened. I raised my child,' he says, pointing at Peter, 'and I left this place. Didn't nurture it, like she did, before—' He stops mid-sentence. We all watch him. 'Healing this space together will lead us to our truest selves. No instant transformations, no miracles. Just commitment. *Teamwork.*'

Families of birds gossiping away is all that's to be heard. Not a word out of anyone.

'Eh, Dad, I'll go get the picnic chairs.'

'Yes, thank you, my boy.'

A moment passes before people start to acknowledge one another, pairing up, talking in clouds of cold breath.

Rosie – mid-chew of her cheeks – comes over to me, searches my eyes for something. 'How you feeling?' she asks, her voice low.

I blow my own cheeks out in response and balance on

my heels. I don't know what to say. I'd very much like to be asleep. But here, I get to look at and talk to Peter. So, I'm putting up with the standing even though sickness and exhaustion and depression all want me to be horizontal.

'Same,' she replies, thinking she's reading my mind. 'Still don't know why I'm here. I don't *need* something like this. But it'll give us something to do together.'

Her lack of self-awareness is embarrassing. 'Yeah, you are way too well-functioning to be stuck here with us. Sickened for you,' I say sarcastically.

'Jenna. Come on. *I* don't need a support group. I just need to not be stressed about my family. About you. I'm here for *you*.'

'You're here because Peter wants you to be here.' She kicks at the dewy grass. 'And his dad. I mean, they obviously think you need help,' I add. 'Plus, David was your doctor, so—'

'Would you stop! This is about you and your problems – OK? I'm just – I'm trusting that this is a good idea, that it'll—'

She stops talking as the Dolans – father and son – appear with fold-out chairs. While David opens them out and places them down one by one to form a circle, Peter asks if anyone wants tea or coffee. Alice and Irish-rugby-player boy both want tea with two sugars. Milky coffee for Rosie and for Peter's willowy friend. Nothing for the others.

'Jenna?' Peter prods.

'Water?' I ask him, hands together in mock prayer.

He winks, and again I get that feeling like I'm dead and

he's one of those electrode things that shocks your heart into beating normally again.

Yes, I'm pathetic. But you knew that right from the get-go.

We all take our seats: kids, day one in a new school. Wilderness vibrates around us. David brings a hand to his chest. 'I'm aware this is all very unusual, but stay with me. It'll all be worth it. At least, that's the hope.' He pauses. 'To start, I'd like us to get to know each other for a bit.' He struggles with the tight pocket of his jeans, removes a mint-green pebble. 'My wife brought this back from her travels in Russia – it's from the Ilmensky mountains. She calls it a stone of truth.'

The hunky, burly chap flicks his nose and rubs his hands against his thighs, like he's feeling out of place.

'Each week, we'll take turns holding it, and it will help us to open up to one another.' David holds the stone firmly between his index and forefinger, in spite of his arthritis. 'The alarm on my phone is set to go off at noon today, and that'll be our signal to get started. Tasks will vary from week to week. A late lunch will follow our efforts, every Saturday at 3 p.m., in a café down the road – a lovely place called Seasons run by a dear friend of mine, Minnie. Then Peter will drive everyone home, and on that drive, I'll be giving out some homework – books to read, worksheets to fill out. So, if anyone needs to use the bathroom, please go in through the back door and take the – the – first right—'

'Sorry, *sorry*,' the pregnant girl begins in a nasal voice, 'you said – about us getting started – doing what exactly? Sorry, really, *sorry*, I, I just, I didn't expect it to be, so – I mean, how are we supposed to make a difference here? Is one day a week enough?' She looks around at the weeds and the dead foliage and the utter state of the glasshouse. Her nervousness makes my heart thump.

'Ah. Jordanne. Everyone, meet Jordanne, a neighbour of ours, and a big fan of my son Peter's work!'

Weird name. Even weirder to invite a fangirl along . . .

Rosie shakes her foot as he finishes speaking. It's a physical manifestation of her anxiety that I recognise all too well.

'Dad. Don't – don't bring that stuff up,' Peter says under his breath, but it's obvious that everyone hears because they all go quiet. 'I mean. Yeah.' He's louder now. Moss runs to his side and Peter robotically pets his head. 'I know some of you like my songs, and – that's – real cool –' he halts between words, shares a nerdy thumbs up, his eyes exploring the grass in the middle of the circle, 'but I – I don't want to be that guy out here. *That* guy is one of the main reasons *this* guy needs . . . something like this. Performing a version of yourself online, opening yourself to . . . well . . . it's not a recipe for great mental health. I know. Shocker.'

'No autographs or selfies, people, you heard it.' An animated voice to Peter's left saves him from having to dance the 'feel bad for me, I'm famous, it's so hard' dance. It's his friend, from the photos online. 'I'm Nathan, by the way, so, yes, *hi*.' A slight south-Dublin lilt. His legs are crossed and his hands are folded neatly on his long thighs. His nails are painted red and his skin gleams as though he maintains a complex twelve-step skincare routine. 'I've never done anything like this in my life,' Nathan says, 'just putting that out there. But I trust Doctor D to help me sort through my shit.'

David slaps his leg, evidently delighted that people are finally talking. 'Yes! And look at that, you don't even have *the stone . . .*'

Nathan smiles cheekily. Looks around. 'I'm assuming we're all here for different reasons, but we probably have more in common than we think,' he goes on. 'Sure, we don't all have a million Instagram followers.' He smirks at Peter, bunches up his lips. 'And *hopefully* we've not all had our – nudes leaked.' His voice shakes; a crack in his confidence. 'That shit bites you over and over again. Doctor D knows.'

David pushes out a soothing laugh. 'Thankfully, the world hasn't been subjected to stills of my naked body. Only my poor wife has had the displeasure of seeing it.' Again, he looks up at the house. His eyes tell the story of a man trying with all his might to hold himself together. We all laugh politely, apart from Alice. She seems unsure whether or not laughing is a safe activity. The giggles dwindle after a few seconds but David's eagerness to plunge himself into this – whatever this is – only grows. 'Ah, Tadhg! You next,' he prods. 'Tell us something about yourself. Anything at all. Oh! Maybe we could play two truths, one lie. A solid icebreaker!'

Tadhg, the handsome rugby-player type, grabs at the string of his hoodie. He's clearly uncomfortable. I see it in how he fidgets, how he scratches his nose. 'Right, so.' Deep voice. Country accent. Monotone. A pause. 'My folks are still together, so they are. I. Eh. Oh. I studied abroad. And, eh, well, my girlfriend, she, eh, she, like, she killed herself. Last year.' He picks at a rip in his jeans as he speaks. I feel the blood in my veins turn cold. I can sense Rosie turning towards me, and my eyebrows furrow in frustration. Doesn't she realise all these people are looking?

But they're not.

They're looking at Tadhg.

Tadhg apologises for throwing that out there without warning while I just think: wow. She really did that. His girlfriend. She left Tadhg behind, and now he's here with all of us because he's obviously got nothing better to be doing, either, because she's gone. Fuck.

I glance at Rosie then quickly look away: she's a deer in headlights and I'm the car, moving in agonising slow motion.

'Izzy, then. Seeing as we're all getting right to it,' David says as he looks towards the thin girl, a vision of calm in the face of all this heaviness, 'how about you tell everyone why you're here?'

'How about you tell everyone why *you're* here, first?' Izzy replies, affection wrapped in sass on stilts. She chews her gum with an endearing grin on her face to let everyone know that she's teasing. 'David,' she announces to the group, 'was my GP, but we've kept in touch since he retired, or, well, I've hounded him and he's been sound enough to reply. *My thing*,' she goes on, 'is I can't eat food, and everyone I love thinks I'll die before my thirtieth birthday.' I'm unsure where to plant my eyes so I look up. The family of magpies that fly overhead sound like helicopters in this ghost quiet.

'There's no real reason for it that I can pinpoint,' she goes on. 'My childhood was awesome and my family rock: nothing terrible has happened in my life . . . it just is what it is. And that's me! In a nutshell.' Izzy blows a bubble and lets it pop over her badly chapped lips.

'Good woman, Iz. That self-awareness,' David says, looking at me, pointing at her, 'is a step towards freedom. It's all too easy to be ambivalent or ignorant about one's problems, much more difficult to develop real awareness, but it's absolutely necessary. This – here,' he gestures outward, 'is just another step to climb.' He nods at Izzy. She smiles.

'Floor is yours now, Doc!'

David looks around. 'You're all being very brave, sharing your stories – it's only right I do the same.'

We wait for an uncomfortably long moment.

'Where to start. Ah! One . . . odd thing they never prepare you for when you train to become a doctor is that you'll eventually be able to accurately self-diagnose. It can be a bother when there's something really wrong, let me tell you. I – I experience what we refer to as complicated grief.' He sighs. Starts to well up again. This time a fat tear falls and I have to look away from his face. I desperately want to reach for my e-cig, but that would be rude . . . right? Oh, fuck it. I grab it and I vape into the inside of my leather jacket, pretty sure nobody notices – they're all too busy staring at the crying man.

Peter pulls his chair closer to his father and places an arm on his shoulder. Then he takes over for David. 'It's sort of when feelings of loss and stuff, none of it goes away even after loads of time goes by. Like – for me – after Mom passed, I was numb. I felt angry. Guilty even, thinking I could've saved her somehow. I'd smell her clothes and I'd stare at her name on my phone, at the last message she sent me, asking what time I'd be home at for dinner. I'd convince myself I could hear her in the next room singing to herself. *Blondie*. Always Blondie, ha.' David's tears stream as he stares at Peter's shoes. 'But after a while, reality sank in and I – moved on. That's what we do. It's natural, it's important, to – move forward. Dad will tell you. Hasn't happened for him, though.'

'I'm, I'm sorry.' Tadhg says it. David acknowledges him with a gentle nod.

'Dad isolates himself. He thinks about Mom all the time, avoids reminders . . . that's why he's not been back here. Sure, we're not in the house, but even *this* – it's a huge step. I'm proud of you, y'know.'

David doesn't bring himself to look at Peter. There's no embrace. He just tries with all his might to keep himself from unwinding further; his hands are bunched into fists, like he's squeezing his pain to keep it inside.

'Dad sometimes says stuff like that he wishes he went with her. I've caught him talking to her, even though she isn't here . . .'

My sister and I lock eyes. It's clear that where I feel concern, Rosie is considering her own lack of discernment in pushing me into this situation.

'That's enough, son.' David says it as warmly as he can. 'Today is just for hellos. That's more than a hello on my behalf. But now we all know that I'm in this as much as the rest of you are. I, too, *need this*. To engage with the problems and the joy of others so I can – get out of my head, my – my grief. There's medical value in what we're about to start here. I worked as a doctor for forty-odd years; that doesn't mean I'm immune to life's problems, neither the physical nor the mental kind.'

I imagine being so candid. It makes me nauseous.

'Anyway,' he goes on, 'Alice! Alice here is our very own horticulture expert! Her home once boasted a truly magnificent garden. A dear old friend. Maybe you'd like to speak next, my love?'

Alice, the older lady with the curly hair sat opposite him in the circle, seems to close up a bit in her seat, like a flower blooming in reverse. Honestly, it's like she shrinks four inches before our eyes. She shakes her head, arms crossed, looking nowhere but directly at David.

'OK. Not ready. That's OK. No judgement here. Anyone else? Rosie, perhaps? Another neighbour of ours, everyone. These two are sisters, actually.' He points us out. I clutch the sides of the chair like I'm about to fall away from the earth into the sky.

'Ah! I can tell,' Nathan says, eyeballing us. 'The likeness!'

'See, I thought they looked alike too at first,' Peter jumps in, 'but, now I know you both separately, I can't see the resemblance any more. You're both so different.' He stares at Rosie as though to ensure her feelings aren't hurt, and I jump around my own brain, ecstatic that he sees me as my own person.

'What are you on, man? They're the spitting image of each other. Eyes, lips, cheekbones, it's all the same. Genes, man! I need to see the mother. Maybe she'll turn me straight.'

'We do get that a lot,' Rosie says. 'Sorry . . . so, I'm Rosie, and I'm just here for my sister, Jenna.' She points at me with her elbow, keeping her hands buried under her armpits. 'Just as, like, a cheerleader. Really nice group, actually. I see we have our work cut out!' She beams in an unnatural way and eyes the glasshouse.

David just looks at her.

'Um, and, well, yeah, I suppose I tend to get a bit anxious myself. I'm a carer. For my – our – mother. She's not well, and going out to her so often – I go see her every day – it takes a lot out of me.'

I shrink away from the guilt that raps on the door of my subconscious.

'So being here, it might do me a bit of good, too. We'll see!'

Her words reek of insincerity. She said herself that she 'doesn't need' a support group. This is just Rosie looking to avoid rocking the boat; she's a people-pleaser through and through.

'Jenna?'

'What?' I don't realise I've said it out loud until it's already out of my mouth, a word pumped full of resentment.

'Your turn,' Rosie snaps.

To keep the peace I nod meekly, look around, grasp at what to say. I need to walk a tightrope right now – between the Jenna that Peter knows and the Jenna that Rosie knows.

I need to introduce a Jenna that this lot will think they're getting to know but who really doesn't exist at all; I need to cover the real me in layers of bubble wrap.

Sock puppet and hand master, I make myself say things. 'Jeez. How am I supposed to follow up all that . . . vulnerability? Me, I'm just a bit lost, really.'

They all wait for me to keep talking. Peter is leaning forward with his hands together, hanging on my every word. I hear the smack of Rosie's tongue against the top of her mouth, as if she's about to jump in and expose me, so I add: 'And I've been on anti-depressants for, well, ages. Upped the dose after a really hard break-up. Not feeling much better. So, I'm here.'

'Good woman,' David says, saving me from Rosie's big, stupid mouth. 'Disclosing that,' he says, 'takes a lot. Little story for you. I had this patient years back. Overwhelmed at work. He came to me, clinically depressed, needed some time off. Bit of time off, that's all!' David says, throwing his hands up. 'He felt awful simply saying it out loud. Admitting it. The man had been working eight hours a day, five days a week for *decades* and we think that's normal because we all just – well, we agree it's normal, like we agree that a €5 note is worth €5 when in reality it's a little slice of scribbled-on cotton fibre.' He has a point. Nothing natural about the hamster wheel. 'And of course, I wrote *depression* on his sick note. "Do you have to put that down?" he asked me. This red, puzzled face. "If my manager sees that, I'll be fired," he said. Begged me to write down that he had a virus. And I wouldn't. It felt wrong to lie. But he lost his job. *Lost his bloody job.* I could've protected him by lying, because the truth . . . it makes some people uncomfortable, doesn't it?'

Some *mm*s and nods and tuts.

'It's not as bad these days,' he goes on. 'People talk more, mental health is better understood. Some of my son's wonderful music touches on—'

Peter bends his neck. 'You had one job, old man.' He says it light-heartedly.

'What can I say? I'm a proud dad.'

'*Cute*,' Nathan chirps.

'Your dad is right,' Jordanne says, her hand resting across her abdomen. 'Sorry, I, I just mean, different generation and that. Some of the stuff you explore through, through your songs . . . it's so . . . emotionally complex, like, your whole *Mortal* EP. Sorry, not trying to embarrass you, it's just, you share your vulnerability and every time you do it helps to normalise that for someone else.' She's turning ruby red. 'Sorry, ha, should I stop?'

If this girl says sorry again, she'll be sorry.

'It's OK,' Peter says, defeated, pretending he isn't.

'Do you really have a *million* followers, then?' Izzy asks excitedly.

Peter, all modest, makes the kind of face that says yes in the humblest of ways.

'That's so cool. I have thirteen thousand two hundred and something, myself.'

'Are you a – what you call it – an influencer?' he asks.

'*Everyone* is an "influencer" these days,' Nathan interjects.

Izzy doesn't boast the same humility as Peter. 'Well, I am!

Maybe *you'd* call me a "micro influencer",' she says to
Nathan, 'but I'm growing fast. I got over two hundred
followers this past week alone.' She beams with pride, looks
at Peter. 'Loads of companies want to advertise on my page.
I have some haters, of course, but sure, look at me! They
hate to see me pose in cute outfits and get paid for it. And
to them I say *fuck you*. I might not look fab but this kawaii
dress is fab and I need money for uni.'

'What do you study?'

'*Pffft*, boring. What I've *really* always wanted is to sing, like
you,' she says.

Before Jordanne has a chance to tell us about why she's
here, the conversation lifts into the air like a balloon. It's
gone. It's all about Peter and Peter's career. It grows smaller
and climbs higher and his ears are turning pink and I want
to tell everyone to shut up. I want to take him by the hand,
to wander into the fields, just us. I want to tell him that I
see past all that; I want him to appreciate me for it . . .

David's alarm goes off. He claps his hands and has us all
gather near the glasshouse entrance. 'Today, folks, we
sweep. We clean. We tidy. We lift off any algae that's taken
hold on the glass. We'll begin to clear that metre-high jungle
of nettles and hogweed over there, and all this, we'll do right
through Christmas!'

I can almost hear my sister swallow her distaste for
everything David just said.

'I'm not banning mobile phones – however, I'd much prefer
if you all put them away. If you can't trust yourself to leave
your phone alone, might I suggest that you don't bring it at

all. Alternatively, I can collect phones in a plastic bag and store them in the van.'

'Oh, good! I'm so glad, I hate phones –' Jordanne starts.

I see Rosie's face distort – the worry in her eyes as she examines her perfectly manicured hand clutching her phone, wrapped in a pretty OtterBox case, and Peter trying to conceal his amusement.

'Before myself and Peter gather today's tools, I'd like each of you to take a little stroll around – we're going to attempt to briefly abandon the five-sense prison.'

Nathan makes a face, probably thinks nobody's looking. I like him already.

We catch eyes. He leans towards me as David spouts platitudes about the power of nature. 'Akin to their owner,' he whispers, framing his own face with his hands, 'my house-plants always shrivel up from a lack of attentiveness. Flora and I do not get along. Starting to think I might not be cut out for this . . . I just wanted to do Peter a solid, but . . .' He sucks air between his front teeth.

David overhears. 'Change isn't supposed to be easy, Nathan. We're here to tear our roots from the soil so we can replant them elsewhere, somewhere they can deepen.'

'Whatever you say, hun.' Nathan's voice is all affection.

David smiles. 'Listen – to what's outside, to what's inside. Feel the ground under your feet, feel whatever emotions arise. Be present. Be patient. *Really listen* to whatever comes up for you. It might be anger, hate, sadness, resentment – just *don't hold on to it*, whatever it is.' His eyes fix on my sister. 'Doing that helps nobody. Acknowledge and feel, then let go. The feelings aren't yours. They're part of *this*, all of this,' he finishes, flailing his twisted hands up once again. 'Letting go is of paramount importance.'

I ready myself to feel nothing.

A cold couple of minutes pass me by before I stop watching what everyone else is doing. I notice a couple of daisies – they're the only ones I've seen in the garden, so I assume they've begun their yearly fade away. I decide to pluck one. With my back turned to the rest of the group, I play a little game of 'he loves me, he loves me not' down on my hunkers, picking one petal from the flower for each phrase; the phrase said as the last petal is picked is regarded as the truth about the intentions of 'one's beloved'.

He loves me not.

No shit.

A while later, somewhere around the back of the glass-house, I find this tiny mushroom. Just one. It's much darker than the white button mushrooms I'm used to seeing in the shops, packaged in plastic, so I almost miss it. To pass some time, I sit down beside it, my back against tree bark. It's the first living thing I've not felt self-inflicted pressure to perform to in God only knows how long. I stroke its little cap and think about how I've been performing around my sister. Perhaps I've even been performing to myself. I reflect on my multiple selves – Jenna the cat mother, Jenna the jobless, Jenna the sibling, Jenna the artist, Jenna the lousy daughter, Jenna the captivated next-door neighbour, Jenna the tenant, Jenna the ex-student – and I wonder how many Jennas exactly are keen to close the curtains on this life, this ability to reach out and feel the warts of a lonely mushroom.

Over lunch in Seasons café, David hands us out these sheets of paper with boxes to tick and sections to fill out in our own time. Up top – under a bolded line about how everything said amongst group members must be kept confidential – is this long, boring block of text about how we're to learn about nature and the seasons, about one another, about community, about how to be 'mindful', blah fucking blah. There's a table too, with statements like:

While walking, I am aware of the sensations in my body.
I can talk easily about my thoughts and opinions.
I judge my thoughts as good or bad.

Rating options run along the right-hand side and go from one up to five – one representing 'never' and five meaning 'always true'. It'll be incredibly easy to lie in my answers.

I'm sat beside Alice. She's filling out her sheet already, big Hermione Granger head on her. I pretend to be reading my own page, but I have a nosy at hers. She rates 'I criticise myself for having irrational emotions and thoughts' as 'always true' and I wonder what she's thinking, though of course I don't ask her.

My hand immediately shades in the 'always true' option for 'I find it easy to discuss my thoughts and feelings with other people'.

At Auntie Bridie's funeral, I remember thinking I'd rather

be in the casket than delivering a eulogy (Mam made me prepare one, and reading it out loud in front of people was hellish). Not much has changed – and it won't, I already know it won't. No point in dropping disappointing truth bombs via annoying questionnaire, is there?

I'm here because I promised the divine creature beside me with the glasses pushed up to the top of his nose, asking me what I'd like to order, that I'd come. I can be truthful with myself and that's surely what matters.

I mentally pull on the Jenna costume I always wear for Peter; spending time with him is like going on holiday and leaving the real world behind. Obviously, this crush – any crush – won't make my depression dissolve into the ether; I'm not so naïve. But I might as well enjoy the view as the sun goes down.

ROSIE

I breathe and I breathe but no oxygen is coming in. My body makes me yawn for air but I can't finish the yawn – it's a half-yawn, and now I'm nervous that I'll suffocate, that Mam will be left alone tomorrow in her bed waiting on me to bring her tea, to wash her, to bring her spaghetti Bolognese on her tray. My chest is tight, so tight, like there's a rubber band crushing . . . everything!

I tried to talk to Jenna tonight. Just about the project, mind, not even about Peter or Mam. I asked about how she's finding it now that we have two weeks under our belts – what she thinks of the group members and if her back is as sore as mine and if she's as nervous about the amount of stuff that David's expecting us to accomplish in seven short months – but she just scrolled on her phone, shrugged her shoulders, capped her sentences before any meaning whatsoever could be extracted. And all I could think about as I watched her – feral-haired and fading away before my eyes – was Rachel.

Tadhg's Rachel.

Panic rises like hot air.

Jenna, dead on the couch. Jenna, dead in my arms.

I can't breathe.

Frantic, I pace around my bed. She's on the other side of that wall and God only knows what's going on in her head, what she's keeping from me . . . Why can't she just talk to me? Am I so terrible? Couldn't she just walk a few metres to find me any time she's feeling particularly low?

I need to safeguard every medication under this roof. I need to hide the knives; I need to pour out all the spirits stored away in the cupboards . . .

Everything feels sharp inside me, everything shakes, ten thousand tingles inside my every pore. And there it is, now: the compulsion for sexual preoccupation that I almost always experience when I feel a panic attack coming on. My eyes search madly until they settle on my laptop, closed over at the foot of my bed.

A gateway to an endless supply of free porn.

I need some mindless escape and porn is always there for me. It's the best distraction that I have at my disposal: easily accessible pleasure, the promise of complete immersion, of no rejection, of a pause on all negative emotion. Heart hammering, I lunge at my bedside fan. White noise! As well as ensuring that Jenna hears nothing, it'll cover up the reverberation of emptiness that's guaranteed to linger when I'm done.

JENNA

Rosie must have gone to bed. She's not once interrupted me with knocks on the bathroom door.

With my back against the radiator, I'm cutting – using the razor she uses for her legs. Only little cuts, so the pain can leak out; little cuts every now and then make living just about tolerable.

She didn't even say goodnight.

When the deed is done and I sting, lighter than I was moments ago, I pull my freshly pricked knees close to my chest and pore over Izzy's Instagram feed for something to do. She's shared picture after picture of her confidently and cutely posing in various brightly coloured emo-style outfits. Some of the pictures are sponsored by clothing brands, and I can't quite get over it: the exploitation of a young woman's visible illness and the hundreds of comments telling Izzy that her body is 'goals', evidently feeding her eating disorder. One of them writes about how she purposefully chooses bruised fruit to bring to school as it offers her an excuse to 'remove calories'. Twenty-three people have liked the comment.

The caption under Izzy's most recent post – a selfie with a black and white filter, clearly taken at Avalon next to the garden's sole bare apple tree (which we watched Alice prune only yesterday) – reads: 'Will I ever be happy again tho?'

My eyes flick through the top comments.

YAS GIRL WHERE ARE THOSE EARRINGS FROM?
Omg omg SLAY the fishnet gloves are giving me LIFE

Then I spot a comment beside a distinct profile picture of Nathan, from the group. His is seemingly the only one that addresses the seven devastating words forming the question under her photo.

It's like billions of people got together and pinkie-promised
to pretend to be happy all the time. And then, there's us
;) Here for the no-BS captions, but also, you MUST drop
a tag on that highlight! I can't wait a whole week to know
what brand it is!

His comment is like a kiss on the cheek. I click his profile and notice that he's already following me, so I follow him too. Then I go back to look at Izzy's selfie again.

The saying goes that when you photograph people in black and white, you photograph their souls. I want to draw

Izzy using charcoal. As a gift. To let her know I'm not just another one of the thousands of people looking at her. I know what it's like to be looked at, but not seen. I *see* her, and I'll prove it.

ROSIE

I arrive to Mam's with cinnamon swirls and a rare good mood. Peter booked us a hotel room for tonight, an early Christmas present. And not just your bog-standard double room in the local. He's got us the fanciest room Dublin has to offer – the Princess Grace Suite (named in honour of Grace Kelly, who frequented it back in the day) in the five-star Shelbourne hotel, €7,500 a night.

I *know*!

Honestly, I hadn't even considered getting him anything. Exchanging gifts isn't really 'casual thing' territory, is it? Of course, this is a sex-related gift, and he can well afford it, so I'm more than happy to accept it with open arms and open legs. Maybe I could get him something silly? A massage candle. Some edible body paint. Something that can't be interpreted as anything other than a fun little 'I'm really enjoying sleeping with you' token.

Jenna thinks I'll be staying in Mam's so I get to vanish

completely off the map and into another life for a bit. I'm glee on legs. Deliriously excited. *Finally*, something just for me after three whole weeks of work and Mam, and Jenna throwing me daggers for the Night of the Ambush, and hauling myself out to that monstrosity of a glasshouse. Garden work is exhausting in and of itself, but throw in all my other responsibilities . . .

Mam eagerly watches me brew our Sunday-morning coffees from the kitchen table like she always does. 'What's with the pep in your step, pet?'

'Sounds like a tongue-twister.' I don't want to tell her about the hotel. If I have to sit through any more enquiries about whether or not we're 'going out' I might actually burst into flames.

'You're like a cat about to pounce – keep going up on your toes.'

I plate up our pastries and join her, using the plates to cover up tea rings stained into the wood. It always annoys me that Mam won't use coasters. 'Don't remind me of Bertie. Caught him chewing on my favourite Kate Spade bag yesterday!'

'Don't change the subject,' she says, her voice smiling while I slice her swirl into six smaller pieces to make it easier for her to lift to her lips.

'Ah, it's just the – you know, the group thing we're doing.'

'What about it? Thought you hated that.'

I sit and warm my hands against the mug. 'I do. The climbing bloody ladders, the blocked guttering . . .' I roll my eyes and sip my coffee. 'Yesterday was terrible, Mam.

My skin is in bits from all the nettles and the midges. But. Well, I should say, there is something satisfying about . . . *finishing*. The food you eat after working up that sweat, it's the most delicious thing you've ever tasted. I've been daydreaming about this swirl since yesterday afternoon.' I go to take a bite.

'That can't be what you're all buzzy about – a silly bite of pastry.' She taps my leg with her foot. 'Go on. Tell your mam. Nothing much happening around here, as always.' She flicks a sad bit of hair from her face. I feel guilty, like I should have loads of fun, juicy gossip to bring so Mam can live vicariously through me. She won't approve of the no-strings-sex stuff, though. If I told her that, she'd tell me to stop being a little tramp and grow up. I need to twist the truth if I'm to have anything to offer at all in the way of conversation.

'Well, there's . . . a really gorgeous fella in the group.'

Her face lights up like sunshine bursting through white linen. 'A man! You never said! Or is he new, this one?'

Peter made a private Facebook group for us all to interact outside of Saturdays called the Bird-Shit Palace Brigade, and Tadhg was the first of the lot of them that I virtually stalked. Found some drop-dead-gorgeous shots of him in his GAA shorts. I tried to chat to him yesterday (we sat beside each other for the post-session lunch – Peter was opposite us, closely observing). Tadhg, eh, he's not a man of many words, which, honestly, is how I usually like them; I make an exception for Peter because he's preposterously sexy *and* because he's easy access. I'd almost certainly be sliding into Tadhg's DMs if it wasn't for the fact that he's grieving what happened to his girlfriend. Still – *any* talk of a potential suitor will lift Mam's spirits. It's the whitest of lies to imply genuine interest in him . . . no big deal.

'It's the chap who lost his girlfriend.' I take a sip of my coffee and watch her search the far corners of her memory for the long discussion we had about everyone David had gathered together out at Avalon.

She shakes her head slightly, confused. 'You never mentioned.'

I want to tell her that I did, but when I point out her memory lapses, I can ruin her whole day.

She starts to eat. 'Oh, come on, tell me!'

'Sorry, Mam. Must have forgotten. To cut a long story short, this fella . . . God, it's terrible . . . his girlfriend killed herself.' Mam's eyes are like two full moons. 'This gorgeous blonde. Had a look at her on Facebook. She was studying to be a teacher. Loads of pictures with her mates on nights out. She seemed . . . happy.'

'Well, we both know the Facebook is all bullshit anyway,' Mam says softly. 'That's very sad, pet.' She pauses for a beat, straightens her spine. 'How old is he, so? Where does he work?'

I laugh into my cup. She's already sizing him up as husband potential. 'Looks around thirty. It says on Facebook that he's an electrician.'

'At least it's a stable job. No kids, then? No ex-wives?'

'I hardly know him,' I say with a laugh.

'Show me a picture, on the Facebook.'

I do. She gasps and tuts and gushes about how gorgeous he is.

'What you do is you move *slowly*. Let the man grieve, Rosie.' She says it with her eyes fixed to his face smiling up from my phone screen. 'Right now, he can't see the forest for the trees. He can't see how brilliant my daughter is. But he likes blondes. That, we do know.'

I can't help but smile, too.

'After he's stood up, wiped off the rubble, *you* ask him out. See, men love confident women. Oh, if I were twenty years younger . . .'

We eat and I humour her till she tells me she wants me to wheel her to the corner shop for some bits and bobs. Picking a magazine is one of the highlights of my mother's week. I help her into her stairlift so I can dress her; she always opts for one of her nicer outfits for these little outings. I catch her struggling with a small applicator sitting on the table at the side of her bed: rose lipstick. Lipstick – for the twenty-odd minutes she'll be out of the house! I help her apply some to her bottom lip then she smacks them together to spread the pigment.

As I push Mam through the postcard-pretty streets of Stoneybatter, Christmas-tree lights glimmering through sitting-room windows, talk turns to Jenna. 'Your sister uploaded a lovely drawing the other day on the Instagram, did you see?' she asks over her shoulder at me. '*The Spider Queen.*'

I look down at her as her wheelchair rattles through puddles and pavement cracks. Grey roots are already visible after last month's dye job. Better fix that up for her again later. 'What's that?'

'That's what she wrote underneath it.'

'No, sorry, before that, what did you say?'

'Jenna. Drew a person!'

'You on about her Instagram?'

'*Yes*, love.'

'She uploaded something?'

'Didn't I just say she did?'

'But she hasn't posted anything in—'

'Weeks! I know. Been desperate for anything from her. Waiting *ages*, I was. God love her. Such a gifted girl. She should sell her pictures instead of working in that salon around all those chemicals!'

Salon? I raise an eyebrow. Another memory lapse: two in one morning. Bit worrying. 'Did she follow you back yet? On Instagram?'

'No, no. But that's OK.'

I frown. 'Well. It's not really OK, is it? You're her—'

'*You're* not a mother, Rosie. You wouldn't understand.' With her fingers loose, Mam attempts to pull her scarf tighter to her neck.

I hate it when she uses that against me. 'I don't need to have pushed a tiny human from my vagina to recognise ignorance. Here, let me.' I stop to tuck her in a little more against the cold. Big Jim from over the road waves at us from his doorstep and makes small talk with Mam, something about how excited he is for the holidays to be over and done with, but I'm not concentrating any more. I'm trying to decide on a lingerie set to take with me to the hotel later. I ordered this black lacy two-piece from Ann Summers with fake diamond detailing – the model wore it with this look that screamed *add to basket* – but my red bodysuit from Savage X Fenty really flatters my figure *and* it's more comfortable.

We move along once Jim goes back inside.

'What were we talking about?'

'Jenna.' My mind is still elsewhere.

Mam gets stern with me. 'Oh, yes. *Listen*. Jenna's my baby. I give without expecting anything back. That's motherhood. She doesn't have to follow me on the silly phone if she doesn't want to.'

You expect everything of me, I want to say.

'When you were a teenager, with your first phone, you'd never answer if I called. Then you'd ring me back about fifteen times needing a lift after one too many,' Mam scoffs.

Does she actually forget how old Jenna is? Or that she hasn't seen her in years? Is this the MS?

'You'd be in the shower for an hour and somehow you'd still come out stinking after running up the bills! But that's teenagers for you. Go easy on Jenna. I've been through all this with you already.'

Everything tightens. My face, my chest, my fingers around the chair grips.

Crap.

Don't snap.

Cling to cloud nine.

Think of later, of Peter . . .

Change the subject!

'Who was the drawing of?'

'A girl. Thin. Black hair, big eyes. It's a very nice picture. Must be one of her friends.'

Sounds a lot like Izzy, who definitely isn't 'one of her friends'. Well, I can't imagine Jenna's made a friend in the group before me. She's as *quiet* out in Avalon – meanwhile I've been making loads of effort with everyone! She and Izzy sat together at lunch after our last session, probably followed each other online . . .

'I'm sure it's – lovely,' I say, straight-faced.

'Have you been in touch at all? You two used to be so close, Rosie.'

'Jenna is staying with me, Mam, remember? We're both going to the same weekly group sessions? The gardening?'

She takes a moment to gather herself. 'I know that.' She wipes at the slight creases in her coat. 'Well? Have you two been getting along?'

'Yes,' I tell her as we close in on the shop. 'Everything's fine,' I say as we make it through the front door. 'Fairytale of New York' plays low in the background – Vincent-with-the-thin-hair-combed-over-his-shiny-head at the till probably turned it down because he's fed up hearing it: the shops have had it on repeat since bloody October. Mam turns to Vincent and grins at him, and I make sense of the rose lipstick. I veer her towards the small aisle with the boxes of cereal and tea-bags.

'I won't ring her,' Mam says randomly, probably thinking

out loud. I wish she'd express a millilitre of bitterness – that
she'd complain about Jenna not coming to visit her.

'Why?'

Mam kicks her left foot out to signal to me which shelf to
bring her to. She keeps her voice low, presumably so Vincent
won't hear us. 'Teenage girls,' she starts, 'like boomerangs,
always return . . . if you give them their space. Maybe one
day you'll start your life, a family, and you'll realise that! She'll
come to me when she's *ready*. Trust your mam. Hmm.' She
looks at the top shelf, far out of her reach. 'Bran Flakes, please,
pet. *Stomach is at me . . .*' The last four words come out in a
hush. Mam waits for me to fetch her preferred fibre source
before she carries on. 'By the time your sister is twenty-one
she'll be out here with us on a Sunday and we'll laugh together
about all this – silly distance – over a roast dinner!'

I want to show Mam a photo of Jenna's twenty-*second*
birthday party from her tagged photos on Facebook, her
looking completely out of it after smashing her face into her
birthday cake, fake eyelashes hanging off, mascara everywhere. I want to tell her what her very absent darling
princess said about being terrified of ending up like her. I
want to throw the box of Bran Flakes at the ground and
scream at the top of my lungs that, actually, *I have a life*,
and that the more she hammers away at me about having
kids the further from broodiness she pushes me. I want to
walk away and leave her here so I can unleash on Peter's
pelvis: wild sex is the best rage medicine.

'You never know,' I say instead, calmly. 'What else do you
need? How about some prune juice?'

When we go to pay, Mam fiddles with her purse. I spot the edges of an envelope inside the cash pocket. I ask her about it on the way home. She tells me Auntie Bridie sends her 'a few bob' every month from her late husband's massive pension.

'Nothing this month, though. Maybe things are tight.' She frowns, vaguely worried.

I don't have it in me to tell Mam, again, that Bridie is dead, to cause her to relive the pain that comes with finding out your sister (and best friend) is gone forever. I don't want to tell her the money is from Jenna, either – or that Jenna is broke and will probably be on the dole for quite some time. To my knowledge, she's not sent out a single CV. Instead, I ask Mam what's on telly later and if she'd like a bath before I leave.

I curl my hair, apply my make-up with meticulous care, dot the perfect amount of Jean Paul Gaultier perfume onto my wrists and the sides of my neck – enough that Peter will catch a subtle whiff up close, but not so much that my presence will choke passers-by. I pack an overnight bag: clothes for tomorrow, condoms, water-based lubricant, a silk nightdress, cleansing balm, tinted moisturiser and a lip and cheek stain to extend the post-orgasm glow well into tomorrow. I also pack my GHD hair straightener, which I use to add 'effortless' loose waves. In the end, I decide to wear nothing but sheer black stockings held up by suspenders around my thighs and my most expensive heels. I imagine Peter's face in the lamplight when he sees I'm nude underneath my heavy red winter coat . . .

My nipples threaten to break off during the taxi ride to the hotel, it's that cold, but I don't care. This is the stuff I live for.

We're given champagne on arrival, butler service, the works. The place is all crystal chandeliers and marble floors and I never want to leave! Our suite has an antique dining table, fireplace, *two* double bedrooms just for us, two bathrooms, beautiful art everywhere and is all decked out in Christmas decorations. I squeal as we stroll through the rooms, connected by soft hand touches at all times, giddy on the high of novelty.

Peter drops his overnight bag. He looks out the windows while – feet away – I prepare to unbutton my coat. 'Damn. The room overlooks the park, Rosie. Look!'

As soon as he says it, memories of David saying the word *suicide* on the bench down there swim in my mind and a fist of sickness punches my stomach. I work fast to push the mental images aside – of his face, of the pills, of Jenna at home alone on the couch. I push all the air in my lungs through my nose, drop my coat to the floor and cup my breasts. They feel full, heavy.

'You come here,' I say, all coy.

Peter turns his head. As soon as he sees me, his lips part, and his eyes narrow, though I can see his pupils grow as he slowly looks me up and down, like two big drops of black ink soaking into parchment. There's nothing like that look of desperate want from a man – dizzying suspense as my palms rotate on my nipples, as I watch him watching me.

'I – I,' he tries.

'Don't talk. Just fuck me,' I beg in a whisper, tightening my legs together with anticipation, reaching for his hands with mine, freeing my breasts.

'Rosie. I wanted us to spend some time—'

I don't let him finish. I just kiss him, his tongue ready for mine, wet and soft. He moans. It's an orchestra playing me my favourite song. His hands caress my hips and pull me closer. I slowly rotate them in his hands, grinding, tempting him with everything I have while I kiss, harder and slower.

Peter pulls his mouth from mine. When I see him trying to gaze into my actual *soul* I focus my eyes on his mouth. I try to kiss him again. He's not having it.

'I'm starving for you, you *know* that, but—'

'I can tell,' I say, gripping at the evidence through his jeans, tongue between my teeth.

'But, can't we, like, watch a movie or something? Cuddle? Order some food and chat while we eat? Then—'

I plant gentle kisses along his shoulder and collarbone as he speaks. 'I'd much prefer we eat each other.' It's no more than a whisper. I can't calm myself down – his scent drives me wild, the pheromones! It's so overpowering: firelighters under my nostrils. I need him. I don't even want to sleep. I just want all of his weight on top of me, all the time; I want to straddle him, holding his hands down as he pretends to try to break free, I—

I stop. He's tensed up. He's mute, and his body, unresponsive. I step back and cover my breasts again, reaching for the flesh inside my cheek with my fang teeth, adrenaline coursing through me all of a sudden, like my arousal turned to anxiety quicker than butter melts on heat.

'Can we sit for a minute?'

'Peter, I'm naked and I'm horny. What's the problem?'

'Well,' he says, eyes widening, 'I just, I thought that tonight, we could—'

'*What?* Act like some old married couple? Snuggle up in bed and share a brownie while we fall asleep watching *Star Wars* in our fucking pyjamas?'

He sighs. 'I don't want to do this again.'

We've been here before. Peter trying to be all lovey-dovey while I just want to *get off*. I stomp then (as much as a person *can* stomp in heels) over to the immaculate, elaborate bed and plonk myself down on it, crossing my legs and planting my chin on a fist. My excitement from earlier – about this being some sort of escape from everything that's going on – begins to drain.

'Come on. Don't be in a huff! Just talk to me. What's this all really about?' He sits beside me, but I shuffle a few more inches away from him.

'What are you talking about?'

'This . . . mechanical, *uhh, I don't have feelings, I'm sex mad* stuff?'

'Are you actually mocking me while I'm sitting here without bloody knickers on? In the *hotel room* you booked for me – the girl you're sleeping with? Mocking me for trying to initiate sex?'

'Stop being dramatic. I'm just saying. You never want to just chill. Hang out. Do normal stuff. Be intimate. And I'm

not talking about you-gripping-a-pillow-while-I-pound-you
intimate. You won't even . . . look, *never mind.*'

'I won't what?'

'Want to go there?'

I purse my lips. 'I do.'

'You won't even make eye contact, when we . . . never.
Just . . . what's it about? Make me understand.'

Oh, sure! It's only my inability to trust or to depend on
other people; my fear of getting too close to literally anyone;
my intolerance for any and all situations in which I sense a
possibility of abandonment; the worry I'll feel rejected if I'm
ever really *seen*. 'I just don't want that, with anyone. Thought
I made that clear as day,' I tell him.

'Ouch.' He grips one hand with another. 'There's more
going on up there,' he says. 'I'm not blind. Get it off your
chest. That's the whole point of the project, and, I mean,
look, *I've* got crap going on, too.'

'You can't compare *your* crap to *my* crap.'

'I'm not trying to—'

'What awful thing happened to *you* today, then? Go on.'

He remains calm in spite of my attitude. 'Well. There's
this meme going around about me online, about my new
song "Can't Breathe".' Oh, here we go! He's so incredibly
tone-deaf – ironic, considering his musical talent. 'One of
my real dedicated haters sent it to me, you know the one
that keeps setting up fake profiles?'

I blink in response.

'Anyway, it's this picture of a Volkswagen. A Volkswagen,
Rosie! As if they *know*! They photoshopped in fogged-up

windows, with "can't breathe" drawn into the condensation. Imagine the effort put in to make that . . . I'm so paranoid this person knows about the proj—'

I interrupt. 'Are you for real right now?'

'What?'

'Peter, Mam is seriously ill; meanwhile, Jenna . . . she wants to . . . you're comparing apples and eggs here, mate.'

'You *asked* me—'

'Yes, and you've made my point for me.'

He runs a hand through his hair. I hear the sound of him swallowing as he thinks. 'Problems are relative, Rosie. Someone will always have it worse.' He looks at the carpet, unsure of his own conviction. 'I'm allowed . . . to . . . to worry about my *career*. I've worked hard for it. Nothing was handed to me. Besides, it's not just that stuff. My dad—'

Enough of the heavy talk. I'm bloody *naked*. He's not going to take this night away from me. I desperately need a break . . .

'At least take off your jacket?' I say, softening my tone. 'I feel like a lemon here!'

He observes me; I watch the stern expression melt into one of mischief. I've coaxed the smallest hint of a smile out of him. 'How about I remove a layer for every five minutes of solid conversation?' As he speaks, he slowly starts to unzip the collar of his silk bomber jacket.

I bite my lip. 'Can't you just ditch the clothes now and talk to me over breakfast tomorrow morning? Is that a fair compromise?' I ever-so-slightly open my legs.

Peter sighs, defeated and desireful. 'I give up. You win,

Walker.' He removes his glasses and throws them across the bed. Stands up. I breathe heavily as he takes off his jacket, jumper, T-shirt, jeans and underwear. 'Lie down,' he orders, as he pulls the box of condoms from my bag and breaks the seal with his teeth.

I do as he says. 'Something I do want to hear. You, telling me what to do.'

Peter expertly rubbers up and climbs onto the bed. He sits on his hunkers, looming over me. 'What if I tell you to let me in – even a small bit – even just for tonight?'

'In *here*, you mean?' I spread my legs proudly so he can see the lovely job I've done with my new razor.

That moan again. It brings out something animal in me. He ruffles his hair. Bites his lip. 'You're impossible.'

'You have thousands of girls out there lining up to "let you in". Girls who'd kill their families to play Scrabble and, and, I don't know, bake apple tarts with you.' I lift my legs up as I speak and he rubs them, like they're part of a guitar he's bid big money for. 'I'm not one of those girls, Peter. And you like that. You like this secret world we have.'

'I like it. I just know there's so much more to it, to you, but you—' He breathes deeply, overcome with excitement now, his face against my calf, the Lycra brushing against his cheek.

'I won't let you have all of me and you hate it 'cause you're famous and you're used to getting everything you want.'

A sharp inhalation of breath. He tenses up again, his eyes glued to my abdomen. A switch has flipped. I feel walls come up, invisible and fast. I was only being cheeky! He usually has a sense of humour . . .

'Right. Let's do this your way.' Peter's energy has shifted completely. He pushes my legs apart. 'Wider,' he commands.

'Mm-hmm.' He just looks at me, all bare, knowing how feeling admired gets me ready for him. This lets me know that he's still in there somewhere. For a moment, he traces nonsensical shapes across the skin where I've removed any trace of pubic hair. 'Me first, please,' I ask cutely.

Peter lowers himself. He holds his body up beside me with his right arm while he focuses his eyes on my lips and with his left hand, he feels for the warmth between my legs, allows his fingers to be slowly enveloped by my wetness. Usually he massages me until orgasm – never entering with his fingers. I can't come this way.

'This is for me, not for you,' he whispers, his lips inches from my ear, his hot breath and dirty talk driving me wild. I can almost hear his singing voice when he talks all low and husky like this. 'I'm making sure you're completely ready so this feels good for *me*.'

This is off-script for us.

A new little game to play.

I welcome it.

'Use me,' I beg. Peter's fingers push in and out of me faster and faster. He tugs them forward and backward then, as though to gently stretch me out. The feeling that he's treating me poorly arouses me beyond measure, perhaps because I feel safe within the confines of play, perhaps because, deep down, I feel that this is how I deserve to be treated: a hint of masochism. A surge of stimulation flows fast, right through the core of my body. Before I realise it's happened, Peter's climbed on top of me, eyes closed, he's sliding himself inside me, driving his hips forward, deep and hard. He fills me up until there's nothing left inside – only him. The knot within me dissolves in fire.

When it's all over, Peter lies beside me for a bit, looking up at the ceiling, expressionless, like he's surprised with himself, like he's physically here but mentally in another hotel room with another version of me – one brave enough to look into his eyes for more than half a second. After he stops panting, he robotically asks if I'd like some water. I say no, to be as undemanding as ever, though I really do. I'm parched. I want to curl around him with my head against his chest but I won't allow it – it's just the endorphin rush trying to overthrow me. He rolls across the massive bed to check his phone and I slink off to the bathroom to masturbate to the first decent video I can find on the PornHub homepage.

It's not just that I need the full release – I do, desperately – but I also need to distract myself from the ambivalence I'm feeling.

It works – for a glorious five minutes.

When I'm done, I return to the bed to find Peter fast asleep, facing his phone.

JENNA

It's mid-December now and Alice is planting what David tells us are bare-root roses while he hangs a bird feeder, which he says will attract hungry birds to pick off overwintering 'rose aphid' eggs. *Pests*. I don't think I've ever spent more than five seconds thinking about their existence, yet if they vanished from the earth, all ecosystems throughout the world would collapse – according to David, anyway.

'There's much to be learned from a pest. Persistence can be wonderfully helpful!'

Nathan, arms crossed, says, 'I beg to differ. There's this bartender – *not* my type – who's been sliding into my DMs for the past three years. I've made it abundantly clear that I'm not interested. The only adjective I'd used to describe his *persistence* is *creepy*.'

A five-minute conversation about how David always thought *DM* meant *don't mind* ensues – eventually, he somehow stirs the chat back to pests and the creepy-crawlies in the grass below our feet.

'*Creepy*, yes, that's what I'm talking about!' Nathan claps as he speaks, to emphasise his words.

Everyone laughs.

'Each one of them has a unique personality, you know,' David continues. 'June taught me to respect them. "No fly spray", she'd warn me when we first moved in here – "no *casual* spider murdering".'

Bar myself and Rosie, the rest of them appear to have really taken to the project, even doing a bit of homework between sessions. Peter fills the bird bath with fresh water from the garden hose while my sister and I watch blankly, the pair of us completely unprepared to contribute in any meaningful way. I think she feels like a right eejit having landed us in this situation, you know. Growing up, we didn't even have grass out the back. If I wasn't so depressed, this scene would be fairly comical – us two in our wellies.

Izzy chirps about how she researched flowers online for over an hour last night, while Alice looks on proudly. With Alice on hand to help using her finger (she points a whole lot, still never talks), Izzy puts in an order of summer-flowering bulbs using David's debit card – she's only allowed use her phone for the order. David gently reminds her that it needs to be put away again till lunchtime, which Izzy doesn't seem too happy about. When he handed over her mobile in its glittery case I swear to God, the girl frothed at the mouth. I know the addiction well.

Izzy loved my picture, by the way. She actually shared it

on her Instagram story the night I tagged her, and loads of
her followers clicked through and followed my art page. En
route here this morning, she made a point of showing it to
everyone, and when we poured out of the bus, she linked
arms with me, asked me all about my art, how I learned,
who inspires me . . . She showed more interest than Rosie
has since I moved in. For a brief window of time, I felt
motivated and good about myself, though the fresh supply
of positive feelings already appears to be dwindling, just like
it always does.

My head doesn't want me to have nice things.

Nathan offers to clean David's tools after making a dirty
pun that David doesn't understand, and as I observe him,
I can't help but see some of myself in him. I imagine
he was a sad kid who grew up to be a funny adult; his
overcompensation through humour screams *trauma*. The
last therapist I entertained for all of two sessions pointed
out that I kept making jokes: she told me it was a sign of
my resilience, prodded me for details related to any neglect
or abandonment I might have experienced as a child, before
warning me that – shock horror – it's not possible to be
funny all the time and that I shouldn't rely on humour as
an antidote to pain. As Nathan reads from the battered little
book on composting that Tadhg borrowed from his dad, I
wonder about the pain behind Nathan's incessant joking.

He 'teaches' us how to compost David's veg plot, to the
right of the glasshouse, like he's performing in the Laughter
Lounge.

'Now watch, my loves, "the pile", she must be kept moist,

then – once every week or two, which really isn't often enough, is it? – we must turn and mix her with our "pitch fork",' he says, winking, 'which will ensure that she heats right up . . . Oh, it's getting hot in here, Doctor D!' Nathan inserts the garden hose between his legs and sprays the compost. The girls giggle at his use of innuendo while I imagine what might be buried underneath it. The best-case scenario is that he's trying to fake it till he makes it, that he wants to come across like the torment of having his nudes leaked hasn't in any way impacted him. I'd be willing to bet on Bertie's life that this side of Nathan – king of the double entendre, the sexy survivor – was born with his pain.

It's a morning of dirty jokes and dirty work. I don't mind the work – it's something different – but I can tell by her huffing and puffing that Rosie hates every second.

I break from spraying dormant oil on the apple tree – which apparently prevents fungal infestations and moths from attacking it over the winter – for a swig of water. Weird how a bit of hard, physical garden work can transform a simple plastic cup of water into literal goddess nectar. I can't even remember the last time I thoroughly enjoyed drinking a glass of water. When I've absorbed every last drop, I wipe my mouth and watch Peter.

He's *off*, you know. I can't put my finger on it but I know something's up. He stands beside me to drink some water himself and I notice that I can't smell his cologne. There's stubble on his face, too, forming an ugly little shadow over his top lip. He's usually clean-shaven. I try to wind him up about how he'd be cancelled for destroying the environment if people knew he was buying plastic cups, but he takes no notice of me. He's watching Moss. The dog is slumped by the back door of Avalon, listless. His lacklustre chestnut coat looks rougher than it did only a week ago.

'Sorry, sorry, I'm listening. It's just – he won't chase his favourite tennis ball.' It's on the ground beside him, all chewed-up. 'I've thrown it three times now. Nothing.'

I ask Peter what's wrong with Moss. He tells me he's not sure. 'He's limping on his right leg. That one.' Peter points, blank-faced. 'Started a few days ago.'

Moss's lethargy makes me think of Bertie back home, sleeping somewhere dark and out of sight. Feline language is a funny thing. Cats don't only purr when they're happy: they do it when they're in pain, too; I often hear him before I see him. All I've wanted to do is hold him and be with him through whatever he's experiencing, but he hardly ever lets me pick him up any more. The thought crosses my mind again, the one I keep dodging as I can't fathom being responsible but, well, the vet might be able to make the whole thing less painful for him . . .

Peter kneels beside Moss. Pulls off the mucky glove he's been using to clear out pots and planters, runs fingers through his floppy hair. 'He let out this sort of whimper earlier when Dad lifted him into the van, before you guys joined.' An invisible string seems to pull Peter's head then. He searches the garden with his eyes. I follow his gaze once it fixes. He's looking at Rosie. She's over by the glasshouse talking to Tadhg.

I do a double take.

There's something in Peter's stare. My fists clench into little balls. The only reason my nails don't pierce my skin is because I've chewed them all off. He's looking at Rosie in a way I've always longed to be looked at by . . . anyone.

Hawk-like, I watch Rosie, all frizzy from drizzle, wearing Alice's spare raincoat that's much too tight on her and some horrible-looking waterproof trousers she ordered online, misery embodied as she shovels with Tadhg.

'So, compost. What *is* compost?' I hear her ask.

'Eh, well, eh, it's – rabbit manure, so it is.'

She looks disgusted.

She's so difficult, high maintenance . . . why would Peter be . . .? Wait.

Hunkered behind Rosie, I spot Jordanne – the right nervous one – wringing out a soggy grey rag she's been using to get rid of paint from the glasshouse. From behind, you wouldn't know she was pregnant: she's shaped like a teardrop, her activewear like a second skin.

Peter has the face of a man lost in a desert who's just spotted a mirage, just-licked lips a little parted, eyes dopey, pupils massive.

'It's not sexy work, this, is it?' I almost jeer it. 'Dirt-crusted fingernails. The classy scent of algae . . .'

Peter keeps staring. 'Hmm?'

'You can do better. Anyway, can't imagine she'll be up for much once she pops that one out.'

His eyebrows do a weird dance then and the spell is broken. He looks at me. 'Sorry, what?'

I feel my own arms wrap around my layered-up body as if to contain me against myself. 'Babies. Not your vibe.'

'Jenna. Say what you mean. We've talked about this.' He pets Moss as he says it.

'I am!'

'Be more specific.'

'Jordanne.' It bursts out of me. 'She's your mystery woman, isn't she?'

Peter's mouth hangs open in a stunned kind of way.

'I saw the way you looked at her just now.'

'But I wasn't—' A tight-lipped smile. 'I was just . . . daydreaming.'

He's lying.

'Jordanne is . . . well, she's a fan. I don't date fans. I told you that. And – you said it – she's pregnant. With her boyfriend's kid. I don't need a kid – I have *Moss*.' Peter, his tone flat, circles the conversation back to the dog as if it didn't happen at all. His features twist with concern.

I'm not letting him change the subject. 'Can't you just . . . tell me who she is?'

'She's private.' He shrugs, like exercising boundaries is a piece of cake. 'You've not asked before. Why the sudden inter—'

'Go on. She'll never know you've told me.'

'Stop it. My ears are *burning*.' Nathan joins us, a walking exhale. He pulls a small compact mirror from the pocket of his puffer jacket and holds it up close to his glowing complexion, sticky with perspiration, then delicately pats at his smile lines and at the wrinkle-free skin under his eyes.

'By the way, mate, this is *bullshit*,' he says, dramatically fanning his fingers so as to gesture at the entire situation, his expression serious. 'You could fry eggs on this fucking face. I didn't wear Charlotte Tilbury to sweat it all off! Proper black foundation is diamond dust. The fatness of the price tag on this.' He points at his face, licks his lips and runs his baby finger along each of his eyebrows before clicking the tiny mirror shut. 'I just had to clean inside the roof of *that thing* with a mop and I'm so done.' He throws the glasshouse a filthy look.

'No, you're not. Seven months, remember? You signed a contract.'

'Shut up. So, who were you losers talking about just now?'

Static rushes to my face. My hand automatically pulls my vape to my lips.

'The dog,' Peter says dully.

This is my chance. They're friends. Nathan will know something. 'We were talking about Peter's mystery woman.'

Nathan glues his eyes to Moss and avoids mine like they'd blind him. 'Sorry I asked,' he says.

A weird tension manifests. Fire on ice. Nathan knows something.

'Didn't go well, then?' Nathan prods, still looking at Moss. But his eyes slowly migrate across the frozen grass to . . . where my sister stands, now metres away from Jordanne.

'Let's not. Please.' Peter squashes his lips together so tight as to imply that we're not getting another word out of him. Frustration snaps and pops inside me, hitching up my stomach to the bottom of my throat. Thoughts swirl at a thousand miles an hour.

I survey Rosie. I really hadn't wanted to listen to the voice inside screaming at me about this because *of course* I knew; down in the deep water of my brain, I knew. But something in the shallows of me refused to acknowledge any of it – that Peter could be attracted to Rosie and not to me, that she'd keep something so big from me while living under the same roof . . .

This brain of mine. It's cursed. I've been lounging in fantasy land, ignoring the door sign.

Rosie. And Peter. My *sister* and *Peter*. I'm weightless. Numb. Even my pounding headache pauses its beat. Memories sway, leaves in wind: all the times I lied to the pair of them about all kinds of things. Barriers to keep the truth out. Acquaintances wouldn't go there together but lovers surely would. I know how vulnerable sex makes a person . . . I've *been* that person. I've spoken about the unspeakable when my wires have been tangled up with someone else's. My mind conjures images of the pair of them venting to one another about how terrible I am and I feel a gush of nausea in the pit of my stomach.

Nathan starts talking about a Christmas party. Asks if I'm going. Keeps talking. His words are like smoke – I can't catch the details, only that it's happening here, that David doesn't know about it, that's it's going to be 'epic'. My head feels like it's been dragged under water. I say something to excuse myself but I'm not sure what words actually come out.

I'm not even sure if they notice me leave. I hope they

don't, but . . . no, obviously they notice. Three people are two, within seconds. What's *wrong* with me?

I'm stinging. Everywhere.

It's not just thoughts of them together choking me. It's how I feel about myself. How toxic a place it is inside me and how I can't just be – sane, like *oh, you two are into each other, that sucks and I'm a bit jealous but I'll get over it*, and so it is, on with the day, the week, the month. No. I hang onto some guy I hardly know like he's a life raft and I villainise my sister – like she's had an affair with my boyfriend, even though whatever it is has obviously been going on long before I showed up. I feel it, even now, this desire to . . . lash out.

My eyes and feet take me to a discolouration on the garden floor – a little path. I think I hear my name but I'm not sure. That's the senses dulling again. The sound of birds goes blunt, everything before me is charcoal-grey, the people and the trees all around me are just silhouettes, Rosie twists herself around Peter through the fog in my brain, and I want to release what's hurting me: myself.

Around the back of the glasshouse, I find that one mushroom again and I sit with it, my back against the bark of the nearest tree. But I can't stay still. The taste of vomit and the bubbling of more. I claw at the base of my neck, piercing the skin under the bad shave job I did under my ponytail, half-wondering why no one has followed me back here. I shouldn't be left to my own devices. Not right now.

Spiralling, stinging, face burning, I search the base of the glasshouse for broken windows and loose shards of glass, manic now. I'm glad nobody is around to see me – that, I tell myself, over and over, to a mental projection screen of Rosie and Peter laughing at me. Something bright orange and brown is moving in my peripheral vision. A plump little robin. It pauses on a patch of earth sparse with grass at the base of the glasshouse's spine. A passionate melody rises up out of the tiny body and so I focus my eyes. By its feet, the cork of a bottle juts out of the earth.

I'm losing it, aren't I?

Because for no reason at all I decide that it's vital that I dig it up immediately. Don't even ask! I literally fall to my hands and knees . . . hungry soul. I crawl over and take my bloodied fingernails to the muck. It's a small glass vial caked in wet crud. The robin, now perched on a branch high above my head, tweets at me, and at me. I know he's tweeting *at* me. Automatic, I wipe my sleeve against the vial. The glass is purple tinged and clear, and . . . there's something inside. Curled-up paper.

I look up at the robin. I swear he's looking right back.

A rock sticks out of the grass only a few feet away. I crawl some more, breathless now, and I smash the bottle against the most pointed part of the rock. Fragments of glass fall all around and I smile through fresh tears. Brilliant bird! I need to cut my flesh until I feel calm again. *Thank you, thank you, bird* . . .

More twittering.

'*What?*' I ask aloud. No embarrassment. Only impatience, unfiltered.

The robin flies down and lands right by the piece of paper,

pokes at it with the shortest and thinnest black beak I've ever seen. Like there's nothing strange at all about this, I say, 'Oh, yeah. Right.' The tightly rolled scroll is ruled copybook paper the colour of tea stain. I press it out against the front of my thigh. There's some blue biro scrawl and I read it. Time stops. The stinging stops. The projector in my brain turns off. Infinity draws a long breath.

Five short words.

It's only up from here.

Gooseflesh all over. I look at the broken glass, my vision clearer than mere seconds ago. I look for the robin, but he's nowhere. I look around. Far-off voices – Nathan singing 'Lucky' by Britney Spears while Izzy laughs and joins in. David asking someone where I've gone. I delicately roll the scroll back up, secure it in my jacket pocket and bury the glass shards with my dirty welly.

ROSIE

'**M**om told me the flowers that used to grow along there were edible, you know that? She said they had "magical properties", actually convinced me to make a wish while chewing one and I swallowed the thing whole.' Peter says this to his dad, one hand on his hip and one holding Moss's tennis ball, trying his best to act nonchalant after avoiding me all day.

We've not spoken since the morning after our stay in the Shelbourne.

David scrapes out the filth he's gathered from the glass-house floor from a dustpan into a black sack. 'Ah yes. The daylilies,' he says. 'June tried to sway me too but unfortunately I wasn't having it. Well? What did you wish for?'

I watch Peter. His eyes smile. 'I didn't think . . . words, like "I wish", but I, eh—'

'You think in images? You're right-brained!' Jordanne pipes up, wiping dew into the leggings of her thighs after weeding with Tadhg (the bloke still rarely says a word! Just shows up, does as he's told – he'll answer you if you ask him something but you'd be forgiven for forgetting he was here at all. I only ever notice him skulking behind people because he's that bloody *gorgeous*). 'Creative, artistic types are right-brained!' Jordanne is far too enthusiastic. I hate it. 'Sorry, sorry for listening . . . just thought you should know – apparently being right-brained means you're emotional. A storyteller!'

'Is that a real thing?' Peter asks Jordanne.

'Yeah. I read it. In – an article.' She rests her hands against her belly. Pregnant women always seem to do that. I wonder why. 'Go on . . . what did you wish for?'

Peter bounces Moss's tennis ball. 'I thought about Freddie Mercury commanding the audience at Wembley. You ever see that footage? It's up on YouTube.' His words are directed at both David and Jordanne; he's acting like I'm the foliage. I don't like it.

Jordanne shakes her head.

'Queen's show at Live Aid. There'd just been a repeat of the concert on TV. Mom watched it with me after dinner one night, and I thought . . . *yeah*. Imagine wielding that much power. To sing some notes, *EEEEEOOOOO!* To have tens of thousands of voices blast the same notes back at you, in tune. Man! Mom told me to pretend – to sing to the flowers till it came true for me—'

David and Izzy turn to Peter as I hear the shoes and breath of the others approach – it must be getting close to lunchtime.

'Peter!' Izzy exclaims, probably about to say what's on all our minds.

'What?'

'You got what you wished for!'

Peter regards her sceptically.

'Way more people follow you online than went to watch Live Aid, you do realise that? You've had, what, over a hundred thousand people watch you perform songs live on Instagram?'

Peter rolls his eyes. 'That's totally different.'

'How so?' David asks Peter.

'Don't get me wrong,' Peter starts, looking around, 'I'm not, like, whinging that my dead mom's flowers didn't turn me into Freddie Mercury.' He laughs, perhaps realising how ridiculous he sounds. 'But, like—'

Jordanne plays with her zip. 'Sounds like they kind of . . . did.'

Oh, calm the knickers, Jordanne!

'Playing virtual jukebox isn't the same thing as being with all of the people listening to your songs,' Peter says, rubbing the back of his head, 'and . . . and feeling their energy, vibing off it, interacting with it. The live shows I do in the real world are never big or anything. My followers are kind of spread out all over the world . . . like, I'm not mainstream, not even close . . .' Nobody speaks. Peter's face tells me he's suddenly realised that he's complaining about his fortune and that he feels really self-conscious. He clears his throat. 'Don't take out the tiny violins, guys, I'm just – saying. All the internet stuff, really *not* that fulfilling. I need to be close to people who are feeling the music right there with me. Rosie,' he says, appealing to me. He's not said my name since the hotel. 'Tell them?'

I keep my mouth shut and pretend I'm confused.

'I performed at the pub where Rosie works. Nobody knew who I was. And *that* gave me way more of a buzz than singing into a phone camera ever does.'

I sense Jenna's eyes burning into the back of my head. Sibling telepathy. I blurt out, 'Oh, yep. He was great. Loads of claps.' *Don't say anything about the song, Peter, don't you dare say a* word *about the song . . .*

'You're still young, son. Freddie was nearly forty when he played Wembley. Give your mother's magic time to work.' David says it with such sincerity. 'Besides. She's in the soil now. Getting your hands dirty might just speed things along. Maybe you'll fill the 3Arena by the time you're thirty!'

'*In* the soil?' I ask, mildly curious as to what he means but also just really wanting to change the subject. I've not yet lived down the cringe of the Night of the Ballad.

'Precisely that.' David glances out at the garden. 'She's right here, but I can't hear her laugh, or . . . anyway.' He holds his hands up, stops himself. Maybe he's decided he'll cry again if he doesn't shut himself up. 'Just as a tree' – he points at the tallest one in the garden, leaning over us – 'transfers its nutrients to its forest before it dies, my wife is here.' He gestures outward.

It seems everyone has gathered round us now. 'Doctor D,' Nathan starts, eyes wide, 'are you saying there's a dead body in this garden?' Fright holds his fingers to the base of his throat.

'Nate, Mom was cremated,' Peter says calmly.

'And,' David challenges, 'her ashes were scattered all through the garden, the glasshouse . . .' He turns to point. 'Her urn is buried right over there, at the base of the apple tree. We love to share an apple.'

Love. Present tense. There he goes again.

'Aww,' Izzy sounds, 'it's adorable that you talk about her like she's still here.' She resumes gum-chewing and I hold my breath, unable to believe she said that without choking on her tongue. She *knows* he's unwell. Is she being facetious?

'We are not our bodies,' David continues, holding an intense gaze with Izzy, like he's struggling to implant ideas in her head using only his pupils. 'These are just sacks of organs and blood. We're far too attached to this facet of ourselves. How we look, how old we are.' He's perhaps hoping that Izzy will somehow be healed by everything he's saying between the lines. It's wasted hope. Izzy is incredibly sick; she can't weigh more than one of my legs. I'm sure she's very much aware that she could do with being less concerned about her weight. In fact, I doubt David understands anorexia whatsoever! GPs aren't specialists, after all – they're the Jacks of all trades. Handy for a repeat prescription of strong painkillers or for a referral letter to someone who has a clue, but certainly not all-knowing Gods of human health!

David looks away from Izzy and around at the rest of us. 'Ask yourselves this: have we committed to this project because we're hurting physically?' His eyes ask the rhetorical question as forthrightly as his words do. 'Of course not. The pain each of us feels exists . . . *somewhere else*. It's my belief that it's our souls that are wounded. The soul, the very core of emotion, character . . . it is aware of its connection to infinite consciousness, even when we become – disconnected . . .'

Etherealism with all the subtlety of a sledgehammer. It's very odd to hear someone with a medical background speak like this. Talk of souls aside, I guess he's on to *something*: I look at what's left of Izzy up and down. It's certainly not her hands that won't let her eat . . .

'Sorry, doc, but my anxiety gives me *actual* headaches and heart flutters. Palpitations! That shit is physical – it exists *in* my body, it's not in my head,' Nathan asserts. I want to say 'same here' but I also want to blend into the background.

'I didn't say it's in your head, did I? I'm simply asking you to think beyond what's tangible,' David pleads, visibly passionate. Every part of his face and hands are talking, along with his voice. 'The narrative that dominates mental health discourse is *grossly* oversimplified. Of course, physical symptoms are very real, but the emotion of anxiety – the tension, the worry, the intrusive thoughts—'

Nathan's words come out in a tight clutter and heavily punctuated. 'All. In. The brain.' His shoulders are back and he stands tall, like he's now engaged in one-sided verbal warfare. '"Consciousness", you mentioned. Where does "consciousness" come from, if not our *physical* brains. Go on?'

'Ah, but you see, everything comes from consciousness, for it is infinite.'

Nathan double blinks.

'Consciousness is awareness itself; it is everywhere and everything and everyone at the same time. Ask yourself, then – how can it possibly come from anywhere? We each need to look a little deeper . . . this world, this garden, it *is* us, it isn't separate . . .'

Poor Tadhg has the face of a simple farmer who's just been planted in the middle of an orgy in Las Vegas. Jenna makes a fist in her pocket and her eyes wander over the garden: she's as mentally checked out as ever. Meanwhile Alice coyly smiles at David. She is perhaps the only one here interested in . . . whatever he's talking about. He's still going, but I couldn't keep up if I wanted to.

Nathan scoffs. 'No! Sorry, and I love you, but *no*, I'm not able for the—'

'Love.' David smiles as he repeats that word. 'Everything is love.'

'Doctor D! I didn't know you listened to Beyoncé and Jay-Z!'

David looks confused.

Peter laughs. 'It's an album title, Dad. He's taking the piss.'

The lunch alarm finally goes off. 'Time to go, guys,' Peter says firmly. 'Let's, eh, resume, in Seasons . . .'

He absentmindedly throws Moss's ball. It soars through the crisp air deep into the glasshouse. We hear it collide with ceramic. The dog, who's not moved an inch all day long, suddenly pulls himself up, like the weight of the house behind him is on his back. Determined, he sluggishly drags himself – limp and all – over to the door of the glasshouse.

'That's weird,' Peter says under his breath. He calls out. 'Here, boy!'

Moss ignores him.

The glasshouse swallows Moss. Peter thinks out loud about calling the vet. I feel like I should comfort him, but I fight the terribly misinformed urge. If the Shelbourne fiasco taught me anything it's that I can't give him what he needs or deserves. I just *can't*. I'm on page 3 of a new book, fully expecting it to end up in the Did Not Finish pile because every book I ever start ends up on the shelf with a folded-over page corner about a quarter of the way into the story – meanwhile Peter is on page 103, itching to take a peek at the last paragraph, hoping it'll be a happily-ever-after ending.

I observe him as he waits for his dog: familiar soft hands with long, slim fingers; messy curls that I've seen wet, combed, flat, fresh out of bed. My mind wanders to his taut tummy and the trail of wiry hair leading from his belly button down to his . . .

Actually, maybe we could sort things out. I just . . . need to make him understand that I—

Moss barks and snaps me out of my nonsense.

'What's he at?' Peter paces a little, concerned. David smacks his hands together to clean them off, then crosses his arms, an eyebrow raised.

Moss appears.

He trots over to us with the tennis ball secured in his jaw. The limp is gone. Completely . . . gone.

An air of disconcertment. Jordanne gasps. Nathan says something about Avalon weirding him out. Peter doesn't say a word. I watch David cross his hands behind his back and head from the garden with a knowing smile.

On the way to lunch I try to push what I just witnessed from the fuzz of my mind but I fail miserably. Peter's bus feels as though it's slowly closing in on me and my throat is itchy and I can't get comfortable because the bloody *dog* is back there. I hear him panting. I want to ask him how he's able to walk normally all of a sudden, but I'm very much aware that I won't get an answer, and so I chew the insides of my cheeks until they bleed.

We land outside Seasons about ten minutes late. Located in the middle of Skerries town, squashed between a skinny bookshop and a small townhouse, the café is homey and noisy, all rich browns, deep greens and bursts of orange, like it's been painted by a fan of earth-toned Pinterest colour palettes. You walk in to the whack of chai and freshly baked dough, to a friendly glance from the barista – Minnie with the Prominent Front Teeth – to film-score music playing at low volume through retro speakers.

This part of 'Operation Bird-Shit Palace' – being done with the messy outdoor stuff and rolling up here, to warmth and food and chats – really isn't all that bad. Because for an hour or so every week I get to pretend to be a person with friends.

I know that makes me seem incredibly sad: to be my age

and a Paddy-no-mates. Thing is, I *did* have friends before, back when I worked for Aer Lingus. Cabin crew, other pilots . . . well, maybe you'd have described them most accurately as 'drinking buddies', but even though we never really spent time together while sober and in the grim light of reality, I had people I could text and meet up with. Before I was roped into these glasshouse shenanigans, I'd forgotten what it was like to spend quality time with anyone but Mam. I hadn't realised how lonely I actually am. I've been heading down a directionless road with no ending and, now, this new weekly ritual. A path unforged. Variety of opinion and perspective and scent and energy and tone of voice all combining to create something new, providing me something to measure my thoughts against.

Today I sit beside Peter's superfan, Jordanne. Of the group members, she's the closest to me in age, apart from Tadhg. He sits on the other side of me and intertwines his fingers in front of him on the table, eyes glued to the salt shaker so he doesn't have to talk. While everyone else hangs coats and scarves over the backs of wooden chairs, I notice that Jenna keeps her jacket on. She looks out of it.

David leans over my shoulder and asks what I'd like to order. His musk smells like petrol.

'Come here first.' He leans closer. 'Do you know if my sister is all right? She looks like she's here but *not* at the same time – what if she's, I don't know – necked something?'

'Like what?'

'How am I supposed to know? Look at her eyes. She looks like she's seen a ghost!'

'Perhaps she—' Moss barks. Hairs stand along my arms, at the tip of my spine. I look over my shoulder at David but he's looking down at Moss, parked by his legs.

'Is it just me, or does this boy look like he's spent a week with a groomer? He looks ten years younger than he did this morning.'

'It's just you.'

'But the limp! Can't argue that he—'

'David, we need to talk.'

'All ears.'

'No, I mean later. Not *now*.'

'We're here *to* talk. Talking is a core component of this whole—'

I give him a look that says *not now* and he stops, mid-sentence, though he doesn't move along. I realise he's waiting on my order and that Tadhg has probably been half-listening through the chitter-chatter of everyone else. My face prickles. I want something with meat in it – I haven't bought any in the weekly shop in what feels like forever because I know it would upset Jenna. 'I'll have a ham and cheese toastie and a . . . a hot chocolate.' I say it sharply under my breath.

'Coming right up,' he says, and then, keeping his voice low, 'We'll chat tonight, Rosie. On the balcony. When you return from your mother's.' Then, louder, 'Jordanne? What for you?'

I do my best to shake off worries about Jenna and

discomfort over Moss. But it's impossible. The dog, lively, like a pup, breathes against my leg.

I mask a shudder by pretending to yawn.

Half-heartedly, I make small talk with Jordanne to distract myself from the uncomfortable tickle in my chest – I ask about her baby, how she's getting on with the pregnancy, all the usual boring questions you ask someone when they're having a baby because you know they probably want to be asked, because it's a big deal for *them*. 'And when are you due?'

'June!' she exclaims. I know she means the month and not the woman whose ashes we were discussing not long ago, but my mind goes there. Back from ordering for everyone, David sits opposite me and clears his throat upon hearing Jordanne. Moss lets out a little whine as though to get my attention. I won't look at him.

'My first, Harry,' she goes on, 'he has this *perfect* toddler skin. Since I got pregnant, my face has looked like *this*,' she says, pointing at herself, 'like it's been sculpted from a granola bar.'

'No, it doesn't!' Really, it doesn't.

'Ah, it does, though. During the first pregnancy I was all glowing and stuff, so it must be a girl this time . . . apparently they "steal your beauty".'

'And where is Harry now?' I don't mean them to, but my words border on judgemental, as though I've snapped *Why aren't you with him? What kind of mother* are *you?*

Jordanne obviously notices. She seems thrown. 'He's with his dad. Thank God he's fully weaned now – I can finally have a bit of time for myself again. Can't tell you how strange it feels to not have him hanging out of me!'

'Which one hangs out of you? The husband or the kid?' I'm doing that thing where you put on this sort of persona when talking to somebody new to get them to like you, and I am *bad* at it.

She tells me they're not married, fills me in on some frivolous details about her boyfriend. I look closer at Jordanne once we're into the swing of chat. Her hair is frayed, like it's not been cut in years. Chewed fingernails practically down to the nail beds. Threads poking out of her cardigan. Dark circles. And then I realise that she never actually told us why she was joining the group.

I wait for a lull in conversation. 'So, if you don't mind me asking . . . what has you here?'

She buries her hands in her sleeves and avoids my eyes. Looks at David. He narrows his eyes, looks away. 'Ah. No sob story here.'

'None here either.' I tilt my chin up a little as I talk. My words are tinged with defensiveness. 'I'm only here for her.' I nod my head in Jenna's direction.

Jordanne looks at Jenna, then at me. 'You've said.' The way she blinks a bunch of times in a row tells me that she doesn't believe me.

Why do I feel like maybe we're both lying?

'Go on,' I say. 'You never had a chance to say your bit that first day.'

Her eyes water. Shit!

'Ah. Just . . .' I leave some room for her to carry on. Moss moves under the table to sit by her side. She laughs as he places his head in her lap. 'Sometimes it feels like . . . like, I'm "just" a mother now.'

I've got nothing. No words of reassurance.

David raises an eyebrow. There's this sad concern all over his face. Something's off here but I can't quite put a finger on what it could be. He sees me staring and offers nothing but a tight-lipped smile.

'I feel pretty invisible a lot of the time,' she says, raw vulnerability. 'Don't get me wrong. I'm Harry's everything, and that feels amazing. How he looks at me. Sometimes it stops my breath, Rosie.' This is the part where anyone else infatuated with their kids would ask me *What about you? Do you want kids?* Thankfully Jordanne doesn't go there. This simple non-act warms me to her. 'But now, with *this*' – she looks down at her stomach, hidden underneath her cardigan – 'I feel the last of myself slipping away.' She pauses for a beat and I get the sense that she's not talked about this much aloud, if ever. It's like she's surprised upon hearing the words escape her own mouth. 'There's this pressure. Among mothers. Like . . . she who disappears the most cares the most . . . she who, who juggles the most is the best. You know?'

I don't know. Thank *God* I don't know. What do I say? Go get yourself a DeLorean with a flux capacitor?

This is why I don't think I want the kids and the white picket fence. I can't imagine I'd know myself any more between all the cooking and cleaning, the nappy changing and sleepless nights. Sometimes I look at my own mother and compare her to the woman in the old photo albums, the young thing in bright-coloured dresses and ear-to-ear smiles. The only version of Mam I've ever known looks like she's wearing *that* woman's skin: poorly minded human taxidermy. And it's definitely not just the MS. Mam raised us pretty much alone, with the odd helping hand from Auntie Bridie. Apparently our dad was as useless when we were babies as he was when I was old enough to witness his uselessness. Mam said he never so much as offered to give us a bottle.

'Anyway,' Jordanne goes on, 'this is probably really boring for you—'

David clears his throat. It seems as though he wants her to stop talking and I can't for the life of me understand why.

'No, no! Go on,' I say. It's clear to me this interaction really means something to Jordanne. There was a lightness about her not a minute ago. She seems relieved. If the look she has on her face in response were made of words, they'd be *thank you*.

'I just. I don't notice the days go by any more. I never slow down enough to think . . . *Hang on, am I OK?* Have I had a glass of water during the past five hours? Every day is Harry slapping me awake at 5 a.m. Feeding him. Dressing him. Potty training. Discipline. Washing him. Cleaning the house. Re-tidying.'

I remind myself that she's pregnant *again* and I wonder why she'd do that to herself if she's finding it all so difficult. 'It's knackering to simply imagine it,' is all I say.

'Thing is, I don't think it's that stuff grinding me down,'

she says. 'I work part-time too, as an online counsellor . . . in the evenings. After every war zone of a day, I work. Right up till it's time to face-plant onto my bed.'

'What? Like, therapy? You're a therapist?'

'Of sorts. "Counsellor" and "therapist" are often used interchangeably, but they're not technically the same. Therapists have more education. Like, I wouldn't go as deeply into things with my clients . . .' A teenage boy drops us over our hot drinks as we sit, silent, while I consider it wild that Jordanne would need something like this project. I hear Peter and Nathan speaking loudly over one another against Izzy's high-pitched giggling, and I do my utmost to drown it out so I can give Jordanne my full attention. She deserves that at the very least – she looks like she's not slept a full night all her life.

'And, anyway, it's just . . . it's suffocating. This expectation that I've to succeed professionally during my only real down-time while being a full-time mother *and* while keeping a house in order. I don't want to work any more.' She's shocked by her own words. She looks embarrassed, too, like she's just trash-talked someone in a text and then accidentally sent it to them. 'I wish I could focus completely on my family, my home, *myself* without having to drag what's left of me after a long, brutal day of unconditional motherly love into the home office, so I can afford Dublin rent and bills. Butter scraped over too much bread . . . Bilbo knew it!'

Lord of the Rings reference? OK. I definitely like her. Even if she is a lowercase pete fangirl.

'My boyfriend had to mind-wrestle me to sign the contract

to do this' – she eyes everyone at the table – 'because I'm that bad at making time for myself. His company recently hired Tadhg and they became buddies. That's how he heard about it all.' Jordanne looks at Tadhg then. He's seemingly been third-wheeling our conversation, gives me an awkward little nod. 'Rosie. Do you think I'm a . . .?'

'What?'

'A terrible feminist?'

'God. Why would I?'

'For wishing Brian's income covered everything . . .'

I mean, if I were Peter's girlfriend, I'd never have to work, because he's loaded, but I'd work anyway. I like to climb into bed at night knowing that I'm standing on my own two feet and that I'm capable of financial independence. Not that I'd ever want to be Peter's girlfriend. This is just . . . hypothetical. He's literally here, at the same table, it's impossible not to hypothesise using him.

When I don't reply, Jordanne dives headfirst into her justifications. 'We have to live in Dublin for Brian's career, which he loves, and . . . all I want to do is, is to have kids.' She sweetly says it like someone who's yet to experience it. Then she cups her coffee and bites her lip and waits for me to smite her.

'Of course it doesn't.' I grasp at possible responses. 'Feminism is about . . . choice.' I say it even though I'm not sure I believe it: that choice alone holds the key to women's freedom.

'But if it's about choice, that sort of means we don't need significant social change, doesn't it?' she says. 'State support for childcare is lousy. But instead of fighting the system I sometimes just lie in bed at night hoping Brian gets another promotion.' Guilt gobbles her whole, I can see it. 'What I wouldn't *give* to spend night and day on myself and Harry, and on this little one.' She pats her belly and continues to spew her situation as I glug my hot chocolate and think about how I'm so, *so* glad I don't have this shit to deal with.

'Ah, well. Without my family, I'd probably still be addicted to shopping and pizza and attention from fellas.' Jordanne rolls her eyes. 'What a sad life,' she scoffs. 'What I have is a lot more fulfilling, even if it does leave me decrepit come 8 p.m.'

I half choke on a marshmallow.

Tadhg interrupts with a lightning bolt. 'Death. It, eh, it really makes you analyse what life is, so it does.' I turn to him, angling myself away from Jordanne. There's a gentleness about Tadhg. A coolness. His voice is stoic, like the hardship he's faced hasn't bent or broken him whatsoever, even though you can tell that it absolutely has if you take one look at him and really hone in on the tiny details. Jenna has me an expert at recognising depression. Tadhg avoids eye contact; he slumps; his cheeks are hollowed-out Easter eggs; there are tiny stains on his hoodie that signify neglect. He doesn't seem the type of lad to be OK with presenting himself like that, yet he's here, covered in flecks of yesterday's dinner.

Neither I nor Jordanne say a thing in response to him. He's a bluebottle we're hoping to catch with a glass: if we make the wrong move, he'll fly away.

'Losing Rachel . . . it, eh . . . kind of showed me how much time we waste.' He swallows all the spit that's accumulated at the back of his throat. 'Worrying about this thing, that thing. Need to hurry up and finish college. Need to hurry up and buy this house. Hurry up, hurry up and then, sure, it's all over.'

Moss whimpers again and jumps half into Jordanne's lap so he can look over the table. The sound of slobber and nails on wood. All three of us look at him. David turns from the others towards the dog.

Tadhg goes on. 'Hearing you talk, Jordanne. About all that stuff.' He half shakes his head. 'Makes me think of her. Rachel.'

Jordanne hesitates, like she's nervous she'll put her foot in it and end Tadhg's outpour.

'She wanted kids,' he goes on, 'my kids.'

The sound of the floorboard that our chairs sit on tells me that Tadhg's knee is shaking now. David faces us, and I can feel Peter watching from across the way. I wonder if Alice is listening from Tadhg's right-hand side; again, if Jenna is high, because she's just staring at the wall; if the rest of them are ever going to shut up.

'Nowadays you have to have it all. Do it all. You have to get a degree, which costs you time. As well as money. You have to carve out a secure job for long enough to convince a bank to lend you money to get a bog-standard gaff, unless you want to be living with your parents forever.'

I sense Peter curl up. I check, and he has. He's pulled his armour on. I figure he's thinking about how much money he has, that he's feeling too privileged to be listening to Tadhg.

'Rachel had debt. Lived with her ma and da. Went to study late in her twenties. Had this, hormone thing, that, eh, meant having kids would be harder. For her. And I said, "Rachel," I said, "I'll wait. No rush."'

Suddenly, Nathan goes quiet and Jenna looks over and we're all listening to Tadhg. The moment turns. Something changes in the air. A foreign feeling envelops me, like the non-material space we occupy fills with a cloud of teeny spores of white light – surrounding us, keeping everything else out. A forcefield. Protecting us. Might sound like I'm on mushrooms but that's honestly the only way I can describe what being at this table in this moment is like. Words are safe to share here.

Tadhg's voice holds firm while he speaks of his girlfriend's suicide. 'One night we were in bed and she told me . . . said she didn't want to be alive any more and . . . I . . . thought she just needed some extra attention. Thought maybe it was a cry for help. Her saying such a thing. *She won't do that, no way. She's just having a vent.* Dismissed it, I did. As . . . her, just feeling stuck. Or something. And, eh . . .' I wait for a crack, a single tear, but nothing. It's like he's talking about the stock market. 'Seemed like I was right. Because . . . then, we talked about getting married.'

Nathan gasps. 'Oh, *God*.'

'Booked a holiday for the following month. She even ordered a new dress.'

My stomach lurches.

'It was delivered the day she – the day I found her—'

David jumps in, sensing that Tadhg doesn't want to finish the sentence. 'Deep inner sadness is patched over with shopping receipts and false smiles more often than you might know. At times, it's impossible to know how someone's really doing. We've all become so adept at performing – these contraptions are a whole new kind of glasshouse, enabling the exponential growth of emptiness.' David nods at our phones, grouped in the middle of the table. 'I can just about count on both my hands the number of funerals I've attended over the years of patients who took their own lives.' He takes a deep breath. 'Nine too many.'

I really want to look at Jenna but I worry that whatever way I position my features, it'll seem like my face is just one massive finger-wag. She doesn't appear to be in a position to be patronised today. But fuck, I hope she's listening . . . *absorbing* . . .

'And at every one of those funerals, the same sentiments echoed through the church. *What a tragedy. I should've seen the signs.* People can be present for the dead in a way they rarely are for the living.' Tadhg shuffles. He rubs the back of his head. David, sensitive to Tadhg's every breath, quickly clarifies. 'I bring up these funerals because there's something to be learned in examining the regrets that people express when they come together in grief, not to say—'

'You can say it. I wasn't there when she needed me most. Let myself get all tied up with life.' He swallows loudly. 'And her family. They weren't close, which. I knew . . . She only had me, and I—'

David absolves Tadhg in seven syllables. 'You are not

responsible,' he says, resolute and unswerving. 'Tadhg, I tortured myself over my patients who killed themselves. I did. But the fact is that some people wake up and the sun has ceased to shine and . . . that's it. Many *can* be helped, but some, unfortunately, cannot be reached.'

Tadhg tries to retort. He can't. It's as if he's got a thread of spaghetti caught up in his throat and the words can't make their way around it. His knuckles are white, he's gripping his hands together that tightly, but his expression doesn't waver.

I don't know what takes over me but I reach out a hand and I place it on top of his. He exhales. Turns up a corner of his mouth, without meeting my eyes.

'I can only . . . imagine . . . how you feel,' I say softly. I fix my eyes on my sister in an obvious sort of way, so that he might read me. But he doesn't look up. We're not there yet. I slowly pull my hand away from Tadhg's and wait for someone else to take over the conversation.

We eat, we talk, we laugh. David takes a 'backwards selfie' (regular photo!) of the nine of us to use as a header for our group chat. For a full half-hour, I manage to forget about the red dachshund and his apparent round trip through a rabbit hole leading to some canine fountain of healing.

David checks Moss's mouth on the drive back to the city. 'Where's that cracked tooth gone? Eh? You're different, little fella,' he mumbles, stroking the dog along his body. 'She's up to her tricks, isn't she?'

I decide it's unfair to press him with so many pairs of ears listening in so I pretend to fall asleep.

*

It's past midnight. The unopened bottle of Baileys in my fridge (left over from the last time I had a man over – think his name was Arthur . . . no, Alder? Maybe?) called my name all evening while I recounted the day's events to Mam. I cracked it open when I got home. After a couple of deep glasses, I sent Peter a cheeky mirror selfie of my naked, wet body right out of the shower.

Still waiting on a reply.

David tells me Peter is in his bedroom with Jenna as we stand together on the balcony, outside our front doors.

'Oh?' I slow blink, green-eyed and tiddly. I'm glad it's dark: with my arms tightly crossed and in my Barbie pink dressing-gown, all I need is the half-smoked cigarette and the heat rollers and I'm the resident narky 1980s housewife.

'He's doing his thing. Music, you know. Talented boy. They get along, our two . . .'

Moonlight drapes itself over the courtyard below as stars stand together hand in hand above. David tells me it's Orion's Belt through a mouthful of tinned peaches: three stars all in a line, visible at some point to virtually everyone on earth.

'I used to insist to her that they were all just big balls of gas,' David says.

I assume he's talking about June again. 'Well, they are.'

David laughs. His eyes twinkle like fireflies. 'You remind me of myself, thirty years younger. You're like that boy in there, too,' he goes on, referring to Peter, 'steadfast in your convictions.'

I shuffle my feet.

'Let's just say, you're lucky you're not my daughter. If you were *my* daughter, I fear we'd clash somewhat. It's easier to maintain a head on one's shoulders when there's no blood running through the conversation. Peter and I, we snap, you know . . .'

I love that blood doesn't matter to David; he really sees Peter as his own. If only blood had mattered more to my father. I want to tell David that I'd reorganise the solar system to have a dad like him instead of the one I was dealt, but of course I don't, because you don't say things like that out loud. Especially not when you're a bit drunk and *a lot* distracted.

'Look, let's cut to the chase. What'sgoingon?' The demand for information comes out as one word.

David forks another lump of peach into his gob.

'That day, when you told me you wanted to help a bunch of miserable people to—'

'Miserable? I'm sure I used words like distressed. Lonely. *Anxious.*' He eyeballs me as if to imply that this whole charade is for my benefit.

'You know what I mean,' I slur. 'Anyway, we *are* all miserable. Especially that Alice one. My God, where'd you find her?'

'Rosie.'

'What? She never even talks!' Big sour head on her any time I look her way.

'Alice cared for my wife in hospital after a double mastectomy. June had cancer. Did I ever tell you that? Breast cancer.'

Well, now I feel terrible. I crack my jaw as all of my muscles tense up at once.

'Give Alice time, Rosie. You lot are the first people she's been around in many years. Imagine being locked away all by yourself *for years*. Not months. Years! You'd need time to sharpen your social skills, too . . .'

'Whatever, look,' I divert, trying and probably failing to disguise my guilt. I think about Moss, perhaps standing on the other side of that door behind us, listening. Goosebumps rise all over my body. 'When you said you wanted to rope people together to, to—'

'Reconnect. With others. With nature. With themselves, and—'

'Sure, sure, but . . . you never said anything about . . . what it's all got to do with . . . her.'

He leans over the glass railing as he always does when I catch him out here at night, empty tin cupped between arthritic hands. 'I did try.'

I let out an exasperated breath. My eyes do that thing where one eye squints and one eye bulges, when I'm trying to appear less tipsy than I am.

'I said it was June's glasshouse,' he says gently, looking my way. 'I attempted to explain that the whole plan was born of her and her ambition to enact positive change – on multiple occasions – and more than once, you cut me off. Forgive me, but you're not always the greatest listener. You asked very little and allowed me no room to elaborate.'

A father I never had is telling me how much of a disappointment I am . . . That'll get the anxiety going. I want to defend myself: I want to point out all the listening I did earlier, in the café. I want to shout about how I *never stop* listening to my mother, to customers at work, and . . . sure enough, there it is: the familiar sense of electricity running through my veins.

'Anxiety is a siren, Rosie.' He looks up at the night sky. How can he tell? 'You've not been staring it in the face and listening to it. It's a signal from your body, one you'll have to learn to understand if you're to manage the anxiety effectively. Medication only does so much.'

That reminds me. I forgot to get my repeat prescription. Shit! All this business with the group . . . when was the last time I popped a sertraline?

'And if you can't listen to this loud noise roaring from deep within yourself, how are you to listen to – or *hear* – other people? Tell me that!'

My mouth is open and ready to talk but all that comes out is, 'Peter.'

'What about him?'

'He's the one who told me about, well, all of it. The project, the—'

'And my son assured me that he explained that *June* walked me down this path.'

'No.' Or – yes? I shake my head. I can't remember. 'Well, he said "my mom's" plan,' I say, mimicking his slight American accent, 'but he never really talks about her, so I—'

'About *June.*'

'About . . . June.' A pause. I start to fiddle with a loose thread on my dressing-gown. 'So, I assumed this whole – *garden-therapy thing* – was something *she* wanted to do, when she was still—'

'You assumed.'

My anxiety is now high voltage. The flat awareness that David might think ill of me – that I'm uncaring – it stings all over. I force myself to look him in the face and to study its lines, its story, sagging and shadowed. I respect this man. The look in his eyes is one I need to wipe away and quick. 'Sorry. I had a lot on my mind that day.'

Well, I did!

David takes this sad little breath.

'Jenna, my, my mam . . . I—' I stutter, my thoughts swirling like a galaxy on fast-forward.

'Rosie, deep breath. We're simply talking. Your body is all tensed up, and I sense the wind is taking you away from me.'

His wrinkles shape themselves in a way that says *you're a let-down* and, no, I'm not just imagining it. My mam's face does the same thing every time she asks me when I'm going to start a family.

Seconds or hours pass. I feel as though I'm climbing a ladder and a few rungs vanish before my eyes. I'm stuck. David won't want to help me on my climb – he thinks I'm awful! And there was me hoping I could turn to him for help, with . . . Oh, I don't know any more! I gasp for air. I throw both my hands out and grip the cold metal railing. Help. Please help. Help, help—

David grips either side of my shoulders. He turns me to face him. 'All right. Imagine that you're on a rollercoaster . . . and that I'm beside you, challenging you to talk through it, as we whizz through the air. Tell me, what did you have for dinner earlier, with your mother?'

'*What?*' I gasp, and I gasp, and I shiver, and—

'Trust me. It's important. I need to know, right now. Before the ride is over.'

'Oh, for *fuck*, I, eh, eh, mash, some peas, lamb, fuck, David, I—' I try to push him away. I fight against his hands, but he holds me still.

'What kind of peas?'

'Just! Peas!'

'Describe—'

'Frozen! David, *why*—?'

'Please recount – in vivid detail – how you prepared the meal. What brand were the peas, might I ask?'

Calm as ever, he keeps asking me these stupid questions until I've described the colour, flavour and consistency of the bloody *gravy*, until I'm talking without gulping at the space around my head. I become aware of the firm pressure of his fingers through my dressing-gown and of how uncomfortably close we're standing. I feel the sweat on my skin gone cold and the fog clear in my head. My breath slowly but surely steadies itself.

'A little technique that always helped my patients during panic attacks,' David says.

'You never used that on me,' I say, pulling away from his hands, mortified.

'Because I've never witnessed you having a full-blown panic attack before.'

'And you say you didn't do enough for them. Your patients. That . . . actually *worked*! That was brilliant. I'll have to tell Mam to distract me like that.'

He smiles a sheepish smile. 'If someone is sitting right in front of you thinking they're about to die, you help them to realise that they're, in fact, very much alive, and that's precisely why they're panicking. Modern life has a way of forcing our natural stress response to do some . . . gymnastics. *Alcohol* sure won't help—'

I cut him off so I don't have to talk about drinking alone on a Saturday night. 'Just. Please unretire.'

A soft laugh. 'I'm afraid that's not an option. My job was to enable people like you to cope beyond the four walls of my office and I rarely did that, or anything close to that. The health of the whole person matters – physical health, yes, but, Rosie, there are many psychological and social aspects of the care I was responsible for and, in that regard, I failed. Time after time after time.'

I lean my back against the wall between our two front doors and I tilt my head to look up at the sky. After what David said – about my inability to listen – I'm afraid to speak.

'You're a ball of apprehension. Talk to me. You'll feel better. Ask me what you want to ask me.'

A sigh of relief to thank him for the open door. 'Tell me what you mean when you say "it was all June's idea". Tell me why *that dog*' – I daren't say his name – 'left Avalon today without a limp. You weren't surprised, like the rest of us . . .'

David nervously plays with the can between his hands; he's just a silhouette from here but I hear metal on tin as his elbows make subtle movements. 'Moss. I – I can't explain that.'

'Don't lie.'

'Indeed, I have some – ideas, but, well, Peter tells me I'm mad, that I shouldn't—'

Frustrated, I suck on my bottom lip. I wonder if Peter's spoken with my sister about this dog business . . .

'It's June, Rosie,' David says bluntly.

I rub my forehead.

'She reaches out to me. And I just – I cannot possibly begin to . . .'

'Explain.' I finish for him, impatient. He just nods. I want to prove both David and myself wrong about my attentiveness capabilities, so I dip a toe into the turbulent question ocean that's stirring. 'She . . . reaches out to you. Even now? While she's—' I can't bring myself to say it. This doesn't sit well.

'Even now. She somehow prodded us, all of us, into this situation. I've been finding notes from her. All over the place. For years.'

I relax my chest. 'Ah. So, notes she wrote while she was . . . alive?'

'Yes.'

I don't understand. My face tells him so.

'I've grappled with this for some time. Racked my brain. Held memories under a mental microscope. This is going to sound . . . well, my wife . . . she's tapped into something that you and I are not. Somehow, she knows about things before they've happened . . . She always did . . .'

An uncomfortable laugh. I can't help it.

He appears flustered. 'Where might I begin? Ah. Well.

My June exhibited many symptoms of ADHD, which is—'

'I know what ADHD is,' I lie, faintly recalling some documentary I saw about hyperactive children.

'Well, I debated about whether or not to refer her to a psychiatrist – for a full evaluation. I was aware of the stigmas, of course, but the risks concerned me more than the myths. However, when I approached the subject with her, she laughed it off with that fierce laugh.' He smiles to himself in the dark. 'My wife has—'

'*Had.*'

He doesn't correct me. '—a unique way of processing information. When we first met, I actually thought she was rather rude, but she simply couldn't fake a response . . . She would always say what she felt. She acted upon her feelings. Always. I admired that! She detested rules for the sake of rules; she wouldn't comply with one if it conflicted with her internal sense of value. She was inherently strong-willed, my wife. Untameable.'

'But—'

'Please, listen?'

I nod.

'My very first conversation with June set off ADHD alarm bells in my physician's mind. It was the focus subject of my doctoral thesis! And if I hadn't fallen in love with her and considered her perspective, I'd have insisted she get herself onto Ritalin.'

'Her perspective?'

'In time, of course, I shared my concerns with her. But June begged me to instead study mental phenomena which are inexplicable by orthodox scientific psychology, such as—'

'Predicting the future,' I say with a sneer. I can't help myself. The conversation is about to slide off a cliff and I don't like the view down below.

'Well, yes. All right. Take Alice . . .'

'What about her?'

'Alice tended to June in the Mater private, shortly before June died, back home.'

'June died . . . at the house?' I think about the party we're having there tomorrow night and shudder – all the tinsel Peter bought and stashed in my spare room, all the bottles of plum wine and spiced rum we ordered . . . David's none the wiser, as far as I know. I'm pretty sure Peter didn't invite Alice for fear she'd rat us all out. She doesn't talk to us, but we're certain she talks to David when they're alone. Hairs stand on the back of my neck, as if to protest my on-the-spot decision to go along.

David nods. 'Cardiac arrest, after her cancer treatments.' He comes to stand beside me against the wall, settles himself against it. 'It's odd. I spent my whole career in close proximity to tragedy, to death. All the times I attempted to console patients with no understanding at all of the pain of death myself . . . *Anyway*, Alice. June pulled Alice close one night – after having her blood pressure checked, half-unconscious – Alice told me that June whispered into her ear . . .'

He inhales deeply.

'What did she say?'

'"You will save the spider queen, before the burst of baby's breath."'

Moss barks in the apartment.

'I don't – get it,' I say, my shoulders tensing. 'Baby – Jordanne's baby? Or, what . . .'

'Spider queen, well, the meaning of *that* still eludes me. But baby's breath is a flower that June sowed from seeds in our garden. It was the first flower she ever grew herself from nothing. A charming white bloom. So soft. Like her. Grows back every year.' He sighs. 'June – she knew that *this exact group of people* would be involved in *this project* before she—' He can't say 'died'. Or maybe he simply doesn't want to. 'In fact, she herself made it so! I hadn't the foggiest notion about gardening. Alice tells me they spoke at length about plants, flowers, during June's stint in the hospital, and Alice – she knows just when and how to bring life to the garden again. She's an *integral* member of the group—'

'David. Sorry. But this is all so—'

'There's more, Rosie, she—'

'June was, what . . . psychic?!'

'Don't roll your eyes like that, please. My wife was no silly clairvoyant.'

'What, then?'

'She was – she is—' He's grasping. '*Wise to things* – things that both you and I are blind to. She is in tune with – everything. Rosie, you once wore a crystal bracelet, rose quartz. Do you remember where you bought it?'

I flatline.

'I saw it around your wrist in my office.'

'Weirdly observant of you, David.'

'Please. Try to recall.'

'I bought them in—'

'More than one?' He jumps down my throat and practically into my bowel.

'Yeah. One for me, one for—'

'Your sister!' He cuts me off, flailing his empty can. The fork inside it clatters in the dark.

'We found them in town. This shop, Tír na nÓg.' Jenna was only small, and I suppose I thought they'd be, like, I don't know. Sibling bracelets, if that's a thing. I stopped wearing it when we fell out.

'Do you remember who served you on the day, in the shop? In Tír na nÓg?'

I search my mind. 'No. And I suppose you're going to tell me it was June, even though I'm sure it wasn't.'

'No, no.'

'Well, thank God!' I exclaim.

'But she did own the place.' No sound but Moss's panting through the door.

'That's a, well, a coincidence, isn't it?' I'm listening to my own words like they're coming from someone else who's trying to reassure me.

'She first opened that shop at twenty-five. Before Peter came along. No place in Dublin provided services like the healing she performed out back! Granted, she was eventually shut down – the bureaucrats caught wind of her experimentation with psilocybin, from magic mushrooms, which regrettably, like all psychedelic substances, remains illegal here—'

'David! You can't be—'

'Rosie, I *swear* it was all a farce to me when she came into my life . . . but—'

'—serious!'

'—there has to be something *to* all this,' he finishes.

I observe a man so desperate for a sense of connection to his wife that he's convincing himself of things that can't be. David needs this project as much as the rest of them do. We stand suspended in time, breathing, looking up at the stars. I decide I won't interrupt him again, that I won't try to make him feel silly. *Complicated grief.* I really need to give it a google. I've no idea how to respond to a person so knee-deep in pain and delusion.

'June reknit the fabric of the universe back together after unravelling it, so that we could all come together. It *must* be important, the project that we're embarking on . . . each one of us is involved for a reason. I don't know how she did it, and I don't know why, but she's most certainly the reason we're standing here together now, our energies shifting, merging, creating something new.' David takes a deep, slow, measured breath. 'White daffodils decorate the patch of earth where I buried June's urn, under her apple tree, every springtime. Only when they come alive again will I know that I'm succeeding. And I know that because she made it so, she planted that feeling in me. Somehow. Forgive me . . .'

David's crying again. The space between his words fills

with a depth of love so annihilating, I wonder how he actually functions on a day-to-day basis. This man is not OK.

And I've got nothing.

All I feel I can do is try on that thing called listening. It doesn't quite fit: I'm so aware of where it hangs loose around the contours of my body. Time to learn how to tailor. Funny how one interaction can find you, grab you by the scruff of the neck, say *that's it, we're different now* and have you fully believe it.

JENNA

ater that day, I watch Peter sing his song 'Letting Go' into the microphone propped on his desk, shoulders hunched, eyes glued to the editing software open on his laptop screen. He's the Antarctic sun going down before its six months of darkness.

She's had him. He's hers. There's no storybook ending coming my way. Not that I thought there might be but . . . did I actually think there might be?

Dry mouth.

Clenched fists.

My heartbeat, all wrong.

Peter asked if I'd like to see how he records his vocals; I said 'of course'. Anything to not have to look at or hear or smell my sister tonight. His cooing is an almost-distraction from the napalm of my thoughts. Continuous irregular thumping in my chest as I look around Peter's room and think about all the scenarios I've daydreamed in which I'm here for the first time. None looked anything like this – us, with so much space between us.

I eye up my jacket on Peter's bed. It looks how it always looks – covered in lint and Bertie's hairs – but there's something sinister about it now. The lens of my mind slow zooms on the pocket, the one with the note inside. I'm surprised my lungs haven't collapsed with how much I've been sucking the soul out of this e-cig.

Peter stops singing. Maybe I've turned grey – my skin isn't far off being fifty shades on a good day. He's not looking at me, though: he's staring at his phone on the desk. The screen went bright. Frantic, he pulls on his glasses.

'What?'

The pre-recorded backing track plays on without him.

'*What?*' It must be a message from Rosie. This feeling really is gut-churning: knowing about them, knowing they don't want me to know. 'Peter.'

'It's that dickhead again. The one who calls me "lowercase Peter".'

'Oh,' I say, relieved. 'What this time?'

He holds his phone up in front of my face. It's a direct-message conversation on Instagram. I recognise the picture he's been sent as the cover portrait for his last album, *Parades*: a beautiful HD shot of him – just him – all lit by neon light. I can't help but get lost in his eyes every time I see it. Losing patience, I tap my feet against the floorboards. 'I've looked at both your album covers a million times—'

'No, Jenna. Look!'

Frustrated, he pushes his glasses up his nose, sticks his

tongue into the corner of his mouth, points at the image of his face, then again at the album title. It's been photo-shopped. The title – *Parades* – now reads *Aids* – and an eighties moustache has been shaded in along Peter's top lip. They've tried to make him look like Freddie Mercury, I think.

I marinate in confusion for a minute. Peter's eyes dart from the message to the image and back to the message over and over again, like he's trying to break the Da Vinci Code.

I'm lost. 'Is this person trying to imply that you're gay or what?' It's 2019. *Who* still thinks that only gay people get AIDS?

He doesn't answer me.

'This is what you get for being so . . . metrosexual. Dinosaur brains can't handle it. Just ignore.'

'This isn't the usual closet-gay rumours. It has to be about earlier – when I talked about Freddie, my mom's flowers . . . It's too . . . specific!' He jabs the phone screen as he talks. 'This isn't – trivial shit – like a dumb threat about sharing where I live online. This is about the project, Jenna.'

I'm not sure what he's talking about. I wasn't in my right mind earlier; I must have missed some exchange. 'It's just a stupid meme,' I say. 'Social media is a sewer—'

'No, no, no, someone must be tracking my phone, or – or someone from the group is talking. But who?' He's muttering to himself now. 'Not Rosie. Not Dad. Not *Nate*.'

I feel my nails dig into my palms. Peter said my sister's

name before referring to his dad. It's telling. *He's crazy about her. Why her?* I bury the thought badly, so its head pokes out of the grainy ground of my subconscious wearing a wretched expression. 'What's their username? The person who sent it?'

'It's tastyyy_yogaxx. No posts, no followers, following nobody. Not even following me!'

'Eh –' I choke on some kind of feeling. 'You think someone on the project is harassing you online? Hiding behind the – the cloak of a pseudonym?'

'No,' he replies, steadfast, 'but I think one of them is – I don't know, telling some, some friend or family member who knows me, about things I talk about during sessions. And *that* person is fucking with me. Maybe.' While he talks, Peter morphs from accomplished detective into one of those orphaned pups you see in sad animal-welfare ads. 'It's my own fault.'

'Of course, it's no—'

'Stop. Look, I put myself out there.' He's shaking slightly. 'I just have to . . . put up with . . . this kind of shit. My manager, he said . . .'

I make some sounds, half-words that mean nothing, till I find some. 'You sound like one of the people who hate-stalk you. Yeah, you're in the public eye, but I don't remember you ever posting an invitation online for people to harass you. The group is supposed to be a safe space.'

'You read the contract, eh?' He forces a smile through anxious lip-biting.

'I read that line. Top and centre on the front page. Sort

of had to.' My forced, coy smile. 'Look, I accept cookies on every single website, I don't do small print, but I thought the whole point is that we can meet and talk about anything – that what's said is kept pri—'

'Who do you think would go home and recount every last thing I say, to – I don't know – someone capable of doing *this*?'

I think out loud then. 'What if it *is* someone in the group? Running this profile?'

He stands up. Paces, a hand wrapped up in his hair.

'I'm sure it's not,' I lie, 'but—'

'Who? *Who* would do this?'

I say it faster than I mean to. 'Jordanne?'

He looks at me like I'm mad. Shakes his head. I glibly list possible giveaways on my fingers. 'Fangirl. Unemployed mother with too much time on her hands. Maybe she resents you for your success . . .'

Peter's eyes threaten me with disappointment. 'Jenna. Don't be a – she's – she's not unemployed.' I mentally scroll through possible insults he had on the tip of his tongue just now. 'And, dude, *my* mom stopped going to work when she adopted me. When did you become so knowledgeable on what being a parent entails? Rosie told me you don't even talk to your—' He stops himself, but the damage is done. I feel the sting of the slap from that unspoken *mom*.

'I see how it is. Rosie said it, so it must be true. Don't act like you know about that . . . You don't.'

Peter groans. Rubs his eyes. 'Sorry. I'm sorry. I'm just . . .'

'Stressed.' After I say it, I observe my thoughts with

terrifying clarity, like they're on one of those sushi trains
– all the ones I want to pick up and throw at Peter, and the
Mam conversation, the last taboo. Instead, I simply watch
them pass by. Am I holding back to protect him, or myself?
To protect his image of me? *The cool girl?* Why is that
thought – of Peter's obsession with my bloody sister – still
staring at me with that awful look in its eyes? How do I bury
it so it chokes to death on imaginary gravel?

He's explaining himself now: something about his album
launch, in June, and a summer tour . . . says he can't allow
himself to become distracted from his music. He fires his
phone at the bed, at my jacket. Then his eyes do this
awkward dance.

'Would you mind? It's just. I've. Got to . . .' He says so
much without saying anything at all.

'Oh. Yeah. Sure.'

He hands me my jacket faster than he can say awesome
and thanks. Then, 'Later.'

Later. At least there's that.

ROSIE

It's 9 p.m. the following evening. I'm on my third vodka and Coke. Jenna's been vegging on the couch all evening in what I'm assuming is her costume for the group Christmas party: a red clown nose and some heavy eyeliner. Eventually I ask who she's supposed to be. 'Rudolph,' she says, hair a state, outfit all wrinkled. At least she's finally talking again!

'Is this' – I start, concerned that I've gone a bit over the top with my outfit – 'a bit much? I showed Mam a picture of the model wearing it and, you know her, *wasn't a fan*, because God forbid anyone sees my knees, but . . .' I haven't even added the gloves yet. I ordered the *Mean Girls* Jingle Bell Rock Santa costume from Amazon a couple of days ago and now, thanks to Jeff Bezos, I'm a cloud of white fluff and red leather on fake-tanned flesh.

Jenna takes five seconds too long to drag her eyes away from her phone screen. I tug the skirt down as low as it'll go (it barely skims my arse cheeks) and anticipate a raised eyebrow, a snort, a giggle, a gasp, *something* – but she just seems . . . sad. There's more dullness in her eyes than before, and because her face is a bigger-featured mirror of the flat expression I see daily in my selfie camera, it's difficult to observe – almost like seeing myself in a parallel world, slowly fading to black.

'You look amazing,' she says. Not a hint of sarcasm. I feel my chin tuck itself into my neck. It doesn't know what else to do because Jenna has never said something so nice to me as an adult.

I shift my booted-up feet. 'Yeah?'

'Yeah.'

Then I wait for her to notice the thin crystal bracelet around my wrist. Mam spotted it immediately when I went over earlier to heat up leftover stew – took it to mean that we've 'sorted all our differences', that our relationship has magically healed in a matter of weeks, that soon we'll be playing happy families again. I didn't have it in me to correct her, to tell her that we still hardly say two words to one another, that Jenna probably threw her bracelet away, or lost it, or, more likely, forgot it even existed. Like Mam probably will and all.

Jenna doesn't notice. She looks back down at her phone. I pull on the gloves in silence and tell her it's time to head down to Peter's bus.

There are two camps when it comes to Christmas: people who grew up in happy homes – the types to gobble up the sentimentality – and those who grew up with people like our dad. I watched him wrap his fingers in bandages from punching through plaster walls more times than I unwrapped presents. I'm already counting down the days to January first.

That said, the sight before me now would convert the Grinchiest of sorts.

Nathan is dressed as Will Ferrell's Elf and Peter as Billy Bob's Bad Santa – he has the fake beard pulled down around his neck and pretend stubble drawn around his lips, where a cigarette is propped, à la the rather loveable alcoholic conman. The pair of them are gushing from the front seat of the Volkswagen about how they spent the day framing each of Avalon's front windows with fairy lights and twirling them around every branch in the front garden so the place would look like the house out of *Home Alone*.

Tyres crunch pebbles. I tip my nose against the rounded square window to take it all in. All that's missing is silent snowfall.

'I made a banging playlist for later,' says Nathan.

'We even made mulled wine,' Peter takes over, 'but, I sort of made a balls of dinner. Cooking ain't my forte. Apologies, gang.'

'So, it's pizza for mains and Cadbury selection box for dessert!' Nathan, adorable in his pointed hat, unbuckles his seat belt as Peter parks and then shoos us off the bus.

We clamber out. Tipsy already, and under the weight of the biggest false eyelashes I could find in the local pharmacy, I steady myself against Tadhg's shoulder. And as my heels meet the driveway, I notice Peter gawping. Just as he seems like he's about to approach me, I turn back to Tadhg.

'Feel a bit underdressed, so I do,' Tadhg says. The soft light of the garden shows me Tadhg's cheap Christmas jumper covered in sewn-on snowflakes.

'Yeah. I was about to say. Could've at least added a star hat, maybe some baubles to your jumper, to be a Christmas tree. *This* is just pathetic.' I bite my lip and squint my eyes – *flirting*! Vodka always renders me allergic to simple small talk with attractive single men my age. I didn't think I'd pull this shit with group members, honestly, but it's been a minute since I last found myself drinking socially with *anyone* attractive outside of a Tinder date. I'm not sure how else to be.

'Ah. Yeah.' Tadhg doesn't seem to know what to make of me.

'Well,' I go on, 'that scent more than makes up for it . . . What's that you're wearing?'

All bashful now, he tells me it's called Aventus by the brand Creed, and I wonder if Peter is eavesdropping, if he's jealous. 'Rachel got it for me. Before. And . . . wearing it . . . makes me feel like she's still with me.' At least I *think* that's what Tadhg says. I'm so in my own head, I almost miss his words. David's creased forehead appears, as a thought, to scold me. I hyper-focus on Tadhg's lips, like the answer to all my problems is about to come flying out of them. 'Only use it on special occasions. I'd love to wear it every day. But if I use it up . . . well. Then.'

Tightening my grip on Tadhg's arm, I make what I hope

is a soothing sound. There's no solution to how much hurt he's feeling, and if there is, I certainly don't have a notion, but one thing I can be sure of is that saying this stuff out loud is cathartic for him; Tadhg loses psychological weight before my very eyes. 'Looks great, lads,' he says in Peter and Nathan's direction, elongating his spine and inhaling the million tiny illuminations along with the cold country air.

Peter acknowledges him with a curt nod and searches my eyes for something he can't seem to find.

My feelings are all knotted up with the tipsiness; I like that he's jealous, and I feel bad about that. I want him to approach me, but I want to throw my shoes off and run a mile in my bare feet . . .

Giraffe-like, I gangle towards the porch arm in arm with Tadhg, hoping that by linking him I'm forming a forcefield that Peter can't penetrate. That's my immediate plan; I'm not sure I have any kind of long-term plan, or even a night-long plan, and I have no idea why I spent fifty quid on a sexy outfit to impress Peter if this is how I've chosen to behave . . .

Sometimes I wonder if there's someone behind the scenes, running me like I'm a vehicle – choosing when to drive me left or right, deciding how much of a distance I should be parked from Peter Dolan. If you were to examine my thoughts fresh as they come through one of those one-way mirrors you might conclude there's something seriously wrong with me because, right this second, the familiar semi-drunk itch for sexual gratification has me gagging to scope out all of the secret nooks and crannies inside the house, all that might serve me privacy for at least five minutes – and not to delight in Peter, even though I've fantasised about having sex with him in his childhood bedroom on more than one occasion.

Instead, I observe Tadhg – his military posture and his strong jaw, his pillowy lips, his big hands. I run through every possible way he could reject me. I ask myself if I could handle it if he does.

Then I look at Jenna, dead-eyed in her red nose, and for the first time since she burst back into my world, I feel this pull to talk to her about my box of mental bullshit.

Peter prepares to turn his key in the front door as Nathan asks, 'So? What do we think? Isn't it fabulous?'

'He made it from the garden,' I hear Peter's voice say.

'I friggin' love it!' Izzy squeals. She's come as Jack Skellington from *The Nightmare before Christmas* and nobody wants to acknowledge how heartbreaking it is. 'So . . . meaningful!'

Nathan fans his face. 'Thankyouverymuch, thankyouverymuch.'

I only realise what they're talking about because I notice Jenna taking a photo of it on her phone. A wreath made of dead twigs.

'Now, wait for it,' Nathan says, reaching in behind the wreath. A small click. The wreath lights up with a string of seven tiny fairy lights. '*How cute?*'

'Very good, ha-ha,' Jordanne laughs. Her effort, or lack thereof: a T-shirt with 'Santa baby' written across her neat baby bump, only just visible under a heavy puffer jacket.

Tadhg whispers to me. 'I don't get it.' He nods at the wreath.

I lean closer. 'I think it's supposed to be a metaphor or something.'

'Right. Yeah. No. Over my head. Think I need a drink.'

'You and me both,' I lie. Three has always been my ceiling, but tonight, I plan to smash through like it's a thin pane of glass.

I expected an eeriness of Avalon, so let me tell you – this lack of haunted vibes takes me by surprise. If you ignore the empty plant pots and the layer of dust over everything (and the *slight* scent of mildew . . . the cobwebs . . .) you'd probably be forgiven for describing the house as 'homey'.

Peter pours drinks into paper cups. Nathan fills old china bowls with popcorn and Galaxy Minstrels. I unlink Tadhg and roam – in my regrettable heels – through Avalon's downstairs rooms. 'White Christmas' sings out as my eyes scan panelled walls and high ceilings; mahogany parquet floorboards in some rooms and rich, burgundy carpet in others; family photos on almost every wall and surface.

As I walk, I feel her oddly familiar eyes on me. June. She watches from every direction: wide eyes surrounded by smile lines. I expect to shudder or tense up, but instead my entire body loosens out. A framed picture of June with a young Peter draws me to a side table in the hallway. I pick it up, wipe away the dust, hold it inches from my face so I can examine June's hand placed softly – protectively – across Peter's chest, him stood in front of her and dressed in a navy school uniform. She is pride personified with this adorable little boy who looks nothing like her, save for the thick, dark hair. They're stood by a long, wooden table, where it looks like June has been drying herbs and flowers—

A voice from feet behind startles me. I drop the picture before I realise it's just Jenna. The glass of the frame breaks as it collides with the marble floor of the hall. 'Fuck!' I feel my heart in my throat as I turn to my sister. 'Look what you made me do!'

'Sorry, the lads are – ordering food—'

'What are you doing creeping up on me like that?'

'I didn't *creep*—'

'David's going to know we were here. Jenna, this is – oh – fuck me!'

'He hasn't been here in *years*. Calm down.'

I feel her stare at me as I get down on my bare knees to gather up shards of glass. You know how a dog will watch you as you eat? Waiting for you to drop something? Begging for scraps? It's a bit like that.

She's just staring, silent.

It actually takes me a minute to put two and two together. Jenna hasn't had access to anything sharper than a spoon at home since soon after the Intervention . . .

'I'll go – get – a dustpan,' she says, lifeless, leaving me with the mess.

I let out a massive moan and pile the broken glass onto the side table before I snatch at the photo that's come apart from the rest. I notice there's writing on the back. Blue biro. I squint, expecting to read 'Peter's first day at school' alongside the year the photo was taken and a brief description of who's in it and where they are, but it's not that. It's a message.

I always knew the day would come when I'd have to let him break free of this big, old house. It did – time for me to encourage him to make friends and mistakes and memories of his own, but all I wanted was to turn the key, to lock him up with me forever.

This was the day I learned that letting go was to love him wholly.

Your turn . . .

Nollaig Shona x

Letting go.

There it is again.

'It's the same handwriting.' I feel Jenna leaning down beside me, an inch or so out of view. 'Nollaig Shona. That means happy Christmas in Irish, doesn't it? Like it was written today . . . for . . . you.'

I turn to look over my shoulder. Her eyes are two orbs. She reaches into her jacket pocket.

'I found one, too.'

Seven bums are planted on Avalon's vintage leather sofas. 'Walking in the Air' plays in the background, my pizza sits untouched, while Jenna and I both try to communicate wordlessly from across a coffee table after years without practice. I subtly shake my head to signal *we should stop or we'll draw attention.*

I really don't fancy having to say 'My sister thinks June Dolan is sending us messages from the grave' out loud. Especially not right now! It's hard to have faith in coincidence, but not as hard as it is to believe that a dead woman might be communicating with us both separately through biro scribbles.

Talk turns to films. Not even Christmas films – weird films I can't stand, like *Donnie Darko*. I can't pay attention. My head is inebriated mush. All I gather is that apparently no matter which interpretation of the film you choose to believe, Donnie is likely dead in all of them.

Lovely.

More death.

Never in my life has talk of death been so impossible to avoid.

Fidgeting. Slurping. Laughter. A big bunch of misfits attempting to fit the conversation.

Peter's legs are spread wide, separating Izzy and Nathan. He's started banging on about *Vanilla Sky*. 'Then as the movie goes on, you find out that the perfect life Tom Cruise is living is actually a fictional one created by his *own mind* after he signed up for Life Extension . . .'

Nathan cuts in, excited, legs crossed. 'YES!' He licks pizza sauce from his fingers. 'Life Extension is this program that prolongs people's lives, and lets them experience lucid dreams about – whatever they want – sooo, Tom's basically *dead*, living inside his own imagination . . . I'm telling you, my people, it's coming. That sophisticated tech is *coming* before we hit, *mmm*, fifty.'

'Nah,' Peter says dismissively.

'You will choke on that *nah*. When we were born, *these* didn't exist!' Nathan holds up his iPhone. 'Now, you have thousands of fans right there in your pocket.'

Peter raises both his eyebrows. 'And hundreds more who hate me, with 24/7 access to me.' He swigs from a cup of beer.

Izzy's eyes dart around. I see the whites all around them.

Jordanne clears her throat.

Tadhg coughs. 'Wouldn't be my cup o' tea now, that *Vanilla Sky*. I prefer more realistic films.'

'Oh no, it's *so good*,' Jordanne insists, touching Tadhg's knee. 'Penelope Cruz *and* Cameron Diaz,' she says, winking at him. She's admiring his arms. I shift in my seat. I really shouldn't mind but by *God*, do I mind. He's so gorgeous. And she has a boyfriend!

'Oh. Right. Yeah, maybe I'd enjoy it so,' he says with a hint of a smile.

Everyone laughs. I force something that I hope passes for one.

Izzy settles right back into the sofa. With a wry smile and a glass of gin and slimline tonic, she says, 'If I had Life Extension, I'd be as skinny and pretty as Cameron Diaz in my lucid dream. I'd be married to Timothée Chalamet. Food would have no calories and I'd eat everything without putting on a single pound.'

I can't help it – I look at Jenna again. Her eyes are still

on me and I can tell she's as blindsided as I am: her lips have scrunched up into a line. So have mine.

'Isn't that why you're here, my love,' Nathan says kindly, reaching across behind Peter to flick a strand of Izzy's hair.

Her smile is almost bigger than her whole face. 'So, Nate. Give us your "lucid dream",' she orders, 'go on!'

Nathan pout-smiles. Adjusts his posture, sits up so straight he's like an ornament hanging from a Christmas tree. Raises an eyebrow, thinking on it. 'If I could live a perfect life, I'd have a boyfriend. Taller than me. Broad. A babe through and through.'

'Ah, come on. That's crap! You could have that now,' Izzy says, reaching behind Peter to smack at Nathan.

'No, "spider queen", I could not.' A shiver runs through me. David's voice fills my mind, 'save the spider queen'. I want to ask why Nathan called her that, but I don't. 'I can't trust anyone. Anyone.' He clicks his fingers in Peter's face. Peter doesn't look insulted, though – he laughs the casual, understanding laugh of a good friend who fully knows the cavern-wide depth of your baggage. 'In my perfect world,' he goes on, 'I trust a nice boy enough to let him wine and dine me, to introduce him to my folks, to accept a ring on it, to take his last name. In *this* world, they always do me wrong as soon as I let my guard down.' Nathan wipes a finger across an eyebrow and tilts his chin back, glancing around. We regard one another with a small smile. He doesn't know that I understand where he's coming from deeply, but I do.

'All because some asshole put you on PornHub?' Izzy asks

it innocently, but the atmosphere in the room shifts in that one split second. I can tell by her expression that she didn't think the words through before saying them – that the gin loosened her tongue a little too much.

Nathan's jaw tightens like a vice. His eyes are daggers. 'How – *how* did you find out about that?' His persona fractures before us. The voice speaking the words comes from a deep, fearful part of him that's perhaps still a child. The look he throws Peter demands an explanation.

Izzy's mouth simply hangs open. Her huge eyes glass over with water.

Peter says, 'Don't look at me like that, man. I didn't say a word. To anyone.'

Nathan takes a long, slow, deep breath. He sweetly sits back into the couch. Turns face to face with Izzy. '*Out with it.*'

'I, I—'

'Did you see the video?'

'No!'

'Then *how*—?'

'I read about it.'

'Where?'

'In. A forum.'

'*What* forum?'

'Sorry, this is way embarrassing . . .'

'Lucky for you, we've all got shit to be embarrassed about.' His pulse is visible across his temple.

Awkward breaths and shuffles from the others.

'In a Reddit forum about – Peter,' Izzy admits hesitantly.

Peter exhales loudly through his nose, doesn't look at her. 'Listén I just sort of fell down a rabbit hole, I – I swear, Peter, I was only looking after we started the group. Morbid curiosity, I suppose. I—'

'Don't.' Peter waves a hand in her direction, without looking at her. 'What people say about us is none of our business.' He necks the rest of his drink. His Adam's apple bounces to the glug sound.

'What people say about *me* is MY business and I demand to hear it,' Nathan asserts.

Izzy stutters, 'I, they—'

Peter half-slams his cup down on the coffee table and sits back so he's separating the pair of them. 'Look. We were never supposed to know so many other people existed in the world let alone every damn thing that goes through their heads. Every opinion they have of everyone and everything. The internet should be blown up. *Fuck* people who post revenge porn, *fuck* anyone who draws other people's attention to it,' he says passionately, angrily jabbing his index finger at the space in front of him. '*Fuck*—'

'That's all lovely coming from you and all that money you make from this internet we should blow up, my man, thank you for the privileged take, but I want to know what's being said about literally the worst thing that's ever happened to me.' Nathan's face is haunted by whatever memory is playing out in his head. 'Some people don't like you. That's shit, I get it. But *my ex* got me drunk and – filmed us – without my knowledge – and posted it online, to get back at me for dumping his ass – and now, I have zero control over who sees me in my most private of moments because once something goes online, there's no delete button. People re-upload, they screenshot. I mean . . .' He takes a deep breath. '*You* at least get to decide what *you* put online. That right was taken away from me. So, shut up and let the girl talk, yeah?'

It wasn't just a couple of dick pics, then. I imagine strangers having access to a version of me – one with no awareness of a hidden camera pointed directly at me – naked, hammered, incapable of true consent. The thought alone makes me feel nauseous.

Peter hangs his head. Nods. 'You're right. Sorry, man.'

Silence apart from 'Last Christmas' by Wham!

'Go on, then.' Nathan taps his foot on the floor.

Izzy fidgets with her pinstriped Jack Skellington collar. 'People – they were just being super mean, OK? Calling you pete's "BBB" and, well . . .'

'Sorry, I never get time to go online any more. What does that mean? Sorry, *sorry* . . . I'm such a granny!' says Jordanne.

'Oh, it's not, like, short for anything,' Izzy stammers. 'They were just, like, calling Nate Peter's – um, they give people nicknames—'

'Spit it out. What does it stand for?'

'Big black boyfriend.' Izzy's tiny chin barely moves as she forces out the words, unsure if she's allowed to speak them at all. 'I know. They're racist *losers*. It's – anyway, they found – pictures of you guys together on Facebook and, and someone brought up the – the video – that your ex—'

Nathan presses his hand firmly over his mouth. He notices

that Peter is still looking at the floor, so he reaches out and squeezes his leg as he pulls his favourite mask back on. 'Your fans know about—'

'They're *not* my fans.'

Nathan forces a laugh through his distress. 'Your hate followers are your biggest fans. They probably know more about you than *I* do.'

Peter groans into his hands. 'Enough.' He looks up and around. 'We're supposed to be partying but we're sitting here doing what *out there* is for.' He points towards the back garden. I look out the big south-facing window, at shades of navy and pearl. A portrait of June in my line of vision almost waves at me to capture my attention and I'm hit again by what just happened in the other room. My eyes are dragged back to Jenna: two orbs still glued to me.

'I see. You want Doctor D standing over me with his notepad and pencil while I process this. You want me to – pretend like I'm *not* reliving one of the worst experiences of my life all night long! That's some bullshit.' Nathan stands up with a melodramatic flourish.

'You started pretending all on your own. You should really see yourself, man—'

That's when the front door opens. Each one of us hears it. One by one, we turn towards the hallway.

JENNA

David explodes into the house, shiny eyes and muck-caked boots. His amplified voice – effing and blinding – carries through the air, cuts through the Christmas playlist, yanks Peter off the couch.

'The gardaí are on the way, you pile of *fuckers*, how dare you, just wait, fucking WAIT!' we hear David roar from the dining room over the other side of the hall – the first door when you step inside the house. The next door along the hallway leads to us.

I glance around: Rosie's pupils are massive. Izzy looks like she's choking. Nathan mouths, *No, no! How? Fuck!* Tadhg pinches the bit of skin between his eyebrows. Jordanne pants like she's practising for birth. And Peter – he's walking slowly towards the door. He pulls off his Santa hat, plays with it nervously. David appears in the doorway within seconds, chest heaving and holding a shovel.

Peter holds his hands out like his dad is a blood-hungry Rottweiler.

'Dad! Chill. It's *us*. Just us!'

Poor David is so confused to see us. He looks like he's just fought his way through the seventh circle of hell only to land himself at the world's most innocent fancy-dress party: strands of his white hair are stuck to the sweat of his face, his cheeks are as purple as the dirty old fleece he's wearing, and the surprise in his eyes is unmistakable. Wheezing, he opens and closes his mouth a few times, lowers the shovel, wipes the sweat from his forehead.

Spotify switches to 'Stop the Cavalry' by Jona Lewie. The stark contrast between the mood in the room and the trumpets is jarring. I want to vanish into the folds of the couch.

'Frank,' David says, disorientated, 'from – over the road, he – he called me. Told me about – the – lights, outside . . .'

Nathan sits back down ever-so-slowly, whispering, *I told Peter those lights were a stupid fucking idea* at us through fanned-out fingers.

Peter grapples with words. 'Dad, we just – I thought it would be kind of cool for us to get to know each other more, so we'd be a little – I don't know – *looser*, while – and you don't come here, so—'

David drops the shovel on the floor; the sound near deafens me. He looks around, takes in every square inch of the sitting room through eyes you'd swear were blind till a moment ago. They flit from photo to photo of June – from the wall to the mantelpiece – all the while swimming with her ghost.

'I asked Frank how – how he had my number. He said she – *she* gave it to him before our last trip together, Glendalough, you remember –' David says, presumably to Peter, through breaths coming in gasps. '"Keep an eye on the house." That's what she said to Frank. My number, he – Frank had it saved in his phone, after all these years. Imagine that—'

Rosie's eyes beg me to help her escape. Escape then offers itself on a platter when Jordanne – clutching her bump – stammers something about not feeling well, needing fresh air. The pair of them link arms and edge their way past the Dolans, past Peter's attempts to defuse the situation. Izzy and Nathan have positioned themselves as far apart as they possibly can on the couch and both have their arms folded. Tadhg just twiddles his thumbs.

'You thought people broke in? Or—?'

'Of course I did! And it's obviously what your mother *wanted* me to think. So I'd – oh, God help me – I'm – I'm here. I'm. *I'm home.*' His voice breaks. He's trying to be calm as he looks around at the embers of June's life, like he's methodically counting pieces of furniture and objects to see what'll fit inside a hypothetical moving van. His control over himself is tenuous: tears build in spite of his efforts.

'Jeez. Dad, *hey* . . .' Peter reaches for David, who shields himself.

'Should I stop the music, or . . .?' Nathan asks Tadhg.

Izzy pipes up. 'I don't think we should be here.'

'You absolutely *should* be here. You, especially,' David

says. Izzy looks disturbed. He moves towards us, clutching at his chest. 'My wife – there – there is reason to my appearance here tonight, this – this is all happening exactly as it had to happen! I needed to – but I, I couldn't – alone—' His mask of age slips. He cries, like a child longing for his mother's embrace. Snot pours from his nose. He wipes it away with a sleeve. 'I can't believe I'm home.'

Peter guides his dad to the couch, tries to steady him, but David curls up somewhat and sobs with the force of someone vomiting violently into a toilet bowl. Peter then looks at me. It's the first time he's really acknowledged me tonight. Fake-bearded but genuine concern: he doesn't know what to do. It's clear. There's a need in his eyes and it fills me with purpose – lifts me out of the pot I've been stewing in since yesterday. I devour every inch of his face and I ready myself to do whatever he asks of me. 'We need to – do you guys mind if we—?'

'On it,' I say. I wink at him reassuringly before ushering the rest of them out of the room. Nathan tiptoes, Tadhg walks with head hanging and Izzy seems to glide as her wedge shoes take tiny, quick steps.

'Ah, *don't leave*,' David begs, arms wide open. 'June wants us to be here – togeth—' He can hardly speak.

The lights flicker. Izzy gasps. We keep moving.

'Dad.' Peter's voice booms, nervous and impatient. I pull the door behind us, leaving it ever-so-slightly ajar. 'Mom's dead. She's dead.' His words – tinged with emotional exhaustion – come out like a great revelation. 'She didn't orchestrate this because she's *dead*.'

I whisper at warp speed. 'Go to the kitchen or something.
I'll stay, just in case they need me.'

'No offence, babe, but why would they?' Nathan replies,
drowning out David's talk of how death is only the beginning,
of how Peter couldn't possibly understand. I observe Nathan.
He seems deeply shaken, but I suspect that it's nothing to
do with David showing up and everything to do with Izzy
bringing up that the video of him has been circulating
amongst Peter's hate followers. You can see it in his eyes
– the person behind them is commanding his voice and his
body language to put on a front. He examines his manicure.
'Maybe we should bail.'

I don't want to leave. My eyes plead with all three of them.
'This is a big deal for David: it's his first time back in the
house . . .'

Tadhg shrugs.

Izzy crosses her hands. 'He's not well, Jenna. Like, *really*
not well. He's paranoid, like, thinks that June is, like, *living
impaired* or something . . . He literally can't accept that she's
dead.' Izzy's face floats in the darkness.

'Maybe he should go do some proper therapy instead of
relying on a bunch of damaged randos,' Nathan adds.

Tadhg is a horse on a dance floor.

It's too much. I zone out.

I think of the message on the back of the photo that Rosie
found not an hour ago and that look on her face – like it
meant something to her, just as the note I found in the
garden meant something to me.

I prepare to peer through the crack in the door, but

suddenly Peter bursts through and almost knocks me to the floor.

'Sorry, *sorry*,' he says, all flustered. Over Peter's shoulder I spot David hovering by a cabinet full of ornaments. He's got a hand across his mouth, like he's witnessing a space launch.

'We were just about to taxi out of here—' Nathan starts.

'We weren't – I wasn't,' I interrupt.

'No, hang about! Dad's leaving,' Peter says in a hushed voice, 'it's still early, and I'm – I just need a minute. Alone.' Peter looks at Nathan like he's desperate not to fall out with him.

Nathan sighs. 'Doctor D will be fine with some tins in him – tell him he's staying.' He then insists that we follow him down the hall, towards more alcohol. Tadhg joins him, while Izzy heads to the bathroom. Rosie must be with Jordanne outside, making sure she's all right.

I face Peter, full of a clear sense of purpose: *be there for him like he's been there for me.* 'Want to be alone together?' I ask, hoping he remembers our first interaction, hoping he finds me endearing.

'Whatever,' he says. I can tell his thoughts are racing by the way his pupils fly around the place. We step out of view of David and stop feet from light's reach, so darkness shrouds us. 'This blows, Jenna. I just wanted one fun night for everyone. Just wanted to *help*.'

'It can still be fun,' I lie.

'Nah, man.' He never calls Rosie 'man'.

'Well,' I go on, 'just so you know – I relate. To watching

a parent kind of . . . lose it. Our mam forgets stuff *all the time*, I really do get it, and—'

He quietly interrupts. 'You know that feeling? When everything is, like, boiling inside you, and the only way you can, like, cool it all down and stop it bubbling over is to . . . *you know*?'

I instinctively cover up my scars by crossing my arms and nod. Then I realise he probably can't see me. 'Yeah,' I say.

'I feel like that right now.'

'Oh.' Oh? Is that all I've got? Oh?

'I'm not going to do it. But, man, I feel that.'

Iron-clad validation. 'Let's – let's walk,' I start, 'out the back or something. I'm here, OK?'

I reach for Peter's hand in the dark and intertwine my fingers with his. He doesn't pull away. It feels good like nothing else does – not a hot bath, not the kiss of the sun, not the scent of fresh buttery pastry. Peter Dolan, holding my hand.

I lead Peter to my spot around the back of the glasshouse. There's no light pollution this far out of the city; stars gleam above like a million tiny spectral eyes. For a while, we sit together in milky moonlight and listen to the wind in the trees, to dogs barking in the distance. He talks through all of it – David's delusions about June, the hate he's getting online, Izzy admitting to looking through a gossip forum about him.

'I kind of hoped the unlovable feelings would go away one day,' he says, mid-gut-spill about being 'given up' by his birth mother. 'They poured so much love and attention into me, though. Mom baking these elaborate *Simpsons* birthday cakes, reading me stories every night before bed . . . Dad playing with me for *hours* after working at the clinic, like, all day . . . They were awesome. I could never really accept it, though. There's this . . . unworthiness, I guess. Like – how could two awesome people give up so much to look after me, when the woman who carried me and gave birth to me didn't even want me?'

'Peter—'

'She totally did the right thing. She did. I probably would've had the worst life living under someone who didn't want me. But. Feelings aren't logical, are they?'

No, they are not.

'Probably why the internet stuff attracted me . . . easy approval, on tap. But, but it's all so fucking hollow and empty. Like me.' A sarcastic laugh. 'No wonder she doesn't love me back.'

I wait. Bated breath. Eventually, I ask him: 'Who?'

'Ah,' he says. 'It – it doesn't matter. You don't know her. Turns out, neither do I. "Proximity doesn't always breed intimacy": one of Dad's less mental observations.' Peter picks at the grass between us. 'Sometimes I think, is she a stranger? In the same way my regular taxi guy, Dom, is? I'm often next to Dom. I know his face, his coffee order, the kinds of politically incorrect jokes he makes. We chat about everything, from the weather to prostate exams, but we don't *know* each other.'

This is music to my ears. 'So, this Dom could be a serial killer is what you're saying.'

Peter gives me a dopey smile and I feel accomplished. I want to stay out here with him. I want to beg him to stop trying to climb over Rosie's ramparts so I can relax some more into my unhealthy obsession.

I want a lot of things that I can't have.

He soon stands up and brushes off the arse of his Santa costume. 'Let's go back. Those kegs aren't going to drink themselves.' Peter extends his hand to me.

A shuffling from above.

I could swear it's that bastarding robin again. I try to ignore the burning intuition that comes on me, blossoming in record time: *something bad is going to happen.* I battle the feeling back down to the root, but it keeps fighting to bloom and it lingers – all through the night and the drunken morning taxi trip back to town.

Bertie's strangled cries wake me from the world's worst hangover. I immediately notice the blinds are still drawn. There's a lack of fresh coffee in the air, of any stir whatsoever. It's unlike Rosie to stay in bed past 2 p.m. on a Monday, but she's definitely not been out of her room yet. All I can hear over the noise of my brain is the hum of the fridge.

I combine cooked chicken with some chicken stock in Rosie's food processor and pulse to liquify. The smell of it revolts my poisoned senses, but it's all I can get Bertie to eat. Raggedy and famished, he waits by my feet. I sit with him beside the oven and pat little bits of chicken gunk onto his front paws, allowing time for him to slowly lick off each application with his barely functioning and permanently out tongue. Watching him struggle to get a meal into him is heartbreaking; a young Bertie would wake me up with his entire front paw shoved down the back of my throat, he'd be that excited for his breakfast – but now, he's powering down before my eyes. Slow movements and all scrunched up as though to protect himself from life. I place a hand gently by his side – even the gentlest pets seem to cause him pain. I wonder what's going on under the surface, how long it'll take for whatever diseases have him so ravaged to win out . . .

The pain of swallowing makes Bertie purr.

He's the only reason I'm still here, hanging on.

The ticking of our clock has just sped up.

Bertie gives up on my mixture and crawls into the table's shadow. My stomach lurches. I look around for something to distract me from fresh thoughts of self-harm.

Rosie's high heels. They're still on the floor in the middle of the hall. Immediate flashbacks of last night. I open up the Bird-Shit Palace Brigade group chat to see if anyone has posted yet. There's a photo of Nathan – wearing nothing but his boxers and an elf hat – posing in front of the glasshouse, head in a cloud of fog breath, and the caption:

Literally zero recollection of this. Wim Hof who!?

Izzy shared a blurry video of Peter singing 'Thank God It's Christmas' like he's Freddie Mercury – costume off, a marker moustache scribbled onto his top lip – visibly hammered.

I keep scrolling. Tadhg posted a shirtless selfie from bed about twenty minutes ago, along with:

Mad one, lads. Needed that.

Rosie liked Tadhg's post: her name is there in bold right under the photo.

Then she calls my name from her bedroom, her voice raspy. 'Stick on the kettle, Jenna, will you?'

'Oh God. My medicine . . .'

I place a mug full of tea – Mam always called it 'medicine' when we were growing up, even fed it to us as babies – on Rosie's bedside locker, between her glass aeroplane ornament that probably cost a few hundred quid and something I recognise immediately: a rose quartz bracelet, identical to the one in the inner pocket of my backpack, wrapped up with all my cheap chains and loop earrings. There's evidently still some sentimentality stuck to my edges – like gum under school chairs – because I was never able to get rid of it. I wonder why she has it out on display like this. It was in her jewellery box that time I had a cheeky rummage . . .

Rosie's face juts out of a mountain of pillows and duvet. I climb onto the bottom of her bed and tuck my legs into Rosie's baggy 2014 graduation T-shirt. This must be the first time I've been in her bedroom – with her in bed – since I moved in. There's this strange caress of familiarity, like we're teenagers again.

During our years room-sharing we were often some shade of maroon in the face from screaming at one another, or crying. She hogged blankets. I'd wake her with night terrors. We never agreed on which CD to play because her taste consisted of maddening dance-pop like Steps and S Club 7. Neither of us could try on clothes or call a boyfriend or *think* in peace. After I set her favourite strappy disco dress on fire in the back garden (because *she* wallpapered over *my* Smashing Pumpkins wall mural) Mam started telling the other mothers along the road about the civil war causing our whole house to throb, who told their daughters, who spread it all around school, and so everyone knew we couldn't stand one another.

The hard parts aside, that little bedroom with Rosie served as a shelter, too, from the big, scary world, and even now I feel instantly safer having stepped just inches through her very ordinary doorframe.

I notice a new plant on a little table in the corner of her room. It wasn't there before. 'Is that . . . real?'

She looks confused.

'Over there,' I say, flicking my eyes to it.

'Oh. Yeah. It's a peace lily.'

'You bought an actual plant?'

'Part of our homework was to look after a plant. Remember? We got a handout. Like, a month ago – I did remind you.'

I don't want to admit that I never read David's handouts,

or that a lot of what she says to me goes in one ear and out the other.

'Such a dramatic plant, though, I swear! When I forget to water it, it literally *droops* like it's in a bad mood, then if I give it the tiniest sup from my water bottle, it goes all perky again. She looks a bit thirsty, actually . . . She'd probably die if I poured in some of that.' Rosie eyes the tea I made for her. 'Anyway. Where's the cat?'

'Can't pick him up.'

'Why?'

'He's in agony.' I chew my lip. 'I'll take him to the vet when I get my dole.' I look at the peace lily again. 'Rosie, last night – that, that *photo*—'

Rosie rubs at her eyes and interrupts. 'Did I take my make-up off?'

There's mascara all over her face. 'You look like you've been sucker-punched by Rocky.'

Her phone vibrates. Panda-eyed, smirking, she types furiously. I know it's not Peter – they acted like perfect strangers last night. It must be Mam making her beam. My heart sinks in the brine-sour water of sorrow, or jealousy – or whatever fucking awful emotion I've bagged in today's lucky dip.

She throws her phone at the bed. 'Sorry, the photo. Yeah.' She sits up and reaches for the tea, like it's the elixir of life. 'I *was* listening. Sorry. Go on.' Rosie sips. Waits.

'Well. I thought . . . you should look at the note I found again. Maybe you couldn't see how similar the writing is

last night because you were plastered. Literally the same
swirls on the letter Ts! It *has* to be—'

'A thousand per cent not the same handwriting,' Rosie
confidently cuts me off.

'You can't have *more* than a hundred per cent of something.'

Her stupid stare.

'Per cent is literally Latin for parts per *hundred.'*

She rolls her eyes. 'Whatever. There's nothing to talk
about, Jenna. Whoever wrote on the bit of paper you found
in the garden—'

'June wrote on the back of the photo. And it's June's
garden.'

'How do you know she did?'

'Peter told me last night. Well, I asked, and he answered . . .'

Before Bertie went deaf, his ears would swivel when he'd
hear a loud noise. That's what Rosie reminds me of as she
sits forward in the bed.

'June gave David the framed picture as a Christmas
present the year Peter graduated secondary school and
moved away to study music in New York. Apparently, David
was sad about Peter moving away, she wanted to cheer him
up – it was a photo of his first day at school.'

Rosie looks relieved. 'Well then. See? It was written years
ago. *And* that explains the "Nollaig Shona"—'

'But, you were looking at it like it was addressed to *you.'*

She scoffs. 'No, I wasn't.'

She was!

'What makes you think a note saying "It's only up from here" was addressed to *you*, anyway? Probably just kid neighbours playing a game, leaving one another clues, directions . . . it's the name of a song, too! Honestly, Jenna—'

I don't even contemplate telling her the truth. She goes on and on and I avoid eye contact.

'This is the most we've talked in ages, you know that?' Rosie laughs eventually, gulps her tea and reaches again for her phone, on automatic.

I block her hand. 'Don't. Please? Seriously, Rosie, something funny is going on.'

'Ha!' She fights past my twig arm for her phone. 'Should've just taken you out to Moggie's hedges.'

'Wha'?'

'If I'd known a little whiff of supernaturalism was all we needed to get you *initiating conversation* . . .' Mam always told us stories about 'Mad Moggie', the local ghost that apparently flits along the creepy tunnel of beech trees near where our late granny Christine lived, every Halloween. Rosie impersonates Mam. 'It's Moggie! The spirit of the abandoned graveyard beneath the fields . . . *She's gonna get ye!*'

A smile tries to step between my words. 'Rosie, stop. Really. Come on . . . the dog? The magic flowers? These notes? It's all . . . I don't know. Things aren't as they seem in that garden.'

Rosie takes a deep breath.

'I can't see radio waves, but I know they exist. There's – there's *something*.'

She throws a sideways look at her bedside locker.

'What?' I ask, wondering what she's looking at. I follow her eyeline to the crystal bracelet.

'Nothing.'

She knows something that I don't. 'Don't keep stuff from me.'

Rosie slowly and intentionally looks over the skin of my arms and legs.

This is different. I hope my face tells her that, so I don't have to.

Her phone vibrates. A second later, mine does, too; I hear it against the counter in the kitchen, where I left it. Both devices vibrate again. We look intently at one another.

Cat-like, Rosie checks her notifications. 'Oh – oh, God.' She bites the insides of her cheek through the words.

'Let me guess. Another thirst trap from Tadhg.'

She scrunches up her eyebrows. 'Excuse me?'

'In the group chat. Jesus. *I'm joking.* What is it?'

'It's – the chat – shit is kicking off. C'mere . . .'

Hesitant, I climb across the bed to sit beside her, acutely aware of how comfortable her bedding is compared to the couch. She holds her phone out in front of us then scrolls through a long all-caps-speckled back-and-forth between Peter and Izzy.

'Hang on – slower – I can't read that fast!'

'They're killing each other!'

'What happened?'

'I don't – I haven't – I can't—'

'Go to the start of the conversation. It isn't that hard.'

'For fuck's sake, here then, you do it!' Rosie shoves the phone into my hand. 'Quick!'

I scroll back through their comments to one another
– all posted under the video Izzy shared of Peter singing.
Him demanding that she delete the screenshot image
from the same video that she posted to her Instagram
stories, her saying she had no idea it would or could be
taken out of context . . . The exchange just seems to go
on and on and on. Peter's first reply to the post is a
screenshot of a tweet he was sent this morning, liked
forty-eight times. We both gasp before reading what it
actually says, because the accompanying picture -- the
one on Izzy's Instagram story – is of Peter looking like
he's impersonating—

'Hitler. Hitler! WHY is he pretending to be Hitler?' Rosie
asks furiously. Flecks of spit fly from her mouth and splatter
the screen where a high-quality image of Peter stares back
at us – him with an arm raised, the photo cropped at his
wrist. Rosie runs a hand through her hair and says 'fuck'
repeatedly.

I can't help but laugh. 'How drunk *were* you last night?
He was being Freddie Mercury.'

She looks incredulous.

'It's just the *angle*! Sure, it *looks* bad, but—'

'Jenna! Read!'

**just saw @lowercasepete on @spiderqueen111 insta
stories mimicking Hitler, not a good look huh
@3ArenaDublin @Spotify @JohnnyJ do you think this is
funny under any circumstance?**

'Just a troll fishing for likes. He wasn't "mimicking Hitler",
I mean—'

'Peter's tour starts at 3Arena, Jenna, he – he does brand
work with Spotify and well, Johnny Jones—'

'No idea who that is.'

'*He's massive!* Covers news on YouTube, and drama, and
– look, if Johnny covers this story, Peter is, like, finished.'

I snort. 'No, he's not.'

'Look! *Look!*'

#lowercasepeteisoverparty is trending worldwide on
Twitter. I swallow. 'Oh. Oh, right.' I check the hashtag –
Peter's public evisceration.

**No words for that horrific picture of lowercase pete. I am
beyond disgusted. #lowercasepeteisoverparty**

**HOW is anyone surprised that pete is a neo Nazi? The man
is friends with derpiedew and we all know HE loves to
amplify anti-Semitic rhetoric!!! #lowercasepeteisoverparty**

**All I want for Christmas is to see lowercase pete's
face when he checks his phone this morning
#lowercasepeteisoverparty**

I'm a grimace behind fingers.

Let's be real, I was never going to get to design his album
art. It was a fun distraction while it lasted, but of course his
career is going up in flames: everything I come into contact
with does eventually.

ROSIE

I messaged Tadhg about last night. I had to! And according to his recollection of what happened between us, my brain isn't making up the slivers of memory that keep flashing in my brain: abs like alabaster and deep grunts in the blue of night, me chucking a condom – somewhere – after trying to put it on him and failing and settling for everything but penetration. His firm grip of my hip flesh. My performative moans . . .

I desperately want to keep texting him. I want to ask him how he feels. Guilty? Regretful? I want to know exactly where we hooked up and if we made a mess and if he could *please* keep the friendly frolic to himself, but more than any of that, I want to know if Peter is all right.

I need to know.

I sent Jenna to the café around the corner to pick us up some sausage rolls – played up my headache so she'd feel bad for me. Wearing creased, mismatching pyjamas and with

my teeth unbrushed, I wait on the balcony for Peter to open
the door.

Public punishment used to be all the rage. I mean, I'm
pretty sure it was part of the judicial process in certain
countries and that people would pelt miscreants with mouldy
cabbages. One day after having sex, Peter and I had a brief
chat about *Game of Thrones*. Something he said pounds my
memory now. 'Queen Cersei's walk of atonement goes down
pretty much every day on Twitter . . . the only way to survive
the war is to be totally bland and unnoticeable, to *never*
speak your mind.' I remember wanting to ask him what he
meant by 'the war' and, instead, kissing him – tasting his
vulnerability and swallowing it down so it couldn't shine a
light on my total reluctance to talk about, well, *anything*,
anything that might lead to us growing closer.

Peter doesn't greet me. He just unlatches the door and
immediately turns to walk back into the apartment, glued
to his phone. Everything in me fights the urge to look in
Moss's direction; I hear him at my feet, panting in his dog
bed. Ever since his limp vanished, ever since I realised that
David thinks there's more going on in the garden than meets
the eye, the dog has given me the heebie-jeebies. I can't
turn them off!

'Where's your dad?'

'Out.'

'Has he seen—?'

'Only a matter of time . . . it's everywhere, Rosie. They're
– they're ripping me apart. I've turned off notifications, but
I can't look away. It's bad. It – feels like – people are, like

– in my face – screaming at me – I know you think this is *dumb*, I know I shouldn't care this much, but, but—'

He's on the verge of hyperventilating. We move about the apartment – two people trailed by tens of thousands of shadows dotted with pitchforks. It dawns on me that I don't really know how to comfort Peter. He listens to voice messages from Nathan, who says all the right things – how awful it all is, how merciless people can be, how ridiculous some of the messages he's getting are – and shoots off blunt replies laced with stress.

Eventually we settle into a corner of the sitting room. I plant myself on the couch and look up at Peter. 'It'll die down.' I'm trying to be reassuring, but I don't even believe my own words, so I don't expect him to.

'This is a proper scorched-earth campaign to, like . . . *destroy* me. They're sending death threats already. Don't mention how bad it is to my dad,' he warns. 'He doesn't use social media. To be honest, I'm more worried about how *he'll* react to all this . . .'

Peter shows me his phone screen. I don't look. I grasp at things to say . . . I can't handle seeing him so upset or the thought of how worried David might be if he happens to see or hear anything. 'Maybe – maybe it'll be like that thing with Prince William.'

'What?'

'The picture of him sticking up his middle finger at reporters, remember that?'

Peter shakes his head.

'He'd just had a new baby or – or something, anyway, he

was actually holding up *three* fingers. One for each of his children!'

'Rosie—'

'And in all pictures taken right in front of him you could clearly see the actual gesture he was making with his hand, but *one* photographer standing beside Will snapped him and – and it looked like he was only holding up *one* finger, and—'

'Stop. Please.'

He looks like he's experiencing real, physical pain. I sit up straight. 'Look. This is fine! All you have to do is share the full video of you singing and all of this will—'

'You don't think I'd have done that already if I could? Jordanne and Tadhg are visible in the background, and group confidentiality is – I mean, that's why Izzy didn't share the video on Instagram. But I just – I can't *believe* she posted that screenshot without a *fucking thought*! And she's not come online again since, to clear it up, she's just—'

'But if *you* just explain—'

'Nobody will believe me.' His voice breaks. And for the first time, I understand what Peter meant by 'problems are relative'. This isn't a problem I can relate to in any way, shape or form, but I can relate to how Peter is reacting to it. His anguish is palpable. 'Anyway. The internet never forgets . . . every time anyone googles my name, it'll be news articles with my face beside the face of literally the worst person in history.'

I can't argue with him. It's widely accepted as normal now that people's lives end up ruined over resurfaced ten-year-old

tasteless jokes, quotes open to misinterpretation and, sometimes, over complete misunderstandings – things that you
didn't even mean, that you didn't even *do*. I just never think
much on it because it's always happening to strangers, so
it's just not something I concern myself with. I see or hear
about the pile-ons and I think *ooh, scandalous* and I move
on with my days, caring for my mother and working and
swiping my way through Tinder.

Peter paces before me, grasps at his plain white T-shirt,
clicks his jaw, nervously checks his screen. In the dim,
greyish light of morning, it hits me: he's not a stranger to
me. That's why my face is stinging on his behalf. His reputation matters to me because all of his dreams and plans
are built upon it.

'Before Dad left the party, when he was all, I mean . . .
you saw, right? He pulled me aside in the hallway, told me
that *I'd* be his legacy. Me!' Peter's eyes glass over. 'That he
was proud of me for trying to bring the group closer together,
for following my dreams. And now, I'm "the Hitler guy".' He
fake laughs. 'Some legacy.'

Energy gives life to unseeable wires that connect us.
'You don't deserve this. You really don't.' Peter moves
towards me, falls into a heap beside me. Fuck. How do
you be supportive of someone you're sleeping with, who
is in love with you, who you'd like to keep sleeping with
without falling in love, too? Why isn't *that* on the Leaving
Cert curriculum?

Another voice message from Nathan. 'It's just people
wanting to feel virtuous – you know that, right? They think

they're soldiers fighting the good fight against racists and
snobs and chauvinists, and maybe they are, but they don't
care when people get tangled in the crossfire for the wrong
reasons and it's *vile*. Bitches could be rallying together to
take on tech giants or – or politicians with real power, but
no – they're screaming about a bit of fucking marker on
your face without a *clue*.' He huffs into the microphone.
Pauses. 'You say the word and I'll save the day. I'll say what
really happened, I'll—'

Peter forces out the saddest, emptiest fake laugh and
holds the record button. 'Mate, thanks. But I guarantee
you'd end up trending too. I don't want even more people
finding out about what happened to you. Nothing would be
worth that.'

Pin-fine holes puncture my heart: I feel it swell inside my
chest.

Nathan takes a minute to reply. He sends a GIF of two
monkeys hugging and finishes with, 'Put that phone down
for a few hours. And when you pick it up again, block the
pricks. They have the right to use their voices and you have
the right *not to listen*.'

Peter composes a message to his dad, repeatedly hitting
the wrong key, deleting and re-typing. He gives up trying,
locks his phone and sets it aside. He lets his head fall to
the left so that he's looking into my eyes, hair flopped messily
across his forehead, no glasses to protect me from his intensity. I look away.

'State of me,' I say, remembering that last night's mascara
is crusted around my eyes.

'Thanks for coming round. I don't think I – I can't deal with this by myself.'

'You don't have to.' I press my tongue to the roof of my mouth and play with a crinkle in my PJ bottoms. His hand reaches across and his fingers grip my thigh. Peter's skin is much warmer than Tadhg's and his touch gentler. I wish the sting of mouthwash could reach through the back of my throat and into my brain and find the guilt and obliterate it.

'You looked real beautiful last night,' Peter says softly.

'Wasn't exactly going for beautiful.'

'Hot, too.' He says it through half-shut eyes.

I snort. Peter laughs.

'How about now?' I pull a silly face.

His wistful smile massages out the knot in my stomach. 'Smoking. Always.'

Somehow, with Tadhg still all over me, I figure now is a perfect time to kiss Peter, so I go for it. Our tongues slow dance. I find my fingers where his hair meets his neck and I stroke him. My breathing quickly grows rapid and I feel a tug to climb into his lap. I do, and I hold his hands above his head. He doesn't fight me. While we kiss, I gyrate strategically, right where his hips meet my thighs, but soon, all strategy leaves me behind – everything blends into the glossiest red. It always does when we give in and let our bodies run the show; nothing matters, only the pleasure of touch. This is what he needs, this is how I can *help*—

Peter suddenly turns his cheek in to my lips. Takes my hands and guides them together around his neck. He starts and stops talking, his voice haltering. 'Could you – please just – hold me? Please?'

I lean back and gather myself, allowing no time for my brain to make me say anything that might make Peter feel worse than he already does. I pull him close to my chest. He lies against me and scrunches up his eyes. I wrap an arm around his neck, across his shoulders, and I tangle my fingers in his hair so I can caress his scalp. None of it is as alien to me as I expected it would be; it feels natural, like breathing.

I climb off Peter, sit beside him, direct his head into my lap. Jenna soon texts, wondering where I am – I see it pop up, but I don't reply. Peter talks for over an hour about the abuse being sent his way and about his dad, his fears, his shame, hardly taking a breath. And I face my discomfort. I don't butt in once. I don't push the conversation towards sex. Our foreheads touch, our lips meet for sweet kisses between conversations.

David returns home and his shoulders relax immediately when he sees me there with his son. The radio got to him before we could.

Christmas comes and goes in a haze of booze, shit movies, exhausting shifts at Skelligs serving sloshed '12 pubs of Christmas' bar crawlers, overcooked turkey for two at Mam's and pulling 50 per-cent-off cardboard crackers.

Jenna blamed a sore throat for her refusal to join us.

On Stephen's Day, I brought her home some leftovers – *sans* turkey and ham – which remained in the fridge until the stuffing turned mouldy. At some point prior to New Year's Eve, she tip-tapped on my bedroom door in the small hours.

'I can't sleep on the couch, it's too lumpy, and your bed is massive, and you won't even know I'm here,' she said.

But I did know – I just hadn't known how much I missed sleeping next to somebody, night after night. Feeling some-one's warmth and hearing the soft sound of little exhales on cotton. We rang in 2019 together – two toasty cinnamon buns wrapped up in the blue of midnight. We raised semi-cold cups of tea instead of champagne flutes and bonded over our shared desire for the universe to throw us each an entire skeleton. 'What am I meant to do with one flipping bone?' That teased a smile out of her, at least. To keep the smile on her face, I played old *Father Ted* episodes on my iPad until she fell asleep.

David paused the project and all. There hasn't been an Avalon gathering for three weeks now because Peter, our chauffeur, hasn't been able to face people – not even me.

Even though I can't physically see him, I know he's in darkness; his shame-coated fury radiates through the walls while the memory of our last encounter licks the back of my neck every night as I try to fall asleep . . .

My guard slipped. He knows it did, but even though he's armed with that knowledge, he's not called or read my messages. I've not run into him outside on a single late-night dash to the twenty-four-hour Tesco for cheese and wine. But I always hover for a bit and, one night, even pressed my ear up to his front door. Hoping to hear him play his keyboard or . . . something.

Anything.

My new little secret – between myself and my headphones – is that I listen to Peter's songs while I go about my business, and nobody is any the wiser. Tragic, shameful, *I know*. But – I miss him. This is the safest way to indulge that feeling. At least, I think it's safe. Because if nobody *sees* the flame meet the candle then there really isn't any fire to speak of, is there?

JENNA

The midwinter solstice has come and gone, as has Christmas and New Year. It's a freezing cold mid-January day and, in spite of the damp grey gloom, Peter is back behind the wheel, reluctance in beautiful human form. If I didn't know David to be so understanding, so patient, I'd assume that he forced Peter's hand in messaging the group chat last week, citing some divine law, because Peter looks like he'd rather be *anywhere* but here, though I'm sure that in reality he just forced himself to face the heavy rain. That's just the sort of person he is. He gleams with resilience. When you're a lump of coal, chilling in your coal mine, it's easy to spot a diamond.

For a second Saturday running, Peter pulls up outside Izzy's parents' house. I sent Izzy a voice message to check in last week, but she left it on 'seen'. Now, eight pairs of eyes watch out for her from the green Volkswagen.

Peter beeps. Twice. Nothing.

Nathan is sure he just saw the curtains move, but she doesn't come to the door. Nobody comes out in her place to explain her absence, and so we set off into overcast countryside once again, without her.

Regardless of what happened in December, Peter appears just as worried about Izzy as the rest of us are. I imagine not only because Izzy looked incapable of surviving any more weight loss the last time we saw her, but also because she obviously didn't intend for *any of it* to happen; she didn't elect a global jury to come for Peter around the clock. She shared an innocent Instagram post – probably hoping her followers would be amazed by her famous company – and it was taken and run away with. We all watched as the story grew legs and vanished on the horizon and she obviously couldn't have anticipated any of it.

Still, though.

Poor Peter.

He's completely disconnected right now. Him pulling away has become the elephant that sleeps between myself and Rosie. I reach my cold feet around it to press them into her thick moisturised calves as she snores under its crushing weight. He also hasn't addressed the backlash to Izzy's post. The inquisitions have been both plentiful and intense, though Peter hasn't been replying to any comments.

His manager's orders? 'Lay low.' I mean, imagine people telling you every day how much they hope you are suffering? How is any of this normal? How is a person supposed to live through that?

Maybe he was right. Maybe the internet *should* be blown up.

David tells us that he returned to Avalon alone over the holidays to keep the project on track, and I'm inordinately impressed: before November, he couldn't stomach the thought of driving through those front gates on his own. He proudly shows off his progress as we get ready for another group session, fingers and toes like icicles.

'I fixed that blasted wobbly fence . . . Peter used to throw his basketball at it in protest. "I don't want dinner!" "I want the PlayStation!" Teenage boys – monsters, of course. And see there?' He points. 'Bird-boxes! I put them up on four different tree trunks ahead of the nesting season, and some bird feeders there too – peanuts or sunflower hearts for the tits. I finished sharpening our tools,' he turns to show us, almost singing, 'gave all the empty pots and trays one last thorough scrubbing. Today, we must brush the past few winters off that patio – a bit of elbow grease. A power hose will only tear out the grout . . . But first, let us take pride in the progress made together!'

'What progress?' Nathan asks. 'That thing no longer looks like an abandoned drug den – I'll give us that,' he says of the glasshouse. 'But—'

'"But" – what about the shimmer of our lovely evergreens? The trees, and these feathery buggers over here, *we* revived those.' David points to the row of handsome frost-proof containers of varying heights and sizes that decorate the patio, each of them covered in Celtic-knot designs and exploding with healthy foliage. 'Defiant beauties. *Look at them*. They reflect the love and attention we've been showing them.'

'Defiant beauty,' Nathan repeats. 'I'd like that carved into my tombstone, please.'

David pairs us up and doles out various tasks.

Rosie and Jordanne have to remove dead and diseased branches from June's apple tree. My sister throws me a sarcastic 'woo hoo' behind David's back. I was hoping to be paired with Jordanne; it's easy to avoid talking about your own feelings when someone's pregnant – there's never an awkward lull in conversation about the mind-blowing reality of what a female human body can do. Her bump has grown a lot, and I really want to have a feel of it if she'll let me.

'For those of you who still haven't bothered to check out the library books I asked you to read' – I grit my teeth and look at Rosie. She may be keeping on top of David's hand-outs but she has in her hole set foot in a library – '*annuals* are plants that live for just one growing season then die off,' David says.

Feeling unusually comfortable, I let the words 'hard relate' slip out without much thought.

Tadhg throws me a funny look and I immediately regret my words.

Peter and Alice – both mute – start to sow the seeds of 'annuals' in plastic trays.

David joins Nathan in taking root cuttings of perennial plants (ones that 'come up every year from the same root system') and planting them, while Tadhg the electrician and

I have been tasked with installing a working electric heater in the glasshouse to keep frost at bay.

There's something about this particular glasshouse, you know. An aliveness . . . a unique kind of magic. It's the sort of space that threatens to centre you every time you step inside it, as though the structure itself seeks to heal by evoking a strange sense of cohesion of body, mind and – whatever else there might be to each of us.

With my arms crossed against the unfamiliar peace I always feel inside the glasshouse, I watch Tadhg fiddle with wires and a screwdriver. He's pleasant company: doesn't ask many questions, offers up plenty of easy small talk. His eyes are less hollowed than they were when we first met and his cheeks fuller. As I examine him, I catch a mysterious expression on his face, a flash like sun through forest heights: he looked at the clear space in the corner of the glasshouse and this Mona Lisa smile appeared – the kind you can't quite figure out. It wasn't immediately obvious what he was looking at. I double check. Nothing exciting to see there – visible to anyone but Tadhg, anyway.

Alien bravery prompts me to ask him what he's thinking about.

'Eh?'

'I saw you smile to yourself just now.'

'Yeah?'

'Yeah. And now you're blushing.'

'I am, am I?'

'You are. It's the pasty skin. I'm the same – when I have something to blush *about*. Which is never . . .'

'Ha.'

'So?'

'So . . .' I raise my eyebrows. Like magic, they pull some words from him: 'Ah. It's nothing.'

'Tell me.'

'No, no. I can't', he says, glowing now. He fights a smile that's taken over every square inch of his face, but the smile wins out.

'Ah, please. I've had a shit few weeks.'

'How shit?'

I tell him, as candidly as I can, that my cat – my best friend – is dying.

'That's fairly shit all right.'

'So, cheer me up.'

'Ah. I can't talk about it.'

'Why?'

'You know how secrets are. Besides. A gentleman never tells.' Concise, discreet, infuriating.

He checks the heater. Desperate to know whatever he's keeping from me, I wander over to where his eyes lost themselves. There's a stack of bags of fertiliser, a dustpan and brush, hanging baskets for the coming months, yet to be hung . . . Right before I admit defeat and circle back to Tadhg, an empty Durex condom wrapper glints at me just hidden under the dirty, wooden table. It's out of Tadhg's line of sight, but I think it means he got lucky in here, and my heart of hearts tells me it was with my sister.

Rosie has 'liked' everything Tadhg has posted on social media within ten minutes since well before Christmas.

Since the night of the party. She's not said a word about it, even though we sleep beside each other now, and I wonder why she never opens up to me about anything to do with the men in her life. Though, Bridie once said that those in glass houses shouldn't throw stones: our bed is filled with secrets and I'm sure that many of them belong to me.

Implying usefulness – that I'm tidying something – I snatch the wrapper up and hide it in my welly. Peter surely doesn't know about them. I don't imagine my sister to be so cruel as to dump that on him while his career is being virtually slaughtered. And if my suspicion is true, Peter *can't* know. I need to protect him as well as Rosie; she may not love him back, but I can't imagine she'd have hooked up with Tadhg if she'd known what was coming, what Peter would be going through . . .

'Want to talk? About your cat?'

'What?'

'Your cat.' Tadhg keeps doing what he's doing and waits for me to take over. My brain is running a mile a minute. 'We're supposed to bare our souls here, aren't we? It's what David wants.'

What *June wants* . . .

My mind slows. 'Eh, I don't like talking about . . . that.' It's not a lie. I don't. 'The idea of losing someone you love is – well, I know Bertie technically isn't a *someone*, but he is to me.'

'That's all that matters. You don't have to explain yourself.' Tadhg pauses. 'Rachel . . .' He looks around the glasshouse for a bit. Digs the tip of the drill into a groove in the floor.

'You never really talk about her, so I'm sure you get why I'd prefer not to—'

'I have . . . talked about her.'

Barely. 'Not about how it made you feel.'

'What am I supposed to say?'

We stop looking at each other. I hear him play with the drill some more. I examine my nails: it's like I've not looked at them in a whole year. They're horrible, brittle, full of deficiency spots. 'I don't know. Maybe . . .' I grasp at ideas. He's looking to connect and I should facilitate that. 'Maybe – pretend you're talking to someone who is planning on taking their own life. As a sort of – exercise.' Shit. Shit *shit*. What am I doing? 'What would you say to *me*, if I told you I was going to do it tomorrow?'

'You sound like my therapist.'

I keep looking at my hand. *Through* my hand. I wait. I don't know where else to look.

'All right, so. Eh. If you – kill yourself – eh . . . Jenna, this is weird.'

'We're on this project to sort through our shit. To "bare our souls". You just said so yourself.'

'And what about you? Your . . . stuff.'

I breathe. My eyes tell him that it's his turn. I wait.

'Well, right.' He inhales. Exhales slowly. 'If you kill yourself, I . . . don't know where you'll go . . . if there's even a heaven,' he starts.

And because we're not looking at each other, I feel like

I'm in some kind of secular confessional where I'm being personally attacked.

'All I know is that the people you leave behind won't know how to carry on as normal. Because you . . . you can't come back. You're supposed to be around, at the dinner table, in the . . . the passenger seat. But you're not. You decided to leave it empty. Somehow knowing that . . . it makes missing you even harder.'

He's no longer speaking to me. I glance at him. His eyes are fixed on the trees visible through a single missing pane of glass that's still to be replaced.

'People won't just be sad, though. When you're dead. They'll be fucking angry.'

I swivel my wrist and then let it go limp in my other hand. Tadhg didn't strike me as the type to swear, so every time he does, it's like a kitten barking.

I look at Rosie through the glasshouse on her hands and knees, beside Jordanne. They're laughing at something. I think about her complaining later on about how gross her task today was while she removes her make-up. I imagine her having a child someday, and her child having no aunts or uncles. No cousins for play dates. I picture her finding my cold, lifeless body . . .

'"What could I have done to make the pain stop?"' he goes on. 'Because that's what you want, really. Escape. You don't want to *die*. You want the pain to stop. For. The impulse to be . . . dead . . .' He shakes his head. 'It won't last. But if you follow that in a . . . low moment, you . . . you leave people behind. People who'll feel awful things – resentment

– where they only felt love . . . before. It's not nice. I know. But it's true.' He looks at me then. 'The truth isn't always nice.'

I can't even talk.

'Stay here,' he goes on. 'It's only up from here. Just . . . stay.'

'What – what did you just say?'

He swallows. 'Stay?'

'No, before – sorry, never mind.' Blood gushes in my neck. 'That was – you, you did good, Tadhg.'

'I wish I could've said all that to her.'

'I know.'

'Jenna.'

'Yeah?'

'How you feel about your cat, it's not stupid. A broken heart is – well, it's broken, isn't it? Doesn't matter how it got like that. You're waiting for yours to get smashed. That's hard.'

We return to the task at hand in a comfortable, intimate silence but I swear, the glasshouse itself is listening to all of the words we don't say aloud.

ROSIE

I arrive outside Mam's house at twenty to six on Wednesday evening – forty minutes later than usual – because I met Jordanne from the group for lunch. And, well, 'lunch' turned into almost four hours of intense discussion about my messy affair with Peter: him wanting more, me stepping out of my comfort zone and then him shutting me out; perhaps finally hearing the *bad news* bells that inevitably ring out when someone as confused as me comes too close . . . I just couldn't help myself. Obviously, I've tried to talk to Mam about everything that's been going on before telling someone new about it, but all the online stuff eludes Mam completely, so she can't understand the context, never mind the fact that she forgets what we're talking about mid-conversation, and Jordanne is probably the last person on earth I should've talked to – after all, she's practically the kind of pete super fan that the kids these days refer to as a 'stan' – but I had to talk to somebody. Jordanne didn't offer a lick of unsolicited advice and, thank God, she just listened to me, serving as a shoulder and an ear – things I hadn't realised I desperately needed. I've been crawling on all fours through a desert without water. I really need to make a habit of offloading. It felt fucking *fabulous*!

Dotty Byrne's rollers are visible where her head hovers on the other side of her net curtains. 'Hi, Dotty.' Just like that she's gone – Groundhog Day. Freezing, I unlock the door.

'Brought you the paper and a Flake for dessert! How about shepherd's pie?' I plop my key on the side table in the hall and kick off my shoes. My red-cheeked reflection from Mam's wall mirror throws me. I'd better find some time to give my face a paint job before work. I'm really letting myself go to the dogs! Tom's been asking if I'm OK ever since I stopped wearing fake eyelashes. Spending time outdoors in Avalon is making me lazy about my appearance; it feels silly to get dolled up to go and do dirty garden work. On Saturdays I go light with the make-up and throw my hair up in a messy bun, and when you feel the comfort of that one day a week, soon one day bleeds into four more.

When Mam doesn't answer, I shout out for her. She's not in the front room, though the TV is on. Not in the kitchen, either. There are no dirty dishes left over from her lunch, like she's not reheated my leftover stew . . .

'Mam? You in bed?'

Nothing but the drone of the news.

Seconds pass before dread takes hold of me and propels me up the narrow staircase. Wood creaks beneath my feet.

My heart whooshes in my ear, steady and fast. Mam's walker is outside the bathroom door. I call out for her again. No reply. I ram the handle on the door, but the room is locked from the inside. She's in there and she's not responding.

Somehow impassive and without hesitation, I call an ambulance. As I dial, and as I bark at the operator on the other end of the line, the recurring nightmare I've had over the past few weeks crosses my mind, wearing high-vis to prevent me from looking away: me trying and failing to open my own bathroom door, kicking it in, finding Jenna curled up in a ball on the shower floor after an overdose. I really wish she were here so I didn't have to experience this alone; I've gotten used to *not* being alone. When the call ends, I flee Mam's in my socks for help, my stomach in my throat. Thankfully, Big Jim is just in from the building site. The mountain of flesh pulls off his heavy work jacket, piles it on top of his little wife and chases after me. We're running and running and my socks are soaked through. I make it to Mam's landing in a flurry of nothing but thoughts of her on the other side of that door, thoughts of Jenna, Mam, Jenna, Mam. Jim knocks it down with two mighty kicks.

I drag my feet along the turquoise vinyl. Something – probably the smell of antiseptic – is making me feel sick. I stop pacing outside the room leading onto Mam's ward, where a nurse has a curtain pulled around her bed, obscuring her from view. A tall, stressed doctor brushes past me to enter the ward: he's lost in the contents of a page attached to his clipboard. I wonder how many preventable concussions he's had to treat this year so far because of people like me. Because this is all my fault!

Jenna is a pile of pixels in my hand, lit by blue light.

'The hospital reception is – I – can hardly see you,' I tell her, my voice shaking.

'Yeah, you look like a *Minecraft* character on my end.'

'What's *Minecraft*?'

'Doesn't matter.'

I never FaceTime anyone in a non-sexual context, so this is bizarre. I can just about make out Jenna's finger. She's either chewing it, or she's picking at her lips.

'So, how long was she – was Mam – in the bathroom?'

'It seems like she fell not long before I arrived because she came to before the ambulance pulled up. She was all "I just didn't want any lunch today, Rosie" and "I went for my shower before the news because I don't like the news". Meanwhile, there's me slamming on Big Jim's door, picturing her going into fucking rigor mortis!' I nervously laugh, hoping to lighten the mood. The pixels don't laugh back. Jenna wants more information. 'Mam said her feet slipped out from under her,' I go on, 'that she – went down quickly. "Violently", she said. I – I should have been there.' I nod at the phone.

'Where were you?'

I rub the tip of my shoe against a scuff on the hospital floor. 'With . . . Jordanne.'

'From the group?'

'Yeah. I needed . . . someone to talk to.' Jenna's image becomes crisper. I search her eyes, but I couldn't find something there if I tried because it's impossible to make actual eye contact on this bloody app – she's looking at my image and not directly into the camera: the camera would want to be inside her eyeballs for this to be a useful form of connection. She says nothing. I sigh. I start to chew the pockets of my cheeks and I look back onto the ward, waiting for a chink in the curtain to appear.

'So, it's just a concussion then. No fractures, no—'

'Just a concussion. And her neck's a bit – swollen.' It hurts to say it aloud, to know it wouldn't have happened if I'd been there. 'They're keeping her in overnight for observation, and I'll have to stay with her in hers for the next day or so to make sure her symptoms don't get worse. I just don't know what she was thinking, trying to wash herself! I mean, maybe she wanted to prove to herself that she's still capable? Or—'

'Or maybe she completely forgot that you wash her. Maybe her memory loss is getting even worse. An – d – may-yy—'

And just like that, Jenna's image freezes. It's like a virtual wall self-erects between us, blocking the flow of Jenna's vulnerability like it's a harsh wind, like I've not been waiting to feel it sting my cheeks for weeks on end.

I wait. I stutter. She's gone. Seconds later, my phone beeps.

Jenna [20:05]: If you need anything let me know. Not sure I'd be much help in any case.

The offer itself means more to me than anything she could actually do. I don't tell her that. Instead, I fire off a quick 'thank you', and, still nauseous, I return to Mam's bedside.

*

Peter [19:04]: you guys home yet? how's she today? X

Jenna told Peter about what happened to Mam yesterday and he's been texting me non-stop ever since. There's been no acknowledgement whatsoever of the deep gorge between us lately, or the fact that we've been looking at one another across the chasm, week in week out, but Peter's texts are all thoughtful offers and kisses between layers of kind concern. Something tells me he's not messing about – I believe he's genuinely worried about our family and that maybe hearing about what happened to Mam brought him up for air after a long while without any at all.

Me [19:20]: Back in Mam's. We're exhausted. She'll be out for the night . . . we've been awake for 36 hours now! Haven't eaten all day apart from some gone off Skittles from the bottom of my handbag x

Peter [19:22]: want me to pick up a few bits and maybe a Mcdonald's, deliver to the door?

Me [19:25]: Peter. Don't go into a McDonald's. Are you mad? I don't want people hurling abuse at you because of me! There's stuff here. I'll cook. Just need to nap first x

Peter [19:26]: don't, i'm leaving already, i'll use the drive through, will wear my cap, just text me order and your mom's address xx

Me [19:29]: Are you sure? Well, I won't lie I'd murder a double quarter pounder with cheese, a large fries and a strawberry milkshake. Honestly, thanks, I'll pay you

**back! Come to 14 Stoneywey Road in Stoneybatter. It's
about half an hour of a drive with the traffic. And would
you mind checking in on Jenna before you leave? xx**

My message is as nonchalant as I can make it, even though
I couldn't be less calm or relaxed. I agonise over every word
I type. How do I communicate my thawing emotional unavailability while also establishing that tonight is in no way a
significant relationship moment?

Exhausted, I push my phone across Mam's duvet and I
curl up in a foetal position to watch her as she sleeps. Her
chest softly rises and falls in the dark. *Relief.* It never felt
so good. I spy Mam's alarm bracelet on her locker beside
her tube of rose lipstick. I lost count of how many white-clad
nurses asked her why she wasn't wearing one, after finding
out she's got advanced MS – she didn't answer a single one,
just shrugged her shoulders. The thought of Mam explaining
that Vincent-from-the-shop would find the alarm bracelet
terribly unsexy puts a silly grin on my face. I trace the
contours of her cheek with red-rimmed eyes.

What would I do without you?

I cuddle into the warmth of her and immediately pass out.

I keep my eyes on the mountain of food Peter brought me
so I don't have to look at him.

I'm seated cross-legged in Mam's favourite padded
armchair. I have every reason to be comfortable but I
imagine I appear anything but. My foot is flying all over the
place. My nerves are shot! I've just interrogated Peter about

what he told Dotty (because *of course* she saw him outside and *of course* she came out for a nosy and *of course* she asked him if he's 'with me', what he does, where he lives, how he likes his fucking eggs . . .).

'She even noticed the mud on my damn shoes, asked if I'd come from "the cemetery" like she was talking about the supermarket.'

'Arbour Hill. It's near here. Dotty's husband is buried there – she practically lives there when she's not spying out that window.'

'I just said "yeah" to get her off my case. Not really a lie anyway – Mom's ashes in the garden and all. I was out at Avalon with Moss and the well-maintenance guys . . .'

I clench my teeth behind my lips.

'Anyway. That Dotty one seemed real concerned about your mom.' He's sat upright on the edge of a wooden chair that Mam keeps in here – right by her armchair – for extra tea and book storage. Peter's bum is propped against a small stack of battered Catherine Cookson novels.

'She's isn't. Trust me. Mam and Dotty hate each other.'

'Hate. Strong word!'

'They do – always have!' I try to speak without the chewing noises but it doesn't work. I leave my inner savage to fight my ego so I can finish my food.

'Hope she doesn't hate *me*,' he says. 'Then again, if she does, now is about the best time to hate me.' Peter's charming smile, all chin, accompanied by sad eyes. Eyes that have read enough cruel messages and clickbait articles for a lifetime. 'Will I get to meet her?' His enthusiasm staggers me. He's met Harry Styles and Billie Eilish! *As if* he's excited about meeting my mam.

Mouth full, I look away, cover my lips as I talk, so Peter doesn't have to see burger mulch inside the place he kisses sometimes. 'Nah. She's sleeping like a baby up there.'

'I don't get it.'

I swallow forcefully. 'Don't get what?'

'Why we describe people that way . . . people who are, like, passed out. I thought the whole thing with babies is that they never sleep.'

I shrug. 'Wouldn't know.'

He stands up and eyes the stack of old photographs Mam has perched on the edge of her too-crammed bookshelf.

'Fire away. Maybe they'll put you off me for good,' I joke. Nervous post-full-day-in-hospital flirtation is *not* my favourite.

Peter snorts at me and rolls his eyes. The photos are mostly of myself and Jenna when we were younger, wearing denim shirts and halter-neck crop tops; skinny eyebrows and grunge liner; butterfly clips and bumpy foreheads. Then he asks me, 'D'you ever *want* to know, then?'

'Know what?'

'About babies.'

I feel myself go pink in the cheeks.

'Kids. You ever want any?'

I blow my lips while my head sort of shakes itself. 'I – no. No. Don't think so.'

'I don't,' he says, flicking through Mam's pictures. I envy the absolute certainty in his voice. 'I'm way too selfish for kids.'

I think for a moment while I finish my meal. Maybe it's the fact that we're in Mam's house, where I feel so at home, but I find myself wanting to be candid with Peter. Something tells me that this is a turning point for us; that Peter is teetering on the edge of a decision about whether or not he should involve himself with me any longer and that I have the ability to push him forward or to pull him back. I have to be open. Honest. *Myself*. Perhaps then I'll discover what my own heart desires.

I relax back and play with the straw of my milkshake. 'I don't really know what my reason is. Just that . . . it is what it is. I can't quite see myself as a mother, just like I can't quite see my own mother as anything else. It seems like having Jenna and myself became her whole world. She lost so much of herself. And, well, look at Jordanne!'

Big sappy head on him, Peter holds up a cute snap of Jenna and me on horseback down the country. 'I mean . . .' His expression reads: *how adorable*. 'You sure you don't want all that?'

'Believe me, it wasn't so pretty all the time. And – and – starting a family, it's not a thing I should be trying to talk myself into, right? Like, surely if I wanted kids, but just, well, didn't think it was on the cards for me – like, if I was just lying to myself about *not* wanting them (which my mother seems to think is the case) – I'd be trying to talk myself out of it? I'd be trying to come up with all the reasons why I shouldn't procreate, of which there are plenty! I have a roof over my head but I don't have a support network.' I stare off into space and swing my free hand from left to right, to demonstrate the two invisible sides of the seesaw that is my stream of consciousness. 'I have age on my side but I'm not broody. I'm caring but I already care for someone who really depends on me and who probably will until I'm an old woman myself. And I'm sure I could figure out how to earn a living from home at the same time as keeping a baby alive, but I just – I don't want to!'

It's like Peter can sense I'm not done yet. He doesn't pick up the conversation when I pause. I recline even more.

'I list all the good reasons to have a baby in my brain sometimes when I'm falling asleep. It's sort of like reading through all the reasons I should work out – I mean, plenty, obviously – but none of them are ever enough to keep me going to a gym or whatever, so I figure it's just . . . not for me, I'm a walker.'

'Indeed, Rosie Walker.'

'You should do stand up, really,' I joke. He shrugs. 'I want to travel. I don't want to know what to expect week to week. Knowing what to expect every day, for years, hasn't been good for me. And this is real life and I won't get what I want, and that's fine, but, I'm just saying, we all have our dreams. And kids?' I think a little more. 'They change every day, so maybe – *maybe* I'd like that, but . . . your duty as a parent doesn't change: that stays the same. There's no escaping that. Keep them safe, fed, clothed, warm . . . call the doctor, teach them right from wrong . . .'

Peter looks at me, impressed. 'At least you've given it some thought. Just like my mom did. Both my moms. My birth mom knew she couldn't handle it and didn't want it, and I'm glad. Because June, my *mom* mom, she was the best.' He sits on the settee to my right, balances the photos on his lap. 'I blame being an only child on why I am the way I am about kids. Always had all the attention on me. Never liked . . . sharing.'

He watches for my reaction.

I think of Tadhg and I choke on a chip.

'You all right? Need some water?' Peter leans towards me.

I carefully examine his glowing, unlined, beautiful face – as flecks of my spit splash it – for any evidence that he knows about what happened at the party, but all I can see is mild concern. 'Nope. No, no!' I compose myself.

He smiles and resumes flicking through the photos. 'So. You *don't* want to know what to expect, then?'

'No. Life's more exciting that way. *You* know – you live it!'

'Well. I mean, sure. But it's important to have someone to rely on too, isn't it? To know what you can and can't expect – of someone – day to day and year to year.' A fleeting glance. Everything is still but the blood in both our bodies. 'Dad said Mom helped him to grow more selfless. Said without her he'd never have learned to really stop and look at situations from another point of view. None of us are islands, Rosie. We all need a bit of that surrounding land when shit hits the fan.'

I bite my lip as our eyes meet again. 'Is that what we're doing right now? Being each other's surrounding land?'

He laughs. 'I suppose it is, yeah.'

'But you deserve Canada,' I tell him. 'Some massive place. I'm – I'm Iceland.'

'Nah. You're more like France. And that's cool. I love France.'

Love? I look around the room quickly.

'Let's go there some time,' he goes on. 'On me. If only for the food . . .'

A moth in my chest. 'Now you're speaking my language. You're going there this year, right? On – your tour?' My toes curl up under my legs as I wait for him to reply. The last day out at Avalon I found myself daydreaming about what it would be like to be his plus one on the European tour. All of the pasta and croissants, the sunsets and sea breezes, the cocktails and the accents and the breakfast buffets and the smiling at his fans while he signs autographs knowing he's all mine and . . . and then I stopped myself. Because entertaining the thought of abandoning Mam is *ridiculous*; because to allow Peter to get himself wrapped up in a relationship with a headcase-in-denial like me would be inhumane; because Jordanne has inadvertently reminded me over and over again by banging on about his music and all the cool things he's already done in his career that Peter is a shooting star. I was never any good at interception when playing camogie: there's no way I could catch him, even if he's aimed himself directly at me.

Peter hesitates. Taps his muck-crusted shoes against the carpet. 'Yeah. Well. We'll see.'

'See what?'

'About that.'

'The tour?'

'Mm-hmm.'

'Why?'

He picks at the edge of a photo of Jenna showing off her Billie Joe Armstrong poster collection (most of the posters have had everything removed but Billie's head, so it's essentially a terrifying wall of floating Billie Joe heads). 'It might not happen.'

I inhale and forget to exhale. 'But. Wait. Why? Not because of that stupid Freddie Mercury picture?'

He scrunches up his lips. 'Public perception right now is: lowercase pete equals anti-Semitism.'

'But if you just asked Izzy to—'

'I've reached out. She's ignoring me. Avoiding group. I just – I – what the—?'

I notice that Peter's mouth is hanging open. The whites around his irises are visible. He's staring at a photo.

'It's – Rosie, it's my mom! Look!'

He's too busy staring to show me what he's looking at. I clamber across onto the settee and settle myself on his lap, to get a good look. Peter's pincer grip holds up high a water-damaged photo covered in traces of dirt that I've seen multiple times before – Mam regularly whips these pictures out but, somehow, since seeing June's face out in Avalon it never clicked: why she looked so familiar. Two twenty-something beauties with fuzzy eighties hair stare back at us.

'Sweet mother of—'

'*Me!* And you! Ha!'

My mouth opens and closes several times.

'They knew each other, Rosie!'

They look like ABBA's leading ladies: my mam's hair is dyed blonde and June is wearing bright-blue eyeshadow. It looks like they're at a house party.

'This must have been taken years before she adopted me. I can't – how wild is this? I can't wait to show this to my dad! And – hang on. I feel like I've met your mom. She didn't –' his jaw falls '– she's not – I mean, she wasn't a *piano tutor*, by any chance, was she?'

Before I can respond, three loud bangs emanate from above as Mam taps her floor with her cane.

'She must need water. Give me a minute – this is' – I say, in a fluster about the picture – 'I can't *believe* . . .' I stand and make a beeline for the door to the hallway.

'Well, she's awake, so now you have no excuse not to introduce us,' Peter says cheekily, with a smile that reaches his eyes. 'Or *re*-introduce us!'

JENNA

Earlier today, I direct messaged Nathan through Facebook to ask him to meet me after his shift at the bank, where he works. I'm not sure what possessed me to do it – maybe the fact that I found some blood on the floor beside Bertie's food bowl this morning; like, maybe now we're approaching the end of the line, survival mode is kicking in and is on the lookout for grips, like, I'm simply wall climbing out here, like it's really that easy. Peter is the grip I'm too afraid to grab onto, or maybe I already *have* – slippy-fingered naivety . . .

Nathan and I have never spent time together outside of a Saturday, so I know it's incredibly random, but I need to talk about this Peter stuff before I combust. Nathan will tell me straight.

I know it.

We meet at Café en Seine, a contemporary Parisian bar in town full of lavish seating and elaborate chandeliers. One

Pornstar Colada cocktail here costs almost as much as my weekly food shop. Nathan offers to buy me a drink.

'Thanks. I was going to order tap water . . .'

'I love luxury. What can I say?' To my surprise, Nathan pulls an e-cig from his pocket and vapes using a piece of his cashmere scarf to hide what he's doing from the staff. He exhales out slowly into his coat, so there's no evidence in the air. I immediately copy him and blow into my sleeve.

'They don't like us having fun with our chemicals in here. But today was *stress*.'

'I didn't know you vaped too.'

'Well, I want to give up. Only started 'cause I thought this would give me that young-Marlon-Brando-smoking sex appeal, but turns out boys don't seem to go for it. Smoking was never *actually* sexy. And vaping is just – pretend smoking. Pretend non-sexy. It's a waste of money and it looks absurd.'

Give up? Why has it never even crossed my *mind* to give up?

Nathan drums his manicured fingernails against the table. In the glow of red and purple light from the bar he looks more sophisticated than should be possible. He sips his martini and waits for me to talk. After all, I dragged him here after a long day at work.

'Right. Listen. I need to tell you something but I also need you to promise me you won't tell anyone else. *Anyone* else.'

'I know how to keep a secret. Hit me.'

'I mean it. You can't—'

'Jenna, stop. Look at me.' His eyes are wide and serious

and give the unmistakable impression of a person who would sooner take your secret to the grave than pursue five minutes of idle gossip.

I push my bottom lip out and I feel my eyes water. 'OK.'

Nathan manages to drink his entire martini in the time it takes me to tell him how I feel about Peter; how much time I spend thinking about him, how he's helped me through intrusive thoughts. I tell Nathan all the things I've kept bottled up over the past few weeks. How I've always wanted to meet someone like Peter – not because he's famous but *why* he's famous, why people are drawn to him online like bees to flowers in the height of spring. Peter is an enigma. One minute he'll burst into song, do a nerdy dance, and the next, he's inside himself: a turtle in this thick shell of achievements, numbers, expectations, somewhere I'd kill to reside even on cloudy days. I even talk about how I imagine kissing him and living out in Avalon with him all happily ever after . . .

Nathan's face gives nothing away as I drag it all out of myself. I reassure him I've managed to keep a lid on how I feel and – most importantly – that I know about him and Rosie.

'Me and her haven't even talked about it *once*!' I slam a palm against the table. 'I've been living with Rosie *for months* and she's not said a word about being interested in any guy, let alone someone we regularly see together. So maybe – maybe they're just fuck buddies. And maybe it's OK for me to—'

'Hold up,' Nathan says, stopping me. He eyes the bartender. 'Going to need another one of these, love.'

I put my face in my hands. 'It's a shitshow, isn't it?'

'First things first. Has Peter given you any sign that he's interested?'

I speed through the mental footage of our every interaction. 'I held his hand at the party and he didn't let go.'

Nathan raises an eyebrow. 'Before or after seeing his dad have a breakdown, after which he'd probably have held *Tadhg's* hand?'

'After.'

'Nothing else?'

I want to lie but it'll do me no good here. 'No.'

'And you've not told your sister you fancy him. *Why?*'

'Because – she – she's not told me about – them.'

'And what? Is this some sibling bullshit? I'm an only child. Tell me. Is there a competition I'm not aware of? Gold medal goes to the best-kept secret? Don't talk about Fight Club kinda vibes?'

I dig my fingers into the chair. 'I know. I'm fucked up.'

'Jenna, from what I've seen, your sister and him – it's *messy*. Rosie is like me. Can't trust anyone. She's hot and cold, and Peter – he needs tepid water, if you know what I mean.'

'You don't approve of her?'

The squeak of his tongue between his teeth. 'The girl just needs help. So she can let herself be happy. Like me.' He smiles a supposed-to-be-fake smile. 'Besides, you're not exactly "tepid water" yourself. You're in for this garden-group shit, too. Why should I approve of either of you? Peter's my boy.'

'Peter's in the group, too . . .'

'Eh, *yeah*! He's famous. Famous people need all kinds of therapy.'

'David said the group doesn't replace therapy.'

'No. But Peter's already in proper therapy.'

I didn't know that. Peter never said.

'Anyway. I don't think he should be dating *anyone* right now with where his head is at. Your point is moot.'

I huff. I literally *huff*.

I'm insufferable.

'Well, what do I do? What would *you* do? I can't just get one of those memory-erasing machines from *Eternal Sunshine of the Spotless Mind*. How am I supposed to—?'

'Look, look, *look*,' he stops me, sitting his glass down and crossing his legs. 'I don't know what kind of person you are, and I really don't know shit about your sister, but there are only' – he stops to think and to count under his breath using his fingers – '*seven* options available to you right now. Want a rundown?'

I sip my water. 'Go for it. And please be brutally honest! That's why I've come to you.'

He acts overly shocked. A playful smile. 'How dare you imply that I'm capable of being anything but. OK. Option one. You let Rosie have him.'

'Great.' I give him an unenthusiastic thumbs up.

'Maybe she ends up with him, and family get-togethers are awkward as fuck . . .'

'*What* family get-togethers?'

Nathan slow blinks. 'OK, you can't just throw that out

there and expect me to continue with my incredible list of possible solutions to crisis A. What's *that* about?'

'What?'

He rolls his shoulders back. 'The sarcastic tone. Crisis B!'

I consider how I might summarise the entire situation – and my plethora of feelings on it – for this person whom I actually, genuinely want to connect with. I'm fed up of sitting all alone in the dark. I've not even spoken to Peter about this stuff. I don't want him to think badly of me. 'Eh, well. My mother, she got sick. She stayed sick.' I take a deep breath. I want to vape, but I don't. 'I got scared. So, I . . . pulled away. And now I can only assume she hates me. Because what kind of daughter am I?'

Nathan doesn't dig; he allows me room to vent.

'I know it's normal to fear the unknown, and the uncertainty of what might happen in the future, but my fears – of, like, ageing, and' – I swallow – 'physical disability, dementia . . . it runs – deep, like it's glued itself to my bones or something. It keeps me up at night. I have this recurring dream where I – it doesn't matter.' The discomfort of vulnerability begs me to shut up, to turn the lights off so I can sit in the dark alone some more.

'It does matter,' Nathan says. He rests his chin on his balled-up fist. High-beam headlights.

'In the dream, I age – in seconds. I look at my reflection and I'm suddenly old. Grey hair, sagging face, and I need help – for everything. Then I wake, screaming. Covered in sweat. It happens every few weeks.'

'And seeing your mother makes this disturbing nightmare seem real. Because you see yourself in her.'

Intense eye contact.

'And there we have crisis B.' I fake smile. 'That one is for the Bird-Shit Palace Brigade.' I can't tell if I'm being truthful or not: I've not yet felt compelled to be vulnerable out at Avalon and I'm not sure I ever will be. 'Can we *please* get back to . . .?'

'Crisis A. Ah. Where were we?'

'Me leaving Rosie and Peter at it.'

'All right. Yes. Maybe Rosie decides it isn't worth pursuing – which seems to be what's happening,' he says, fingers fanned out. 'And if you step aside, you'll feel great being the bigger person, and—'

'*Or* I'll resent her, and I'll still want to . . .'

He waits. I don't pick the sentence off the floor. 'You'll still want to what?'

I shake my head against myself. I don't want to burden him any more than I already have. 'Just . . . go on. Option two. Give me option two.'

'You compete for him.'

'Come on. Really? He's not the Iron Throne!'

'I'm just listing off all the paths you *can* take – not saying I endorse them all!'

I lean on my fist.

'This one could get ugly, obviously. Would not recommend.'

'Next.'

'You ask Rosie to let *you* have him.'

I look on blankly.

'Option four,' he starts, as the bartender brings his second drink, 'you toss a coin. Leave it up to fate. Eliminate blame from the equation.' He giggles.

'Nate, seriously—'

'Option five,' he interrupts, an eyebrow raised. 'Let *him* decide.'

'Go on.'

'That one is my favourite.' He winks. Sips. 'He'll choose one of you or he'll choose neither of you and then both of you can get on with your lives.'

'If that one's your favourite, then what's left?'

'Options six and seven!'

'And they are?'

'Both of you date him. Or neither of you date him.' He blinks multiple times in a row. 'Option seven is my *second* favourite.' Then he knocks back half of his drink. 'Because at the end of the day, your relationship with your sister might be destroyed here no matter what way you choose to go about it, because you were unlucky enough to fall for a guy who is head over heels in love with . . . your sister. That way, maybe you're both left thinking *what if* but at least you hold on to each other.'

I groan. 'He really is, isn't he? In love with her?'

'I've never known someone so lovesick in all my life. It's disgusting.'

'He . . . shouldn't be. She'll hurt him. I think she already has, he just – he hasn't felt the impact yet.'

My phone vibrates. I glance at the screen. A text from Rosie. I ignore.

'Peter is a big boy. Besides, we all get hurt in the game of love. If life has taught me anything, it's that we stand the fuck back up and get on with it, no matter what.' Nathan examines his many gold rings. I suspect he has a lot he needs to offload himself. 'Peter wants your sister and he's not getting her and he seems fine about chilling with her shadow instead of the real deal. We need to stand back and let that shit play out. Of course, you do you and all, I'm just – you asked for brutal honesty.' He vapes again, dodging the view of the bartender. 'You want my advice? Don't get involved. Don't say *shit*. Talking is good, but some things are better left unsaid. Boys . . . they're real upfront about love when they're *in* it. You know if a guy loves you 'cause he'll make sure you know. And Peter loves Rosie.'

Tears spill from my eyes. I'm as shocked as you are. I mean, I can stand Peter not loving me. Really. But can I stand him loving *her*?

'Shit, Jenna, I'm sorry—'

'No. No. I just – I don't—' I point at my tears, embarrassed. 'But, fuck, it hurts.'

Nathan grabs a serviette from the table and pats my face with it. 'Growth hurts like a bitch, but it's not as painful as staying stuck on some guy who doesn't want you *that way*. Just trust me, Jenna. Peter didn't break your heart on purpose, did he? He dropped that shit without even knowing he was holding it.'

More tears flow.

'So, let's focus on putting the pieces back together, yeah?'

'What about your heart?' I ask him.

His eyes flash. He searches, again, for the bartender. 'My love? Two martinis. Cheers.'

And just like that, I make a new friend.

ROSIE

It's Saturday again and in the shade of Avalon's bare trees, their branches like bronchi breathing a mild wind down on all of us, we huddle around David. He's holding the photo of Mam and June and his eyes are bonfires; David has seen the picture several times this week already, but every time he looks at it, it's like the first time all over again.

I begged Peter not to say anything about the photo, but Peter being Peter insisted on telling his dad. David then excitedly announced it in our group chat, like it's some kind of miraculous sign from June herself that Peter happened upon it at all, and then, *of course*, within hours, everyone insisted that I bring it to group.

Everyone minus Izzy. We've still not heard a peep from her. Peter still parks outside her house every week and every week we pull away without her. Sometimes, her mother spots the bus and pulls the living room curtains – not the most welcoming of signals, is it? According to David,

Izzy isn't even speaking to her parents. We're all at a loss over what to do.

We're supposed to be doing some kind of meditation today while finishing up the last of the weeding – my least favourite task: it's back-breaking! – but they're all way too excited over this bloody photo.

Peter recounts the conversation we had with Mam on Thursday evening, when she had insisted that we both come sit on her bed. Thankfully, he leaves out the fact that she asked him questions like 'Why is a man like you still single?' As he talks about her, Peter beams. He was perfectly lovely to her. It kind of rendered me low on reasons to continue keeping him at arm's length. Seeing him and Mam get along so well did nothing but allow me to taste a possible future, one that might evaporate, might leave me bitter and with nothing but the memory of my mother like a giddy little girl who found exactly what she wanted under the Christmas tree . . .

'And the craziest thing is that Rosie and Jenna's mom taught me piano, *here*, nearly fifteen years ago! She went to secondary school with my mom apparently, and they were friends for years – right up till, well . . .' Peter stops short of talking about the MS, because it's not his story to tell.

I'm not quite ready for the reactions to this. I've spent the last handful of days and nights reassuring myself that it's another remarkable, ridiculous coincidence. Like, it has to be! I *refuse* to entertain the silly notion that there's something supernatural afoot, which Jenna appears to be clinging to. It must be the depression. Both her and David are going through so much mentally, they're probably more susceptible to superstition. Why else would two people so far apart in age and so different from one another in every way, shape and form believe that a dead woman's garden has some sort of . . . fey-like force about it? Jenna even insisted on bringing the damn *cat* with her today, as if somehow the garden will heal him of – whatever is wrong with him! She stuck some grass through the bars of his cage, hoping he'd eat it. Now, the cat is off somewhere in the glasshouse. The poor sod is probably traumatised from the bus ride here.

'It took, like, five minutes for it to click,' Peter finishes eventually. 'Mary looks really different now,' he looks my way, 'I'm sure we both do. I was a right emo back then. But I just couldn't *believe* it . . . What are the odds?'

'That's mad,' says Tadhg.

'Oh my God!' flaps Jordanne.

Alice looks utterly gobsmacked.

When nobody inquires about why Peter was in my mam's house, I finally release the air in my lungs and uncross my arms.

We all spread out a little. David shakes the photo. 'Holy moly, *Mary Walker*. It's marvellous. We're connecting the dots much faster than I anticipated we would!'

This is my opportunity to put the magical misapprehensions to bed. 'What dots?' I ask it as innocently as I can.

Tadhg and Jordanne mirror one another's curiosity.

'*What dots?*' Jenna mimics me. She leans into Nathan, who she is – bizarrely – linking arms with.

I raise an eyebrow.

'You know what he means, Rosie. We all do.'

Moss barks from Peter's feet as David looks over me. 'I suppose you think I'm a daffy old codger too, like he does.' David points at Peter with the photo. Is Peter *with me* on this? 'That's OK. That's all right. This is all part of the project.'

'I – it's unfair to put me on the spot,' I say defensively. 'Surely, I'm not the only person here – aside from Peter – who thinks the idea that we're all here because of June, for "a reason", is a bit, well' – I self-filter on the spot, running through words that express what I mean to say without offending, because I want to say *insane* but I settle for – 'implausible.'

Shuffling feet. Pronounced breathing.

'Have to agree with Rosie,' Tadhg says, standing tall. We stare at each other and silently acknowledge the fact that we're very much physically attracted to one another. It can't be helped and neither of us knows what to do about it, so we've just been ignoring it and allowing it to simply be, without expectation. Pesky pheromones. I mean, I don't even really *know* Tadhg yet. In another time and place, perhaps we'd have bonded emotionally. But this is the world in which not one of us has an available heart to share.

'Ditto.' Nathan looks down at Jenna, whose face has dropped a good half an inch. 'I know *you* think some divine intervention is happening, and that's fine. See, I'm playing with this thing called *tolerance*, 'cause if I don't figure it out, I'll have no one left. Turns out I basically hate most people's opinions . . .' He laughs in an annoying attempt to derail the conversation that we all absolutely need to have together.

'Alice. What about you?' I ask, half-hoping a bolt of lightning will strike her and get her talking. She shrugs her shoulders and mouths something that could be the start of a thousand different words, then she looks at David like a love-heart-eyes emoji.

'Jordanne?'

Jordanne grabs her belly like she always does and looks at Peter of all people. 'I – sorry. I don't know.'

Peter's face can't settle on an expression. 'Well. Obviously, it all seems a bit mad. My mom knew *their* mom,' he starts, glancing at me again. 'She died here, her ashes are here. Moss's leg. We all saw that,' he says, and Moss jumps onto Peter looking for attention. 'Her "magic flowers", my wish after eating one . . . well, that doesn't count. I only meant that as a funny story. And, look, *sure*, Dad ended up getting over his fear of going inside the house because Mom *happened* to have told that Frank guy over the road Dad's number, and we put up all those fairy lights, which made Frank call – but it – that – it's all *random*. There's no reason to get spooked—'

'Not just all that,' Jenna interrupts. 'I found a note. Around the back of the glasshouse. I wanted to –' She stops herself, recomposes. 'I was considering doing something stupid and I found a note that told me not to. It was intended for me, somehow, I – I know it was. Because Rosie also found a message from June, with the same handwriting . . . on the back of a picture, like *this* one' – she says, pointing at the photo of Mam and June – 'at the party.'

'It didn't "tell you not to", and it *wasn't* the same handwriting,' I say. A condescending smile forces itself onto my face.

'It was. I saw and it was.'

'What's this?' Peter asks. 'You never said . . .'

Don't you start! I say it with my eyes, then: 'Nothing. It was nothing.'

'It was *something*,' David cuts in, holding his hands up. 'In my humble opinion, of course. You're entitled to believe what you like. But I've found many's the letter from my wife in blue biro and I know her writing when I see it.'

Sweet mother of Jesus *Christ* . . .

'What did it say?' Peter pushes his glasses up his nose and tries to appear less interested than he very clearly is.

'It was an old letter to your dad, to *you*, David, on the back of a photo. The one of June and Peter on the side table.' They're all waiting for me to tell the story. No bloody way! I'm not getting into the *Rosie and Peter Show Episode 49* with this lot. I can't explain why I was so drunkenly taken aback by reading the words 'letting go' *without* telling them all about the song Peter wrote for me . . .

'It was. But it resonated with you in the moment that you found it, did it not? It is my belief that the message on that photograph was addressed to both of us at different times.'

I step back and bring my fingers to my temples in frustration. 'I know you want to feel connected to your wife, David, but all this, it's – this is, just – what's the word – what's the word – *Peter*, you said it the other day – begins with S?'

'Serendipity,' Peter finishes for me. His goofy smile. God, that wonderful smile.

I feel Jenna's eyes on me like laser beams. 'Yeah. Yeah! All of this stuff . . . it's *chance*. It's not—'

'Never mind this,' David says, flapping the photo. 'You bought two crystal bracelets from my wife's shop!'

'What?' Jenna asks, listening raptly. 'The one you bought me years ago? That was June's shop?'

'Tír na nÓg.' David smiles, then he looks directly at Nathan. Nathan's mouth hangs open.

'Sorry, sorry, what am I missing? *I know that shop!* Sorry, hardly slept, Harry's having a tough time, hard to keep up, I'm in another world, ha . . .' Jordanne rubs her belly extra hard, to remind us all that she's pregnant and exhausted and pregnant and *pregnant*.

I'm losing my patience.

Nathan swallows. 'I – worked there. Two summers selling salt lamps and incense sticks.'

'Oh, come now, you did a whole lot more than that,' David interjects. 'But yes! Nathan worked in June's shop. Customers loved him. Great energy, this boy . . . That's where he bonded with my son.'

Peter looks far too gobsmacked for my liking.

'Sorry, *sorry*, are we talking about Tír na nÓg? It was just off Temple Bar, purple walls, yellow shutters, yellow floors – *that* shop?'

'Precisely,' David says.

'They sold the – the baby tea I used to drink all the time, before Harry came along!' Jordanne's smile reaches her bloodshot eyes.

I'm not able for this.

David starts laughing. He looks at me as if to say *You see?* 'June dried and crushed the tea's raspberry leaves herself, you know, right here at the house! She'd harvest after the dew evaporated, before the plant bloomed . . . That was the trick! We discovered that the leaves turned bitter once it started to bloom, and—'

Finally, Peter speaks some sense. 'Dad, Temple Bar . . . kind of hard to miss a big purple shopfront in the middle of the city. Doesn't necessarily *mean* anything.'

'Oh, but let's continue, then! Alice here—'

'Treated June in hospital and made a flipping "prophecy", OK, OK, we get it!' I snap. 'You've really gone down that rabbit hole, haven't you? You're perceiving a – a pattern – where there is none—'

'Hang on,' Peter starts, 'you treated my mom? Alice?'

Alice smiles so much that dimples appear in her lined cheeks. She nods excitedly.

Peter turns to me. Gathers himself. 'How come you knew that and I didn't?'

Moss barks again.

I start to chew my cheeks.

Jenna has this look on her face that tells me whatever irrational and chaotic thoughts she's been experiencing are being confirmed by this daft conversation. This *can't* be good for her. I'm fit to scream!

David answers Peter for me. 'Your mother, her death . . . I don't like to saddle you with thoughts of that. It was hard enough the first time. Rosie and I had a chat one evening—'

'Prophecy?' Tadhg cuts in. 'What does that even . . . mean?'

'Tadhg!' I snap, throwing an arm out to point at him. '*He* has no connection to June. None at all.'

Everyone's eyes are on him like he's about to divulge the meaning of life.

He shifts on his feet. 'She's right. I don't recognise her.' Tadhg nods at the photo in David's hand that now hangs by his side. 'Never been to that shop either. This is all a bit . . . out there. For me.' He rubs his hands together, clearly uncomfortable. 'David. I thought you just wanted to do some research on . . . whether or not us . . . getting together – fixing up the garden, getting to know each other. If it would – help us . . . with how we're feeling. Not what I expected when I sent the e-mail, but sure—'

Calm flows out from David; his sense that everything is as it should be. 'What e-mail?'

Tadhg's eyes look over at David. Then at me. Back to David. 'For . . . bereavement support.'

David doesn't appear to know what Tadhg is talking about.

'I e-mailed Teaghlach family support services. Found the address through citizen's information . . . was looking for grief counselling. About six months ago. And you—'

'I called. I don't do e-mail.'

'Yeah. But . . . this is – that. Right?'

David shakes his head. 'I'm not from Teaghlach. You—'

'Assumed. Well, yeah. Haven't even logged into my e-mail since you rang . . .'

I look sideways at Peter. He's all ears, all misty-eyed hope. Like the rest of them. I can't believe this shit.

'But, then . . . how?'

'You did some rewiring for me some years ago, yes?'

'In the house there? I did, yeah.' Tadhg pre-emptively crosses his arms against whatever David is about to tell him. 'But, sure, I work a forty-hour week. I've wired half the houses between here and Louth.'

'You left your card, which had your number.'

'So? I never met your wife.'

'Well, she insisted that I keep your contact details. She stuck your card behind a fridge magnet. I found it sandwiched between two photographs with notes from June, photos of our family here in the garden . . . the photos and notes that stirred me down this path! Pulling you all together, choosing *this location* . . .'

Jordanne gasps, like she's just won the Lotto.

Nathan starts clapping.

Jenna whispers, 'I knew it!'

No. No, no, no. 'She wanted to keep his details because he's *an electrician*,' I say derisively. 'It's nice to know a good electrician. They're hard to come by!'

'Why would you just . . . *randomly* ring me. And ask if I want to – enrol in some – group project. To help with – I mean – you *knew* I was – struggling. How?'

'June—'

Before David has a chance to respond, my hands fly up in the air. 'That's it. Enough is enough. Peter, tell him? How is this supposed to help any of us? How is this supposed to help him with his own grief? This – *unhealthy obsession* with June, it's—'

'I'm here. Please don't speak of me like I'm not.'

I ignore him. 'Peter?'

'I'll show you,' Jenna says then, mustering more confidence than I've seen her exude since she moved in. 'Wait, just wait.' She pulls her sleeves back and marches over to the glasshouse. 'Bert! *Psshhhwshhhwshhh!* Bertie!'

'I thought the cat was deaf . . .'

'Maybe he isn't deaf any more,' she fires back at me. 'Bert! C'mere! I have treats!' Jenna pulls a small orange bag of chicken-liver snacks from her pocket.

The cat doesn't come. As much as I want to be proven right, I feel bad – Jenna seems stunned, like it was a sure thing that the crusty creature would emerge, suddenly able to hear her call.

'Just. Hang on.' She vanishes. We all wait together, totally absorbed in Jenna's determination. Seconds pass. A couple of phones beep; others vibrate in pockets and bags. Moss attempts to run at the glasshouse, but Peter holds him back on his leash.

Nathan checks his phone. He confirms the simultaneous buzzing was the group chat.

'Shit!'

'What?' Jordanne asks worriedly.

'Iz.' Nathan glances at Peter. 'She's resurfaced. First time since Hitlergate. Shared a selfie – no message, but—'

'At last,' David starts. 'I've missed our Izzy.'

'Looks like she's – in hospital.' Nathan gulps. 'Look at her feeding tube! OhmyGod!'

'It's the best place for her,' I say. 'This obviously wasn't going to help her, in her condition.' Perhaps my pessimism is merging with my distaste for all of the grand-tapestry talk, but I'm well past caring about insulting David and how he's going about all this.

And now I'm worried all this is going to make her worse.

Jordanne, Nathan and Tadhg prepare a group reply to Izzy. Peter is distracted – he asks David about Alice and her time with June on the ward. But when Jenna appears in the glasshouse doorway, everyone stops what they're doing and looks her way. Walking devastation, Jenna's Doc Martens crunch against the ground as she carries the cat's cage back towards us. The cat is just about visible through rusted bars.

He looks . . . unchanged.

'No luck?' Peter asks Jenna earnestly.

She looks so small in her big boots now. 'Nope. He still won't let me touch him. He – he went for me.' She displays her palm, freshly scratched. 'So. Maybe you're right,' she says to me, wilting. 'Maybe it is all chance. *Luck*,' she says, repeating Peter. All the life that was sparking from her not ten minutes ago is gone.

David hands the photo of Mam and June to Jenna. He winks at her. Whispers something that I miss. 'Right,' he says then, 'animals inside and out of the cold. Peter, please give Bertie and Moss some fresh water from the well – it's finally back up and running. Like I said in the chat, today I'll be teaching you all my *favourite* meditation technique—'

'Finally!' I don't mean to say it out loud, but I don't regret it either. *This* is what we're here for.

Jenna hands Bertie's cage over to Peter and sadly watches them disappear out the side gate.

'Each of you please settle on a word or an object . . . have a think, and pick something you like, because you'll be thinking this same word or object over and over and over again while we rid this garden of these blasted weeds . . . but hear me, it's a year-round job . . .'

Tadhg looks at me, dumbstruck.

Nathan and Jordanne are both at a loss for words.

And Alice. She's up on her toes, desperately excited for the session to begin, like everything we just talked about didn't faze her one little bit.

JENNA

I'm sure you'll agree that Tuesday is the worst day of any week, but this week it simply means I survived another Monday.

At least there's that.

Last night I had the most realistic dream where I came on to Peter. I can't get it out of my head. Awkward limbs on limbs. My tongue searching for his. Licking his teeth. Him half-talking into my mouth. Incisors clashing. An unpleasant shiver runs through me from the memory alone, the kind I feel when I hear two pieces of Styrofoam rubbing together. Me searching for his hands in darkness, him whimpering and uncomfortable . . .

Face down in Rosie's bed, I prepare myself for another entirely unremarkable series of forgetful hours. Nathan's working and there's no group session to look forward to for the guts of a week. The vet can't see Bertie until Friday lunchtime, either. So, there's *nothing*. Nothing I have to get up for right now.

Surely there's more to life than my experience of it so far? Life *can't* be this terrible for all of the smiling people on Instagram. There's *no way* the whole world is populated by Oscar-winning actors! Imagine my life was *The Truman Show* . . . you'd have to pay people to watch. Seriously, I'm bored of being awake already.

I breathe in Rosie's smell on the pillow. Fairy Non-Bio mixed with that too-strong perfume she wears. She's out.

Probably with Peter.

My brain replays the certainty I saw in Nathan's eyes: *Peter is in love with her, Peter is in love with her, Peter is in love with her*; my stomach turns over and over like a pancake.

Time passes.

I'm face up now, looking around Rosie's bedroom at everything she's accumulated and nobody to share any of it with. You know, even when distance had its arms stretched out between us, holding us so far apart that we'd hardly recognise one another upon uniting, I did – deep down – want my only sibling to end up with someone like Peter Dolan. I really, *really* want to be happy for Rosie.

And look, maybe there are plenty of Peter Dolans in the world: men who would love me like that, men with talent, allure, hearts full of goodness. The issue is that the promise of 'maybe' isn't enough to keep me pushing on through this pain any more.

Really. I can't do it.

The hope of a career I'd actually *like*, that I'd be good

at, is hanging on a loose nail: Peter's album launch this summer might completely flop after what happened at Christmas and that album-cover gig – I was starting to believe it might be the only available ticket to a new life, that June really had somehow prodded us into one another's lives so I'd be saved by a rare shot at true happiness. As I've been chipping away at the concept design in my sketchpad I've found myself fantasising about earning a living solely through commissions. But I think that train left early without me on it.

Rosie must be right, about all of it.

At this point I'm not certain the pain would stop even if the universe itself handed me a curvaceous body to flaunt in place of this hipless hell-hole that I live in, and a support network of vivacious sweethearts like Nathan, and my dream cottage with some chickens out the back and a husband like Peter Dolan, and a time machine for poor Bertie. Maybe I'm one of the unlucky few – broken beyond repair. You do hear about them: people who seemingly have everything they need to make it through the years that stretch ahead, yet they just don't feel like they've been cut from the correct cloth, the one everyone else in this world is made from. And without certainty, the prospect of continuing to fight feels – flimsy, so flimsy I doubt it'll hold me up much longer.

The Tadhgs of this world say things like *it's only up from here*. But there's only so much depression one person can absorb without becoming so heavy that they sink.

Like today.

I've no *idea* how long I've been lying here.

And it's just this, every day, while other people get to be pregnant, get to eat ice cream by the seaside, get to have guys like Peter Dolan fall in love with them. The only time I ever feel anything close to how I remember happiness is when we're in the garden at Avalon, fingers in the soil, feeling the rhythms of nature, chatting about everything and nothing – because it's not just *me*, it's *we*; because there, I'm working towards something, and there's so much going on, I don't have time to ruminate like this . . .

Eventually, the ring of a phone that's not mine pulls me up from the water.

I let it ring out.

Again, it rings.

When it starts up a third time, I growl. I actually *growl*. Headaches are a lot to contend with when you can't be trusted with painkillers.

My feet drag me over to Rosie's dressing table, where the light from her phone is visible. I pick it up to turn it to silent and see three little letters on the screen that make my chest ache more than my head already does.

Mam.

Honestly, I hardly remember what her voice sounds like. How sad is that? That little bump on Jordanne's body, growing bigger by the week – like that, I was inside the woman on the other end of the line, someone who still exists, back in Stoneybatter, knowing I've chosen a life without her in it.

I feel oddly impelled to answer. Just to hear her voice one last time. Fear holds me still. My hand hovers over 'slide to answer'.

Fuck it.

I've nothing to lose, do I?

My finger swipes over glass.

She's . . . hysterical. 'Rosie? Rosie, pet! It's Bertie – he's *here*! After all these years! God help me, am I going mad? How could he possibly have found his way back here? I thought you girls keep him *inside*?'

My heart rate rises. 'Mam, calm down – can you say that again?'

'Your sister's cat, Bertie! I swear, it's him – out the back!'

Mam can't tell our voices apart. She never could. She sounds so upset. 'Describe the cat?' I ask, disbelieving.

I tear through the apartment looking for Bertie as she talks. 'No tail. Long fur . . . creamy, and raggedy, the darker bits around his ears and face, dark legs, *it's him*! Poor divil looks shattered, Rosie. Come early today. I can't let him in, my allergies . . .' Her voice is full of sympathy. 'And after that fall, I'm afraid of my life to get down on my hands and knees – but he looks like he could do with some water. He looks like he's walked five hundred miles, this one!'

In cat miles, the two and a half miles between Grand Canal Dock and Stoneybatter probably is about five hundred miles.

Bertie isn't here, and the front door was left ajar.

I tell Mam that I'm on my way.

ROSIE

Nothing exists outside of Peter's bedroom. Narrow beams of light across the ceiling and bursts of colour up and down the walls. His stuff and his scent and this kiss.

Soon, nothing exists – only us – my hair and dewy skin, his fingers stroking my cheek like he's combing grass.

'Is this so hard?'

Part of me wants to make a silly, dirty joke – that actually *yes, Peter, why it* is *hard, har har* – but I shh the urge. I know exactly what Peter means, even though I barely know how to put words to it. We've spent the whole afternoon having sex, something we've done *countless* times before: the same sexual acts, the same general behaviours, but something's different this time. There's a different intention behind the sex. Visceral affection guides my every move. I've finally succumbed to what it is Peter's been craving and he's delighting in teasing me: this eye contact is easy, like breathing.

Peter's lying on top of me with his jeans only-recently-pulled-up back down somewhere around his ankles. He pushes himself into me slowly as the tips of our chins touch. He has his head tilted back, so he can watch how my eyes change – they seek every little detail while he holds himself still inside me for a beat: the most exquisite of long pauses. I arch my back and thrust my hips every time he pulls from me. His kaleidoscope eyes are all I can see, and then they aren't his eyes because we've gone somewhere else. We aren't any more. He makes love to me like a song. We taste each other and pant with yearning for more, more.

Wet lips on smooth flesh.

Upside down, inside out.

A – a thump?

Wait.

I'm back in my body. My heart hammers as the room comes into focus.

Peter is upright – gripping his forehead – making a loud and long *ahhhhhh* sound.

I catch my breath. 'How did you manage that? The headboard?'

'Over-excited,' he breathes. 'Forgot – about – surroundings.'

'Aw, God love you.' I laugh.

Peter's body jolts. It's like I just shot him in the chest with a revolver. He peers through the fingers clamped around his face. 'I love you, too.'

Anxiety shoots through my middle. My eyes widen as I

become aware of my thoughts again. They're building up in a big pile on the conveyor belt . . . 'What?'

'Huh?'

The shift between us is dizzying.

'You said – I said . . .'

Peter bites his lip.

'I just meant – *God love you* – as in, you know, expressing sympathy – your head – that sounded painful.'

A humble nod. He must have misheard 'God love you' as 'God, I love you.'

Why doesn't he look as awkward as I feel?

'I do, though, you know. Love you,' he says.

I realise that I do know; that it terrifies me, so much that I can't even speak. But I don't have to. He reads me like I'm his own lyrics.

'Now. Where were we?'

'I'm not sure,' I say softly. 'But I'd like to go back, please.' Eye contact during sex and 'I love you' might be on the same continent, but I'm pretty sure there are still plenty of rivers and lakes and forests between them . . .

At least, on *my* map there are.

I might not be able to lay it all out on the table like Peter does, but here, in a tangle with him, my body can say to Peter what my brain won't allow my words to say: I love you and I love you, it's *frightening* how I love you. Words can lie, even thoughts can lie, but bodies don't know how.

JENNA

I didn't bring Bertie's cage to Stoneybatter. Something about the sorrow in Mam's voice told me *this is it*: he found his way back to his first home to die somewhere familiar.

Just . . . don't ask me how he managed it.

The garden didn't heal him. It was all in my head. This is an independent incident. It has to be.

White ribbons of cloud curve above Stoneywey Road. I ring the doorbell, the very same flecks of white paint spotted across it after all these years of missed calls, missed birthdays, memories that never had a chance to be. I wait for my mother to let me in and I wonder what we'll say to each other. Will she go quiet? Will she shout at me? Will she even recognise me?

The click of the front door. Mam stands there with her walker, like the past five years didn't happen at all, like seeing me in the doorway is nothing new, like I've done nothing wrong whatsoever. Her eyes are pink from the cat allergy and her hair's still bottle red . . . she's got that same old housecoat on – the one with the pilling in the armpits and the big cocoa stains all over the flaps that sit against her thighs. 'Come in here out of that cold,' she says, looking up at the white sky, all glassy-eyed concern, 'before yer one in there accuses me of letting you catch pneumonia.'

I find a comfort in her voice that I don't remember appreciating before. It melts away the tension in my shoulders, my neck, my jaw. Sure enough, Dotty's little eyes are just visible through her net curtains. 'You can't catch pneumonia, Mam – it's not contagious,' I start, wiping my shoes across the battered welcome mat.

'He's been struggling for air this past half-hour,' Mam says, leading me through to the sitting room. It's completely unchanged apart from the feature wall around the fireplace – it used to be ugly floral wallpaper but Rosie has painted it lavender. I can tell Rosie did it because there's visible stains throughout the paint due to poor wall preparation, and there are bubbles all over it: it's a Rosie job if ever I saw one. 'Sit down there for a minute first, get heat into your bones, will you? You'll catch your death out there like that.' She flaps her hands and looks disapproving of my outfit choice.

The fire is smouldering. 'How did you manage that?' I ask Mam, eyeing the fire.

'Emma did that, pet.'

I swallow. I don't want to admit that I don't know who Emma is. It's embarrassing – not only that I've not asked Rosie anything about what's been going on in my mother's life, but that a stranger has to come to help Mam when I'm usually horizontal, scrolling online, free as a bird . . .

Mam grabs a wool coat she had strewn over the couch and throws it at me.

'Um, so, where is he?' I ask, catching it.

'The shed. In his spot. Sorry, I'm not dawdling, I just – it's cold, and—'

A smile breaks across my face. 'I'm a big girl now.'

'Bigger than I remember.' She scans my face. Her lip quivers. 'Besides, motherhood doesn't end when your child grows up or – if they don't visit for a while.'

A while, she says. Without words, I pull her coat onto my body to the crackle of the fire. Then I look at Mam. I really *look* at her, and challenge myself to see her as she is, not just as a psychic's prediction of what I might become. I see a kind-hearted woman clinging to an aluminium frame, trying to keep her baby warm.

'You'll always be my baby girl,' she continues. 'And Bertie. He's your baby. I know that, and I'm – I'm *so sorry*.' Her voice breaks. 'Come on. You'll want to be with him. Fetch some clean blankets from the hot press, drop some milk in a bowl. Even if he won't drink it, he'll know we're thinking of him.'

The creak of the shed door. There, beyond the hedge trimmer, the old broken chairs, the cobweb-covered childhood relics, Bertie huddles in his favourite corner, where he slept for most of his long life, his laboured breathing the only sound we can hear apart from the distant thrum of a lawnmower.

Mam isn't able to make it very far into the shed but she does her best – parks herself on the side of the hot tub Bridie loaned us. Nostalgia like lightning: it saw very little daylight, that thing – turned out that none of us liked to get our bare, pasty arses out under the ever-watchful eye of Dotty next door, who Rosie and I dubbed Sauron one Halloween after we saw her hanging out the top window to try to see who found the ring in the barmbrack. I remember Bertie's show-off saunter, us cheering him on after winning scraps with Dotty's cat, Phyllis . . .

It wasn't all bad, was it?

Mam makes herself comfortable. 'Go on. I won't be going anywhere,' she assures me.

Down on the filthy shed floor, I make a bed for Bertie and place the milk bowl as close to his face as I can get it. Gently, I place the backs of my fingers against his forehead. So cold. He doesn't even flinch. I lie down a few inches from him and try to take in every last hair.

David taught us to think of a mantra – a word or phrase to repeat, as a tool to help release our minds – and said that repeating this mantra should prevent our minds from drifting off in other directions. It didn't work for me the first time, out at Avalon, but I try it again now while looking at Bertie and thinking the word 'safe' over and over again. This time, it works. I'm one with the vibration of Bertie's purr. Ready as I'll ever be for his passing. Eventually I start humming a song to soothe him – something from some old musical that I can't even remember the name of.

'Oh, Jenna. This is a very peaceful goodbye for him.'

Mam's gentle voice is like a balm. 'Love knows no boundaries, even death, as they say.'

I turn to Mam and keep my voice soft. 'That sounds like something David Dolan would say. June's husband.'

Mam looks confused.

'Rosie found that picture of you both together . . .'

'Oh yes, June Judge.'

My face goes blank. Here it comes: the dreaded reality, the fear that slashes at me from the shadows in my nightmares.

'I mean June *Dolan*, who was married to David Dolan, he was a doctor. She ran a business in town. Rosie said you two were old school friends . . .'

'Yes, June Judge!' Mam reiterates. 'Judge was her maiden name. We did the Gaeltacht together every summer. She spoke Irish beautifully.'

I sigh, relieved, and lean on my hand, amazed still that a coincidence like this might be real. 'What was she like?'

'Ah, June was – something else. All the boys fancied her, you know. I was awful jealous. She had the big hair and the mad laugh. She sang, she – she was a free spirit. Never cared about what people thought of her. I envied that.' Mam flattens her hair then refolds her arms. 'Sometimes I'd play piano and she'd sing, and all eyes would be on her. But she appreciated my playing. She asked me to tutor her son. He was a dream, that boy. Patrick. Or maybe he was a Paul? But he took to it like a duck to water.'

Mam's lapse in memory tries to faze me but I don't allow it. 'It's weird,' I say, focused on June, 'I never met her, and

I know so little about her, but it's like I *knew* her, or like
– like I know her now. Does that sound stupid?'

'You're not a stupid girl.' Mam smiles at me. 'You know I
still talk to Bridie when I'm here on my own?'

'Oh yeah?'

She nods. 'If something funny happens, I'll tell her out
loud. I say goodnight to her when I'm going to sleep.'

In a world where I make it to old age, am I as close to
Rosie as Mam was to Bridie? Bertie's lungs make some
awful sounds, pulling me from the thought. 'And do you
ever feel like – Bridie—'

'Hears me? I know she does. She doesn't answer, but
that's fine.'

Just like that. So sincere. 'I have this feeling that June
was fun and strong-minded. Thoughtful. And it's not just
because David talks about her so much . . .'

'She was thoughtful. You girls nowadays, you share your
– your quotes – on *the Instagram* – well, back in our day,
we'd have to find quotes in books, fold the pages, or you'd
bookmark them, to re-read them. June loved to translate
her favourite quotes into Irish, and she'd mark them for
people she cared for. I still have some inside, on the shelf,
books she gave me, quotes she shared with me that she
thought I'd like—'

Bertie bellows. It snaps me out of the belief, beckoning
once again . . .

'It's OK, little guy. You're OK.' I readjust myself so that
my head is super close to him. His breathing has slowed
right down.

'Sing for him again, pet. He liked that.'

Then it happens. Right there, in the dirty old shed, I bid farewell to my four-legged rock. The planet doesn't implode like I expected it to, but a special kind of sadness stuffs me full: the bitter cold of death touched by the hint of warm, slanted light I didn't expect to radiate from my mother. I curl into the foetal position and cover my face as my body shakes with sobs.

An eternity passes before I sit up and cover Bertie's still, age-worn body with a clean towel.

What now?

It's darker. I'm thirsty. Do I go home? Stay here? When does Rosie get here?

Mam breaks the silence. 'Is fearr an t-áthas ar chruinniú arís ná an pian a bhaineann le scaradh.'

'Sorry?'

'One of June's quotes, that,' she says. "The pain of parting is nothing to the joy of meeting again." It's Charles Dickens.'

My head spins. She remembers that, and she can't remember Peter's name!

'Bertie has just moved along, is all. There aren't many words for it, pet, but you understand that, you – you *feel* June. You'll feel that little fella, too.'

All I can do is listen to her, blown away by her lightness and how much I need it. When I lived here, Mam would come alive in these rare moments of sharpness, and back then, all it did was instil me with so much fear for her next episode of forgetfulness. But now, I find it a beautiful thing to behold: she's still in there!

She stands up off the hot tub slowly, leaning against her walker. 'Still have June's copy of *Nicholas Nickleby* inside, one of her favourites. It's funny you should remind me of June Judge tonight, Jenna,' she goes on, mystified. 'Those words – "nothing to the joy of meeting again" – they got me through these past five years without you. I even wrote them in the back of my address book. And they were bang on the money! My God am I glad to see you again.'

It sinks into me slow, like rising damp, that Bertie meandered back here with the purpose of bringing my mother back into my life – that he wanted to pass the torch to someone else, so I'd consider hanging on. *Maybe I am losing the actual plot* – a cat couldn't know they were saving a life, couldn't know a person so well. Am I overreaching? I must be.

By the fire, I tell Mam all of my unfounded suspicions about what's been going on with David and the group. She might forget everything I'm saying, but for the first time in my life that awareness doesn't hold me back. It's not like I'm going to suddenly start rocking up every weekend for tea and scones, or texting her about my day-to-day musings, but it's as though I'm suddenly capable of hearing the crisp, clear voice of my intuition and it's telling me that this is somehow important.

We don't embrace; there's no big conversation about how much of a disappointing daughter I've been: it's just shared contemplation and the consolation of my mother's presence.

ROSIE

Nothing could have prepared me for the sight. The pair of them! Eating cheese toasties! Together! Smiles on their faces, nonetheless.

I should be thrilled. But I'm only nerves on legs.

I rocked up to Mam's at the usual time, pure floating for the first time in God knows how long after my afternoon in bed with Peter. And before I even had a chance to say hello, Mam asked me to join her in the hallway, closed over the kitchen door, hushedly told me – in no uncertain terms – that family 'don't come with conditions', that I need to 'forgive the past' . . .

Sure. Nothing to see here, folks! Well, the cat is stone-cold dead out the back, and we've not spoken to each other in forever, *also* we're speculating about whether or not a woman who died four years ago had (well, *has*) some kind of magical powers. But it's all good! Carry on with yourselves!

My foot is shaking under the coffee table. Mam is in her

armchair; myself and Jenna are on the settee, feet – and worlds – apart. I want to move the conversation away from the Dolans in case Mam brings up my non-relationship with Peter.

Jenna still hasn't got a clue.

'And you better hear me when I tell you I was a sceptic! But, listen, I'd have tried *anything* for the pain, so I said, "June, go on. Give me a go." She brought me out the back of Tír na nÓg, had me lie on – "a plinth", I think she called it. She dimmed the lights and put on this nice CD and then, well, she moved around my whole body, holding her hands at a distance from my skin as she moved – like this,' Mam gushes to Jenna. She's on about some kind of woo-woo spiritual healing crap June was into.

Jenna is all ears, her back straight and her eyes massive.

'She held my head in her hands, popped them under my neck – right here – she held my hips, my knees . . . but she focused on my back. I'd told her it was at me – small kids will do that to you, pet. You'll know, one day!' Mam laughs.

I eyeball Jenna to suss her reaction.

'Yeah. Maybe,' she says. The liar. If *I* can't bear the thought, I'm not sure how *she* can. She can't even clean up after herself, never mind giving birth. The judgement whips out of nowhere and behind it, holding it, the realisation that this is actually a good sign. Jenna is talking about a possible future. Of course, she might just be indulging Mam, but I can't imagine that she'd express a false interest in something as big as motherhood. And come to think of it, she was always one for baby dolls, while I'd play with toy cars and mini dinosaurs . . .

'Then, when June placed her hands on my lower back, I felt this – this *heat*.'

'No way,' Jenna says, overly enthusiastic.

My foot is shaking so much now, I worry my shoe will fly into the air and smash the TV.

'Yes way! Then, June asked me to turn over on to my front. Again, when she laid her hands on my hands, I felt this intense heat!'

'Wow!'

'I remember she told me to wear the colour deep red, for healing – and to eat red fruit and vegetables, like apples and red berries, and peppers, and radishes – and to light a deep-red-coloured candle. She said it would provide me with strength and boost my energy and even make me feel more connected to my physical body, which I was *really* starting to hate because it was failing me.'

Oh, please.

'The colour has become significant for me. I have this red heat pack upstairs that smells of roses – I can warm it up in the microwave, to throw across my shoul—'

'I bought you that,' I say flatly, interrupting the intense gaze between the two of them.

Mam looks at me like she's a balloon I've tried to stab with a pin. 'I know you did, but – my point is just that – the *colour*—'

'You don't eat fruit. Or veg. You *never* light candles. I'm sorry, but you're both desperately looking for signs here and I'm just, I'm *really* struggling.' I squash up my face and wipe my palms against my jeans.

'We are not!' Mam seems to be playing up how insulted she is to appear to side with my sister. 'Maybe *you* are dismissing signs as—'

'Oh, "signs" me hole. Mam. You're *in pain. All the time.*' A flurry of compensatory blinks.

'If whatever June performed on you worked, you wouldn't have MS, would you? You'd be symptom-free, always. You'd be out there living your life, teaching piano lessons, maybe dating Vincent from down the shop. But you're not.'

'Rosie. Jesus Christ.' The look of disgust on Jenna's face would curdle milk. 'Do you have to be such a—?'

'Such a what?' I sense that I look a little manic.

Mam claps her hands together. 'Enough. I've waited a long time to have you two here with me, together. And Rosie, by all means, have your views. But *we* feel that June – she had a part to play in us sitting here together now, and that's not us being a pair of ninnies, is it, Jenna?'

'We? It's "we" now?'

'Stop being so uptight. This is basically Bertie's funeral, and you're ruining it,' Jenna says solemnly.

This is all just . . . too much. I genuinely can't take the two of them gawping at me like this. 'The cat was ancient—'

'*Bertie.* Look, you wouldn't get it. You *eat* animals.'

My ears turn hot with a shame I never feel while eating a Big Mac. 'Eh . . . so does she!' Childishly, I point at my mam as I realise: I'm regressing. It's like a dormant part of

my brain has been activated, like all of my repressed resentment is gasping for fresh air. Mam gets all flustered, and
seeing that makes me feel terrible. 'Here, I'll head,' I say in
a breath. 'Jenna, be a pet and clear up the dishes. It's only
been *years*. Think it's your turn.'

I slam the door.

Slam it!

What. Is. Wrong. With. Me?

As soon as I'm outside and free of Dottie's eyeline, I send
Peter a voice message. 'I'm staying over tonight. Bagsy big
spoon.'

JENNA

Izzy's return that Saturday is a welcome distraction from my grief. None of us expected to see Izzy again, but Peter drove by her family home again this morning anyway, and there she was waiting by the front wall, hunched over her phone, like today was first day back to school after summer holidays. Peter pulled in, hopped out and wrapped his arms around her. I watched through the window as Moss jumped and barked around them, straining to hear the words being exchanged over the radio, afraid to blink in case I missed something. Curiosity ate that much of me I'm surprised I didn't make it to Avalon as thin as Izzy.

Rosie appeared to be in the same boat: I watched her from one row behind, ferociously chewing her cheeks, staring Peter out of it, with poor Tadhg to her right trying his best to catch her attention.

Izzy hasn't gained any obvious weight – she's as emaciated

and yellow-skinned as ever, the pallor impossible to disguise with makeup – but there's definitely something different about her. For one thing, she doesn't join us in our tasks right away. She used to be rearing to get going more than any of us. I steal a few looks from the back door, where I'm pulling on wellies, as Izzy glides into the middle of the recently cut grass of the garden. Bizarrely, she pulls off her buckle-covered platforms to walk barefoot. Two laps around the glasshouse (and an array of funny looks thrown behind her back) later, Izzy re-joins us.

'The world can really hear itself think out here, huh.' She chews gum as she speaks; it smacks off her words. 'I missed this – *in there*,' she says of the hospital. 'The days never end in there. You forget what reality sounds like. All the birds are accounted for, anyway. My wee pals!' She looks up into the trees, where the resident choir of birds sing from. Now close up, I notice the sheer amount of pink lip gloss Izzy has doused herself in today. Way more than usual. It's completely at odds with how erratic she appears. I suppose she could've worn the extra make-up to shield herself from the inevitable questions. Nathan, direct and wonderful as ever, acts like everything is perfectly normal. Within minutes, they're discussing the backlash she received after posting the moustachioed photo of Peter.

'I made my Instagram private. You guys probably didn't notice because I have you all approved. The spon con, it's just not worth it,' she says of her paid-for outfit posts. 'People said I was – glorifying the holocaust,' she chokes. 'Like, for real. It was the worst week of my life. I'm such an idiot for posting that photo . . .'

'Nah. The internet has just grown some teeth, and you got bitten,' Nathan says. 'I've been there.' He clears his throat. 'As you know.'

Peter reaches his hand out and gently grips Izzy's shoulder. 'Nate is right. It's not your fault, Iz. I was mad, yeah, but I wasn't mad at *you*.'

She toes a blade of grass, keeps her eyes fixed on her feet. 'But it's done so much damage to your public image.'

Peter stiffens. 'Well. Look. Shit happens. I'm *here*,' he looks around the garden, at our progress, 'because I want to learn to give less fucks about what people I don't even know think about me.'

With Peter's effort, Izzy mellows out as the day goes on; he goes out of his way to put smiles on her face by telling tales about how plants have sex – which, apparently, is a thing. He goes so far as to write an on-the-spot song about bisexual plants while we sow sweet peppers, cucumber and tomato seeds. Izzy laughs her head off, seemingly as dazzled as Jordanne by Peter's unusual burst of energy. He even has Rosie smiling.

Over the other side of the glasshouse, Nathan helps me to start off some basil seeds in pots full of moist compost, to go on the windowsill. The pair of us need to google how to do it. We beg David for our phones, giggling like schoolkids mid-exam who think studying is for losers.

'It's really *not* that difficult,' David says, and shows us how it's done. 'Perhaps the time has come to actually *read* the books on the reading list?' He winks at Nathan, who blows David a kiss after promising to go to the library this week for the fourth time since group started. There's more chance of him coming out as straight than reading *The Complete Gardner's Manual*.

Nathan mists the batch of seeds he's just sown and watches David shrink on his way towards Peter, who's now in the middle of a full-blown stand-up routine about the sex life of clitoria flowers – a pig in shit, *smothered* in attention.

'Alone at last,' Nathan says in an exhale before vaping like this life depends on it.

I finish sprinkling seeds into another tiny pot. Trying to ignore Peter's distant voice is like trying to smile while getting bloods done. But I promised Nathan – and myself – that I'd distance myself. I also promised him I'd try to give up vaping too, but my e-cig is calling my name from my pocket, in the most alluring voice . . .

'So. I think I've finally finished working on my tier system of who here is the most fucked up,' Nathan goes on.

'What are you like!'

'Eh, Sherlock Homes with a better *wardrobe* is what,' he says. 'Well. Wait. I can trust you to keep this to yourself, yeah?' His eyes look me up and down. Then something flickers across his face, a kind of self-awareness taking hold. 'Sorry. Brain thinks everyone's out to get me. It's a constant battle.'

I just offer him the most reassuring look I can muster.

'OK.' A sharp inhale and an even sharper exhale. 'Not sure how acquainted you are with Jordanne . . .'

'I've not spoken with her much yet. Rosie gets on pretty well with her – said she's nice.'

Nathan grits his teeth and breathes through them.

I look at him. He's opening his eyes as wide as they'll go. 'Say it!'

'It's just – it's proper sad, Jenna. You'll think I'm the world's biggest bitch in a minute but I'm just *really uncomfortable* with stuff like this and I can't *not* tell someone and I—'

'I know you, I *get it*, just . . . talk.'

Nathan leans towards me. 'You know how she talks about her son Harry, like, *all the time*?'

'She's a mam. Of course she does.' An image of my mam permeates my mind, her gentle smile, by the fire, with her cup of hot chocolate.

'Was . . .' he says darkly.

I look at Nathan and wait for him to finish his sentence. He doesn't. 'Was what?'

'*Was* a mam.'

I look over at Jordanne, rubbing her pregnant belly, tears of laughter in her eyes as she watches Peter flounce around, telling some story.

'She wouldn't accept my Facebook friend request and that made me curious, 'cause we click,' he explains. 'I thought, what's up with that? Found her on Instagram. Page private. Found her *boyfriend's* Instagram . . . no new posts in, like, two years.'

'You little stalker.' I'm watching Jordanne, waiting for the bomb to fall.

'Found her Twitter. Nothing much to note, just retweets

of charities and shit. But she'd shared a YouTube video link
. . . She has her own YouTube channel . . .'

'No!'

'Well. Nobody watches. But she still posts videos – just
her cleaning her make-up brushes and organising her wardrobe – camera like a potato – five views—'

'Oh, come on. You take forever to get to the—'

He shushes me. 'So, I click into her playlists. And she's
not made her favourites playlist private. It's full of videos
she's bookmarked—'

'I'm familiar with how YouTube works . . .'

'Well.' Nathan blows his breath through his lips so they
flap. 'She's saved all these videos about grieving the death
of a child – from bereaved mothers.'

My throat feels like it's closing up. 'That doesn't mean—'

'*Shh!* I clicked into one of them – it's this lady who is
fall-ing-a-part,' he clicks his fingers to each of the syllables,
'talking about how her kid died when she was six of a rare
heart condition. Anyway, I scroll down to read the comments.
Damn *essay* from Jordanne! Thanking the woman for posting,
talking about how her son died in a car accident.'

'That's – just – that's devastating.' I watch Jordanne smiling
and try to imagine the places her mind has been to. Her
hands are wrapped protectively around her stomach, her
something to live for. The image of June with her arms
around Peter in his school uniform flashes in my mind.
'Maybe she was lying. In the comment.'

'That would be even more fucked up. Who *pretends* their
own kid died?' Anyway. I asked Doctor D about it. He said

that he won't speak on behalf of any of us, blah blah, but he didn't deny it, so my guess is that he knows. Beats me how this is going to help her face up to the truth.' He waves a gloved hand at the glasshouse. 'All *I* know is we need to help her feel safe enough to come clean.'

My eyes follow David as he monitors the rest of them, hands behind his back. I wonder if he's playing his own game of pretend as a coping mechanism, or if he truly believes in the things he's talked about, and I consider whether or not the answer really matters if he's coping, all the while helping others to walk through the fog.

'Where do I rank on this tier system of fucked-upness?' I ask Nathan.

'Do you want this friendship to last or not?'

We're headed to lunch in Seasons café. Rosie is up front in the bus beside Peter this time. I've caught him looking over at her three times already and we've not been in here five minutes.

I'm down the back with Nathan. David and Alice are seated right in front of us, then Izzy and Jordanne ahead of them and Tadhg the next row up, on Moss duty. Tadhg is much looser than he was at our first group session. I smile to myself as he whispers endearments into the dog's ear.

They're winding Peter up about the shenanigans at Christmas now: Nathan, Tadhg, Jordanne and Izzy. It's the first time since everything happened that the dust has settled enough for any of us to feel able to draw shapes in it.

'Ah. Man,' Tadhg says. 'Seriously, though. A joke, it is. That people just . . . believe the headlines.'

'Many headlines are simply summaries of facts,' David protests.

Peter drums his finger on the steering wheel. 'Dad, he's not saying *all* headlines are bullshit. Just that *some of them* are bullshit. I'd actually argue that *most of them* are bullshit. Because you click in and you scroll down and you read the small print and it's got nothing to do with the damn headline, and—'

'Yes! *YES!* Sorry! Ha, sorry for cutting you off,' Jordanne says, 'but this is *so true*. You see this all the time as a parent.' Nathan grabs my arm. His eyes look ready to explode out of his head. 'Headlines that play on our emotions, evoking our deepest fears about our children, and we'll always click because if we don't, there's this voice saying "You're a bad parent, you saw those big scary capital letters and – and you didn't click!"'

At least she didn't mention Harry. Oh, the poor woman. Primal empathy wears me like a glove. This numbing of her pain through avoidance of the truth can't be good for her; by numbing the dark, she's got to be numbing the light, too, surely? I have this overwhelming desire to help her feel her way through the labyrinth of pain she's been skirting her way around, even though I hardly know her. It's completely bizarre, like some tribal part of my brain has been activated through spending time with these people week after week.

'Headlines don't really matter,' Izzy starts. 'People believe what they want to believe, at the end of the day.' She blows a bubble with her gum until it pops back over her lips, the pink gloss now mostly swallowed and, in its place, a gooey white film of dead skin.

'Our Izzy is correct. Many of us have a powerful, deep-seated need to support our personal favourite ideology or worldview. Some of us think intuitively when we see head-lines, while others are far more reflective in their thinking.'

'No shade, Doctor D, but what you're getting at is that some people are more likely to believe in conspiracy theories and paranormal BS, while the rest of us live in the real world,' Nathan says, leaning against the chair in front of him, where David sits. He flutters his eyelashes at David, who looks back at him, at a loss for what to say. 'Ms "under-score" spiderqueen, which team are you on?'

Izzy giggles. 'Depends on the subject!'

I notice Alice pulling at David, who discreetly tries to calm her down. I wonder what that's about as Peter jumps in, that cartoonish smile just visible in the rear-view mirror. 'Think what you like, Nate, but Diana's death was no accident. I'll debate any of you into the ground on that one.'

Rosie shakes her head and pinches the skin between her eyes.

Tadhg loudly agrees in his culchie accent.

Jordanne chirps her doubts to Alice, who looks puzzled.

'*Of course*, lowercase Peter is a tinfoil-hat wearer! I suppose you also believe the moon landing was faked?' Izzy exhibits her pre-hospital air of confidence as though, through the project, she's found a burrow to hibernate in till spring

returns. 'I mean, this *is* the guy who makes Hitler gags, so
we can't act surprised, can we?' Izzy says it playfully, swinging
her phone around, making light – once again – of the whole
messed-up situation. A couple of them laugh and join her
in trying to lovingly goad Peter. But as the scene unfolds,
I notice the hairs slowly standing up all over my body in
salutation of the dawn of a long-buried memory – information
I'd assumed inconsequential at the time.

I shoot Peter a worried look.

The colour drains from his baffled face reflected in the
rear-view mirror. He's tilted it so he can see Izzy clearly.
Hysteria swims in his eyes. I've never seen him look like
this. Not in any photo or memory or daydream. 'What did
you just call me, Iz?'

'Sorry?' She looks up. 'I was just – being sarcastic . . .'

His frenzied expression causes her to go quiet for a few
seconds.

'Can't we call you lowercase pete any more?' She quickly
fixes her hair, flattening it against her face, and drops her
phone a little. 'You quitting or something?'

'You didn't call me that.' Everyone's listening. Rosie tries
to talk but Peter gets there first. 'You said lowercase *Peter*.'

'I – I didn't.'

'It's *you*, you – you—'

Before anyone knows what's going on, Peter swerves the
bus in to the side of the road and parks.

'Get out,' he says, his knuckles turning white as he grips
the wheel, like it's his composure.

'What's wrong?' Rosie asks him, all confused.

David smacks his knees. 'What on earth is going on?'

'Get out,' Peter repeats.

'Me? H–here?' Izzy stutters. 'Why?'

'You know why.'

'It's not—' she starts, then lets the sentence fall away.

'Son, what is—?'

Nathan half stands up. 'Why you mad, man?'

'Sorry, *sorry*, I – I don't understand what's—'

'Get the FUCK out.'

Doors slam and people move and there's raised voices and I can't believe it. I hide my face in my hands. Izzy's high-pitched cry from the side of the road snaps me out of my spiral and I look out the window. Peter's taken her phone. He's typing and swiping and she's trying to get it back from him but he's walking away from her too quickly for her to catch up.

Nathan is freaking out. 'Aw, shit – man, *shit* – she's only out of hospital, man—'

'He can't just leave her here. It's *out of the question*! What in *God's* name . . .? Why, Alice, I've never seen him like this in all my years—'

I'm not sure what comes over me then. 'David, I'll stay. Get Peter out of here, away from Izzy . . .'

Rosie shoots me daggers. 'Tell us what's going on, right now.'

'Just take Peter home,' I beg her. They're all waiting for me to explain. 'I think – I think Izzy's been harassing Peter online. Not using her "spiderqueen" account, though. Anonymously.'

Everyone just stares.

'I'll explain – I just – I'll call a taxi, make sure Izzy gets back to her parents.'

Out of nowhere, Alice turns to face me, firm with purpose. She says nothing but, somehow, I'm overcome with the understanding that she'll be joining me. She touches David's arm and locks eyes with him, which seems to dissolve his apprehension. She nods, he nods back, slightly breathless – probably the stress of hearing Izzy crying and Peter shouting on his watch.

I examine Alice's face: grey-tinged skin and jowls and visible blackheads and never-plucked eyebrows surround the kindest eyes.

'It was leading to this, eh, old girl?' David asks her in a hush.

She clears her throat. I hold my breath. '"Save the *spider queen*",' she says to David, her unfamiliar voice hoarse. 'Izzy's username. Our Izzy.' Her eyes dart around as she thinks intently. She looks back to me. 'I don't have a phone to get us out of here, but I'm assuming you do. I've been waiting for this moment for a very long time, Jenna.'

David's head bounces.

'The fuck?' Nathan says, grabbing my leg. 'Jenna, *what*?'

'You – don't – you don't have to understand. I'll call you later, yeah? We *really* have to go,' I say. Peter's voice rises against mine in the distance as both he and Izzy walk up and down the stretch of grass and trees outside, having it out.

'But—'

'Look, Alice might be the only person who can get through to Izzy. If we're wrong, we're wrong, but we can't know unless we go out there and try.'

David beams at me.

Nathan grasps for words as we all watch Peter come at the bus like a bull at a matador. Izzy slumps onto the grass, a rag doll. Her long black hair hides her face from our view but it's clear from how her slight shoulders bounce that she's sobbing to herself.

Alice totters off the bus like it's any other day. Shellshocked, I follow. Peter doesn't even look at me when I brush past him; I can just about feel the heat rising from his skin and he shouts 'Fuck' again after slamming the door. I hear Rosie demand to know why he's kicking Izzy off the bus, but he doesn't answer her. He takes off into the afternoon, just as winter's sun shows her face.

One time I absentmindedly watched a documentary about how most online trolls unmasked turn out not to be strangers after all. This tangerine-coloured, middle-aged man with a blond quiff dramatically told the camera that, more often than not, victims of the most twisted of anonymous bullying have personally met the culprits. But I could never have anticipated this. Izzy! Not in *a million years*. She's the friendliest, loveliest woman . . . and with her own virtual demons to slay. My brain can't wrap itself around the thought that – all this time – she's been hounding Peter using fake accounts.

She's trembling. Furiously typing on her phone. Eyeballing us like we're about to shout at her, too. I hang back like a lost duckling; meanwhile, Alice sits beside Izzy on soggy winter grass. Only then do I realise we're outside someone's front garden: some kids are hopping on a trampoline about twenty metres away. One of them has stopped and is watching, finger up her nose. She shouts that she's going in to 'tell Mam!'

Alice pulls a balled-up tissue from the pocket of a heavy cardigan she's wearing underneath her raincoat. She offers it to Izzy, who swats it away.

'My dad's going to pick me up – don't worry about me,' she snaps, wiping the snot away with her sleeve. 'I don't want to talk about it and I don't want pity!'

'How about a story, then?' Izzy drops her phone, stunned to hear Alice speak for the first time. 'I've always liked you, Izzy. I never had a daughter, always wanted one, and over these past few months, I've found myself thinking, *yeah, I wish I'd done that, wish I'd had a daughter*, looking at you taking to everything like you have. This is hard for me, all right. David, he's the only person I've spoken to – out loud – for donkey's years. As he's said to me many a time, "Nothing worth doing is ever easy", and – this project is teaching me that.'

Izzy rubs her eyes, like Alice is a ghost, like she has to ensure she's seeing straight. At the same time Alice's words evoke something in me. I try to steady myself as one of my veiled desires creeps like a vine from inside my heart and wraps itself around me before snapping, making a sound like thunder to catch my attention – one I've definitely heard before, but maybe depression had its hands over my ears for a while.

I want a daughter.

A kid.

My own kid.

Someone to live for, who'll be around after Mam, after *me* . . .

Izzy bobs her head just as the woman of the house with the kids appears in her doorway, the small child shouting, 'Look, told you, told you! Stranger danger!' We all shoot them apologetic looks – the most curious threesome you'd ever see sitting right outside your house of a Saturday. I wave, hoping the mother leaves us alone. She beckons for her kids to come inside and near-slams the door shut.

Alice rubs the dry skin of her hands together. 'Izzy, I was a nurse, once upon a time. It's how I came to know David and his lovely wife. Loved my job. Was good at it, too. Irish nurses are among the worst paid in the world, you know, but – I felt rich. I felt . . . *rich.*' She repeats herself. Pauses. 'I had my house – left to me by my parents – and my job. I was the richest woman in Dublin. I took up crochet and pottery, I filled in the crosswords in the paper, I practised Pilates in my sunroom, I made raspberry scones. And I was good to people.' She points, to emphasise that last line.

Like there's a sleeping baby nearby, I tiptoe over to them and crouch down on my hunkers.

'But I didn't want a husband or a wife. Didn't want anyone. Anyone but a daughter, one day, *maybe.*' She observes Izzy. 'And that was something that my colleagues had to "contend with", God love them. My desire to be single.'

We both hang on Alice's every word.

'A few of the girls on my ward decided . . . there must be something very wrong with me, because every woman wants to get married – she couldn't possibly be content by herself.'

'So – then – are you – do you mean, you're—?'

It appears that Alice hears words that Izzy doesn't even say. 'I'm just . . . me. Never felt I had to explain myself to anyone. I'm just happy to be alone.'

That seems to satisfy Izzy. She nervously waits for Alice to go on.

'A rumour was started about me anyway, something silly: that I had in fact been married, that my husband left me because I was "frigid". Everyone I worked with was hearing this about me, asking questions, cracking jokes – imagine that, going in five days a week and waiting for the passing comments and having to repeat yourself over and *over* again. And now, I know you might think, *you knew it wasn't true, so why would you quit your dream job?*'

'You quit?' I don't mean to, but I hear myself ask it.

'More than a decade ago now, yes, I did. Trust was eroded between myself and the people that I worked with. That's no laughing matter. When you don't believe a person can be honest about something unimportant to the task at hand – caring for sick people – you start to question if they can be trusted with patients, and that they did. My profession- alism was called into question. "Frigid Barnes" can't take bloods, she's an alcoholic, she's *mad*. My favourite place in the world became my living hell.'

Izzy slow blinks. 'Why are you telling me all this?'

'I offer this with humility and understanding, dear. Granted, I'm not aware of your cache of offences but I *do* know that something you've done has deeply hurt that wonderful boy.'

Izzy's face contorts with shame, like she's realising what she's been doing is far more revealing of her own true character than of Peter's.

'Whatever it was may not have seemed serious at the time to you, but the impact on our Peter, that's clearly significant. The look on his father's face . . .'

Izzy's bottom lip comes out. She throws her eyes my way, self-aware, exploring my face for judgement. I hope she can't see any; I hope I'm hiding it well.

Alice takes a sharp breath, like the memory she's holding in her mind is heavy and barbed. 'The woman who started all of the rumours about me – she was someone who had been a guest in my home. She drank wine at my table. I holidayed in Paris with her family . . . We were friends. Good friends. One of my co-workers eventually informed me out of sympathy – bear in mind, I was breaking down in the bathroom on a daily basis and news was getting around.' Alice crosses her hands like she's praying for the strength to keep talking. 'When I found out who it was, my whole world-view ran off on me. Up was down and down was up. This person had posed as a trusted confidante even just an hour before, offering to give me a lift to the post office over lunch-break.'

'And this was all just . . . out of the blue?' I ask. 'Your friend turning on you like that?'

Alice shakes her head. 'My friend was – unfortunately – unhappy in her marriage; she envied me my liberty. Got drunk one night, told me . . .' Alice leans back, tilts her head; the sun coats her in light, and she squints against it. 'I expect she hoped that dragging me down would pull her higher. She wasn't a bad person. Bad people don't exist. But people who do bad things, they're everywhere. And – every moment of every day, you get to choose whether or not to be one of those people.'

'No,' Izzy says, defeated. 'I'm just a piece of shit. Say it. I already know.'

'Hey. You're not,' I start. 'What *you did* was shit, though – Alice is right. But your behaviour isn't – that isn't – your *identity*.' I find myself needing to hear my own words. 'Can I ask – why? Why Peter?'

Izzy hugs her pencil-thin knees to her barely there body and I can't help but want to hug her.

'I don't want to – look, I'm not ready to – have I fucked it? Like, how can I ever face him?' She looks like she's been stripped bare of her clothing and is desperate for a blanket.

'I like to imagine that there's a parallel world in which my friend apologised to me and set things right in the hospital – told them all the truth. A life where I didn't spend half my forties hiding at home, paralysed by the thought of . . . getting close to anyone again.' Alice sighs. 'I can't get those years back.'

'So, just apologise? That won't do anything, he won't *care*.'

'In nursing, I learned never to make presumptions. You don't know. All you can do is try.'

Izzy plays with her phone. 'I . . . no, I can't. I just want to go home.' She says it completely deadpan.

Alice shrinks.

Then, as though none of it happened at all, 'Will I ask my dad to give you guys a lift home?'

ROSIE

'Just stop, will you? I'm trying not to speed. I – *fuck*!' Peter elbows the window. Somehow, it doesn't shatter. His glasses fall down his nose and he pushes them back up, visibly embarrassed by his loss of cool. His anger hits each of us harder than the blast of rolled-down windows on a motorway. He turns the bus's audio up full blast, like he hopes it'll drown out his thoughts.

When we park, Peter silently jumps out of the bus, thrusts the keys into Tadhg's chest and walks in the direction opposite from the café, hands pulling at his hair. Everyone clambers off apart from David and Nathan: they're engaged in a heated conversation down the back of the bus.

We watch Peter grow smaller as he storms along the street. 'Poor lad,' Tadhg says into my ear. 'I knew he was dealing with a lot. But – imagine finding out someone here . . . was . . . the cause of – all that.'

I catch a whiff of Tadhg's cologne: the same one, the one Rachel gave him . . .

Peter needs to know about us.

The thought of it coming from anyone else, or in any way other than from my mouth, with intention, is too much.

'What should we do?' Jordanne asks, visibly stressed and rubbing her belly. 'I feel so *bad* for him. I'm used to dramatics, ha, I mean, I have a two-year-old, but this is – I'd go after him, but my boyfriend is picking me up early today. Harry isn't well . . . needs his mammy. Tadhg – maybe *you* should—'

'No, no, I'll—' And then it bursts out of me like a fucking Jack in the Box. 'Tadhg, we're, Peter and myself, we're sort of, a' – I swallow – 'a *thing*. So, I should go.'

Jordanne splutters. 'Oh! So, it's *official* now—'

I give her a death stare. She stops talking.

Tadhg sits with my words for a few seconds. 'Yeah?'

My eyes are glued to the ground, but I decide that Tadhg deserves a look at them, so he can decipher whatever's there for himself. 'Yeah.'

He licks his bottom lip. 'Well. I'm happy for you both.' He really is. The man's face is incapable of lying.

This is unfamiliar territory. Really, I didn't plan to tell him, to admit aloud how I define my relationship with Peter when I'm still not sure how we got here. I'm still very much processing my truth privately, the truth that I'm very much in love, the truth I've attempted to deny, week after week after week. It dawns on me: perhaps I'm telling people we're 'an item' to quickly plant some roots in case Peter changes

his mind after I tell him what happened with Tadhg, in case
he rips *it* from the ground, before it's had a chance to grow
into whatever it might one day be.

I call after Peter. He doesn't slow down. So, I run. I catch
up. And I take his hand. He jerks, surprised, and immediately
looks back to check if the rest of them can see us. They
can. All four of them are talking and stealing glances our
way. David smiles. I smile back. Peter wraps his arm around
me and we carry on along the pathway.

We sit on the beach. Choppy water under a grey sky. Peter
talks about how Izzy gave herself away as his most venomous
hate follower. How her phone – unlocked when he grabbed
it from her – had a shortcut on the home screen to a Reddit
page full of malicious rumours about him, 'the lowercase
pete masterpost'. He tapped it and discovered that she was
logged in: the account that started it all. Izzy has apparently
been setting up anonymous account after anonymous account
across social media to send Peter a barrage of abuse, about
everything – his music and his looks and his every opinion
made public, and always including a verbal wink, to increase
Peter's distress. She would call him *Lowercase Peter* instead
of *lowercase pete* to make him aware of her dedication.

'Kind of like a graffiti artist's tag. It drove me *mad*, every
time I read it. And then she went way too far . . . my dad
. . . my *mom* . . .' Peter vents until he's calm enough to
loosen his shoulders out.

I take off my shoes and extend my legs. 'How come Jenna
knew, about . . .?'

'You never really wanted to know. I mean, we can have that conversation, but you're not going to like what you hear.'

'I'll just have to deal with it, won't I? Because I'm in this now.'

He turns his body towards me. 'Really? Because—'

'I don't know what it is, but I just feel . . .'

'Rosie, I'm – crazy about you, you know I am – but if we're going to do this, *really* do this, you're going to have to learn to give me a bit of space – to . . .'

'Do exactly what you're doing right now? Peter, you've been talking for, like, half an hour – you know that?' I smirk. 'And I *have* been listening.'

How about that. I really have.

'Well, yeah! I'm afflicted with verbal diarrhoea, OK? Let me' – he giggles, looking at my face with a mixture of mischief and longing – 'let me shit everywhere, all right? Whenever I like.'

Our noses touch. He's so silly and *so great* and I've never been more terrified in all my life.

'How are you laughing right now?' I want to laugh with him, but I can't. Because I know what's coming. And it's not a bit funny.

'Because I'm sure I can get through just about anything with you by my side.'

'Even this?'

He doesn't take his eyes off me. 'Look at you. Finally letting go, pretty lady.'

I pretend to retch. 'We're not there just yet, right? Don't—'

I cover my face. And I can't help myself. I start crying into my hand.

'Oh, shit. Rosie, *Rosie*, come back to me,' he says, and places a finger softly under my chin so I'll lift my face. I pull away.

'You should know something.'

When he doesn't reply, I look at him expectantly.

'I'm listening.'

I bury my feet in the sand because I can't bury my actual head. *Pull it off like a plaster.* I compose myself. 'Something happened between me and Tadhg at the Christmas party.' *The plaster catches on the scab*: Peter double-takes, moves away from me. Faces the sea. Touches his chest, like he's checking that his heart is still beating.

So much time passes before he says anything that I manage to use David's distraction technique on myself to pre-empt a panic attack: I ask myself what I'd be having in Seasons if we'd gone; I think about what Jenna and the girls might be talking about, and what Mam is reading right this second, and—

'Do you like him?'

Ah, how do I answer that honestly?

'Rosie.'

'Define *like*.'

He blows out a load of air through his nose, but in a frustrated kind of way – not like he's about to shout at me. Peter makes me feel safe enough to be completely transparent. 'He's – I think he's good-looking. I'd go for him on a night out if I were, you know, *on the hunt*. But, Peter, he's not—'

'Where?'

My forehead presses into my palm. 'The . . . glasshouse.'

He winces. 'Damn, *really*?'

I remain still as the island out on the skyline, the only bit of colour in front of us for miles. I feel horrible.

'How many times?'

'Oh,' I gasp, 'once! Peter, I was *hammered*—'

'So, so he took advantage of you—'

'No! *No*, no, he didn't. I wanted it, I—'

'Was it – like – kissing? Sex?'

The words *define sex* almost slip my lips. 'No, no.' Peter leaves me that bit of room to be completely open. 'But – we tried. We did everything but – *that*.'

He stands up. Walks around aimlessly, like he's short-circuiting. Sits back down. 'And – have you guys been, like, *talking*, or . . . or . . .'

'Tadhg isn't exactly a conversationalist.' Surprisingly, that's enough to pull an unenthusiastic chuckle from Peter.

'Well, that's that,' he says eventually.

Everything is nausea. The ground falls out from under me. I can't hear the waves any more, I feel like I'm underwater, I'm full of water and it's coming out my eyes again, I apologise, like my whole life depends on it . . .

'Rosie, stop.' He strokes my leg. 'You – told me. And I'm – glad. Well, *ha*. I'm not glad it happened. I'm glad, for one, that he's not here, because I'd have punched him and that dude would take me *down*. The size of him. His shoulders are . . . impressive.'

I'm still crying. Not crying-laughing, just . . . full-blown
blubbering.

'And I'm glad that you aren't letting us start this off on a
lie. It – it doesn't count. Nothing before *that*, back there on
the street, in front of my dad, nothing before *that* counts.'
Peter takes my face in his hands and holds my head to his
chest. His heart pounds like a hammer against my cheek.
'I just – how am I going to face him every damn Saturday,
acting like this doesn't bother me . . . I don't think I can *do*
that.'

I lick and flick away my tears. 'Can I play you a voice
message he sent me?'

Peter squeezes me harder than I presume he means to.
'Rosie—'

'Do you trust me?'

He holds me tight. 'Today is really *fucking* testing me.'

I wait for a go-ahead.

He kisses my forehead.

Loaded with adrenaline, I fumble with my phone and find
my last direct-message exchange with Tadhg. I tell Peter
that hearing this will help. He holds his breath as I press
play.

Howya. Is this working? Yeah. Sorry . . . here, I said I'd
voice message you 'cause it's quicker and I'd feel weird . . .
typing this out. There are no hard feelings. Or anything like
that. I wasn't expecting this to keep going. I'm . . . you know,
I'm still not over Rachel. What happened. But, like, God. I
needed . . . something. Something to prove to me that there's

a future without her. Thought I'd just feel so . . . guilty, if I, you know . . . with anyone. Honestly, I know we were both pissed off our heads, Rosie, but – Well, that, it's done more for me than any medicine so far. The past two nights I actually slept. It's been over a year of . . . insomnia. So . . . Just, thanks.

When Tadhg's voice stops, I notice my face is wet again, but these tears aren't my own.

That's when it hits me, like the waves on the shore. If we're going to be together, Peter also needs to know about Jenna's feelings for him. I decide to allow him a few more minutes to calm down before I complicate an already complicated situation even more.

And then I tell him.

He's still. He tells me that he had a feeling, but that he'd hoped it was the trolling-induced paranoia bleeding into his relationships.

'I want this,' Peter says, squeezing my hand, 'to last. So. We're going to have to play this one real damn carefully. Because we both need that girl to be OK.'

JENNA

Bertie has been gone for over a month.

But I'm still here.

Sure, look, I'm as surprised as you are.

After two weeks spent on the shed floor, wrapped up and rotting in a cardboard box, Mam suggested that I bury Bertie out at Avalon. David was more than happy to let me, so I did, around the back of the glasshouse. I wanted the patch of earth right at the base of my favourite tree for him; everyone suggested much prettier, more visible spots, but I insisted.

Mam *also* kind of cornered me into a pinkie promise on the night that Bertie died: to paint a picture of the garden and the glasshouse for her and to add to it week by week, so she can experience it through my eyes. Mam wholeheartedly believes that there's real magic afoot and near-begged me to finish out the seven months, not only for myself, but for her, too – pure convinced that June can help her and all . . .

After how useless a daughter I've been over the past few years, I figure it's the least I can do.

'One more thing to hang on for, one more thing to add to your pile of good things,' Mam said. 'It might be a small pile right now but, sure, look, focus on the pile, ignore all the rest, and as we say, everything will be grand!' *Grand.* Irish slang for *OK, fine* or *adequate* or, depending on the situation and tone of voice, anything from *great* to *terrible* . . . Essentially, she's right no matter what! I can't peer into the future to see which flavour of grand is ahead, but my job now is to just wait and see.

I made a start on Mam's canvas this week: a light sketch of the landscape and the glasshouse, with pencil. There really wasn't enough going on in the garden to justify using anything but some green watercolour for the grass and the trees, some rich reds and browns for the soil and the tree bark, but somehow – already – it's time to invest in some new paints.

The arrival of spring took me by surprise this year because I genuinely never expected to witness nature's pendulum swaying into another new season. Spring air even *tastes* different.

Wet lawn soaks through my blue jeans. Beside me, Nathan heralds the start of a new growing season the only way he knows how. 'In school, we used to call these yellow flower things piss-in-the-beds.' He swings a dandelion in my face. I swipe at it with my weeding knife, like we're in a duel. 'The other kids warned me, "Play with them and you'll wet the bed!" Ignored the bastards, obviously, but never when Johnny from around the corner was allowed to come to my house. Couldn't have my childhood sweetheart thinking I was a pisser.'

It's a Friday. David wanted us to come a day early this week for some reason. He's not said why, and none of us asked. I'm just glad to be here: the grass is growing, bulbs are flowering, a sweet scent lingers in the air and birds are finally building nurseries in David's bird-boxes.

He stands over us. 'The modern French for dandelion is *pissenlit*,' he tells Nathan, 'which quite literally means *piss in bed*. Fun fact – dandelions are actually a diuretic! People brew them, drink them in tea . . .'

I think of the 'skinny teas' that influencers hawk on Instagram. And then my brain automatically connects some dots and lands on Izzy.

Much to Peter's relief, she never came back after that day on the side of the road.

During every conversation winding up back on the topic of Izzy's sins and related abandonment of the group, David fiercely defends her, insists that we allow her 'the chance to grow'. 'Some plants thrive in shade,' he said. I don't think Peter appreciated it at all.

'Nathan, leave some of them alone, will you? Dandelions provide nectar and pollen for insects. We'd best tolerate them where we can.' Alice. She's still talking. Ever since she started, she's not shut up!

'Wait. If *they're* dandelions,' Rosie starts, 'then what are the – white blowy things? *Those* things there?'

Peter laughs. 'They're Jinny-Joes. I used to pretend those were little microphones.'

Rosie has been in *great* form lately – lighting lovely candles around the house, loaning me her fancy silk pyjamas, offering to fill up her hot water bottle for me when I have period cramps . . . She even baked (underdone) vegan brownies. But the not-so-charming part of all this is that she thinks I'm blind, or stupid, or both: it's *painfully obvious* that her and Peter are getting serious and that she's terrified to bring it up with me. I've been racking my brain as to why, because there's absolutely no way that Nathan ratted me out.

He's one of the good ones.

'Jinny-Joes are piss-in-the-beds, you twat,' Nathan teases. 'They're the same plant!'

Peter stops planting blueberries. 'Pipe down, greenthumb.'

'He's right, love,' Alice says. She pulls one from the earth. 'A dandelion will change dramatically over its life cycle. It bursts from bud to this yellow sunshine before shrivelling, then it emerges again as a white-haired elder . . . a bit like us, eh?' Alice elbows David and they have a giggle. 'Those wispy, fluffy-looking bits are called *pappi* – they're seeds, and they'll sail through the air to make new roots in the earth . . .'

David's face relaxes. His skin is paler than usual and slightly mottled. 'Makes you contemplate. The intricacies, the complexities of nature . . .' He coughs. Doesn't look like he's really looking after himself, to be honest. I'm sure he's still reading right into the night-time without eating anything that Peter prepares for him.

Across the garden, Tadhg takes a break from planting Colleen potatoes. I watch as he kneels down to observe a few dandelions bunched together – all at different stages of their life cycle – and I picture one blooming in reverse: starting out sparse and dead-looking then, somehow, transforming into the golden beauty in Nathan's hand. Flowers seem so much more mesmerising now. I never appreciated them before.

'Harry *loves* to blow the seeds!' Jordanne pipes up. She's *massive* now. Her bump has really 'popped', as they say. But every time she mentions Harry, I feel my blood run cold. 'My parents always told me that they were fairies and that when you blow, you make a wish! So of course, that's what I tell Harry.'

David briefs us on our progress so far and suggests that we stay on a little later today. 'After all, we're getting a few more exquisite minutes of daylight now with every evening that passes – why not make the most of that? Spend some more time out here, breathing in this magnificent fresh air? Eh?'

Something won't allow me to take my eyes away from David; he's perspiring even though it's not that warm, and he suddenly seems to be short of breath. The veins in his neck are distended, and his pupils are dilating. Nobody else is looking at him – why is nobody else looking at him? I shake Nathan, whisper to him to sneak off to the boot of the bus, to where David keeps our phones, and I tell him to call an ambulance.

Nathan looks at me like I have ten heads.

'Don't ask, and *hurry*,' I add.

'Excuse me, I need to use the little boys' room,' Nathan says and slips away. Nobody bats an eyelid. Everyone is either chatting or fully absorbed in what they're doing. Everyone looks content. And isn't that why we're here? We're only halfway through the project, and it's *working* – this *can't* be about to happen, and yet I feel it: I'm attuned to everything that's going on in this garden in a way that I never am anywhere else.

David stumbles. 'Forgive me,' he says, 'just my headaches, that's – June, love—' And he comes down on the grass beside me like a bag of timber.

'Shit, Dad!' Peter jumps to his father's side. He's coughing up what looks like blood, but it's pinker than that. Blood-tinged mucus. 'You're all – hey, you're clammy, what's—?'

Tadhg quickly appears, throws himself onto his hands and knees, feels David's pulse. Peter stares at him, his eyes like two holes in his head, exposing his innermost fears. So she actually told him . . .

'His heartbeat is off,' Tadhg says. 'This happened to my da. We need an—'

'Ambulance! On the way, Doctor D! They're on the line!' Nathan shouts it as he runs to where we all huddle around David.

'How?' Rosie asks. I explain that I had a feeling. She doesn't give me her usual disbelieving look – she just seems relieved, goes to lean beside Peter, palms to her forehead. Jordanne grips Rosie's shoulders, her face contorted.

'Oh my God, oh my God,' she repeats, 'he's going blue, *he's going blue*!'

Stoic as always, Alice notices how panicked Jordanne is. She rubs her back and says calming things into her ear.

David tries to talk to the operator. He can't. He silently slips out of consciousness. Painless peace.

I hold my breath, so too does the garden; the air stops moving for all of five seconds.

'Quick, hand me the phone,' Alice says firmly to Nathan, whose hand has gone limp beside David.

'We can't wait on an ambulance,' Peter snaps. 'I'm going to have to put the foot down – the hospital is half an hour away and there's roadworks on the motorway. We'll go the backroads. Tadhg, help me move him into the bus?'

'No, no, don't, just wait,' Alice starts, but Peter doesn't acknowledge her. She takes the phone call across the garden so she can hear the operator speak.

'Might be dangerous, lad. The ambulance has equipment in the back. They can start interventions on the journey, and—'

'Please! We've to act fast, I *can't* lose my dad. I can't—'

'Mate, this is a medical emergency. If we drive him, there might be more delay, and—'

'We'll get there faster if I drive!' Peter shouts, fear and fury. 'Look, if you're not going to help me, I'll move him myself—'

'Right. No. Your call. I'll help.'

The pair of them – together – carefully hoist David's body. Nathan is about to go open the gate for them when he stops dead. He's looking past me. At Jordanne. 'Girl, either you smelled too many piss-in-the-beds or you're going into labour.'

Her water has broken; the grey of her leggings becomes darker before our eyes.

'I'm – I'm – sopping. I'm – *no!* I'm only thirty-two weeks. *It's too soon!*'

'Good thing there's an ambulance on the way, then. Everything's going to be OK,' Alice whispers to her. 'I was a nurse. I'll keep an eye on you. Let's go sit down inside, shall we? Call your boyfriend? Peter, give me the keys.'

My sister, gobsmacked, pulls me aside, tells me she's going with the boys. 'Stay with Jordanne, will you? I – I have to—'

'Rosie, I know.' I hope it somehow encapsulates everything there is to say, so I don't have to say any of it: that I know about her and Peter, that I know she knows my heart, that I know about her and Tadhg and how *sick* it probably makes her that she'll have to be alone with both of them. After all, that's how we got through our teenage years together. It's much easier to be sisters when you can read one another's subtext. But maybe easier doesn't always mean better. The conversation *has* to happen, sure – but absolutely not as filling sandwiched between medical emergencies. I search her eyes for understanding.

There it is. A knowing nod. That's all I need.

ROSIE

Peter is driving, I'm sat beside him and, behind us, Tadhg hovers above David, who is stretched across several folded seats. No small talk. No real talk. Just two guys who I've shared saliva with and the life of the closest thing to a dad that I've ever had hanging in the balance.

'Take a left here,' Tadhg says, pointing.

'It's a right, man. I've driven here before, when Mom was in hospital.'

'That was ages ago. I'm telling you. Go left. Otherwise, you'll end up adding on, like, twenty minutes with the one-way system.'

Peter tenses up. I half-expect him to leave the decision up to me but, surprisingly, he swallows his pride and turns left at the very last minute.

Nobody says another word until we arrive at A&E. Tadhg was right in the end. Peter claps him on the back to thank him – a little harder than he might have if he were anybody else in the world.

JENNA

We have our taxi trail the ambulance all the way to Drogheda hospital. The driver almost refused to take us because of Moss, but when we explained what had just happened, he said, 'Fuck it, get in.'

Each of us takes a turn minding Moss outside – there was no getting past the front desk with him. After three hours of no updates on Jordanne's condition and of reading terrifying pamphlets about a variety of things that can go wrong with the body and the brain and wanting to *tear my hair out of my head*, it's my turn on dog duty.

I'm doing laps of the car park out the back of the hospital – to release some of my pent-up energy – when I spot Alice by the sliding doors, asking a stranger for a cigarette. She leans back against the stone wall and exhales a thick cloud of smoke.

'Hey. You're a smoker?'

'Was,' she says, looking at me all guilty. 'What happened to your vape pen? Haven't seen you use it recently.'

I actually can't remember making the decision, but I just sort of stopped using it before my e-liquid ran out. I shrug. 'Gave up.' An irresistible impulse comes on me to bite the bullet: to speak my truth, however bluntly, to someone – *Alice* – because something has shifted, something worth vocalising. 'Figured I might need my body now that I've decided to stick around for another little while.' I pause. Wait for her reaction. Her attention is powerful. She doesn't wish to interrogate me – I can tell – but it's clear she hopes I'll elaborate. I realise I'm not ready to. Not yet. So, I go on. 'No point in bombarding it with all kinds of chemicals . . .'

'Good woman,' she starts, her eyes ecstatic. 'Anyway, nicotine itself is toxic, did you know? It raises your blood pressure, spikes your adrenaline and, believe me, adding apple-pie flavour doesn't change those facts.' She says it right before she tokes. Looks at me with the smallest smile. 'I'm glad you're not feeling done with life just yet, Jenna. I mean, look around, all these cars, all these people coming and going, all here so they can stay alive. Perspective is helpful, that's what I'm learning, getting to know you all, your stories. Everything you've all been through. This is my old haunt, you know. Actually, I'm out here because I'm trying to dodge ex-colleagues – the place is *swarming* with them.' She sucks on her cigarette like it's life support. 'If you'd have told me a year ago that I'd be standing here now . . .'

'*This* is where you worked?'

Her face softens. 'The fears we don't face become our demons. June knew that. She had no demons because she had no fear. I'm going to finish this cigarette, and I'm going to go in there, and I'm going to sit in that *miserable* plastic chair for as long as I have to for that *poor* girl. Challenging times lie ahead for her. Postpartum is no joke. And she was really starting to love the project. Its cessation was supposed to line up with her baby's birth . . .'

I'm about to prod Alice to see if she knows about what happened to little Harry when Rosie appears, mascara cheeks and red-rimmed eyes. 'You're – you guys are *here*? But – the bus – I've walked around this car park so many times with Moss and I didn't see it . . .'

'Peter parked out on the road, we – he wanted some time alone with him, to say – goodbye – he—' Rosie starts, but she breaks down mid-sentence and reaches for me.

'Aw, pet,' I hear myself say, and I hold her. She bawls into my neck, her arms – familiar and unfamiliar – hug me so tight it almost hurts.

'I can't say it! I can't!' She struggles in my arms without letting go of me, a gutted fish, pulling my whole body in every direction with her. Behind Rosie, a shadow comes over Alice's face. She peers at me through a haze of pain. 'His eyes changed! Right in front of us! He was there and then he was, he's—'

Alice closes her eyes. 'He's gone.' Finishes her cigarette. Stubs it out against the wall. She waits for Rosie to control herself.

'I don't understand. He was – fine,' Rosie starts, rubbing

her eyes. 'Wasn't he? "Pulmonary embolism" they said. Peter's allowed stay with him a while before they move him – to—'

'The mortuary.' Alice sighs. 'He wasn't ready to tell the poor lad. Besides, David was sure he'd last until we finished this thing.'

'What do you mean? Isn't an embolism a – blood clot? A – *sudden* thing? How could he have known?'

She bends down to pet Moss, who is cuddled against Rosie's leg. It's like he senses something's up. 'Nothing gets past a dog; would you look at him?'

'Alice?'

'Sorry.' I notice now that she's stopping herself from crying. 'Last year, David was diagnosed with a large and aggressive tumour at the base of his skull. He visited me one day after I called him – too scared to sign for a package that I really needed, too terrified to answer my own door. We ate soup; he told me it was attached to his spinal cord, therefore inoperable; we spoke of the best plants for bees, I believe, and shared some bread pudding.'

We both just blink at her.

'He was at risk for something like this to happen . . .'

Rosie looks like she's floating through space. 'What about chemo?'

'He was offered a treatment plan, but in reality, nothing could be done for him. The prognosis was lousy, girls. David knew his decline would be precipitous. That's when he decided to get to work on the garden.' Alice hides her face so we can't see her tears fall. She wipes it, looks back at

Moss, right into his eyes. Rubs his flank. 'David wanted to make the garden beautiful again, wanted his own ashes to be scattered there, with June, and for his urn to be buried with hers. After he'd written his book, of course.'

'What book?' I ask.

'About the project. David somehow knew it would be transformative, for all of us. It already has been. Whether you believe it was all down to June or not. Look at me, *here* of all places, talking to two young ones! The shared mission, being in nature with other people . . . it's touching all of our lives in profound ways. Without David, without each other, we might have continued up and down the same old paths. He wanted to write about *that*, all of that.'

Neither of us says anything. The thought of such a book never ending up on shelves is just too sad.

'Even had a working title . . . *Missing Links*. He wasn't satisfied with that, though. He was waiting for the perfect title to strike him—'

Rosie's face is ghost white. She looks at me like I'm her oldest friend.

We excuse ourselves and sit together on a bench nearby. Rosie lays her head against my shoulder. A few moments pass. Rosie cries. I think about the idea that I'll never hear David's voice again and it doesn't feel real. I think about my mother. And Peter, and how glad I am that he has my sister.

Time to think out loud. 'Sorry I've been so—'

'Shit? Same here. Jenna, this is just . . . well, it's horrible, isn't it?'

I nod. I *mm-hmm*. 'I'm not ready to go through something like this. Mam—'

'Neither am I, Jenna. *Peter* certainly isn't. Nobody's *ever* ready.' We watch patients and visitors coming and going for some time. Then she starts to ask me a question she's probably been dying to ask me for months. 'Can you, I mean, would you mind coming over with me sometimes to Mam, for—'

'I'm going to move back in with Mam,' I say, stopping her. 'What?'

'Yeah. I decided literally just now.' It's true. There's nothing I want more in the world right now than to hug my mother. 'I've let enough time slip away. And – you deserve a break.' I think about the birds of Avalon and how they share the load, protecting eggs, bringing food back to the little baby birds. 'You need to focus on . . .' – after a deep breath, I release that part of me that is iron consumed by rust, by the disease of jealousy – 'Peter. He'll need looking after. It's just going to be him now. Him and you.' I squeeze her. 'For a long time, I hope.'

Her body shakes against me. She takes my hand and holds it so tight, I'm afraid she might break it off. My peace of mind then wraps itself around the both of us as the wind picks up, as Alice cuddles Moss in the distance, as sirens roar, as the texts pour in from Nathan.

We soon rejoin Alice. All three of our phones vibrate and beep at the same time. It's the group chat. A selfie of Nathan and Jordanne (flat on a bed in the background, her thumb in the air) and:

How's Doctor D? Little preemie GIRL alive, mama is stable! Emergency C-section. J's boyfriend is still on the way, baby J is in NICU. J for JUNE. She's calling her after the lady of the garden herself! xxx

Her boyfriend must have missed the birth . . . he was on a job in Cork when he got the call, apparently. She must have been so frightened – going through that all alone. I get a private message from Nathan, too. I tilt the screen, so Rosie and Alice can't see.

Mama's up here saying how she can't wait for everyone to meet Harry . . . HELP! Lying by omission is NOT my forte. The girl can tell I know something's up! I'm freaking, Jenna. What do we do? I think she's having a serious mental health episode, but it's not my place to fill these jolly midwives in on the truth because I'M NOT SUPPOSED TO KNOW . . . I'll say it again. HELP.

'Should we tell them about—?' Rosie starts.

Alice shakes her head. 'No, no, not yet. This is one of the most special times in Jordanne's life. We can't take that away from her. Oh.' She bunches up her face. 'Jordanne *loves* the project and she's been like a niece I never had. It's been helping her more than either of you might be aware. She'll be just *devastated*—'

'You know then? It's actually true?'

Alice hesitates. Waits for me to keep speaking.

'About Harry?'

'You mean Hugo?'

My eyes search hers.

'*Harry* is the one that survived.'

I didn't anticipate that I'd cry when I saw the little boy curled around Jordanne in the hospital bed. The ward is dimly lit and quiet. We enter one at a time, so as not to overwhelm her and the other new mothers. Alice wanted to come in first, but she's a bit shaken after the bad news, so Rosie and the boys are looking after her.

'Careful, hunny, careful, Mama has an ouch on her tummy.'

Harry smiles up at Jordanne and asks if he can kiss it better.

'Not now, chicken. *Look!* Another new friend!'

Jordanne's boyfriend nods at me in acknowledgement but I can't pull my eyes away from Harry; he looks at me like I'm a Teletubby. 'Green hair!' he says gleefully, before erupting in wild laughter.

I tug at a few stray bits of my low messy bun. 'Ha, yeah, how did *that* happen?' I pretend to be shocked.

'Green is – is – is – for *monsters*!'

'Harry, pet, this is Jenna, and she's *not* a monster,' Jordanne croaks, beaming at me. She looks like she's just run a marathon. *Pet*. There it is again. I missed being someone's pet. I'd very much like to have someone to call pet, one day.

'C'mere, mister. Toilet break. Let Mammy talk to her friend,' Harry's dad says.

'Nooooo,' Harry moans, and grabs onto Jordanne even harder.

'I'll let you press the button in the lift.'

'Yeahhhhh!'

They leave together, and I take over the visitor's chair. Jordanne swigs some water.

'Oh. My. *God*,' she starts. 'What a day – can you actually believe it? That was so scary. "We're going to have to cut you open." Just like that! David taught me this technique for staying calm and some breathing exercises, and thank God, otherwise I'd have *lost the plot*. The breathing kept my mind calm, but my body had other plans. And now, they're going to have to keep June in for a few weeks . . .' Jordanne looks devastated.

'It's beautiful that you're calling her June. Really. Such a lovely name.'

'Well, she was due in June and all but, *you know*,' she says, whispering now, like she's saying things she shouldn't, 'as the weeks have gone on, I've started to come round to a lot of David's, well, I'd have called it nonsense before, but, well, there's something in it, and I'll always look back on this pregnancy and think of you lot, and that garden . . .'

I smile a true smile.

'It's all been *so* good, for me. To have you guys, to have something out of the house . . . that's *mine* . . . and . . .'

I lean forward.

'Look, sorry, I'm so emotional, *sorry*, it's the hormones, it's *everything*,' she says, tears pouring. 'This baby means *everything* to me, my world. I felt that I had to be calm through that pregnancy. I couldn't let *anything* go wrong, because I've, I've let things go wrong, before . . .'

My heart is pounding. I see myself reflected in her eyes, my regret for cutting my mother out of my life, for ignoring her for so long, my determination to make up for it.

'I – my – my son, he had – a twin – a brother – and I've not told you this, and I'm sorry, I don't know why I'm telling you now, but I need friends, *real* friends . . .'

I don't look away for a second.

'One afternoon I was walking my boys in their – in the buggy, the old buggy, the double one.' Jordanne doesn't even wipe her tears away, they simply flow. She doesn't look around the room as she speaks, either, she just gazes at me, the lid fully removed. 'A car mounted the pavement, some man on his phone, I *fucking hate* phones, Jenna, *I hate them*, so much.'

Thankfully, I tucked mine away before sitting down . . .

'Hugo was only one. And that – that's really why I'm on David's project. The things I told you all, they were all true but, really – this project, it appealed because, I suppose, well, I read . . . It's important to manage stress while pregnant, and I don't want *anything* to happen to my June, my little baby, and now, *listen*, I felt so – guilty – that I was there when David fell, and I got so worked up—'

'You can't, Jordanne, it's not your—'

'Wait! I'm not finished,' she whispers, and looks around, at nurses coming and going from the other bedsides. 'Pull the curtains for me, will you?'

I do as she asks. Then I pull the chair nearer to her and listen closely.

'I'd developed severe preeclampsia, Jenna!'

My dumb face just floats. I don't know anything about pregnancy. Not a sausage.

'It's this – it's dangerous for pregnant women. June could have stopped breathing inside me or, goodness forbid, I could've died, leaving Harry with – no mammy.' Her eyes are wide-open windows in rain. 'I had no symptoms! Well. I thought they were just regular pregnancy symptoms. My last appointment, I had to reschedule it because Harry wasn't well, so it wasn't caught – and – what I'm *trying* to say is—'

'What happened today might've saved your life, your baby's life.'

Compulsive nodding. Then she lets out a huge breath. Presses her palm to her heart. Says she can't wait to tell David about this fortunate stroke of serendipity.

When I finally swap out with Alice, everything hits me with the force of a gale, and I let myself cry in my sister's arms for the first time in my adult life.

ROSIE

Peter's knees buckle when he sees me. I swaddle him in wordless love, this precious heirloom coming apart at the seams, eyes raw from crying.

'You look how I feel,' I whisper. We're nose to nose now, wet with the realisation that David is in the room and, at the same time, nowhere to be found.

We sit beside the bed where David's body lies. I can still smell *him* off his clothes, off his hands: musk like petrol and fresh earth.

Peter takes my hand. Our fingers hang intertwined between two plastic chairs. I can almost feel him wrestle with the words attempting to form at the tip of his tongue.

'Dad wouldn't have wanted to die here, Rosie.' His voice breaks. I want to absorb the agony pouring from him. 'He'd have wanted to die at home, at Avalon. In the garden. Where Mom is.'

'She was his home,' I agree, tightening my grip on his

hand, 'but he – he believed, I mean, you know, that she was always with him.'

Peter sniffs. 'This is going to fucking suck.' His hand near-crushes mine. I do my best not to flinch. 'Dad always described death as *natural*, you know, when I was growing up, trying to understand his job. But as he said himself, after Mom, it feels . . . anything but. Feels more like a bomb going off in slow motion.' His eyes well up. He bites his lip. Inhales fast. '*How* is he dead, Rosie?'

I love him. Goodness, I love him.

He keeps hold of my hand and uses his other to slough away the tears. Turns his head slightly, to find my eyes.

I'd rather it come from me than a coroner, so I tell Peter everything that Alice told me. About David's cancer and the book he was working on.

He was already privy to the book plans. 'Maybe he told me because he hoped I'd finish it for him, if he – if – but I can't write a *book* . . .' His voice trails off. He observes his father's body for another while in quiet contemplation. Then: 'Do you think there's anything to any of it?'

'Any of what?'

'You know.' I presume he's acknowledging what my sister and some of the others believe – about June and the garden. What is he hoping I'll say? All I want to say is words he longs to hear: that his parents were star-crossed – born to love one another and to bring us together and to spark this great, healing fire that burns bright for the lives they touched and that *we* touch but, of course, I don't believe any of that. You tell the truth in love, don't you?

'I – I think there have been an amazing number of coincidences, but . . . that's all.'

Peter blows out his cheeks. 'Right. Yeah.'

'I really *wish* I could say—'

Peter pulls his hand away from me and mentally checks out of the conversation. Within seconds he's got his phone out, Google open. I can't help but glance at the screen. Elbows on his knees, he's frantically searching 'brain cancer' alongside words like 'delusions', 'hallucinations', 'personality changes'. Less than a minute passes before he locks his screen and sits back in his chair.

'Of course. I mean, *obviously*.' Peter fixes his eyes on David's shoes, caked with dirt from the garden floor. 'He was imagining things. Because . . . he was sick.' Peter's eyes give away his brain as it tries to solve an unsolvable equation. 'Do you believe in God, or anything like God? Anything that can't be proven to exist?'

'Eh.' Fuck. 'I know my mam does. She believes in something bigger than us and I think she just calls it *God* because that's what she was brought up to call it but, really, "God", "the universe", "higher power", it's all the same to me. Religion and spirituality – they seem to exist to make people feel better about,' I swallow, 'dying. I mean, I've always thought that faith is kind of just . . . something people use to avoid reality, because reality is so *hard* sometimes.'

Peter wilts.

'Then again,' I continue, 'the belief my mam has, in, well, *whatever* – it's made her life better. It doesn't really matter what I think because . . . she has faith, and she benefits from it. I believe *that*.'

'All the stuff Dad believed, about Mom . . . you think that maybe brought him some, some—'

'Listen, Peter.' I pull my chair even closer to his so I can lean my head on his shoulder. 'Your dad told me that he wasn't at all that concerned with 'why'. And through him, to appreciate how much *why* doesn't matter. *What is* – in any one moment, for any one person – that's much more important. David wanted to impact what *is*. That's what we need to remember him for. Because he did what he set out to do, regardless of what *you* believe . . . what *he* believed . . . he made a difference in all of our lives. He was on to – something – and it doesn't matter where the project – all of it – came from if it had the desired outcome, does it?'

Peter cries softly into my shoulder. 'Please help me,' he asks eventually.

'With what?'

'To keep it going. To finish what he started. I can't do it alone.'

I hold his gaze, beautiful even in its fear and sorrow. 'You aren't alone any more.'

JENNA

We buried David's urn beside June's, in the soil at the base of Avalon's apple tree, which is now, finally, starting to bloom; fragrant pink flowers lovingly hang above the daffodil-dotted final resting place of the Dolans, against shades of crocodile, juniper and pine. I wonder if they're happy with the harmonious aesthetic and if they were free of any doubt that they'd be together again like this, here, eventually.

After Peter flattened the earth above his parents, the tightened circle of myself, Nathan, Peter, Rosie, Tadhg and Alice decided to camp in the garden. Peter and Nathan pitched an old tent that June had stored away in the shed, once upon a time, for music festivals. We brushed off the cobwebs, filled it with cushy pillows and blankets. We hung some of the Christmas-party fairy lights using Sellotape. In June's spirit, we sang and we danced next to bright, hot coals in David's old brazier; we sent Jordanne drunken video updates in exchange for adorable newborn pictures, and we talked about David until the sun came up. There were belly laughs about his eccentricities, his love of tinned fruit and purple clothing, and tears – mostly from Peter – for the man's hidden burden, for the pages of the book that he'd never get to write.

Almost two months have passed; two months of blizzards and unexpected floods, two months of getting to know my mother all over again before I move back home, two months of tending to frost-damaged plants with toughening hands and of turning our shared world right side up again.

This morning, six of us form a circle in the grass to the right of the glasshouse. It's in much better shape than it was on our first day here: the broken windows have long been replaced with new, shiny, spray-paint-free ones, and the wooden tables inside are lined with pots filled with plants that grow taller by the day. You can see the little splodges of green through the glass from where we sit now.

'So, moustachio. What's next?' Nathan asks, flipping the toe of his pristine loafer at the sky.

Peter has his legs crossed, and his dad's battered project journal in his lap. 'Well,' he starts, humourless and haggard. Rosie sits to his left. Concern for Peter has her biting the side of her lower lip. Last night, she and I watched *The Notebook* in bed. 'He's like . . . the version of Noah after Allie has fucked off,' she'd said of Peter. Aside from the fact that he hasn't shaved since David died, he's also seemingly forgotten how to laugh. But I suppose the fact that he hasn't sold many tickets for his upcoming tour really isn't very funny

– he's considering cancelling it altogether, even though he knows that's the last thing his dad would have wanted.

Peter goes on, monotone, 'I, eh, I found a scribble in Dad's handwriting, here, look . . . in the margin.' He unenthusiastically shows Nathan the journal. 'It's . . . indecipherable.'

'Lavender, babe.'

Peter just stares.

'That there says *Lavandula angustifolia*. Means *English lavender.*'

'How do you know?'

'Because I don't need glasses. You should really try, like, wearing them. Remember those things you used to have on your nose every day?'

'I meant *how do you know what it means*?' He's impatient. Tired. Grief with arms and legs.

Nathan stretches his long body across the grass. 'I read every book your dad recommended on the reading list. Cover to cover. Alice, back me up?'

Before Alice can respond, Tadhg jumps in. 'I . . . eh . . . I keep lavender beside my bed.'

Peter – ever the gent – fights a grimace, but I see it lurking, hiding.

'Tiny bottle of it. It's great. For . . . calm. Reduces stress, and anxiety.' Tadhg leans forward onto his knees. He's so much more confident in our presence now that he's used to seeing us every week. 'Helps me sleep,' he finishes. 'Actually, it's *one* of the only things that's helped me. Since . . . you know . . . Rachel.' After he says it, he shoots my

sister a look. Though it wasn't a look meant for me, I understand it. She recently admitted what happened between them
at the Christmas party – proudly played me the voice
message he sent her about how transformative their little
fumble was. *Now*, any time Rosie mentions Tadhg, I hum
the chorus of 'Sexual Healing' by Marvin Gaye and she
literally turns *magenta*. A smile threatens my face. I look at
my shoes.

'Yeah?' Peter acknowledges Tadhg. His knee bounces
under David's journal.

'Yeah.'

'So, we'll plant some,' Peter decides, nodding. 'Yeah?' He
looks to Alice for reassurance. He answers himself, nodding.
'Yeah.'

Two boys trying to play house. You can feel it in the air,
though: Peter's inability to change the past and the mighty
power that holds over him. An awkward moment passes
wherein Alice blinks a lot, looking from Tadhg to Peter and
then back to Tadhg. She's probably the only one of us who
still doesn't know.

Because of course I told Nathan.

'We can plant an English-lavender hedge over there, along
the side of the house, maybe,' Alice says, all sprightly,
unaware of the complex dynamic between the lads. 'It'll need
the full sun to thrive! But I believe we should. We'll make
good use of it. Lavender can be used sparingly in cooking,
similarly to rosemary, and as a lovely garnish for salads,
desserts . . .'

There's no way Peter could have kept this thing going

without Alice's support. His shoulders relax as she takes over the steering wheel.

Time slows. We sit in our den of nature, our sanctuary, and listen to Alice talk. My eyes are drawn to my sister, who doesn't look one bit out of place here any more. She's all red cheeks and a wild tangle of hair. Being outside suits her almost as much as love does.

I thought maybe their love would turn my interest in Peter off, but the switch hasn't flicked yet: I've tried my best over the past few weeks to conceal how often I look at Peter from Rosie, reaching for all the oldest tricks in the book: peripheral-vision eyeballing; observing him before promptly glancing away, as if I'm not bothered by his presence. I surrender to my admiration for Peter and it guides my chin, encouraging me to look around. To look at all of these new people in my life, people who matter and who make me feel like I matter, and at the garden, slowly coming to life – there's been a concerted, combined effort to drag me through the dark. And now, I'm here. Alive. With sunlight touching my cheek and birdsong filling me whole. With porridge in my belly and a trip to see Mam to look forward to. With fresh air in my lungs and an ability to find things to smile about. The light at the end of the tunnel doesn't emanate from Peter alone.

'So, who wants to go first?' Alice asks, prodding us towards the divulging of our 'truths' as David used to call them: our stories, perspectives, experiences, the things that keep us up at night. She holds the pale-green stone of truth out before her.

I look around to see who's up for offering themselves as tribute this week. Then I see something that makes my heart skip a beat in my chest – eyes that aren't quite alive but aren't dead, either. A tiny white face hidden in a mess of chequered hat and scarf, slowly approaching us from the side entrance to the back garden . . .

Izzy!

Nobody else has noticed her yet. Izzy pouts her lower lip at me like a three-year-old looking for a cuddle. She fans her face with her hand in a weak attempt to keep the tears back. A gasp. People hear and, finally, they look up.

'Shit,' Rosie whispers.

'Ah. You *made it*,' Alice says warmly.

Izzy's giggles are wrapped in layers of apprehension and her long thin legs in thick black tights. She creeps slowly towards us. 'Dad got lost, like, five times on the way. He's waiting for . . . me . . . outside . . .'

We each turn to Alice, who appears entirely unsurprised. But Peter doesn't. He's sat beside Alice facing Izzy, and he's frozen – looks like he could be sick. All colour has drained from his face. He's gripping David's journal like it might serve as a shield. 'She's – you're not welcome here.' His leg shakes. His eyebrows scrunch.

Izzy stops in the middle of the grass. She crumples a little before hugging herself. Her big eyes flicker with regret, with embarrassment, with shame. 'Gosh, I'm sorry, I – I'll go, I – Alice, this was a *stupid* idea, I—'

Alice stands up. She takes a step forward and opens her arms to Izzy.

'Alice, excuse me, but you – you don't get to – just—'

'Hear the girl out, boy. I beg you! Hear her out.' She takes a deep breath. 'Let her put this right. It's what your mother wanted.' Alice pulls the stone of truth from her pocket, plays with it.

Rosie rolls her eyes. I decide then and there that I need to say what I'm thinking, out loud, even if it means discomfort, even if it means getting into trouble, because, honestly, what's the use in buckling up for the ride of life if I can't so much as turn the fucking keys? My story is connected to Izzy's; they're both part of the same grand mosaic of tales – and I have the power to alter how the final piece looks, if only I speak up.

'Peter, please,' I beg. 'We all deserve a second chance, don't we?'

He doesn't look at me.

'You saw the potential for growth in *me*.'

'Jenna, *you* didn't set out to *destroy* someone . . .'

'Oh, but I did destroy someone. I destroyed my own mother.'

Peter averts his gaze from Izzy. The rest of them are still, listening. They're perhaps in shock. I mean . . . *I've* never taken the stone. Not once have I fully participated here. Seeing Izzy was the spark I needed.

'My mother has been telling me how depressed she was to know I wanted nothing to do with her,' I say, daring to be vulnerable – unworried and calm. 'For a long time, I wouldn't answer the phone when she called me. My own mother. But guess what? Last night, she drank hot chocolate and watched me paint. Because of this . . . *us*. This garden. I know it. I'll take that stone, if you give it to *her* first, if you just let her talk, if you just . . . listen.'

I don't have to say any more than that. Peter softens slightly, says nothing, waits for Izzy's next move. I look her way; her eyes thank me with a heavy blink and slanted eyebrows.

The grass thrives against her heavy black boots. She edges towards the circle and sits just outside of it. Moss then stands from his position at Peter's side and trots over to Izzy. He rests his head where her ankles meet, prompting silent tears from her. Then Alice hands her the stone of truth.

'A warning,' Izzy starts. 'I've not planned this out, it's going be a, just a, stream of consciousness, so, enjoy the tea while it's hot.' She's nervous. So nervous. She closes a hand around the opposite wrist and keeps her eyes on Moss. 'So, um, I've been like, harassing Peter online for the guts of two years.'

Nathan makes a noise with his breath to signal his disgust.

Izzy manages to ignore it. 'I was a fan of his, like, I *idolised* him, but things took a turn in my personal life, which I won't go into just yet, if that's – OK.' She squeezes her wrist tightly, so tight it looks like it could snap off her body. 'I needed to regain some sense of . . . control, I guess. Controlling my food was just the tip of the iceberg. I was between years at uni, with no hobbies and no girlfriend and no kids, so I had all the time in the world. It all started with online gaming. Do any of you . . . play?' She looks around. None of us nod or make a peep. 'Right. Yeah. "Read the room, Iz",' she says to herself, in a funny voice. 'Well, I started out hijacking people's accounts in this one game and – and, stealing their items. Then, life became all about arguing politics using fake accounts on Twitter but, well, arguing with other faceless slugs got real boring *real fast.* And the boredom drove me crazy. Life was just *boring boring*, so boring. Then Peter,' she goes on, pausing to pull her hand away from her wrist so she can hold Moss's paw, 'released this one song I wasn't impressed by – actually, let's be real, I was just super jealous of the girl he picked for the music video.' Izzy laughs at herself. I glance in Peter's direction. He's leaning back on his hands, watching the girl who unravelled his career petting his dog, and his expression is completely unreadable. 'I decided, hey, I'll let him know through one of my fake accounts that he was in fact contributing to body shaming by hiring a super slim actress, which, I mean, *duh*, he wasn't. You . . . you weren't, Peter. I was . . . projecting.'

'Go on, love,' Alice says, when Izzy's words dry up.

'Anyway, Peter, he . . . replied. Just this nice, short reply. And it was invigorating to be *noticed* by someone like him. Addictive, actually.'

Peter sits forward as if he's about to interject, but Izzy starts to talk louder, faster.

'I wanted to be known. I wanted him to talk about me in his real life to his friends. That's where I really wish I'd stopped . . .' Izzy looks up. She looks at Alice. 'If something is repeated often enough, it can pass for the truth.' Then, cautious, she looks at Peter. 'I'm not sure *why you*, exactly, but, well – Sorry, no, I do know why. Here I am at it again. *Sorry.* Give me a minute.'

'Iz,' Peter starts.

'OK. You were pursuing music like I always dreamed I would but – I didn't. I wanted you to feel how I felt. So, I, like, sort of latched onto you and I wanted to watch you . . . fail? Yeah.' She closes her eyes against the tears that build up. 'That's what I wanted. I extended every insecurity I ever had onto you. I even, eh, like, *stalked* you. A lot. Like, hardcore, actually. Found out where your dad worked. Persuaded him to take me on as a patient. That's how I ended up . . .'

Peter's mouth is hanging open. He looks disorientated. 'Here. How you ended up *here.* So, you could send me abuse from across the table in the café and – and – watch me quivering. So you could see me jump after every notification while driving you home. You . . . you . . .'

Izzy breaks. Her whole face contorts and her body wracks with an onslaught of tears. The cries are devastating. 'It made me feel alive! I didn't know how else to feel . . . alive.' Sobs break her sentence apart. 'But, Peter, after I got to *know* you, I wanted to *stop.* Genuinely. I'm not heartless! As bad as all this sounds, I'm not!' She wipes the delicate skin beneath her eyes with the back of her sleeve. 'I felt, like, *so* bad. He's this real good guy, you know?' Izzy looks around, seeking agreement.

Anger meets pity on Rosie's face.

'He cares about people. Keeps his head down. Turns his heart into art. But by that point I'd – God, this is *so* . . .' She looks at Alice in desperation.

'You're doing great,' Alice assures her.

Izzy composes herself. Rolls her shoulders back. 'I had, like – I suppose you could say *recruited* – hundreds of other people through Reddit to go hate on you, Peter, for, like, every little thing you did. We'd go to town on your live-streams with negative comments, hoping you'd talk about it – about *us*.' Izzy looks to Nathan, to Tadhg, to me, as she relieves herself of this secret life she's been living. 'We'd reply mean shit to his other followers. We'd get together and dislike bomb his videos, and we'd say the most inflammatory things we could about him to . . . bring him down, to where we were.' She nods to herself. I can't tell if she planned to say all of this before she started talking; it seems to me as though she's discovering more about herself with every sentence that flows. 'I stopped, Peter. I did.' She looks at him again. 'But the train of hate I created kept on going and going, and when I posted the picture – you all know the one – well . . . I'm so sorry that I posted it. I never dreamed things would get so bad, and – it's not like I deserve any sympathy, because a few months ago I'd have eaten it all up.' Her voice shakes like the leaves on the trees all around us. 'I'd have been sitting in bed, eyes inches from my phone, having a – a victory circle jerk with my forum "buddies". I *know* that what I did caused you a gross amount of pain.' Moss whines, as though to express Peter's hurt. 'Your music was your escape after what happened to your mam – to June – and now you've lost . . . well, I just feel so bad. I can't eat the little bit I usually allow myself, and I can't sleep.' Her voice is tiny now. So tiny and delicate and genuine. 'It was all just so unfair and wrong in every way and – yeah, I'm sorry. What I did wasn't . . . harmless messing around on my phone. Alice has shown me . . . bullying, its scars can last a lifetime, and being out here, with you guys, with all this' – she strokes the blades of grass by her shin – 'has shown me that my phone, it's – bad for me, so bad for me. It's part of why my own body is eating itself alive; it's a tool I'm using to harm myself and to harm good people, and I'm just – I'm done. You know when you're completely just *done*? I don't want to be a weed. I want to be a – I don't know – some pretty black flower. A "Queen of Night" tulip.'

I attempt a laugh, hoping to break up some of the tension. Izzy looks appreciative.

'I read about flowers and shit now. Instead of . . . trolling. Because your dad changed my life, Peter.'

Peter clears his throat.

'And, sure, I made your life worse for a while but . . . I hope I can make it better again.' Only then do I notice that Nathan is on the edge of himself – looking from Peter to Izzy. 'Let me clear your name. Let me explain the missing context behind the "Hitler" picture. People online are so *fickle*, they'll forget, they will, and – Peter, I know you're angry. And you should be. So, I'm here to, to . . .'

'You want me to forgive you.'

Moss pants. Nathan swallows loudly. Izzy fidgets. Peter pulls his hands to his face only to notice a caterpillar crawling along the knee of his jeans. He extends a finger so it can crawl into his hand.

'So, you lie to my dad – to me, to all of us – you dismantle something I've worked towards *for years* before it even happens, you ruin the last bit of time I had with my dad, and . . . what? I'm supposed to just let you get away with it?' Peter closes his fist around the caterpillar.

'Oh, Peter,' Alice says, 'she won't get away with anything.'

Nathan scoffs at Alice. 'Please.'

Alice takes no offence. 'I mean it. Everyone has to live with the consequences of their actions.'

'Some don't,' Tadhg adds, to everyone's surprise. 'Some . . . don't . . . live with the consequences.' Obviously talking about Rachel. 'But . . . that doesn't mean there isn't . . . lasting damage.' His eyes burn into Izzy. Maybe he's worried about her dying and leaving her family behind, leaving us behind. Should we be worried? That can't happen. *We can't allow it.*

Alice nods. Continues, directing her words at Peter. 'My old friend, the friend who . . . stole *my* job, *my* life, she saw me that day, when we were leaving the hospital, after . . . she wrote me a letter. And trust me, Peter. She didn't get away with *anything*. Don't you think our Izzy has suffered enough?'

Peter's fist shakes. His lip shakes. Rosie places a hand on his shoulder.

Alice kneels before Peter. 'What she did was terrible. But the pain inside you is terrible, too. Grief for your parents, grief for your reputation. It's destroying you. It's stealing time away from you and this *magnificent* woman,' she says of Rosie.

Rosie finds her voice. 'Forgiveness . . . is just about letting go, isn't it?'

Peter looks at her. They say so much to one another without saying anything at all. His eyes seek Alice. 'I don't know how.'

She looks helplessly at Peter's fist, where the tiny caterpillar is encased, like she's terrified he'll crush the critter. 'Just say the words. That's a start.'

Peter looks at Nathan then for what feels like a lifetime, like he's waiting for approval, like he's wondering if it's even possible to form the right syllables and if any kind of act of atonement from Nathan's ex – the guy who wronged *him* so desperately – would ever elicit forgiveness from Nathan. Eventually, Nathan tilts his head back, misty-eyed. He smile-pouts through tears, nods briefly and stiffly. 'If *you* can say it and mean it, maybe I can too.'

Peter's lip trembles. He gasps for air. For a moment, he looks as though he's about to speak, but no words come out. He slowly, silently mouths *I forgive you*, and then opens his hand, so that the caterpillar can move forward, so that, one day, it might go on to radically transform its body, emerging as a butterfly.

ROSIE

Last week, I bought my sister an easel for her birthday. Her eyes lit up like Disney fireworks. To see her whole demeanour transforming over something so bloody simple brought me more contentment than any online checkout or clothing delivery, more gratification than any Tinder hook-up or private porn marathon.

Finally, I feel like I have my sister back. It's really her! The giant shadow that trailed her has shrunk to doll-size and I'm now able to imagine a world in which it no longer exists.

In spite of the breathless, muggy days of May, Jenna looks forward to Saturdays more with every week that passes. She's been sat on a stool in front of her easel all morning under one of Avalon's big windows, lost in flow, working on a painting for Mam. Her forehead creases now as she fights the distraction that is Nathan and Izzy running around and splashing water from the garden hose at one another instead of watering the plants, two overgrown children.

'Holy crap, Jenna! That's something else . . .' Peter says it. He leans beside her to examine the canvas.

'Yeah?' Jenna doesn't flinch. Her hand is held out before her with a tiny paintbrush as she adds dots of violet with meticulous care.

I think Peter's finally fallen from her pedestal: Jenna no longer turns to goo when he talks to her. I'd rather not admit how much this pleases me, so I never let on that I've noticed. And even though I've been learning how to peel back the many layers that I've wrapped myself in while out here in the garden, while with my sister, my mother, my *boyfriend* (!) – it's still a universal truth that some things are best left unsaid.

'Usually, I take a mental image before we leave, so I can paint while Mam watches,' she tells Peter. 'Mam loves seeing it evolve as the garden does. I'm trying to make little changes week by week. But . . .' She trails off, squints her eyes, bites her lip. 'I wanted to wait for the right amount of light to catch the colour of the irises. See that beautiful purple, there?' She points across the garden, to where some of the flowers we planted as part of the project have bloomed in their beds; purple petals bathe in the dappled light coming through the gaps in the tree canopy above. 'I can't get enough of this almost-blue. It's stupidly nice looking.' Jenna pulls away from her canvas and hovers a finger above the area she's working on: a nail-polish-free forefinger highlights the intricate detail I'd never usually notice in a painting – different colours and textures she's used to make the flowers come to life.

'This is really, *really* good,' I tell her. 'You could be selling pictures . . . If this was in a shop, I'd buy it!' It's only half a lie – someone, somewhere, *would* buy it.

She turns to me. Her eyes are big, wistful. I think she's about to say something but, instead, she gives me the smallest hint of a smile.

'Wait a minute,' Peter says. We both turn to him. 'What about . . . *this*? For the cover?'

Four very similar eyes blink at him, all dumb.

'My album!'

It's as though the promise of having her work immortalised on an album cover hasn't crossed Jenna's mind in a long while: she double blinks, like she's just woken from a dream. She almost seems confused, and I don't understand. The promise of being featured on Peter's social media propelled her forward at the start of the project – I thought that was why she consistently followed through on her commitment to these sessions. But you'd be forgiven for thinking that the prospect is news to her. I guess her 'why' – or whatever incentive is shaping her weekly choice to board Peter's bus – really did change somewhere in the haze of all the gardening and growing, the cleaning, the chatter.

'Hear me out,' Peter goes on. He's not noticed the head on Jenna. Instead, he's running away with himself. That grainy little video that Izzy posted, revealing the reality behind Peter's ruination, and the swift 180-degree shift in public opinion – it really has perked him up. He's decided to push forward with the album launch and the tour, even though he knows it might not be as successful as it could have been because of course, some ears will remain forever lost. 'White border around it. The album title up top in black font . . .'

Jenna stutters. She doesn't know what to say. I jump in instead.

'What *is* the title?' I gently elbow him as I interrogate. 'Fed up of you being so secretive about it all—'

'Hey, it's supposed to be a surprise! For the launch! You don't want to hear all the songs before then because—'

'Actually, I bloody well do! I don't want to find out you've written some . . . *symphony*, about – my – formerly unhealthy relationship with sex.' I feel my face heat up. 'Don't look at me like that,' I say, wagging my finger. 'Some musicians do stuff like that! Everything on the radio is about sex nowadays.' Peter giggles dopily. My brain forces me to mirror him. 'Don't you laugh, mister. Beyoncé released songs about how Jay-Z cheated on her . . .'

'Ah, Rosie, they use music as a form of relationship therapy. Putting all their feelings out there helped them. Also helped their bank accounts. Hey. Maybe I *should* sing about your' – he clears his throat – 'coping mechanism of choice . . .'

'I'm warning you, Dolan.'

Jenna smirks at her canvas.

Self-deprecation feels so damn good. It's ten steps up from where I *was*, at least.

I don't recall feeling so light, like I might lift off, a feather on a zephyr. To watch my sister take pleasure in something;

to feel comfortable joking about my compulsive sexual behaviour and to have the weight of that *shame* off my back; to see someone I'm in love with excited about his work, planning for his future, and to feel *safe* in love somehow – like self-sabotage isn't lurking around the corner and like I'm worthy of having something as great as this relationship . . .

I'm aware – it's not earth-shaking stuff. I've not won the actual lottery or cured cancer, I've not written a *New York Times* bestselling book or even a *shit* book, but this feeling is somehow more revolutionary. It's peace. It's hope. It's *oneness* – a word I've never before been close to capable of understanding.

I brush my palms against my jeans and look around, enjoying the chorus of birdsong like which I've not heard since childhood. The garden is near pristine and its beauty is abundant. Together, we've outsmarted the seasons by growing fruit and plants in June's old glasshouse, restored through our sweat and goosebumps, our callouses and cancelled weekend plans. Its frame serves as a skeleton to so much life – inhaling and exhaling and changing day by day. Strawberries and tomatoes blow me kisses through the glass from their pots and hanging baskets. Luscious trees sway softly, like they're waving, inviting anyone with eyes to exist in their presence. After a morning of trimming and pruning and weeding and of unearthing potatoes that *we* grew – ever-guided by Alice – I take a deep breath and realise that everything is coming together as David hoped it would. The garden is coming alive, like Jenna, like me.

Tomorrow and yesterday don't exist in Avalon, so I get to just *be* – where I'm standing – and to dismantle my walls brick by brick, at my own pace. I get to taste life and enjoy it and I get to find out how it feels deep in my belly: sometimes good, sometimes bad, but always *something*. Out here, money doesn't matter so much. We're all less wrapped up in how we look here, too: at the end of each session, every one of us climbs into that bus with dirt ingrained under our nails and with hair stuck to our faces in sweat and we laugh about it. We deal with the conditions given to us and we adapt when we don't get what we're expecting. And when someone messages the Bird-Shit Palace Brigade chat asking project-related questions about meditation or journalling or garden maintenance or if they're venting or simply looking to connect . . . someone replies. *Someone* cares.

It's not divine intervention. It's not 'the universe'. June isn't behind any of this synergy. I'll tell you what's up: we're all experiencing a long-earned break at the same time. That's all. That's what I think! And I'm going to relish every moment of it. Making love to Peter until midnight and letting him hold me as I fall to sleep. Reminiscing with my little sister and hearing her sing in the shower again. My mother's joy every time she hears my sister's name. The fact that I don't know where I'll be in ten years because why should that be so scary? I don't know what the future holds, but now I know for certain that I hold my own future – I took Jenna in, I decided to dedicate myself to . . . *this*, I took Peter's hand and let him in. I finally learned how to let go.

Peter snaps me out of my thoughts with a whip. 'I'll give you something, OK? The album title.'

'Go on, then!'

'I'm calling it *Glass Houses*.'

I cock an eyebrow.

'It's mostly about – all this. Everything my dad wanted to write about. This place. Our stories. All those letters my mom wrote.' As if our minds are one, he responds to my words, unspoken. 'Or . . . didn't write. But, whatever.' He shrugs at me. 'It's just music. Art. And *this* – this is art.' He eyeballs the canvas again. 'Let's pool our damn talents and push this thing into the top ten,' he says, to Jenna this time. 'Dad believed his book would offer people some – hope, but I also get the vibe from his journal that he, he—'

My sister stipples her paintbrush against the palm of her free hand. 'What? I mean, I know *she* thinks it's all cods-wallop.' Jenna smiles at me. 'But I don't. I won't laugh.'

Peter looks from Jenna to me. He goes weak under my gaze. 'I think my dad believed that writing a book out here – inspired by his plans unfolding, inspired by Mom – would heal a lot of people. Literally. As if – the words – would absorb – her – *power,* her magic or whatever.' He seems uncertain, and a little embarrassed. Am I making him feel that way? 'I mean, look!'

Peter pulls David's journal from his jeans back pocket, opens a page – its edge, folded over. 'Apparently, Dad found *this* message on the back of a photo . . . says here it was from Mom.'

I trap the words that try to burst from me somewhere in my gullet. Instead, I breathe and I listen.

'I can't find the photo anywhere. I've literally turned the apartment inside out looking for it but . . . nothing. So, this is all I have to go on.' His finger traces messy scrawl. '"It'll serve as centre stage. They will grow fast and tall, like sunflowers. Thank you, thank you, the world will thank you, my dearest love! J x"'

'And?'

'"The world will thank you",' he repeats.

'What am I missing?'

Jenna and Peter beam at one another.

'You could record your songs in the glasshouse,' she starts. 'It would give it a real unique sound, and you never know. *Maybe*, when people listen—'

'Ah. I see,' I start. I can't help myself. 'Santa is coming to town. You two are my children and I'm to go along with the farce, with the morally ambiguous *lie*—'

Peter wraps an arm around me. 'The myth of Santa can *totally* survive the truth, you know. Christmas would still be exciting and fun to a kid, even if they knew where their presents were coming from.'

'I call bullshit.'

'Jordanne told Harry it's all pretend – and *he* loves Christmas!' Jenna says.

Peter nods, enthusiasm embodied. 'Kids pretend to be astronauts and cowboys and – and Spiderman,' he declares, pushing his glasses up his nose. 'A bit of fantasy never did anyone any harm. You don't have to *believe* to join the buzz train . . .'

He nuzzles my neck. I squash my lips together in playful protest.

Izzy appears in my peripheral vision. 'I do believe in fairies!' she shouts. 'I *do*! I *do*!'

Nathan joins her. He giddily dances through the grass on his tippy toes. They repeat the line over and over in unison. Tadhg and Alice laugh as they approach us with buckets of fresh spuds. That's when I roll my eyes as far back as they'll go.

'Right, right. *Glass Houses*. At least it's not *My Girlfriend Is a Nymphomaniac*.'

Later that night, when I return from Mam's – leaving Jenna there for her first overnight back at home – Peter plays me some demo recordings of his new material. We're both naked, and I'm not quite sure where I end and he begins.

The music he's created for his new album is enchanting. It's unlike anything he's put out before.

'People are going to adore this, Peter. But not as much as *I* adore you.' I keep my voice low; we're so close, I could whisper it and I might still burst his eardrum. His pupils dilate, black holes. 'Look at me go. Telling you! To your face!'

Peter runs a finger along my nose, brushes my cheek, kisses me. 'You're in every note,' he says eventually, his voice heavy with emotion.

A snort escapes me. 'Sorry. It's not . . . the romance. *That* I'm learning to deal with. I just don't understand – artsy talk. Not from you, not from Jenna—'

'You don't have to. You don't have to understand how a song was put together to enjoy the sound of it. You can't play any of these instruments. But they still make you feel something.'

A single tender note takes over the pulse of bass: it hangs in the air, and shivers run along my spine and across my shoulder blades. I nod my head subtly.

'You felt *that*, yeah?'

'Yeah.'

'That was Dad. He's in every note, too. And Mom, she's – between the lot of them.'

I only look at him. Our breathing synchronises. He plays with my hair, tucks a strand behind my ear. Dopamine floods me as we talk ourselves to sleep: we discuss the ins and outs of his tour and how he wants me to accompany him; whether or not I might quit bartending and consider retraining to be a pilot; how his therapy is going and how my sister has miraculously agreed to allow Peter to set her up with an appointment with his *very-in-demand* psychotherapist, Garon. Peter will cover the cost: payment for the right to use Jenna's painting of the garden and the glasshouse on his album cover. All the while, the rough recording of *Glass Houses* plays on repeat. My consciousness dims. I prepare for the best sleep of my entire life.

JENNA

During the couple of decades since I was born, with the birth of the internet, the whole of the world changed – probably more than it did during the hundred years that preceded the ability to google, depending on how you measure societal and personal and social and physical change, of course. And as I sit cross-legged now on this early June day in the shade of the glasshouse with lush, daisy-dotted grass cushioning my arse and Jordanne's curly-haired, gap-toothed little boy, Harry, running circles around me, as I point out the swallows weaving playfully through the air, as I explain to him that the little robin appearing periodically over to our right is on the hunt for insects to feed its young, I find myself thinking about how Harry probably can't even imagine a world without internet access, like the world I remember from my own childhood . . . like the world we occupy here, in June's garden. I'm sure – if Harry were a little older – he might even argue with me about the possibility that a world without iPads and YouTube Kids ever existed in the first place. He wasn't alive, so he couldn't know. I'd forgive him for his ignorance in the same way I've forgiven myself for my own.

See, I was just about still alive when you first came upon me all those months back, but I wasn't really living at all. I breathed vape, not air, and I ate food that I never enjoyed, and I followed people online that made me feel worse about myself, and I never *ever* went outside and got my fingers dirty, never tasted rain as it pitter-pattered around me, never felt the tickle of a ladybird across my hand. The single tree in the courtyard below Rosie's apartment once looked how I felt – sad and bare. Now lush and green, I acknowledge it every day, for it is living – just like I am.

This is living.

The sky is crystal clear and blue as our resident robin's eggs. My sister and Peter are cast in sunlight through the glass, with honeymoon-phase smiles stapled into their cheeks – they're setting up Peter's little keyboard and his mic, so he can perform for us through the open door of the glasshouse ahead of a livestream to celebrate *Glass Houses*, which launches tonight, at midnight. I have champagne on ice in the kitchen and a pride-soaked, gushy Instagram caption ready to post – all about Peter's resilience and, of course, the album cover. *My* painting. It turned out a bit bloody SUBLIME, if I do say so myself.

Rosie is wearing the twin of my thin crystal bracelet. We didn't even plan on it. But it is what it is.

Alice and the boys – Nathan, Tadhg – are arguing over

whose vegetable patch turned out best. Nathan is flailing a turnip around by the stems like it's a pair of knickers.

Jordanne – back on her feet after birth and genuinely thriving – wears baby June in an olive-green sling. She helped Alice to prepare a simple mouth-watering picnic for the lot of us to enjoy today, in celebration of making it to the end of David's project. Metres away on Alice's massive orange-chequered blanket, chopped tomatoes that we've grown from nothing gleam beside a stack of freshly buttered bread. One of our basil plants from the glasshouse hangs over plates of pasta and potato salad and, beside those, bowls full of washed veg from our beds. Paper cups filled with elderflower cordial form a circle around the lot of it. Izzy appears from the kitchen and delicately adds a decorative copper plate – it's the lavender tea cake that Alice baked this morning using *our* lavender. One corner of the cake is missing. I notice the crumbs at the corners of Izzy's mouth.

An abundance of life swells around me as I exhale: bees and insects and birds and trees and flowers in all of their glorious hues – and that baby's breath, white and light and airy, creeping up the borders of the garden with delicate sprays of tiny five-petalled white flowers like fragrant mist, and all of these wonderful, flawed, busy people. Then she waves over at me from her wheelchair, positioned by the birdbath – the one person who I couldn't be here without, in her rose lipstick and her favourite satin scarf. I feel myself beam with her, like we're two headlights on a dark country road.

Mam demanded that we bring her with us today. Just last

night after a chipper, she watched me add a little Jenny Wren to the canvas – as a last touch – and I swear to God, the moment I finished the dot of the wren's teeny, tiny eye, the woman fell apart at the thought that she might never get to come here, to experience the garden first-hand, because soon Peter will be off on his tour – leaving Alice to maintain the garden on her own time. We'll no longer have our free weekly rides in the bus that just about transported Mam's wheelchair here in one piece!

'I'm going back to my mammy now,' Harry tells me, before waving in my face.

I wave back playfully. 'I'm going back to *my* mammy, too!'

'Copycat!' He sticks out his tongue and is gone in a whirl.

I could have a child of my own. It's a dream I fall into bed with every night now: I melt into sleep soon after my head touches the pillow. The gardening, the good thoughts, the art and the friends and the memories I'm making, it's all power, like electricity, and me – a battery on charge after a winter running on empty.

I sit in the grass beside Mam and my hands decide to make a daisy chain, something I've not done in well over a decade – I make a slit in the stem of one daisy and insert the stem of another into it.

'Oh, Jenna, pet,' Mam starts, her hands softly crossed in her lap. 'This garden's vitality, its vigour . . . I feel better here than I have in a very long time. Nothing aches. *Nothing!*' She opens and closes her fingers, as if to demonstrate something I can't possibly see, because I can't feel what she feels. 'Thank you for letting me come along.' Mam nervously looks from Tadhg to Nathan to Alice. 'I just, I hope they don't – I mean – I hope I *look* all right.'

I retell her all the things I've already told her about the group, just in case she's forgotten. My capability of looking after her has come back to me like it's a bike I've not hopped onto in years but that I'm still very much comfortable on. 'Mam. Everyone's glad you're here. They all know. About . . . how much the three of us have been through. Dad and your – illness – and how we didn't talk for so long. How Rosie and I . . . fell out. We all talk here, about . . . *everything*. There's no judgement from anyone. It's great. And they're good eggs, I promise.'

'I know, I know, only – you know me. I don't see people any more. Since Bridie, I've been a bit of a – shell – of myself.' Mam sniffs. 'It'll be nice to spend time with people other than Rosie for a day.'

I can't help but break with laughter at the way she says it. 'I see. I've already become the favourite—'

'I don't mean it like *that*! I – just – oh, *you know* what I – I'm not playing the game of *favourites*.'

'Ah, Mam, I'm only winding you up!'

She's staring at Alice's roses. 'My Rosie is like one of those roses, there. Beautiful and thriving – in spite of all the thorns. And, oh, she can be thorny! *You* know, pet. And *you're* like . . .' her eyes scan the garden floor before settling on the daisy tucked behind my ear 'a daisy. One of Ireland's most wonderful wild plants – wild but *durable*. You keep going. Both flowers, similar in ways, but a rose will never be a daisy and a daisy will never be a rose. You don't see them . . . competing, do you?'

'Nope,' I say with a smile. 'They just . . . bloom.'

Mam, satisfied, nods. She looks around. Allows herself to become distracted. It's as if she's been dying of thirst and someone's planted her in a pool of filtered drinking water brimming with essential electrolytes. She beckons me closer, points at the apple tree and bites her lip. 'I can't tell you why for the life of me but I feel that I *need* to eat one of those apples, once they ripen. Paul will surely have me over again, for the harvest, when he's back,' she says of Peter. 'And I'd very much like to pet – *the dog*.' Her eyes flash, like Moss might carry some otherworldly power in his coat. 'And . . .'

I raise an eyebrow. 'Yeah? What's your third wish, Aladdin?'

'Hmm. Maybe – maybe, Paul—'

'*Peter*.'

'Maybe he might let me have a go of his little keyboard?'

'But you don't play any more, I thought? Rosie said—'

'*Of course* I still play,' she scoffs. I can't tell if she's experiencing a memory lapse or if this is simply more of the 'magic' she keeps harping on about. 'Wheel me in there to him, will you? I want to play a little tune for you, one that you'll remember from a long time ago . . .'

At a leisurely pace, I push Mam through the garden and through the glasshouse door. Peter immediately looks up as the well-swept floorboards creak against Mam's wheels. She asks him outright for his mini keyboard – bold as brass – like a version of her that lives only in my memory.

'One sec, Mary, let me get it down for you.'

'No, boy.' Mam mutters it as she wiggles in her wheelchair.

Rosie throws her hands up in the air. 'Ah, Mam, careful now, remember – it's a bad day, your *leg*—' she starts.

Mam *shh*s my sister. 'Pet, let me – let me just—' Mam then stands up near-straight and completely unassisted. She holds the wooden table of the glasshouse for support. Her eyes look more awake than they have all my life. She cracks her fingers and says, 'Right, Jenna, you tell me if this one rings a bell!'

Peter, Rosie and I watch her, mouths open and eyes almost falling out of our heads. My heart thumps as a charming melody massages the very soul of the garden – us, and the air, and the soil. Mam plays *perfectly*. Not a single bum note. It takes me a minute but then I recognise the song as 'The White Rose of Athens' – buried treasure! She used to play it to us before bed after a long day of work.

When Mam finishes, everyone claps. Nathan wolf-whistles. Harry requests 'Baby Shark'.

'I'm afraid I don't know that one, little man,' she tells him. Rosie belly laughs. She *never* belly laughs. And Mam looks at me. And I'm – happy. So happy. Happy that I lived, that I've been built anew from rock bottom, that I get to see my mother with her chin up in the air like this.

June is right.

It's only up from here.

ACKNOWLEDGEMENTS

I pitched the original idea for *Glass Houses* (*The Secret Garden* for adults!) to my wonderful editor – Joanna Smyth – back in 2019, before the world changed forever and before I fell pregnant with my now toddler. Joanna's unfailing support through such uncertain times helped me to keep writing and I cannot thank her enough. I wrote most of the book from that place between asleep and awake, with my son either in my uterus or in my arms, and so Joanna deserves a medal (Emma and Aonghus too for the copy-edit and proofread!) for helping me to knock it into shape. I'm a better writer for their hard work.

During both the pandemic and my introduction to motherhood, I had the fortune of being surrounded by wonderful people, many of whom can be found between the sentences of this story. Nicola and her art; Amanda and her gardening; David and his stoicism; Jessica and her vape and her adoration for her dog and her candidness, always, when it comes to mental health; my dear friend Calum, who was 'cancelled' for something he didn't do; Sandra and her invisible illness; Hannah and her excitement for parenthood; Paul and his friend group, who greatly contribute to his happiness; Fran and his love of music; Bilbo and his kitty problems. Andrew and Caoimhe – usually reading different books every time I see you both! The mental image of you guys reading proof copies of *Glass Houses* in bed together and 'having a race' propelled me through the edits!

A massive thank you to Johann Hari, for your incredible book about depression and anxiety, *Lost Connections*. The story about 'Dog Shit Alley' served as the primary inspiration for the story of Avalon and the glasshouse and the Bird-Shit Palace Brigade. Your work has helped me more than I could ever even begin to explain.

Mostly, thank you to my husband Thomas – the Sam to my Frodo. You contributed substantially to the development of the plot of this mad story and without you there's no way that this story would be what it is. Without you, you *incredible* father, I couldn't have kept writing while working *and* mothering. When I was so tired that I called my left arm 'my main arm, my big arm', when I was absolutely certain that I couldn't possibly finish writing a book, you pushed me forward. You listened, you encouraged me, you read my words, you shared your thoughts. Thank you, thank you, thank you.

And thank *you*, if you've ever read one of my books or watched one of my YouTube videos or even if you simply leave me supportive comments online. You are why I get to have the pleasure of holding this book in my hands. And what a pleasure it is!

THE BESTSELLING AUTHOR

Melanie Murphy

One milestone birthday.   Two little words.

If Only

A lifetime of possibilities.

Erin wants a fresh start.

With her thirtieth birthday coming up, she's taken a long hard look at her life (the job she hates, the wedding she just cancelled) and concluded that it's basically a mess.

If only she knew where to begin.

A trip to her hometown in Ireland to visit her beloved grandmother is a welcome escape from her disappointments. But, there, Erin also finds an unexpected solution to her problems, in the form of a magical family heirloom. No more of the 'what ifs' she's been tormenting herself with – now all she needs to do is whisper two little words and she'll be able to see for herself what might have been, had she chosen a different path.

But as Erin gets caught up in one 'if only' after another, changing her life proves more complicated than expected. And she starts to realise that, by chasing dreams and searching for an easy fix, she might be missing out on what's right in front of her...

Available in print, audiobook and ebook

HACHETTE
BOOKS
IRELAND

'I'm just a nitwit girl who's sort of stumbling through life learning that we all have our own roads to walk – but that it's still valuable, and rather lovely, to hear about other people's journeys...'

Filled with honesty, wit and wisdom, *Fully Functioning Human (Almost)* – part memoir, part life guide – will show you the real Melanie Murphy: warm, fun, positive, honest, a girl who's got this whole adult thing down. *Almost.*

Irish YouTuber Melanie Murphy regularly chronicles the ups and downs of her life on her popular channel, discussing topics such as sexuality, skincare, social media and self-esteem. Now, in her first book, she looks with her trademark humour and down-to-earth honesty at the experiences that have shaped her.

From learning how to manage her online life, to giving up on the idea of perfection, living with anxiety and the lessons she has learned about relationships, Mel shows us that difficult times can teach us the most about who we are, and by learning to value ourselves, we can overcome whatever life throws at us.

Available in print, audiobook and ebook

HACHETTE
BOOKS
IRELAND